DEATH'S EMISSARY

EMILY DEVEREUX

ALTERSPHERE PUBLISHING

To Samantha,

For being the first person in my life to read this book. Thank you for your everlasting support.

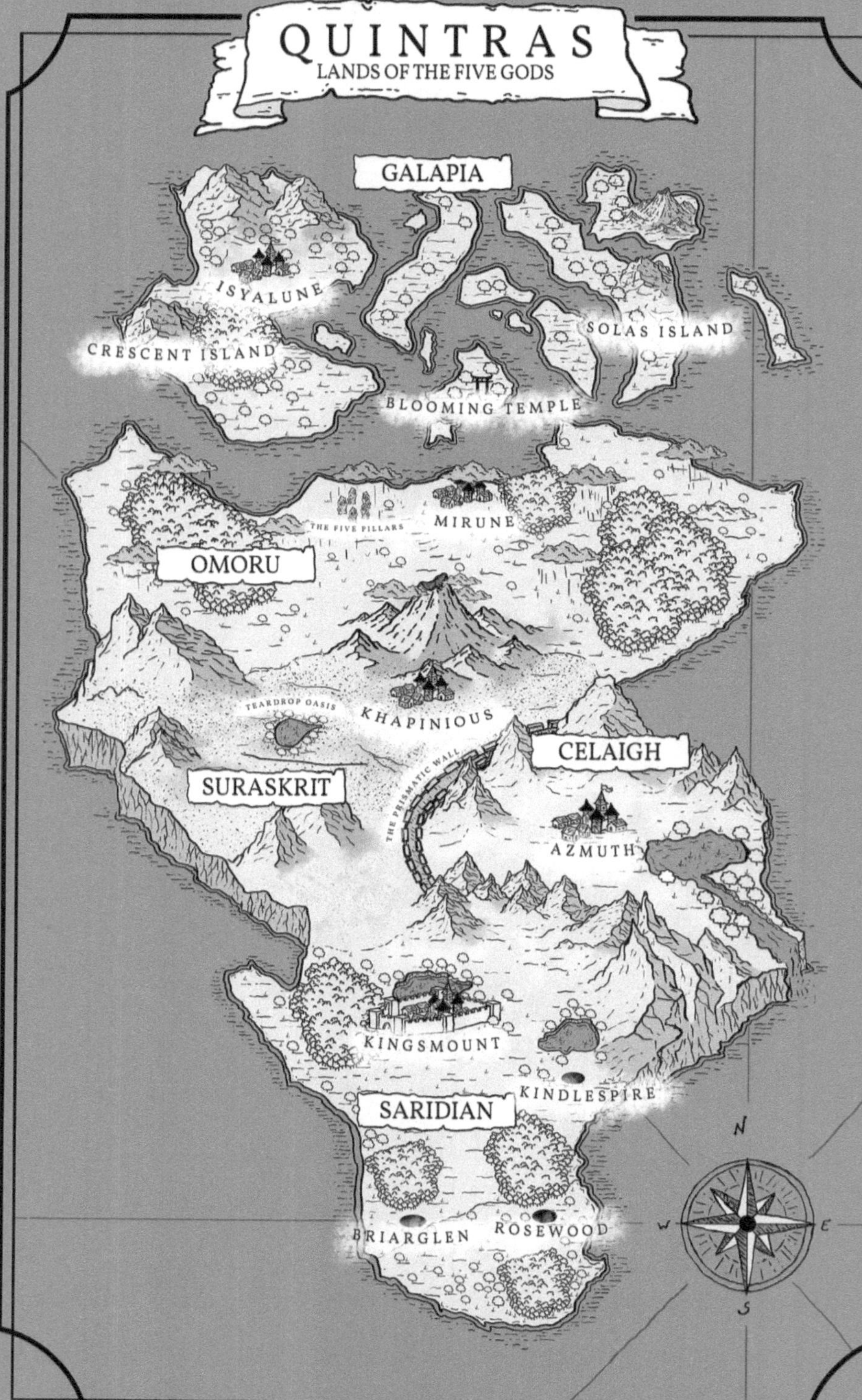

QUINTRAS
LANDS OF THE FIVE GODS
GALAPIA
ISYALUNE
CRESCENT ISLAND
SOLAS ISLAND
BLOOMING TEMPLE
THE FIVE PILLARS
MIRUNE
OMORU
TEARDROP OASIS
KHAPINIOUS
SURASKRIT
THE PRISMATIC WALL
CELAIGH
AZMUTH
KINGSMOUNT
KINDLESPIRE
SARIDIAN
BRIARGLEN
ROSEWOOD
N
W
E
S

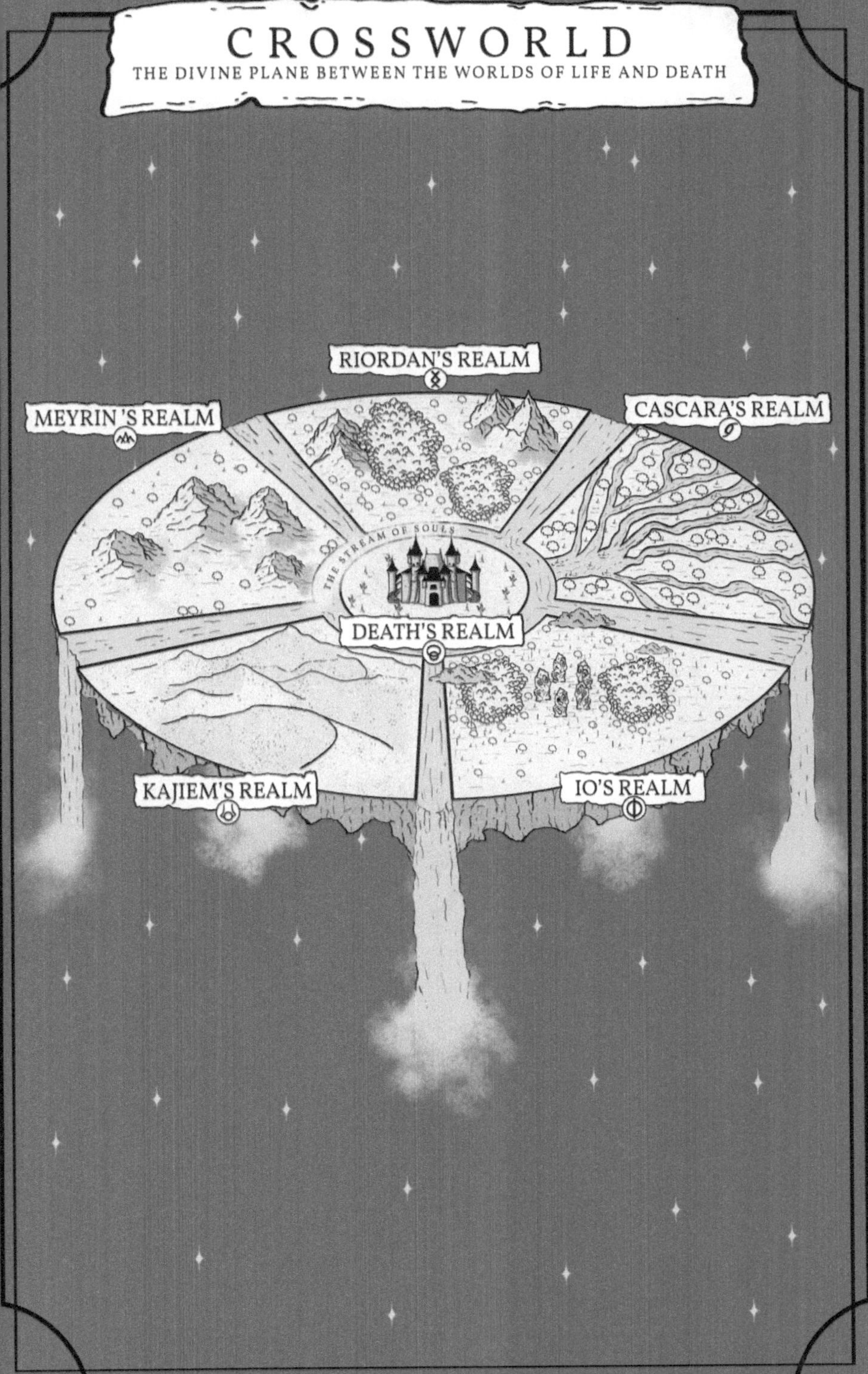

CROSSWORLD
THE DIVINE PLANE BETWEEN THE WORLDS OF LIFE AND DEATH
MEYRIN'S REALM
RIORDAN'S REALM
CASCARA'S REALM
THE STREAM OF SOULS
DEATH'S REALM
KAJIEM'S REALM
IO'S REALM

Prologue

Back home, it was winter. But here, in the plane that separated the Worlds of life and death, snow did not fall.

That fact didn't make Kiera's journey any less wretched. Though she tired of the snow that had coated Saridian for months, she wished the swamp she trudged through was frozen over. Instead, she had to slosh through the murky water, chilled to the core as she pressed her way past stiff reeds and sharp tree branches.

Darkness fell, stealing away any discernible variation in the landscape. In the distance, twin moons rose above Death's castle. Each panted breath toward it filled Kiera's lungs with sulfurous air. She was acutely aware of the burden she bore: her daughter, a decade too old to be carried, was clutched protectively in her arms.

If this journey did not go well, it would be the end of her child's life. Pain echoed within her chest. *I won't let this happen. Not again.*

Finally, Kiera's destination towered high above her: Deianira. A shiver crawled down her spine as she approached. The castle's massive obsidian doors always made her feel inconsequential. Feebly, Kiera managed to press a palm to the dark stone without dropping her daughter. Lines of silver radiated outward from her touch, across the surface of the stone, and the doors silently swung open.

Kiera's limbs threatened to give out as she wove through the castle's convoluted halls, but she made it to the throne room where her patron god awaited. At the end of the lengthy carpet leading up to the dais, Kiera collapsed.

"Please," she choked out. Her daughter rested on her lap, unmoving. "Save her."

Death rested upon her simple wooden throne, remaining engrossed in the examination of her long braid rather than looking down from her dais. The color of Death's hair always reminded Kiera of blood.

Blood. Kiera was bleeding, but her daughter's wound was more urgent.

The god was silent as she considered the plea. It had been years, decades since the divine being's presence intimidated Kiera enough to make her shake, but through exhaustion and fear, her body trembled now. Death was weaker than she used to be, though her aura of power still felt overwhelming to a mere mortal. Right now, Death's weakness was a problem, if anything, though what Kiera feared even more was the god's decisions. They weren't as close as they'd once been, and she could rarely predict her god's whims... especially in matters relating to Kiera, herself.

Death finally deigned to speak. "I *told* you having a family was a mistake. All you did was give him a target."

"Spare me the lecture," Kiera spat. "You know what I've lost, all in the name of saving you. Without her, I'll have nothing."

Death rose from the throne, her green eyes blazing now that they'd locked onto her subject. Her rising voice echoed off the bare walls of the desolate throne room, almost seeming to make the stone tremble. "You have nothing because you have accomplished nothing. Where are my results, Kiera? Riordan is still out there, terrorizing me." She glanced down and waved toward them. "And you, apparently."

Kiera clenched her jaw. "I'm close. I have a lead."

"You have *nothing*," Death repeated. Her voice was deadly soft now, like a dagger pressed lightly to Kiera's neck. "And I won't waste my energy."

"Riordan came after me personally. You don't think that means something?"

Death's face was stone. Impassive. Unyielding. "Then tell me."

Kiera took a breath, steadying herself for the tightrope she'd have to walk to avoid incriminating herself. "You were right to suspect Angelise. After she left, she made some... discoveries."

A new intensity sparked in Death's eyes. "Tell me *everything*."

Kiera looked down at Scarlet and stroked some dark curls out of her much-too-pale face. "While my daughter is caught between this World and the Nextworld? No. Save her first."

Death descended back onto the throne. "And why, exactly, should I save her at all? She's nothing but a distraction to you and your work."

Kiera suppressed a scream. The wetness seeping through her cloak was warm—not the swamp water she had trudged through to get here, but her daughter's blood. She didn't know how much time Scarlet had left. What she did know was that Death's sudden nonchalance was feigned. The information Kiera held was exactly what the god had been seeking: a way to truly kill another god, not just release them from their current physical form.

"Eva, please." It had been a long time since that name had touched Kiera's lips. She had to appeal to the human part of this half-divine being. "You know my suffering. Your energy may be limited, but you're stronger now than when Viridian—" Kiera choked back a sob. "Than when I lost Viridian. Scarlet still has a chance. If you save her, I'll tell you everything."

Death's expression darkened. Kiera's tattoo, the two overlapping circles on the back of her right hand, began to burn. The pain made Kiera grunt involuntarily; it was an unpleasant reminder of the magic that bound her.

"You really think you can bargain with me?"

"So be it. Use our bond to compel me." Kiera's voice shook. "But if Scarlet dies, if you *let* her die, I'm done."

"Done?" Death's eyes widened for a moment before she smoothed her expression back to neutral.

"Ange broke her bond. I can do the same."

"You wouldn't." Death's voice was small. Tight. "We had an agreement."

"We did. But if you make me choose between you and my daughter…"

Death pursed her lips. Kiera held her breath.

"Saving her is not so simple. With my powers strangled—"

"Even if you don't think she'll survive, I beg you to try. Please. For everything we once had."

The moments it took Death to contemplate were an eternity to Kiera. "Fine," she said finally. Bitterly. "I will try. But the information comes first."

Kiera spoke quickly, her heart caught in her throat. "Ange gathered a small group of mages. Others that were willing to break terms laid out in the Magus Treaty."

"Artificing?"

"Yes."

"Bold." Death's hand went to her crystal pendant. Kiera was surprised she didn't turn to anger; the god did not look kindly upon artificing. "The artifact they made, will it work?"

"Do you have any doubts that Ange will accomplish whatever she sets her mind to?"

The low growl that escaped Death's throat reminded Kiera she'd hit yet another sore spot. "No. I suppose I do not," Death said. "But what exactly *has* she set her mind to?"

Kiera bristled at the question. Firstly, because her daughter's life slipped further away with each passing moment, and secondly, because she couldn't afford to botch the delicate process of extracting herself from Ange's plans. "I don't know." It was the simplest lie she could come up with. "I'll find out. And I'll find the artifact. But right now, Scarlet is running out of time."

"Just promise me one thing: when you do find the artifact, swear to me that I can trust you with it."

Kiera forced a lump down her throat. The last artifact Death entrusted her with—well, it was gone. She had made sure of it.

"Kiera?"

"You can trust me."

Death stood and stepped off the dais. She leaned down and placed a hand on Scarlet's pale forehead. "You know that crossing to the Nextworld is not the worst fate."

Kiera thought her chest would burst open with the pressure of her frustration. "She's sixteen. It's hardly her time to cross. You can't tell me there's nothing—"

"There is one thing I can do. I'm sure you've thought of it."

Kiera's heart skipped a beat. "You can't make her an emissary."

"That is the deal. That's *always* been the deal. If I spend my precious energy, I need something back."

"That *something* was my information."

"No. You know well enough that your work for me is in exchange for your own life."

"I'll find you other recruits. Please, anything else."

"Your only task now is to find that artifact."

Death could be ruthless, but she wasn't heartless. Kiera had seen her kindness, long ago. Now her god was spiteful, unwavering, and carried a fairly legitimate grudge against Kiera, but she had to believe that Death had a speck of humanity left.

"I've sacrificed my happiness many times over for you. My daughter's life and freedom is all I ask in return."

Death's face was frozen, her expression unreadable. "At this point, I will only be able to save her if we share a bond. It's the simple truth." She withdrew her hand from Scarlet's forehead. "And maybe, instead of being a distraction, she can be a form of insurance. If you complete your duties, Scarlet won't have to step into the fray."

A wave of nausea overtook Kiera. "I won't force this life onto my daughter."

"If you want her to have a life in this World and not the Next, this is the only option. Ultimately, she'll have to decide for herself whether or not to take the deal. It's the same choice you had."

Kiera stared at the fragile girl bleeding in her arms. Her only remaining child. Kiera had sworn to protect her. From Death, from Riordan, from the unbearable weight of duty. The life she'd given Scarlet wasn't a normal one, but at least she had kept her safe. Until now.

And so, it had come to this: Kiera could protect her daughter from death—the crossing of souls—or Death, the god who had grown so bitter. But no longer could she save Scarlet from both.

Kiera's heart ripped with the impossibility of the decision. The inevitability of it. *This day was always going to come, wasn't it?*

She looked up at her god, life and death incarnate, and took a final breath before speaking the words that would seal her daughter's fate. The words that would break her and every promise she'd ever made to herself.

"Prepare the ritual."

CHAPTER 1

*S*carlet... *you're here.*

The words woke Scarlet with a jolt. Every bit of her body ached fiercely, radiating from a point on her back. The pain was overwhelming, but it only took the space of a breath for adrenaline to take over. She kicked the blankets off and haphazardly rolled from the bed to the floor. Her landing sent excruciating shockwaves through her.

Who had spoken to her? The voice was familiar, but not her mother's. Was there danger?

The floor was cold. Stone. That wasn't right. The cabin's floor was wooden. She wasn't home. Wasn't safe. Her eyes adjusted to the near-darkness and she took account of her surroundings. The room was musty, small, sparsely furnished, and as far as she could tell, she was alone in it.

She had her back to a raised bed with a straw-filled mattress. There was a wardrobe hewn from dark wood, a matching bookshelf with bare shelves, and a dusty full-length mirror next to a vanity. A door was to her right, and to her left was the window, partially covered by thick red drapery. Where it was not covered, moonlight spilled into the room.

Scarlet pressed her eyes closed and took a shaky breath. Filling her lungs hurt; everything hurt. *What happened to me?*

Last she remembered, she and her mother were in their current hideout, an abandoned cabin that was deep in the woods. Now, she was here, injured, and it appeared that someone had tended to her wounds. Underneath the nightgown she had been dressed in, she felt dressings covering the wound on her back. Her right hand was also wrapped in linen. Both her palm and the back of her hand pulsed with a dull pain.

Carefully, she stood. The movement caused her vision to blotch and fade into gray for a few long moments. She stumbled to the window and pulled the curtains back the rest of the way. She was in a tall tower, though she couldn't make out much of the landscape below in the darkness. Just some bare trees, and a river not far off, moonlight glinting off the flowing water.

Wait, is that a second moon? One of the moons was a crescent, a sliver just big enough that Scarlet could make out its faint yellow glow. That one was familiar, expected. The other was full, its shine a shade of violet. That one was alien to her. The sky was oddly colored as well—even in the darkness, Scarlet could see that it was a purple hue rather than blue.

She wasn't in the World.

Scarlet shivered. *So, I'm in the Crossworld... or, am I dead?* She didn't know if injuries, or even her body, would carry over into the Nextworld if she had died. She doubted it, but no one knew what awaited souls who crossed over. Unfortunately, due to her mother's insistence that Scarlet know as little as possible about her emissary work, she didn't know much about the Crossworld either.

Mom, she thought next. *Is she here? Is she okay?* She needed to find out more.

Every movement cost Scarlet dearly, a single step causing what felt like a full year's ration of pain, but she scoured the room. The wardrobe creaked as she tugged it open. There were a couple of dresses hanging in it. They smelled musty; Scarlet doubted anyone had worn them recently. She was about to close the wardrobe when she spotted her boots in the back corner. She pulled them out and tugged them on. Her boot sheath still held her dagger, which she was grateful for in this unknown territory.

Better equipped, Scarlet swung open the door, which led out into a hallway that had the same dark gray stone walls as the room. The hall went in both directions. At random, she turned to the right and began to explore. The air felt moist, and blue luminescence emanated from light motes in metal sconces placed at regular intervals. It was a magic Scarlet was familiar with. Creating orbs of light was one of the few pieces of magic her mother allowed her to learn. In times like these, she desperately wished her mother would relent and teach her combat magic. But after what had happened to—

S... Scarlet? You're here...

Scarlet froze. She hadn't heard that voice in years, but now that she was properly awake, it was impossible not to recognize it. "Viridian? *Viridian!*" She glanced both ways down the hall, but she saw no one. "Where—how—"

Suddenly it occurred to her, that since Viridian was dead, and if she was hearing Viridian...

Her whole body shook, either from the intense pain that plagued her or the fear that she was already dead. She waited, but Viridian didn't respond.

Alternative theory: I am simply going insane. Scarlet took one last glance back the way she had come, and continuing to see no one, decided to press forward. She had to find out as much as she could before her body gave way.

Soon, she was lost in a maze of stone and doors. The layout of the castle confounded her. Some halls stretched from one end of the castle to the other, and some were only a few feet long before splitting off into two or three directions.

She imagined that a castle would be lavishly decorated, but this one didn't live up to that expectation. There were no ornamentations, nor anything to distinguish one hall or doorway from the next. She tugged at each door she passed, finding most of them locked. The unlocked ones led to barren, dusty rooms. *What is this place?*

Eventually, she came across a room that wasn't abandoned. A library, full of shelves upon shelves of tomes. Scarlet dipped into the room, practically salivating at the sight of the vast rows of books. She'd never seen a collection of knowledge like this. These books would not hold the answers she currently sought, but it took everything in her not to start pulling them off their shelves.

"Knowledge is power," her mother once told her during an argument. She said it like it was a bad thing.

"Powerful is exactly what I want to be," Scarlet retorted.

Her mother only shook her head.

"What's wrong with that?"

"Power doesn't make you safe," her mother replied. "Trust me."

Those words always rang false in Scarlet's ears. How did ignorance and lack of self-defense measures protect her? She detested every moment that she felt helpless, the pinnacle of which was this very moment. She was alone, injured, in an unfamiliar place. Or maybe she had already been killed.

You're not dead yet, Viridian said. The words emanated directly into Scarlet's head. *But you're missing pieces.*

Scarlet jumped, and as a fresh wave of pain exploded from the center point of her back, immediately wished she hadn't. She sank to the floor, using a bookshelf as support but was careful not to lean the injured portion of her back against it.

"Then... then how am I hearing you?" Scarlet asked, shakily. "Wait, and what do you mean by 'yet'?"

I don't know. Part of you is there, in physical form. But part of you is here, too.

Scarlet grasped for words, trying to process the entire situation. "I... I miss you."

Scarlet. I miss you too.

"I don't... I don't know what's happening. Where I am. Where you are. I don't know what to do."

I don't know all the answers either. For now, I believe you are safe. Rest. Heal. I will try to return some of your pieces while you convalesce.

Rest. That sounded good. But was it even possible to find her way back to the room she'd woken in? There had been so many twists and turns, and everything in the hallways looked exactly the same.

The tapping of footsteps snapped Scarlet out of her brooding. A woman entered the library. Scarlet tried to pull herself up, but her energy flagged, so on the floor she remained as the woman approached her.

Her eyes were green and sharp, contrasted against her bright, true red hair. At the end of her thick braid, a single black feather dangled. Her brown skin hinted at a Suraskriti or Omorui ancestry, though Scarlet had spent her life in the insular Saridian and couldn't make an educated guess at which. Underneath a black cloak, the woman wore simple, neutral-colored clothing. A bright clear crystal hung from her neck, and she had two piercings—a pair of turquoise beads pierced high up on each nostril.

The woman looked down at her. While she was neither tall nor short, the immensity of her presence made her tower over Scarlet. Her aura was unlike what Scarlet had experienced from any mortal mage, containing a power far more immense. Scarlet was in the vicinity of a god.

Not just any god. Death.

"Scarlet," the god said, examining her. "You should not be up yet."

Scarlet thought she'd choke on her words, but then they tumbled out. "I didn't know where... where I was. And my mother, if she's here too, and—"

"She is not," Death said. "Come. You need to rest. I will take you back to your room."

The back of Scarlet's hand burned underneath the wrappings. Agitated, she itched it through the bandage, but it gave her no relief. "Where is she?"

"I said, **come.**"

The burning sensation became unbearable, like a red-hot brand pressed against her hand. Though she didn't intend to, Scarlet found herself standing. The pain receded as she acquiesced to the demand and followed Death out of the library.

"You know who I am, don't you?" Death asked as she led Scarlet. Scarlet nodded.

"But you don't remember our agreement?" Death said under her breath, perhaps to herself. She made a sweeping gesture. "This is my castle, Deianira."

"Deianira," Scarlet repeated. Probably she should have kept her mouth shut—this was a god she was talking to, and whatever that pain was, she didn't want it to come back—but still, she couldn't stop the question from coming out. "Does that mean something?"

Death stiffened. "It is just a name. The point is—get familiar with it. The castle. Kiera's return has been delayed, and you will be staying here for the time being."

"Is she alright?"

"She will be fine. But while she is gone, I will be training you. It is past time you learned to defend yourself."

"You're going... to train me?" Scarlet said, slowly. "You're going to teach me magic?"

"Yes."

Somehow, they had already arrived back at the room Scarlet had woken up in. It seemed impossible to have returned so quickly.

Death led her into the room, and Scarlet sat down on the edge of the bed. Her limbs were heavy and her pain threatened to overwhelm her consciousness. She fought to stay awake, to get a bit more information.

"What agreement were you talking about?"

"I suppose I should not be surprised that you don't remember. You were quite far gone when we made it."

Scarlet's hand tingled again. Not painfully, but strange. A prompt? Gently, she unwrapped the bandages. On her palm, a diagonal slash ran from the base of her index finger down to her wrist, scabbed over. It emitted a dull pain.

She flipped her hand over. On the back was a symbol, tattooed in black ink. Two circles, overlapping.

"An emissary tattoo. When—how—"

"It may come back to you in time," Death said. "You agreed to become an emissary in exchange for your life. I needed the binding to keep you from crossing over. Kiera never would have allowed it otherwise."

Scarlet couldn't interpret the wry smile on Death's lips. She tried to let this new reality set in. All her life, her mother had shielded her from her emissary duties. Even more so after Viridian died. Now, Scarlet was an emissary too, bound to do Death's bidding.

Knowledge and power. It was everything she'd ever wanted—but from her mother, who was gone. And though knowledge may be forthcoming, she still knew little about the origins or purpose of the conflict between Death and Riordan, a feud she was now firmly stuck in the middle of.

"When will you start teaching me?"

"As soon as you are recovered."

"And my mother—where is she?"

"She is on an important mission for me."

"Is she coming back soon?"

Death waved her hand in a dismissive gesture, sharp nails glinting in the light. "Yes, yes, she will return. In the meantime, I will keep you busy. Sleep now. The more you rest, the sooner we begin your education."

As Death exited, she closed her fist and the light orbs in the room dissipated, leaving Scarlet alone in the darkness.

Scarlet's body shook; pain, fear and desire intermingled into a concoction of anxiety. She was in the Crossworld, she was separated from her mother, she was going to learn magic, she was an emissary of a god, and somehow, she could hear the voice of her dead sister. It was all strange, a blend of wonder and distress. In this moment, she wanted nothing more than sleep—a respite from the overwhelming aching of her wound and the contradiction of getting everything she wanted in all the wrong ways.

CHAPTER 2

"Drink this." Dante handed the man a bottle containing a thick, red liquid. "Two swigs a day until your cough is gone. It won't taste good, but it should help."

The man, Glenwal, gave both the bottle and Dante a quizzical look but nodded. "And if it don't get better?"

"Then come back, and Ferrick will take a look at you."

Glenwal nodded again. He was a farmer, and a traditional kind of man—one who would more readily accept treatment from the town's veteran healer rather than his scrawny, teenaged apprentice. Glenwal thanked Dante, pocketed the bottle, and made his way out of the clinic.

Glenwal's farm neighbored Dante's family's farm. It had been some time since Dante had spent his days toiling in the family fields. He was grateful for that. Not that farming wasn't an honorable profession, but Dante wasn't cut out for it. He was nearly seventeen, but still scrawny.

Sometimes he felt he was the complete opposite of the other boys in town. They were all broad-chested, tall, and kept their hair shorn short.

Then, there was Dante—shorter than average, too slight considering how much he had been working on the farm, and shaggy blond hair that he had to brush out of his eyes far too often. While the longer hair could be annoying, he liked it better than the more popular short style that never seemed to suit him. Still, he made sure to never let it grow past his chin. There was only so far past the norm that he could stray before people considered him *too* weird, and then surely his parents would scold him.

As the afternoon wore into evening, Dante's eyes drooped. Ferrick had kept him late once again. *How many days in a row have I gone home in the dark now?* There was always something to do. Brew a concoction to repel the bugs that had invaded the greenhouse, hassle the weaver for more gauze, and so on.

Some days, Dante did these various tasks, other times Ferrick set him to study a particular section of a book or, as today, stay at the clinic—really, the front room of Ferrick's house—in case someone in the village needed medical attention while Ferrick ran errands.

Dante never complained. Every moment he could spend away from home was a relief. Plus, Ferrick had agreed to take Dante on as an apprentice at no cost, which was unprecedented, so Dante did his best to make himself an asset. There was no way his parents could afford an apprenticeship fee.

By sunset, Dante was worn thin. Finally, Ferrick returned, frazzled—not an uncommon state for Dante's master. He stumbled around the clinic, reorganizing supplies in a seemingly random fashion. In between Ferrick's sessions of mumbling to himself, Dante asked if there was anything else he could help with that evening, praying he could go home to rest.

"No, no, nothing else," Ferrick said. He examined one of his bottled concoctions by the light of an oil lamp, probably trying to discern what the unlabeled liquid was. "You'd better get home, actually. I will speak to your parents tomorrow if the situation requires."

"If the—? Wait, what's going on?"

"If the situation requires, boy!" Ferrick repeated. He stumbled into his supply closet, continuing to mumble to himself and loudly rummaging through the mess.

Dante sighed. It was impossible to get information from Ferrick when he was in a state like this. He was a good master, if somewhat eccentric. *I'll have to figure this out on my own... but if it involves my parents, it can't be good news.*

Dante fetched his coat and left the clinic. The bitter wind tore at him as he walked along the cobblestone road that led him back to the farmhouse. Winter was over, technically, but spring in Saridian was only slightly more forgiving. This region was infamous for the thick blanket of snow that graced the land for an unmerciful portion of the year.

He wondered what it was like to live somewhere else, a land that was warmer and where he didn't have to worry so much about trying to fit in.

Each time he walked home from Ferrick's clinic he passed a particular crossroad, the site of the accident that had changed his life. Last summer, he was still resigned to his fate as a farmer. But then, out doing errands, Dante saw a carriage wheel break, causing the whole carriage to tip over. He had watched in shock until Ferrick grabbed him, pulling him onto the scene. Ferrick had directed him in aiding the four injured passengers.

After it was over, Ferrick praised Dante, which surprised him—working under pressure had never been his forte. But this he had done, according to Ferrick, quite aptly. Aptly enough that Ferrick waived the apprenticeship fee and convinced his parents to let him leave his farm work. He kept showing promise and worked hard to prove himself to Ferrick and his parents.

None of Dante's successes made his parents fully accept his new path in life. His father dreamed of Dante following in his footsteps, carrying on with the farm that had been his father's, and his father's father's before that. His mother was less opinionated, but chronically agreed with his father to keep the peace. Plus, the farm hadn't been doing as well the past couple of years, and Dante knew losing a free farmhand was a big blow.

His parents' disappointment left him feeling guilty. But working for Ferrick was the first time he had ever felt *competent*. He had an amount of confidence that he had lacked previously. At the very least, he had overcome his soft-spokenness enough that people didn't constantly pester him to speak up anymore.

As Dante was about to turn the corner that would lead him out of the town and toward his family's farm, his friend Milo pounced in front of him.

"Did you hear?" Milo was bright-eyed, full of more energy than Dante could tolerate in his exhausted state.

Dante sighed. "Hear what?"

"Soldiers."

Dante became acutely aware of his heartbeat pounding in his ears. "Soldiers?" He glanced past his friend, trying to see if anyone in blue and gold uniforms was headed toward the farmhouse. He didn't see anything, but the farm was a way off, still.

"Yeah, right here in Briarglen. Can you believe that?"

It was a small village, far south from the northern capital of Kingsmount, barely of note. Soldiers didn't come here, not without a reason.

"D'you know what they're doing here?" Dante asked. Suddenly, he wasn't sure what he did with his hands, normally. He crossed his arms, uncrossed them, then shoved his hands into his pockets.

"Word is they're recruiting for the army." Milo raised an eyebrow at Dante, apparently noticing his nervousness. "Look, don't worry about it. I'm sure of all people, they wouldn't want you." He punched Dante's shoulder good-naturedly.

Enlisting was low on Dante's list of ways to get out of this place. In fact, it wasn't on the list at all. *This must be what Ferrick was alluding to.* His master had been offering to help convince his parents to not send him away. There hadn't been mandatory conscription since the Magus War, generations ago, but the king still kept a standing army to enforce the laws of the land. Soldiers were paid well, and it was no secret that his family was tight on coin.

But right now, the idea of his parents pressuring him to enlist was his secondary concern. "Hey, look," Dante said, "Have you seen my sister?"

"Nah. She wander off again? I can help ya look for her."

"It's fine," Dante said. "She's... she's probably back at home by now."

He sent Milo on his way and hurried back to the farm. As he slipped inside the beaten-down farmhouse, he could hear his parents arguing in the kitchen. When he heard his name among their squabbling, he quietly shut the front door and crept closer.

"—never take him," his mother was saying. "He's not suited to that kind of thing."

"They'd train him to be," his father responded. "Lira, you heard how much they're paying now. We need the money."

Dante's stomach churned.

"We aren't desperate yet. We could give it more time."

"That may be so, but you remember... the *incident* as well as I do. It wouldn't hurt for him to have some extra supervision."

"Ferrick seems quite pleased with him," his mother said. The compliment would have warmed Dante's heart, had there not been a careful restraint to it. "Maybe—"

"I've made up my mind," his father snapped. "That boy needs to do something useful for this family."

Dante tried to tiptoe back out of the house unnoticed, but he forgot to omit the creaky floorboard from his path. As the wood squeaked, his parents fell silent. Dante's father slammed the back door on his way outside, and his mother peeked her head out of the kitchen.

"So," his mother said. She paused, fidgeting with the fraying edges of her sleeve. "You heard all that?"

"Enough of it."

Dante saw the sorrow in her eyes.

"Your father—he just wants to be proud of you—"

"He could be proud of the work I'm doing with Ferrick."

"It's respectable work," his mother admitted. "It's just, not what he had in mind for you. And—"

She cut her sentence short, but Dante knew her thoughts were going toward the "incident" his father had referred to.

Dante wiped his sweaty hands on his trousers. "And what do *you* think?"

The question was edging on defiant, not a tone he often took. But he had to know. If his parents were of the same mind, there was little hope of weaseling out from under their expectations.

His mother retreated to the kitchen to continue scrubbing a dish. Dante followed her, but she didn't look at him when she answered. "I think it might be good for you to get away."

"To 'get away'?"

"From Zandra. I don't want her to end up—" She waved a hand vaguely, as if that could communicate her meaning. In this instance, it did.

Bile rose in Dante's throat. "She won't. She's not... like me. And I've kept my promises to you."

I hate the lies I have to tell.

His mother wrung out the rag. She said nothing. Even if he was being truthful, she would never believe him. It stung, but he supposed he deserved it.

"Where did Dad go?"

"To look for Zandra. She's been out too long. Again."

Dante turned to go back out the front door. "I'll go help."

His mother caught his arm. He could feel her concern as if it trickled in through her touch. "I'm sure your father can handle it."

Dante shook himself free from her grasp, and despite her protests, he left. If soldiers were here, and Zandra was missing, she wasn't safe. Protecting his sister was one of the few situations in which he would risk provoking his parents' wrath.

He knew all of Zandra's hiding spots, he just had to find her before someone else caught her practicing magic.

Dante headed straight for the forest path, the one that he and Zandra took when they picked wild berries. It was growing dark, and long shadows reached ominously across the trail. Once past the still-bare bushes, Dante reached the thawing creek and turned off the beaten path. He made his way into the thicker underbrush, branches prickling through his sleeves as he shouldered them aside, until finally, the trees gave way to a small clearing.

Their secret hideout. As children, they'd played here often. They'd also had to make excuses to their parents about why it had taken them so long to fill their baskets with ripe berries. Zandra was still making excuses; Dante knew he couldn't mess around anymore.

He'd been right to look here first. Zandra was at the other side of the clearing, kneeling in the snow. As Dante approached, he saw her thick eyebrows furrowed in concentration. The air around her hands shimmered and distorted as she moved them slowly from her feet, up to and over her knees, and then each of her arms. When she was finished, she shook her hands as if to dry them, and looked up at Dante. He could see the magic clinging to her body, resonating from her.

She smiled at him. "I thought you might catch up."

"Zandra." He tried to think of anything to say that he hadn't said before, but couldn't. "You have to stop doing this."

"It's harmless." Zandra glanced around the clearing. "We used to have fun here. Building shelters, playing games, telling stories."

"This isn't a game."

"You're right." There was a serious note in his little sister's voice. "It's not a game. It's more important."

"It's against the rules, against the law—"

"The rules are ridiculous!" A blast of magic resonated out from Zandra as she flung her arms up in frustration.

Dante recoiled as the magic hit him, sending tingles down his arms and knocking him back just a little. "If someone sees you—"

"If someone sees, *they* should be afraid. Not me."

Zandra turned away from Dante, bent her knees, and leaped at the tree in front of her. She jumped higher than should have been possible and caught a branch a few feet from the ground. Easily, she pulled herself up onto the tree's limb and perched there, towering over Dante.

"I'm not going to hide my whole life," Zandra continued. "I have the gift, and I know you do too."

The gift. Dante wondered where she'd heard that phrasing. He had heard it a few years back from a traveling trader, one that had a rare license to cross the border to do business outside of Saridian. He told tales to the children about how in the other regions, when a child developed nascent magic, they were said to have "the gift".

The trader scoffed at that, of course. Because here, in Saridian, it was a curse. King Riordan had decreed that magic was for the gods, not something to be sullied by mortals. Humans couldn't be trusted with that kind of power. The "gifted" among them had to eschew their powers.

Dante clenched his fists. "Come down. There are soldiers here. You can't play around with magic, it's too dangerous."

"'It's too *dangerous!*'" Zandra mocked. She spun around on the branch, hooked her legs around it, and then leaned back to hang upside-down facing Dante. Her blonde hair dangled down to her elbows, swaying along with her momentum. "Look, I appreciate you pulling out the big brother act. But it's time to stop lying to yourself. You're like me."

Dante had heard that fewer mages were born in Saridian than in other regions. To be born a mage here was a rare fate, but it happened. And if you were one of them, you could never slip up. Your life depended on it. "Please, just come home, before Dad or the soldiers find you."

"Show me some magic first." Zandra grinned and swung herself back on top of the branch, then used a combination of impossible leaps and sure-footed climbing to gain altitude. Dante's stomach dropped in direct proportion to the height she ascended to.

"Zandra!" Dante had to yell for his sister to have any chance of hearing him. "I'm not bargaining with you. We'll talk about this after the soldiers leave."

"You let everyone run your life! They control you. If you never take chances you'll—"

A sickening *crack* broke off Zandra's sentence—the branch holding her weight snapped, and Zandra crashed through layers of the canopy before beginning to plummet, a deadly free fall where the ground would be the finish line.

Time slowed for Dante. He'd seen this happen before. In his dreams, this scene had played out over and over. It always ended a bit differently, but the outcome was always the same. In a split second, he saw each potential scenario flash in front of him.

Zandra on the ground, body twisted unnaturally.

Zandra crashing into Dante as he tried to catch her, severely injuring them both.

Zandra caught in the branches, blood dripping from her body, hanging lifelessly.

So many nights he had awoken in a cold sweat, bloody images seared into his memory. He couldn't lose his sister. But he wasn't able to stop her and now she was going to die.

He couldn't hold it back anymore—as his sorrow took over, so did his magic. It burst forth from his palms, a rush of tingling energy, shimmering in the air before him, useless, all magic was good for was getting people killed.

Then his instincts kicked in. He could sense what to do and he let his desperation guide him. Dante imagined a shell, a magical shield around his sister. With all the force he could muster, he sent the energy toward Zandra and willed it to protect her in the moment of impact against the ground.

The magic obeyed, materializing as a glowing barrier, a thin wall of light that took the force of the fall instead of his sister's fragile form. The shell shattered into fragments that flashed brightly before dissipating around

Zandra's prone body. As he ran towards her, Dante hoped that the shield had been the only thing to break.

She can't be hurt. She... she can't be dead.

Zandra was still, very still, but her body wasn't contorted like Dante feared it might be. He knelt at her side and brushed the hair away from her face. Her eyes were open and she seemed conscious, though distant.

"Zandra. Zandra, can you hear me? Are you alright?"

Zandra's eyes became more focused and she took Dante's hand, squeezing it feebly.

"I thought—I thought I was dead," Zandra said. It was all she got out before tears welled up in her eyes. Dante pulled her close as she began to sob.

"It's okay. You're alright, you're safe."

After a couple of minutes, Zandra's breathing steadied. She looked up at Dante, tears still brimming. "You protected me. I knew you were a mage, I *knew* it." After a shuddering breath, she added, "We used to tell each other everything."

Dante wanted to protect her from this, only he couldn't. Not when she was a mage too.

"It started a few years ago," he told her. "When I was twelve. And I was like you. I thought, maybe, that I could get away with it. I could be careful." He closed his eyes as he relived his memories. "Then Dad found out. He... wasn't easy on me." Dante had gotten a beating that day, the worst of his life. "He made me promise to never use magic again, but he didn't turn me in. But if he finds me again..."

"You won't get another chance."

"No. And you might not get a chance at all."

Zandra paused, then continued softly. "Being a mage. It's part of who I am. We can't abandon that. Not forever."

"We have to."

Another pause, longer this time. Dante knew his sister well enough that he could see her brain ticking, her mouth opening and closing silently as she tried to find the words on the tip of her tongue. "I saw the crystal, Dante. That thing Dad found next to the creek. It was broken already, so he threw what was left of it into the water. He said it might be dangerous. But you found the pieces and put it back together, didn't you? With magic."

A jolt ran down Dante's spine. Panic, followed by a heavy dose of shame. "You saw it?" If she did, someone else could have. He should have been more careful. Better yet, he shouldn't have fixed it in the first place. It was the only time, up until saving Zandra, that he had broken his promise to forsake magic.

Saving his sister's life happened so fast that it barely seemed like a choice—though he would have chosen to save his sister regardless. But holding onto some magical crystal thing had been wholly on purpose, and it hadn't been worth the risk. Guilt overtook him every time he thought of the useless crystal sphere, the memento of his failings.

"I saw candlelight from your room, late. Thought I caught a whiff of magic. A couple different nights. So I snooped. Under your bed is not a good hiding place, by the way."

"You shouldn't have done that." Dante felt violated by Zandra's poking about his room, but he tried to quench his anger. Not the time, not the place—just like being a mage. "Aren't you too old for snooping?"

"Shush. You want me to be serious about this, don't you? Well, I'm being serious. They can keep telling us it's wrong, that King Riordan decreed that only he should have these divine abilities, blah, blah. But that doesn't change the fact that we are mages. We can't deny that. I won't let my power go to waste."

"Maybe one day, you can leave Saridian and go somewhere else where magic is accepted. But you'll never live to make it to that point if you run around like this, if you try to be a mage right now. I want you to be happy, Zandra, I do—but I also want you to be *safe*. So please, promise me you won't keep doing magic. Not here."

A long moment of silence passed between them. Zandra sniffed and used her sleeve to wipe her face. "You think you're so wise. You're only a couple of years older than me," she said. The half-smile she wore seemed forced. "Okay. I mean, I'll think about it. Good enough?"

"I'll take it."

Zandra's mouth twisted grimly. "There's really soldiers here?"

"Yeah. I haven't seen them yet, but Milo did." He almost mentioned that their parents wanted to ship him off with the soldiers when they left, but he didn't want his sister to worry about that unless there was something to worry about for sure. He'd double down, put in some extra time on the farm on top of his duties at the clinic, and get Ferrick to talk them down. Maybe if they heard, one more time, how good of a healer he was... well, maybe it would finally mean something to them. Something more than the coin and peace of mind they'd get by sending him away.

Despite not knowing his secret worries, Zandra said, "When I leave, come with me. Be a mage with me."

"Zandra—"

"Think about it."

Dante nodded. His promise was solely to placate her. He wanted out of Briarglen, maybe out of Saridian, so he could be safe... but actually becoming a mage? Magic seemed dangerous even without the risk of being caught by soldiers. Zandra's fall only proved that. Maybe Riordan was right to ban mortals from using it. Either way, Dante was no mage. He was barely capable in mundane matters.

Zandra put on a brave face, but as Dante gave her a hand up he felt her trembling. *Could this close call put her on a safer course?* Scared as she was in this moment, he wasn't sure it would last. His sister's determination was rooted deep. For now, he was grateful that she'd survived. Somehow doing the wrong thing, using magic, had saved his sister.

Dante couldn't stop the growing knot of anxiety. This nightmare had come to life, and it was far from being the only disturbing scene that haunted his dreams. The images were becoming more vivid each night. He could hope that it was a fluke that he had foreseen this event. A coincidence, or a one-time divination.

He could also pretend that his dreams weren't what had driven him toward the crystal shards his father had dumped into the creek, causing him to painstakingly search out each piece, following the faint trail of magic that radiated from them. He did this despite any logical reason and against his better judgment.

But he had to do it, to stop the endless dreams—where each shard shone so much brighter than in reality, and he picked them up, over and over in his sleep, until he finally gave in and did so in his waking hours.

His dreams taught him how it felt to put the shards of crystal together, how they fit, and how to bind them back together with magic until it was once again a single item—a perfectly round crystal sphere. It had been an obsession to make it whole once more, and then once it was... there was nothing. The crystal suddenly didn't feel any more magical than a sack of potatoes. Regardless, he couldn't bear to throw it away, so he stashed it under his bed and tried to forget about it.

Those dreams ceased, and the regular cycle of nightmares continued to play out, instead. Zandra falling. Flames, everywhere. Screaming. Briarglen, in ruins.

He could feign ignorance, but deep down he knew: life was only going to become more dangerous.

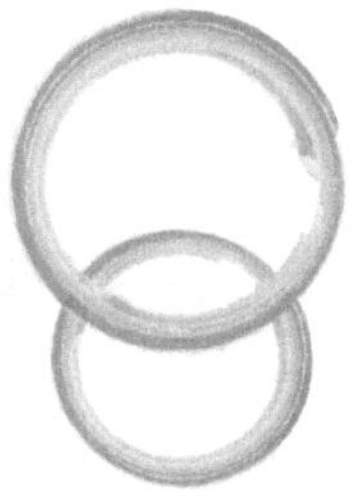

Chapter 3

As Scarlet slept, her unconscious mind summoned a tangle of memories and dreams.

She heard her sister's voice and saw her family together, intact. They traveled down a winding road. Her father had an arm draped casually around her mother's shoulder, and he laughed at something she had said. Viridian was the same age that Scarlet was now, calling her younger sister along, a young Scarlet bounding behind them.

But Viridian would never get older, she was immortalized at sixteen. The four of them would never be together again.

Scarlet dreamed about the raven—no, the god. There was a sensation as if she were floating down a river. Or perhaps, she was part of the river. She had no body, and her whole self was dispersing into the water as it flowed. Her destination was close.

Black feathers fluttered against a hazy, purple sky. An outstretched hand pulled what was left of her from the stream. There was a deal. She could live. She could have what she wanted most: power. All she had to do was trade her soul—

—then she was falling. The descent seemed endless. Everything around her was darkness. Flames lived in her fingertips. If she could just summon them to light her surroundings, maybe she could do something. But she was frozen, falling; she couldn't muster her magic. She screamed into the void, helpless to do anything to save herself.

Finally, there was silence and peace. Rest. Calm.

A voice broke through it. *Scarlet.* It was Viridian. Her words were urgent. *You've been asleep too long. You have to wake up. You have to find Mom. Before... before—*

Scarlet snapped awake. She sat up in bed, testing the limits of her body. Her back ached, but it was more tolerable than the first time she'd woken. Her bare feet, one at a time, made contact with the stone floor. Cold seeped into her feet. Though it was unpleasant, Scarlet was grateful for the chill, it steadied her as she rose.

She shivered. *How much of that was a dream, and how much was real? Is Mom in trouble?* Her joints ached as she moved. Maybe she had been asleep for a while. Days? Hopefully not weeks. How bad exactly were her injuries, to keep her laid up this long?

She stumbled to the floor-length mirror and wiped the thick layer of dust off of it. Then she took off her nightgown and unbound the dressings that kept the injury on her back clean. She looked over her shoulder to examine her wound in the mirror. Near her left shoulder blade was a circle, a couple of inches in diameter with thin tendrils branching out in every direction and splitting off even further, like bolts of lightning.

The scabs covering it were pure black, and where it was beginning to peel, the skin underneath was darkened as well. She would have to get used to the starburst scar; it seemed inevitable that it would be permanent. A small price for survival.

What exactly happened? Viridian said she was going to try to help her while she slept. Did that mean she might be able to remember now? She sat back down on the bed, closed her eyes, and tried to bring her memories back into focus.

The fragments began to piece together.

They'd been hunted. Scarlet's mother pulled her out of bed with shaking hands. Enemies approached their cottage. Scarlet had never seen her mother in such a frenzy. Usually, she was fearless under pressure.

Panicked, they fled the cabin, making their way through the forest surrounding their cottage, her mother using magic to conceal their retreat. Thick conjured mist spread around them, and their tracks faded into the snow after each step.

Normally, when they were obscured, it was alright to speak quietly. But when Scarlet began to ask questions, her mother put a finger to her lips, eyes wide. This was the moment Scarlet realized how much peril they were in. They'd been chased by her mother's enemies before.

But not like this.

The hunter closed in, so they abandoned stealth in favor of speed. Scarlet tripped on tree roots, barreled through branches, her mother yanking her forward—until a single figure had appeared in front of them. A man on the other side of the snow-covered grove, silhouetted in the light of the moon. Not just a man. A god. Scarlet could feel his aura pressing in on her, even over the distance. Her mother froze, grasped Scarlet's hand so tight it hurt, then suddenly let go.

"Run. Don't look back."

Scarlet, in opposition to her mother's plea, froze. Her breath came out in visible puffs, swirling in front of her before dissipating into the night. The mist her mother had conjured likewise dispersed into the forest around them.

Hiding was no longer an option.

"Scarlet. *Run.*"

"But—"

"Go!"

Scarlet stood paralyzed for one last moment. *I can't leave her to die.* But neither could she help. She turned and fled further into the woods.

Her chest started to burn with the exertion of plowing through the snow and pushing aside branches, with her fear and frustration acidic, eating at her core.

She should have taught me to fight.

A sharp scream resounded through the forest. Scarlet stopped short, taking a glance back toward where she had left her mother behind. She was too far away now, she could only see trees and darkness.

A sob grew in her throat, but she stifled it. There was no time to cry. She had to keep her silence and escape, or—

Or she could try to save her mother. But how? Scarlet crouched and pulled her dagger free from her boot sheath. It wasn't magic, but better to have a weapon than not. Staying low to the ground, Scarlet crept back toward the glade.

She didn't have a plan. She was probably about to get herself killed—and if, miraculously, they survived, her mother would probably kill her for coming back instead of running to safety. It didn't matter. Scarlet couldn't live with herself if she gave in to cowardice and let her mother die.

The trees began to open into the clearing. Scarlet circled around, doing her best to stay covered by branches and brush until she caught sight of the god. He wore a cloak patterned with mottled colors, which would have given him camouflage deeper within the forest, though not against the stark white of the snow. At his feet was Scarlet's mother, crouched over on her knees, holding her balance with one hand planted in the snow. Her other hand was pressed against her chest, above her heart. From her distance, Scarlet thought she saw blood dripping onto the snow.

As Scarlet moved to place herself behind the god and as close as possible while maintaining her cover, she found that she couldn't look at him directly. Every time she tried, her gaze was shunted to the side. A unique trick of his magic, no doubt.

She was close enough to hear him speak now. "I won't kill you. At least, not yet. But you will live in a world of pain until that moment comes: the moment I have everything I need from you."

Scarlet's grip on the dagger tightened. Could she throw the blade into his back? She'd practiced such a thing, but he was still too far for her to be confident she'd hit her mark—especially without being able to look right at him. But perhaps all she needed was a distraction to give her mother a moment to retaliate.

"Torture me or kill me now, it makes no difference. I'll give you nothing." Her mother's voice was thin.

The glowing pulse of magic appeared in the man's hand, pure energy coalescing into a deadly bolt. "Perhaps I'll save myself some time then."

As he raised his hand to throw the energy bolt at Kiera's face, a primal yell unwittingly escaped Scarlet's throat. She flung her dagger at the god and charged forward after it. The blade missed its mark, whipping by his left side. The god's bolt likewise failed to hit, but clearly on purpose. It struck the ground next to Kiera's hand, forming a crater about a foot both in diameter and depth. After releasing the energy, the god spun toward Scarlet, and she found herself suspended mid-stride.

"*Scarlet!*" Her mother's cry awakened Scarlet's guilt. She was a fool; she should have run. Now they would both die. Scarlet had risked her life for nothing.

With a flick of the god's hand, Scarlet fell backward into the snow. She rolled onto her hands and knees, preparing to get up, but then—pain blossomed from her back. The energy held in the magic bolt that hit her resounded through her body, forcing her to convulse and writhe in the biting cold of the snow. Her blood felt as if it were boiling, an agony beyond anything she could have imagined.

And then, nothing.

And now, one deal with Death later, she was in the Crossworld. Somehow, her mother had thwarted Riordan after he took down Scarlet. *So all she needed* was *a distraction after all. She made it out.*

Scarlet took a deep breath, separating herself from the memory. She looked down at the new tattoo on the back of her hand. Another cost of survival. It wasn't just ink that'd been injected into her skin; she could feel magic running through the marks.

Her mother had explained that emissary tattoos were what connected an emissary to their patron god. Scarlet could feel that connection when she concentrated. Death's ominous presence lingered somewhere in the castle. Her stomach churned. The pain that had flared through her tattoo when Death ordered her to go back to her room had only gone away with her surrender.

Recalling that loss of control made her shudder.

My turn to need a distraction. She turned to the window and pulled back the blinds. This time, daylight shone in through it. The castle seemed to be planted in the middle of a swamp. Patches of land interspersed water that looked green—or perhaps teal—with algae, even from up high. Scattered across the landscape were reeds and trees with winding, twisted branches without leaves. As she had ascertained in the darkness, the sky was purple. The brighter daylight hue made Scarlet feel like she was in an odd dream world.

She'd spent enough time asleep. Her limbs were weak and heavy. When had she last eaten? Her stomach was tied in knots of anxiety, but even so, it growled for sustenance. Where could she even find food?

Scarlet turned to her door, considering another excursion out of her room. Immediately, a folded note on the ground caught her eye. It seemed to have been pushed into the room under her door. She snatched it up, her eager curiosity overcoming the stiffness of her body.

It read:

Scarlet,

When you wake, please come to find me. We will continue your healing process. Also, I have proper food for you if you are up for it. Directions to my quarters are on the back.

-Bronwen

Who in the World was Bronwen? Her healer? Apparently, someone who had food. At this point, that was good enough for her. Scarlet turned the note over. On the back, as promised, was a map showing her a twisting route from her room to another.

Whoever Bronwen was, she didn't want to meet him wearing the nightgown she had been dressed in. Scarlet pulled open the wardrobe, wondering if her hopes for better clothing would manifest as quickly as her hopes for food seemed to. She was disappointed to find that the wardrobe only contained the musty dresses that had been there the first time she checked it. She grabbed the purple one. It was a unique color, purple dye was hard to procure. After putting it on, she looked at herself in the mirror.

She'd never worn a dress. It had never been practical. At any moment, she and her mother could have been in danger and needed to flee. Plus, it's not like she'd had any formal events to go to. It had been a long time since she'd looked in a mirror, too—and she'd never seen a full-length one like this before. Suddenly, staring at her own reflection, she felt self-conscious.

Am I pretty? It wasn't something she had ever worried about, and it was a strange thought to confront now. She smoothed the dress where it ruffled out awkwardly. It fit her body well enough, though it was a bit long, and weird to see herself in. It had too many layers of skirts. Dresses would continue to be impractical, especially if she was going to be learning how to control her fire magic soon.

Scarlet took a breath. *Okay. Good enough.* Referencing the map, she made her way to Bronwen's room. She was glad for clear directions, though even with them she nearly turned the wrong way down the winding hallways that occasionally looped around each other. *What a strange design.* Her head was spinning and the pain in her back had doubled by the time she reached the indicated door, though it hadn't been that long of a walk. She hesitated at the door for a moment, then knocked.

A man opened the door. He looked older than her, probably in his twenties. His hair curled down to his cheeks and matched the brown of his eyes. There was something soft about his gaze; totally opposite of Death's piercing stare. It threw her off. He broke into a smile when he saw her.

"Scarlet! I'm so glad to see you up. Please, do come in."

She let the man lead her inside. The room was large, with huge windows letting in natural light. It was the first room she'd seen in the castle that wasn't dark and sparse. There were decorations—rugs, cushions, tapestries—and so many plants. It was *alive*, filled with color, and a bit overwhelming. Scarlet couldn't take it all in. "Could I sit?"

"Yes, of course."

He took her over to a sitting area in the corner of the room, and they each sat on a couch, opposite from one another. Scarlet glanced out at the window behind her and then turned to face the man.

"I'm Bronwen," he said, "as you've probably assumed, given my note and all." His voice, like the rest of him, was gentle. It was clear that he intended to calm her, but somehow the contrast between Bronwen and everything else she had experienced since she'd first awoken left her more perturbed, if anything. *Maybe I'm just being cynical. Waiting for a twist that isn't even coming.*

Scarlet took a breath. Now that she was sitting, her mind relaxed a bit more at least. She caught a glance at Bronwen's hands. One of them had the dual circles emblazoned on the back. "You're an emissary?"

"Yes. I'm Deianira's caretaker. And, occasionally, a caretaker of guests, such as yourself."

Right. He'd implied as much in his note. "Death didn't mention you when I... met her."

"Death is like that sometimes. Preoccupied."

"Oh." Scarlet picked at a cuticle absently in the brief silence that followed. "You said in your note that we'd continue my healing process?"

"That's right. I'm a healer, so I've been aiding in your recovery. While Death saved you from the brink of, well, death... you needed some additional help to ensure your stability and make your recovery more rapid than it would have otherwise been."

"Wait, you heal with magic?" Not that Scarlet knew many mages, but she did know that healing was a particularly rare talent.

"Yes. My gift was a large factor in Death selecting me as an emissary and as caretaker of the castle. If you would allow me, I will continue healing you. But first—I offered you food, didn't I? Would you like some oatmeal?"

Scarlet nodded, and Bronwen disappeared for a few minutes through a curtain that covered the doorway to another room. When he returned, he handed her a bowl of steaming oatmeal with bright red berries in it. She thanked him and took a careful bite of the hot oats.

"So." Bronwen said, taking his seat across from her again. "I'm sure you must have questions. As you've already learned, Death is not always the most forthcoming. I'll fill in whatever blanks I can."

Scarlet swallowed a mouthful. "How long has it been since I got here?"

"Weeks. Your body needed quite a while to regain its energy, even with my aid."

Scarlet dropped her spoon into the bowl. It clattered loudly. "Weeks?" *Mom has been gone for* weeks? *Viridian was right. I did sleep too long.*

"I'm afraid so." Bronwen frowned empathetically.

Scarlet took her spoon back in hand and took a couple more bites of oatmeal. The berries in it were unfamiliar to her. They were sour, but in a way she found pleasant. "Are there any other emissaries here?"

"Just you and I. There aren't many of us, so Death tends to keep us busy."

"Busy fighting Riordan."

"Not directly at this time, but as an ultimate goal, yes."

"Why?"

Bronwen's brow furrowed. "Your mother never told you?"

Scarlet snorted. "No. She didn't want me involved in... all of this. But now I am, and I need to know everything I can."

"I see." Bronwen leaned back into the couch cushion and took a deep breath. "You grew up in Saridian, right? I'm sure you've witnessed Riordan's influence over his lands firsthand. Unless you worship his godliness and thus wish to appease him at any cost, it's easy to see that his rule is a detriment. Especially as a mage. But even setting his ban of magic aside, he drains the wealth of his people and his land for his own selfish interests. Unlike the other gods, who work for the empowerment and advancement of their people, or, at worst, leave their people alone to do what they will."

"I know all of *that*." Scarlet tried to not sound as irritated as she felt. "But why does Death care? She's not like the other gods either. She's never played a role in the mortal World. This is the first time she's chosen a physical incarnate, isn't it? So why does she care to get involved now?"

"There is, of course, more to it. But that is as much as I can say. Death has requested that I not speak of it to you. I was hoping you already knew more." He furrowed his brows.

Scarlet growled. "I'm an emissary. Shouldn't I know about this fight, if I may be expected to take part in it?"

"I agree that you should know the full reasons for their conflict, but Death must explain it to you herself."

Scarlet finished the rest of her oatmeal in silence, lost in thought.

Bronwen cleared his throat. "Before I send you back to continue resting, may I do a healing session on you?"

"Yes," Scarlet said without hesitation. Walking back to her room seemed unimaginably painful right now, and she was curious about magical healing.

Bronwen got her to lay face down on the couch, and he pulled up a chair to sit close to her. Then he placed his hands just above her injury and began to pour energy into it. The sensation was strange; it caused her skin to tingle and itch. She got lost in the sensation as the healing session wore on and melted away her pain.

But while her body relaxed, her mind refused to. "You said that Death requested that you not tell me some things. Was it... a request, or a *demand*?"

"She's my god," Bronwen said. "To me, a request and a demand are one and the same."

"When I wandered and Death found me in the library... I didn't listen to her right away when she wanted me to come back to my room. But, she did something. And I felt forced to obey."

"Gods can use their power to compel their emissaries," Bronwen explained. "It takes some energy to do, but it is a technique that Death occasionally employs."

"And it doesn't bother you?"

"There are tradeoffs to being an emissary," Bronwen said. "There are benefits, too. I would barely be able to heal without my magic being augmented by Death's power. If you trust that your patron knows best, then you won't feel stunted by their orders."

Trust. *Could* she trust Death? Bronwen had been correct, she had seen enough back in Saridian to know that Riordan's rule was detrimental. The ban on magic, the brutal taxes, the limitations on knowledge... none of it was right. Even if those weren't the reasons for Death's battle with him, defeating him would help free Saridian. Plus, her mother obviously believed in Death's cause.

But still. Being thrust into Death's service while knowing so little about the god herself left her uneasy.

Bronwen took advantage of her contemplative silence to ask a probing question of his own. "Your mother is Galapi, but you grew up in Saridian, is that right?"

Scarlet grunted a confirmation. She had never been to her mother's home region, the Galapia Islands off the north coast of Quintras. Instead, she'd spent her life on the southern end of the continent. She'd never left Saridian—until now. "Do you know my mother well? Or where Death sent her?"

"I've met her, but I don't know her well. And no, I'm not sure what Death's mission for her is."

What was so important that she had to leave even while I was injured? And Viridian made it seem like she was in trouble... Scarlet tried to reach out mentally for the connection with her sister. But there was nothing, not even a hint of Viridian's presence. *Maybe I just imagined it all.*

Though Scarlet was caught up in her thoughts, Bronwen continued. "And what about your father?"

Scarlet stiffened. "What about him?"

Bronwen, evidently picking up on the sharpness in her words, murmured an apology and stopped asking questions in favor of focusing on healing.

After a couple of tense minutes, Bronwen stopped the flow of magic into her wound and then pressed it lightly with a couple of fingers. "Does that hurt, still?"

Scarlet grimaced. Touching her wound or moving around too vigorously still sent strange tingly spikes throughout her body. "Not as much as before."

"Well, you are making progress, though you still have some way to go." Bronwen got up and started sorting through some glass bottles and jars up on a shelf. "I have some ointment somewhere that would be good for your pain in the meantime."

Scarlet sat back up. "Thank you. For the healing and... and everything." She felt guilty for snapping at him, especially after everything he had done to help her recover over the past weeks. Her father was a sore spot, but how would he know that? She reached for another topic, trying to smooth them back into friendly conversation. "How did you end up here?"

"Similar to you. Death saved me and gave me a choice. I could cross over, or I could help her. I chose to stay."

"She pulls that move a lot, does she?"

"Not anymore. Her power wanes, and plucking souls from the stream is not easy. But for a while, yes, many were recruited that way. Death cannot leave, so it was one of her only ways of finding emissaries. She also occasionally takes a Raven as an emissary."

The Ravens. She and her mother visited the nomadic tribe on a semi-regular basis, as they paid well for copies of histories that Scarlet flamescribed, or commissioned Scarlet to reproduce their own texts. The Ravens appreciated the high-quality reproductions and the fact that Scarlet and her mother could be trusted.

The nomadic tribe was openly defiant to Riordan and his laws. They were the last bastion of knowledge in Saridian for anything regarding magic, the other regions of Quintras, and the Magus War. Of course, that made it dangerous to spend time with them, so her mother kept their visits short.

Scarlet had long suspected that the leader of the Ravens was an emissary, but her mother would never confirm it. That was the problem with her mother—the constant limits she set. How much magic Scarlet could use. How much Scarlet could know. Which Ravens she was allowed to speak to, and for how long. It was all, ostensibly, for her safety.

"I've never gotten a good idea of what emissaries do, now that the Magus War has been over for nearly a century," Scarlet said. "I mean, Death's emissaries obviously combat Riordan, but what about other gods' emissaries?"

"It depends on the god. Each still has their own goals. Creating more of their ideals in the World allows their powers to grow. These days, a lot of emissaries serve their region by researching new technologies, whether magical or mundane, or by training others in the practices and ideals of their gods. Most regions don't have their god as a king, as Riordan has placed himself. Oromu, for example, is led by a council of Io's emissaries." Bronwen plucked a jar from the back of the shelf. "Aha! Here is it." He handed it to Scarlet. "It's a little smelly, but you can rub it on your wound a few times a day and it should curtail the pain, somewhat."

"Thank you."

"Do you need a hand navigating back to your room?"

"I think I'll be alright, I still have your map," Scarlet said. As she was about to leave, she turned back to Bronwen. "Do you regret it? Staying. Becoming an emissary."

"I have unfinished business in this World. I wish to repay Riordan the pain he put me through during my first life," Bronwen said.

What did Riordan do to him? Scarlet wondered, though it didn't seem the time to question him further.

"So no, I do not regret my decision. I hope you feel the same in the end, Scarlet."

CHAPTER 4

Every time Scarlet slept, she worried she would re-enter her comatose state that had kept her unconscious for weeks. *Viridian, please wake me if I sleep too long,* Scarlet pleaded. But neither did she continue to sleep days away, nor hear her sister again.

Each morning, Bronwen visited her to perform another healing session. He also showed her the way to the castle's storeroom, which he kept stocked with food and other essentials. After he left, Scarlet spent some time resting. She seemed slightly stronger each day, but she was always the most tired after Bronwen's healing, her body working in overdrive to use the energy Bronwen infused into her to repair her injuries.

In the afternoons, she began to explore Deianira. Bronwen told her she could go anywhere she wanted within the castle, provided it was unlocked. It was an easy enough rule to follow.

Her first stop was the library, though it was difficult to find again. The layout of the castle continued to baffle her. The halls often turned one way, only to force her to turn in the opposite direction only a few paces down.

There would be a long, straight hall with no doors, then several small rooms clustered close together. Scarlet could not fathom why it would be designed this way, and it made it challenging to map out the castle in her mind. She wasn't even confident that the halls weren't changing over time... though perhaps her mind was just muddled from her injuries and how long she'd been unconscious while recovering.

But after some hours of winding through the castle, she finally rediscovered the library's location. Light poured in from the windows on the far end of the library, and she spotted some desks there that would provide a sunny place to perch and study. She grabbed a tome at random from the nearest shelf.

As soon as she opened the book, the smell of charred paper was immediately recognizable. Holding a newly inked book in her hands was an infrequent event, but to examine the work of another flamescribe was an even rarer treat. She ran her fingers down the page, examining the cursive letterforms that another mage had carefully burned onto the paper. For a moment, admiring the craftsmanship took precedence over reading the actual words as she flipped through the book.

Flamescribing was a delicate art, one that Scarlet equally loved and hated. It took immense control to produce a flame small and cool enough to char fine letters onto a page without igniting the paper itself. It was often monotonous, mind-numbing work that left her exhausted. But she also loved the challenge of mastering a new set of letterforms, and the expressiveness of the craft. When she had extra paper, she'd take a break from letters to instead illustrate landscapes or intricate designs of her own imagination.

It was the one kind of magic that her mother allowed her to do on a regular basis. Using magic put them at risk of mage hunters sniffing them out, but flamescribing was a minor enough task that as long as they were living somewhere secluded, her mother had deemed it as undetectable enough to be safe.

As Scarlet grew proficient in her craft, it became their main source of income. Scarlet scribed reproductions of illicit texts that held information about the gods, history books covering the Magus War that the gods had induced to gain more power for themselves, and information about magic in general. Her mother sold these copies to the Ravens—the only group that worked openly against Riordan and that they could trust not to report them. The Ravens did the riskier job of distributing those texts to others across Saridian.

The book Scarlet flipped through was similar to some she had reproduced, in that it spoke of the Magus War. This one appeared to focus on the god Meyrin, and Celeigh, the lands he controlled to the north of Saridian. The section she had flipped to detailed how Meyrin created the Prismatic Wall, alongside his emissaries and other loyal mages. Other books Scarlet had read and copied were much more broad than this, which made it all the more interesting.

She wished she could one day see the Prismatic Wall in person. An immense wall, crafted only of magic, that defended all of Celeigh's borders that weren't already protected by mountain ranges... she couldn't even imagine what it would be like to see a colossal magical structure like that, especially after growing up in Saridian.

As she further explored the library, she found more meticulous records of the Magus War and other events in the history of Quintras, as well as reference books. She began digging into the histories, thirsty for more knowledge of the gods and their emissaries.

The rest of the castle was largely composed of empty rooms, but she did find a couple places of interest. There was an armory, full of various protective gear and weapons. One room, perhaps once occupied by a tailor, was filled with fabric and finished clothing. Scarlet had scavenged a few pieces of clothing, some well-made shirts, and sturdy pants for her wardrobe. *Finally, something other than dresses to wear. I need something easier to move in for training.* She wondered who had made them. *An emissary?*

There was one door she found that she didn't have the nerve to touch. It was made of a dark stone, perhaps obsidian. It matched the set of doors that Scarlet suspected led out of the castle, except those rose many times her height. She had tried to push those larger doors open, but they were shut tight. The smaller door gave her more pause. On the other side, she felt a presence, a dark emanating of energy. Perhaps it was Death, and Scarlet dared not disturb the god, though she doubted the handleless door would respond to her touch any more than the larger one did.

It took less than a week for Scarlet to tire of the routine of healing and exploring the mostly vacant castle. While recovering and soaking up all the new information held in the library had kept her occupied, each turn of the sun made her increasingly restless.

Scarlet was pacing from one end of her room to the other when Bronwen next came to heal her. He paused upon entering, seemingly perplexed by her anxious energy.

"Scarlet," he said carefully, "are you ready for—"

"How long have I been here?" Scarlet interrupted, stopping her pacing to swivel toward him. "You said weeks. How many?"

"Eight, I think."

Two months. Too long. "And my mother has been gone just as long." It was half question, half statement. "I was near death, and she hasn't even come to check on me."

"Death has her doing a very important task, as I understand it. She may not be able to interrupt her mission to visit."

"Or something went wrong."

Bronwen's lips twisted. "Or... or something went wrong," he admitted. "But Kiera is a formidable mage and—"

"And has never left me this long. Not since—" Scarlet stopped. She crossed her arms, each hand gripping the opposite arm tightly. *Not since Viridian was killed.* But she couldn't say it. If she really had heard her sister though, Viridian knew something was wrong too. "She just... wouldn't leave me this long. Not unless something happened to her."

"I... I don't have the details about your mother's whereabouts. I wish I could put your mind more at ease." Bronwen's face was a shade paler than normal. "But for now, it's best if we focus on your recovery, and hopefully news of your mother will come soon."

Scarlet took a breath. "No."

"No?"

"I'm done resting. Death said she would train me when I recovered. It's time."

Bronwen's gentle tone took on a bit more edge. "You've come a long way, but the kind of training that Death has in mind for you... it's intense. I want you at full capacity before facing the rigors of delving into magic, and you aren't ready yet."

Scarlet shook her head, sending her wild curls bouncing back and forth. "It's already been too long. I can't just sit here in bed doing *nothing* anymore. I'm an emissary now, and I need to live up to it."

A new voice cut in. "For what it's worth, I agree with the girl."

Bronwen spun to face the doorway, and Scarlet's gaze snapped into focus behind him, where Death had appeared at the threshold of the room. The god wore a pitch-black robe, trimmed with intricate lace. Her braided red hair contrasted brightly against it.

Bronwen held steady. "With all due respect, Scarlet is not ready."

Death shrugged. "She'll never be."

"The state that she's in, you'll damage her further."

Death pushed past Bronwen and examined Scarlet as she drew closer. "Keeping her idle could be nearly as detrimental." She reached a hand toward Scarlet, who nearly flinched away but forced herself to stand resolute. Death pressed her fingers on Scarlet's forehead.

Scarlet couldn't decide if the god's touch was cold or hot. Her emissary mark buzzed with energy, itchy and invigorating. The bond between herself and her patron god felt tangible in this moment, a rope of energy tying them together.

Feeling the god's presence up close felt like being thrust into space, among the galaxy of stars. On one end of the connection was Scarlet, rejuvenated though not whole, specks of unrealized power within herself.

Her energy was scattered nebulae, a cloud of dust disseminated. On the other end was Death, and Scarlet felt lost staring into her vast well of power. Scarlet was insignificant compared to the smoldering core of power held within the god. It was a star, the sun, so bright it nearly blinded all her senses.

Death removed her hand, and Scarlet suddenly felt empty. It took a moment to steady herself, she felt too light, like the slightest breeze from the open window could knock her over.

This... is the power Death has when she is weakened. *It's more than I ever could have imagined.*

Scarlet blinked a couple of times and realized that Bronwen and Death had continued to discuss the matter while she was in a daze. She focused back in just in time for Death to turn back to her. "Bronwen may or may not have a point," the god said. "Training now could come at a price. You have been struck by a god, then subsequently bound to me. It is a lot to subject your body to. But I also fear you may wither without a focus. You have been left to languish too long—both your mother's doing as well as your recent respite."

Scarlet didn't have to hesitate. "Train me," she said. "I don't care what it costs me."

The next morning, at dawn, Scarlet made her way to the front doors of Deianira, as Death had instructed her to do. Her suspicions that the imposing obsidian doors led out of the castle had been confirmed. She wiped her sweaty palms on her pants while she waited for the god to arrive.

It wasn't long until Death strode down the hallway to join her. She was wearing a light set of leather armor that looked easy to move in. Her red hair was pulled back into a messy braid, and as always she wore a simple crystal necklace, a delicate piece of jewelry that looked slightly out of place alongside the armor.

Scarlet locked eyes with Death, overwhelmed for a moment as she recalled the immense power that the god wielded. *This is it. I nearly had to die for it to happen, but I'm finally going to learn combat magic... from a god.*

She froze for a moment, remembering her first encounter with a god. Face to face with Riordan, she'd been so helpless. Her throat constricted. She wiped her hands again.

"Well, go on," Death said, and nodded her head toward the door.

Scarlet, tentative, reached out and touched the door. The moment her fingers made contact, her hand buzzed with the sensation of flowing magic. Silver tendrils extended out from where her fingers made contact with the obsidian, designs lighting up the stone as the door swung open, silent despite their overwhelming size.

Scarlet stepped outside and took a deep breath of relief. She hadn't realized how confining the dark walls of Deianira were until stepping out into the open swampland surrounding the castle. Death began to lead her away from the castle.

The air here was thin, too light, and more humid than Scarlet was used to. She had noticed that it made her curly hair even more unmanageable than usual. The reeds that sprouted from the moist ground around her were teal instead of a true green. The twin moons were visible even in the daytime, looming over her in the violet sky as a constant reminder that she was far from home.

Deianira sat above the surrounding lands, so the farther away they went, the more swamp Scarlet got inside her boots. They slogged through rivulets and muddy terrain until they were close to the river—the stream of souls. She'd heard about the stream from the books she'd copied, and about how they separated the gods' realms in the Crossworld. Bronwen had indicated that they were in the center of the Crossworld, Death's realm. They were encircled by a river that was fed by the five streams which, like spokes on a wheel, separated the other surrounding realms.

As they drew closer to the rushing water, Scarlet picked up her pace, curious to see the river for the first time. When it came into view, she was disappointed to see that the water itself looked the same as any other river. Then, she noticed it had a glimmering undercurrent. Scarlet could feel the energy rushing within the stream. It tugged at her, almost as if it were beckoning her. Death stopped, which snapped Scarlet back to attention. She glanced around. They had stopped in a mostly open area next to the river, free of the denser plant and tree life that covered most of the swamp. Scarlet's feet were freezing and her heart was pounding.

"Before we begin," Death said, "I want you to know some things."

Am I finally going to get some answers about Death and Riordan? Scarlet wondered.

"I will not go easy on you. At some point, during all this, you might wonder—why? Why suffer, why struggle for this god? I will tell you right now the reason why: Riordan. He is a scourge that must be removed, at all costs."

"Why do you care what he does?"

"If Riordan has his way," Death said, "he will stop me from tending to the cycle of souls between Worlds. This disruption would be catastrophic for both gods and mortals. And if for some reason that is not enough to take up my cause, you are my emissary, and that means he will come for you, eventually. When that time comes, you must defend yourself."

A blurred memory flashed—the silhouette of Riordan in Scarlet's peripheral vision, back in the forest. His power crackled around him, his aura ripping through her even from a distance. She had to run—

But being afraid would only get her killed faster. Death was right. Scarlet was an emissary now. To survive, she'd have to fight. She probably should have run instead of flinging herself at Riordan, before—but how could she have just left her mother to her fate? What kind of option was that? No. Fear wasn't the answer. Or maybe it was, because the thought of facing

Riordan again chilled her to the core. But there was no choice, now. She had to keep pushing toward what she had wanted for so long: the power to fight, to defend herself and her family.

Scarlet took a couple of shaky breaths before she spoke again. "And what about the other gods? If he's that dangerous, why don't you all work together to stop him?"

"The other gods." Death snarled. "They are useless. Self-involved. They don't see him coming, and even if they did, interfering with one another would break the treaty and begin the Magus War anew."

"Then aren't you and Riordan breaking the treaty already?"

"I never took part in the other gods' petty war. So I am neither protected nor hindered by their treaty." Death twisted her braid in her hands.

"Why does Riordan want to stop you from shepherding souls to the Nextworld?"

"That is not his aim, but a consequence of him succeeding in his goals." Death clapped her hands together, a signal of finality even though Scarlet's questions had been dodged. "Alright, let's begin. Tell me what you've learned so far."

"I... in terms of combat magic, nothing. I can make light orbs and flamescribe. I've tried to make some larger flames but... my mother would always stop me from practicing."

Death shook her head. "*Tsk.* Kiera gave you no way to defend yourself?"

Scarlet kneeled and pulled the dagger out of her boot sheath. "She taught me to use this. But otherwise..."

Death snorted. "Oh, useful. If you need to cut a tough steak, that is. That dagger may as well be a needle, for all the help it will give you against another mage."

Scarlet sheepishly resheathed her weapon. *I can't argue that it would be useful in a real fight, but it is the only thing of Mom's I have with me now.*

"So, flamescribing, you said. Immolation magic. You're attuned to Ka-jiem." A grimace briefly passed over Death's face.

"Is something wrong with that?"

"No. No, it is useful. And beautiful. Have you heard of the fire dancers of Suraskrit? In the desert, magic is an art. Much like your flamescribing, I suppose." Death stared out over the river for a moment before continuing. "The other aspect of Kajiem's gifts, which you may have as well, is enhancement. Magic that you can use to make your skin tougher, reflexes quicker. Or someone else's, as enhancement mages often do."

Scarlet coaxed her tiny flame to dance between her fingers. She'd tried to use enhancement magic—behind her mother's back, of course—but had never been able to make it work. "Did you come from Suraskrit? I mean, your human half, of course—"

Death snatched Scarlet's hand, forcing her fingers to close around the flame, extinguishing it. Smoke filtered out between the fingers of Scarlet's closed fist, weaving upward between her and Death, their faces close. "Focus. You must practice discipline above all else. The power you wield is not for free. Magic is taking your life energy and weaving it into physical effects. Negligence can, and will, result in injury. Or, what's probably worse in your eyes: death."

Death released her grip on Scarlet and stepped away. Scarlet tried to center herself and suppress the lump growing in her throat.

"So pay attention," Death said. "No more questions. We'll start with the basics."

Death took her through a series of meditative exercises, urging Scarlet to clear her mind and breathe deeply. Scarlet fidgeted throughout.

Death's frustration at Scarlet's lack of focus became increasingly apparent. She snapped at Scarlet for squirming more than once. "What did I say about discipline?" she growled. "You might not think this is important, but I assure you that it is."

"Sorry. There's... a lot on my mind." *Between wondering about Viridian, my mom, and the dangers of Riordan, how can I be calm? Plus, Mom should have taught me years ago, and now my impatience to use magic, rather than just prepare for it, is costing me this lesson.* Scarlet gave a deep sigh, then made a renewed effort. As intrusive thoughts or worries arose, she did her best to dismiss them and stay in a state of peace.

After Scarlet had sat quietly for some time, Death spoke up. "Reach out with your mind, feel the space around you. Tell me what you sense."

Scarlet drew in a breath, exhaled slowly, and let her mind unfurl and discern the energies around her. The stream of souls and Death's aura were overpowering. It took her a few minutes to hone in on the finer details of the energy flowing throughout this area, at which point she realized something about the Crossworld that she hadn't before. "There's so much energy here, all around. It's not like this in the World."

"In the World, mortals access the divine gift through the veins of magus stone that run beneath the earth. The power of the gods flows through that stone and some mortals become, by proximity, attuned to a god's energy in a way that lets them use magic. But the Crossworld is the divine realm. Here, our power is everywhere."

Scarlet paused to consider. "Does that mean I can use any god's magic here?"

"No. You are attuned to Kajiem's energy and that will not change. Your magic will be stronger here though, and more difficult to control. Hence, my insistence on discipline."

Scarlet nodded, resigning herself to taking the process of learning magic more slowly than she'd hoped. After the lecture, Scarlet certainly didn't want to face the consequences of losing control of her magic.

Before the lesson ended, Death got her to summon a small flame. Death told her to focus on the stream of energy that Scarlet fed the fire with, to be aware of how much power she was using, and how to increase and decrease the flow. Scarlet practiced making the flame roar large and hot, a new and invigorating sensation, and reducing it to a tiny pinprick, a practice she was used to but that indeed seemed more difficult now.

When she returned to her room, she was drained both mentally and physically, but pleased. Even if it was a slow process, it was happening. She was learning magic.

CHAPTER 5

Jarrett sat on a log bench, close enough to enjoy the nearby bonfire, but far enough that he hoped to avoid sparks and smoke wafting his way. He sipped a cup of warm apple cider while other Vanguard members milled about, likewise enjoying the evening.

Saridian had finally given them their first proper day of spring, one that brought warmth to the earth instead of snow, so everyone was in high spirits—thus, a good opportunity to have a party in the town square. Someone had brought out a lute and was plucking a cheery tune from the other side of the fire.

The air was brisk and the moon shone brightly overhead. The warm fire crackled and heated tired bones. The wind kept blowing smoke into Jarrett's face despite his precautionary distance, burning his nostrils. He was intent on ignoring it. Things had been good; better than they had been in quite some time.

"Where's Morgane?" asked Lars. The skinny man took a seat next to Jarrett. "I haven't seen her all evening."

"Home, resting," Jarrett said. "She was feeling under the weather."

"That's disappointing. She should be out here enjoying this night with the rest of us."

Jarrett nodded, though he knew their leader took things too seriously to be able to enjoy a celebration, even when things were going as well as they were.

Lars clapped Jarrett on the back and grinned. "Well, you're the next best thing now, aren't you? It's about time Morgane named you second-in-command."

That brought a genuine smile to Jarrett's face. "Cheers to that, friend." They clanked their cups together, and Jarrett took a long swig, letting the cider warm his belly.

He had been the co-leader of the Vanguard in all but title until recently. The rebellion's cause had been his life's purpose since he'd met Morgane three years back, right as her plans were gaining momentum. Things had stagnated for the past year or so, but lately they were able to bring in plenty of new recruits.

"How are the new mages doing?" Jarrett asked. "Is training going well with them?"

Lars shrugged. "Neera is doing alright. Elden is struggling, he still has a hard time letting himself use his magic, but he'll get there. Eventually. It takes some time, I know that well enough."

Jarrett wasn't a mage, but he understood. Joining the Vanguard was the best thing he'd done, but their way of life took some adjustment. *I wonder if the transition is harder or easier for the mages.* They'd already lived in constant danger, after all. Joining the Vanguard only made it more purposeful.

Saridi mages either avoided using their magic or practiced in secret at great risk to themselves. Here in Rosewood, magic was accepted openly. It was a large part of what the rebellion was fighting for. Of course, being a mage—being anyone—in this town would be a death sentence if the

Vanguard and their dissent were ever discovered by the Tyrant Riordan or any of his loyalists.

That was exactly why recruiting was so difficult. The majority of the kingdom bowed easily to the god-king, whether because they believed he was right in his ways, or because they were too afraid to speak against him. The rebellion force had to be careful in seeking out those that sympathized with them, and wary of each passing traveler.

"What of the less magical recruits?" asked Lars. "Are you hammering the new warriors into shape?"

"You know it."

"The young'ns haven't beaten you to a pulp yet?"

Jarrett glared at Lars. "I bested Leon in a spar yesterday, so don't send me to pasture quite yet."

Jarrett had a decade or two on most of the Vanguard's other fighters. In truth, he was beginning to feel old, but defeating the younger council member—one of their best swordsmen, no less—rejuvenated him.

Raised voices from two other council members caught Jarrett's ear. He twisted around to see what the commotion was. Hera and Korene were arguing a few feet behind them. *Not again.* The two women were often at odds, though usually less publicly.

Korene was on patrol tonight—one of the Vanguard's security measures. He remembered her complaining about missing the evening's festivities. Now it seemed the patrol had come back early.

A tense atmosphere took over the crowd as more Vanguard members noticed the disturbance and began murmuring hushed conjectures to one another. Some of them surrounded Korene and the rest of the patrol, seeking answers.

Jarrett heaved himself up, and rushed over to part the crowd, waving his arms to get their focus. "Settle down. Korene, what's going on?"

Korene tore her intense gaze away from Hera to look at Jarrett. "There's a group camped near the town."

"Potential recruits?"

"No." Korene was firm. "Ravens."

Jarrett strove to keep his face neutral. It would look bad if the crowd saw his excitement. "Really?"

"They want to talk to Morgane. I told them they needed to leave, but they refused," Korene said. A vein in her forehead pulsated. "They'll bring too much attention if they stay."

"Yes, of course. We don't want Saridi military to come poking around," Jarrett said. "Don't worry, I'll take care of them."

"They said they would only speak to Morgane."

"Morgane is feeling unwell, so I'm close enough."

"Honestly," said Korene, "My vote is to take a larger group out and shoo them off. We agreed a long time ago not to work with them. It's too risky."

"It's worth seeing what they want, isn't it?" argued Hera. "All our newest recruits were directed here by them. We're fighting a *god* with an army and an entire kingdom at his back, and we have an active force of what, sixty fighters, a dozen mages? We can't afford to be picky about our allies."

Hera's comment was met with silence and awkward shuffling from the group at large. Her points were decent and though the Ravens had indeed sent them many new members, both recently and in the past, they weren't popular. The Ravens' open hostility against the Tyrant went against the secrecy that kept the Vanguard safe. The Vanguard hid in plain sight, and it gave them time to build, to plan. The Ravens' mere presence in their area threatened all of that.

Plus, the Ravens were... unorthodox. They dressed in black and wore jewelry made of bone. Actual ravens often followed them overhead, as if waiting for carrion. Anyone who had spoken to them said they were some sort of death cult, claiming that Death was a sixth god, and controlled the "cycle of souls", or something along those lines.

Jarrett didn't care how many gods there were, as long as they kept mortals out of their conflicts. The Magus War nearly tore the continent apart, and though it ended a century ago, he wasn't convinced that the gods had ceased manipulating mortals for their own gain.

Korene was the one to break the quiet tension. "You're being naive, Hera. Everything we have turns to nothing if we're discovered."

Jarrett stepped between the women. "This squabbling will get us nowhere. We need to make an informed decision, and that means speaking to the Ravens first."

Hera nodded. "Should I fetch Morgane?"

Jarrett inhaled sharply. There was no way his leader would let him run off to the Ravens, not alone like he needed to be. Guiltily, he was grateful that Morgane was sick this eve. It seemed he was having a lucky streak. "We can let her rest. I'll see what the Ravens have to say and convene with her if the situation requires."

"I'll go with you," Korene said. "I'd like to hear for myself what they want."

Jarrett shook his head. "We have nothing to fear from the Ravens—only what consequences they may bring if they stay. I think I have the best chance of hurrying them on their way if I speak to them alone."

"Alone?" Korene asked. "Take Hera"—she made a sour face—"if you think it's better, or whoever, but go with *someone*."

Jarrett clenched his jaw, and tried to project bravado, not his anxiety. "They wanted to speak with a leader, so I'll go. No need to ruin anyone else's evening."

More than a few people looked at him dubiously, but no one argued further. They knew by now that Jarrett wouldn't change his mind once he'd made a decision.

And sure, Morgane was going to give him a verbal lashing when she found out, but he couldn't squander this opportunity.

Jarrett made sure his sword was belted tightly to his waist—on the off-chance this didn't go as well as he hoped—and set off with a confident swagger.

He ventured out into a last moment of peace in the darkness, under the cover of the stars and the silence of the night. Following Korene's directions, it didn't take long for him to reach the Raven camp.

A dozen hide tents were set up on the border of the forest. Jarrett approached a cookfire wafting the savory scent of deer stew. A few of the Ravens stopped what they were doing to stare at him. They all wore black garments, and their clothes and hair were ornamented with long, dark feathers and carved bone decorations.

It wasn't long until someone came to interrogate him: a girl passed off the bone spoon she had been using to stir the cooking pot's contents and approached Jarrett. As she got closer, Jarrett realized she was older than he first suspected, not a girl, but a young woman.

Her brown hair was pleated, with some sections wrapped in red string or embellished with dangling metal ornaments, bone beads, and feathers. She wore even more decorations than the other Ravens. What caught Jarrett's eye first was the bird skull she wore around her neck, but then he noticed the mark on her face.

A gnarled scar stretched vertically from just below her left eye down to her jawline. A magebrand, though only half of one—her right cheek remained unblemished. Though Jarrett had met a decent number of mages, it was rare to find one that had escaped the grasp of Saridi soldiers.

Once marked, there was little refuge for a mage. Even if they managed to escape before their execution, their options were severely limited. A rare few were lucky enough to find their way to the Vanguard, or, as this woman had, the Ravens.

Jarrett waited for her to speak, but it became clear she was expecting him to make the first move. His mouth was dry. He had waited so long to speak with a Raven. The pressure of his expectations pressed in on his rib cage.

"I need to speak with you," Jarrett said.

The woman snorted. "As we told the last one, bring us Morgane, or no one at all." Apparently, she considered this to be the end of the conversation and started back toward the camp.

"Wait, please!" Jarrett's voice cracked as he yelled out.

The woman looked over her shoulder at him, a pierced eyebrow raised. He cleared his throat and started again. "I'm connected to the Ravens.

And I need information. Please." He could tell her that he was Morgane's second-in-command, but whatever the Ravens wanted from the Vanguard was his secondary concern. This was the one thing more important to him than the rebellion he'd committed his life to, and he didn't want to get sidetracked on complicated Vanguard business before it was resolved.

She turned around fully but kept her distance. "Connected to us *how?*"

Jarrett took off his cowl and unbuttoned the top of his shirt. He pulled down the collar to reveal the tattoo on his chest. Baring his tattoo would be the quickest way to show her his meaning. He hoped the fire light reached far enough for her to make out the image: a raven in flight, placed over his heart.

"So?"

"You're a mage, right? Take a closer look."

They stared at each other for a long few seconds before the woman finally walked over to him. A nervous triumph ran through him. She placed two cold fingers on his tattoo and he felt the tingling probe of her magic.

"Hm," was all she said.

"A mage once told me in passing that—"

"Come with me."

An obstacle passed, and his muscles relaxed. She led him through the camp to the tent at the heart of the temporary settlement. The woman gestured for him to enter, and he obliged. She followed him in.

Inside the tent, an older woman sat cross-legged on a worn rug. Her hair was gray, and her robes were simple. In front of her was a short table, where she was sorting through a collection of herbs. The air was thick with smoke from a stick of burning incense and the sweet smell of lavender.

The elderly Raven barely glanced up from her work. "Fae, what have you dragged into my tent? I told you I wanted their *leader.*"

The woman shrugged. "I thought you might find him interesting." She nodded to Jarrett. "Show her the tattoo."

Jarrett revealed the raven tattoo again. The elderly woman paused her work to look him up and down with an evaluating eye. She sighed and waved a hand at Fae. "You may leave."

Fae gave Jarrett a sidelong glance as she exited through the flap of the tent.

"I am Leandra." She kept sorting herbs into piles on the table as she spoke. "Who are you, and what is it that you want?"

"My name is Jarrett. I come seeking information—"

"You are not an emissary of Death," Leandra interrupted. "Yet, you have a tattoo imbued with her power, or perhaps that of an emissary. How did this come to be?"

"*Death?*" he asked incredulously. The only hint he had to this perplexity was the form of the tattoo: the image of a raven. "I don't know. But I seek answers."

"Sit down."

Jarrett obeyed, kneeling at the opposite side of the table from the Raven. He coughed as pungent smoke from the incense swirled around him.

"I woke up one day with this tattoo. I don't know who gave it to me." Jarrett ran his fingers through his hair, as he considered telling the Raven his full story. But those words wouldn't come. He hadn't told anyone. For some reason, it was just too hard to say. "Whoever they are, though... they took something from me, too. I'd like it back."

"When did this happen?"

"Five years ago."

Leandra finished one last bundle of herbs and looked up at Jarrett. "I'm attuned to Io. I have the gift of insight. Occasionally, I give readings. I see things that others don't. It's possible I can read the magical signature left in that tattoo, and tell you something about the mage who gave it to you."

"Yes, please—"

"If you promise to set us a meeting with Morgane."

Now that Leandra's hands were still, Jarrett noticed the black markings on the back of her left hand. He'd never met an emissary before, but he'd heard of the magically imbued tattoos that tied them to their patron god. Leandra's tattoo was two overlapping circles—he didn't recognize it as an insignia of any of the five gods.

Perhaps Death was a sixth god, as the rumors hinted. Perhaps she had left a mark on him, too, somehow. Now he might finally get answers. His nerves buzzed with excitement.

Leandra held her tattooed hand out to him. "Well? Do we have a deal?"

"Of course."

Jarrett placed his trembling hand in hers. He thought they were shaking hands, but instead, Leandra latched onto his hand with her cold fingers and stared at him from across the table. He barely kept from fidgeting as she seemed to gaze into his very soul, a prying flow of magic reaching into him. Though it was invasive, he welcomed the sensation. If this could solve the mystery, he could finally be at peace.

It was an eternity before Leandra withdrew her hand, breaking the magic that let her examine him. Beads of sweat glistened on her forehead. She drew in a deep breath before speaking. "You won't find what you're seeking."

"What?" Jarrett's stomach dropped. "No, please, you can't tell me there's nothing—"

"It's best if you stop searching. It will only bring you more pain."

"But you know *something*, don't you?"

"I see what this mage took from you."

He froze. So she had seen into his soul, into his mind.

"Getting it back would only cause more pain. Trust me on that. Continue with the life you have now. It will save you the heartbreak."

"*Tell me!*" Jarrett stood and drew his sword in a single motion, pointing his blade at Leandra. He was breathing heavily, his head getting lighter with each breath. "You know who did this, don't you? Tell me their name. Anything you know."

"There is nothing more for me to tell." Leandra didn't look up at the bare steel facing her. She began once again to bundle herbs together with twine to hang on a drying rack. Such a mundane task. So nonchalant, as if none of this mattered.

Jarrett let the tip of his sword lower to the ground. He couldn't get enough oxygen into his lungs. The world pressed in on him, spinning as his vision narrowed. He dropped to his knees before he lost his balance and fell.

What a nightmare. What a continuous, everlasting, godforsaken nightmare. Jarrett let himself collapse completely.

Was that it, then? Five years of searching, only to get so close and to find that he had gotten nowhere. His memories were gone, and there was no way to recover them.

He could forget about the hole in his heart, sometimes. For a minute or two, maybe a couple of hours, on a good day. The first years were the hardest; he'd been a shell of a man. Empty, with nothing to focus on. He had wandered through Saridian, trying to find any hint of himself.

Then, three years ago, he came to Rosewood. He met Morgane as the Vanguard was starting to form. He'd joined and heartily thrown himself into building up the rebellion force, improving his abilities, and helping others to do the same.

Most of the time, he could at least pretend he was happy. He had a goal: to stop the Tyrant from destroying what little he had left. If he didn't have anything to live for, at least he had something to die for.

But each day he lived, he lived in the torture of knowing there was something so important, so essential to himself, that had been missing for the past five years. He just wanted to know who had done this, and why. What could his past hold that someone found it necessary to erase it?

When he came back to himself, Leandra had finished bundling her herbs. "You should go."

Jarrett said nothing. There was nothing to say. Nothing to do. The chance of him overcoming a mage, especially if she was an emissary, was minuscule. He wasn't a mage, and he had no backup. Jarrett knew when he was beaten and he hated that it had been without a fight. He stood, sheathed his sword, and left his hopes behind.

CHAPTER 6

Scarlet was alone in the library. It had become her habit over the past weeks to go read to settle her mind after a long day of training. Today, she could barely concentrate on the words she was trying to read. Her mind kept drifting, too anxious to be filled with much else.

Her brain reverted to examining the letterforms, delicately created by a flamescribe. It had been ages since she'd flamescribed, herself. It was a practice she had enjoyed back when it was the only magic she'd been allowed to do. Now, she wondered if it would be satisfactory, in comparison to the fireballs, energy bolts, and other magics she'd been learning and drilling on endlessly.

Restlessness and curiosity drew her to a stack of blank paper on one of the library's desks. She sat and snatched the top sheet, then stared at it in all of its emptiness, pinprick flame ready at her fingertip. What to write, or draw?

After a moment, she began tracing out a map of the Crossworld. There hadn't been one in any of the books she'd been through yet, a fact that had irritated her. She wanted to know everything she could about the Crossworld, and yet there'd been so little. The books were mostly histories of the various regions of Quintras and chronicles of the Magus War, which were interesting enough—more knowledge than she ever could have found in Saridian. Yet her mind was never sated.

She sketched out the center island, where Deianira stood. The circular river that surrounded them split off into five sections. She had pestered Bronwen to tell her which direction each of the gods' realms lay, so she added the appropriate topography to them. Forests and fields for Riordan's, a reflection of the landscape she had grown up in. A desert with the occasional oasis for Kajiem, the god she drew her fiery roots from. Grasslands and a jungle for Io, the god of knowledge and healing, to which Bronwen was attuned. Sturdy mountains stretching across Meyrin's realm, echoing the god's protective nature. And, finally, scattered islands made up Cascara's realm.

Cascara. The god her mother was attuned to. Scarlet found herself with a new piece of paper in hand, her mother's face appearing as her hand moved across the page. Sharp eyes, angular nose, her hair curly like Scarlet's, but shorter—

And then it hurt too much. Her heart hammered a heavy beat. Her fire couldn't be contained to a pinprick any longer. An outburst of flames flashed before her face and the paper she held disintegrated into ash. In her frustration, she stood and threw a second round of fire, more concentrated this time, at the desk. The wood was too resistant to catch aflame, but the top of the desk smoldered, and the rest of the paper stack burnt up before her eyes. She managed to grab the map she'd drawn, left to the side. Its edge was crisped, but otherwise, it was left intact.

A buried thought surfaced. *Why did Bronwen have to bring up my father?*

It had been weeks since the topic had been prodded at. It was the smallest pinprick in her armor, and Scarlet had been careful to tread around the breach in her mind, but as time went on, and her mother still hadn't returned or sent a message, had given her nothing—the comparison was becoming difficult to avoid.

Her father had left without a goodbye, and now, so had her mother.

Her whole life had been spent crisscrossing around Saridian. Friends were scarce, and short-lived, if present at all. It didn't help that she'd inherited her mother's Galapian looks—her black hair and sharp features were an oddity in Saridian.

When she was younger, she'd always had Viridian, at least. Her sister had been her best and only friend. Scarlet longed to hear her voice again but was becoming more and more convinced that her sister's voice in her head had been imagined during her recovery.

Her old life had felt empty. Viridian dead, her father's fate uncertain, her mother shoving her into the dark at every possible moment... It was deeply lonely, frustrating, and often uneventful. In the Crossworld, she was learning magic and had endless books to read. It kept her busy and satisfied in ways she had craved for years. But the loneliness had its claws in her deeper than before.

Not to mention the fear. Her mother knew what leaving without a goodbye would mean to Scarlet. But she'd done it anyway. And she'd stayed away. There were only so many things that that could mean.

And if Death won't give me answers, then I'll have to get strong enough to find them for myself.

For the most part, Scarlet's magic lessons took place outside the castle. Occasionally, Death would instead take her to a room full of dummies and targets. Today, Death led her through the castle and took a turn toward neither of those locations.

"I'm running a gauntlet today, aren't I?" asked Scarlet.

"Observant, aren't you?"

Scarlet hesitated to accept the potential compliment. She couldn't decipher it as sarcastic or genuine.

Death glanced back at her. "Think you have it all figured out, now?"

Scarlet had learned that answering a question, when that question was asked by Death, was its own kind of test. "I think I know most of the castle."

Death snorted. "How many levels does Deianira have?"

"Five."

"Wrong. This is just like magic. There are things you don't even know that you do not know. Don't get too confident."

Scarlet grimaced. Did Deianira have a basement? Or were there stairs up to another floor that she had yet to discover?

Death stopped in front of a door. "Give me a moment," she said. "I have a couple of adjustments to make before you come in."

Scarlet sighed and waited as the god slid into the room. Her wrong answers might have bought her a harder test. This would be the third gauntlet Death had sent her through. The past two hadn't been kind; she'd needed visits to Bronwen after both.

In the first, Death had set up a maze within a large room. Scarlet navigated it while Death ran along the tops of the temporary wooden walls, just above Scarlet's head, shooting bolts of magic at her. There'd been little room to dodge, so it was a true test of her ability to spot-shield with magic, one of the main skills Death had been teaching her.

The flashes of magic that Scarlet sent out to block the attacks lasted only a moment, so the timing was a crucial element of spot-shielding. If she were attuned to Meyrin instead of Kajiem, she'd be able to create long-lasting shields. There were moments she wished for the ability to do so, though she wouldn't trade her flames for anything.

Along with trying to shield herself from being pelted by Death, she'd had to navigate through the maze. It didn't help that there was a time limit. Scarlet wasn't sure how Death had done it, but the god had rigged the floor to grow hotter over time. Scarlet, barefooted, had to get out of the maze before her feet were charred. By the time she escaped, she'd taken a couple of hits from Death, and her feet were blistered.

After all that, Death hadn't seemed impressed.

For the second gauntlet, she was blindfolded. It was an obstacle course, with walls to climb and nets to crawl beneath. That too had the additional complications of Death attacking her, though with slower-moving energy orbs than last time. It gave her time to sense the energy as it came at her and the injuries they caused were less acute. It didn't stop her from gaining a new set of bruises and a sprained ankle when one knocked her off the top of a wall.

At Death's goading, she did manage to limp over the finish line of that gauntlet as well. Even with Bronwen's healing, she could barely walk the next day. Bronwen would have had her rest for a few days if it were up to him. But it wasn't. Death's training happened every day, without fail.

Scarlet resolved to escape the next gauntlet unscathed. Or at least, less scathed. No doubt this next test would be even more difficult, but Scarlet had been honing her skills. The desire to excel burned as hot as the flames that she summoned at will.

Death came out of the room. "Scarlet. This isn't just a test, but a lesson. And it's a lesson you'll learn well if you want to keep living."

Sure, that's not ominous at all.

Death gestured for her to go through the door. Scarlet slipped by the god into the room, which was pitch black. Before she could ask Death what her goal was today, the door between them slammed shut.

She let her magical senses unfurl through the room, reaching for anything that might give her a clue about what to do. Immediately, something felt off, though she couldn't pinpoint what it was.

She summoned a flame into her palm. The fire flared up bright, then dampened substantially. Feeding more energy to the fire only made it incrementally larger again. Scarlet frowned. Something was strangling her magic.

Darkness pressed in, it felt almost tangible as she took a few tentative steps forward. The light of her flame barely cut through, she could only see a couple of feet in front of herself. Then, she stepped through something she couldn't see, but could feel. A screen of magic, biting each inch of her skin that came in contact with it. On the other side, she collapsed.

She'd been drained. Her flame was extinguished and she was panting like she'd just finished a long run. The darkness was absolute. She drew herself up, trying to regain her composure. Scarlet tried to call another flame to her hand, but the magic that flowed within her had run dry. All she could muster was a tiny, candle-sized flame.

"Death?" Scarlet called out, only to find that she couldn't hear her own voice. She stood and stomped down hard with her boot. That resulted in no sound either. In her resulting panic, she lost hold of her pinprick flame, leaving herself in total darkness once more.

Death had managed to take away her sight as well as her hearing, and she could barely sense anything with her magic in this state. It took a conscious effort to keep her breathing steady.

So what was this, then—a mental test? Or was Death about to start firing energy bolts at her?

You think you're in control, Scarlet. The words pulsated from her emissary bond, Death's words resounding directly into her mind. *But you're not.*

Scarlet clenched her jaw and scanned around the darkness for any hint of an attack coming toward her.

Even now. I've ripped away your senses and your powers, and you're still looking for a fight?

I'm not going to give up, Scarlet replied through her bond.

This isn't about giving up, but giving in. You barely know how to hold control of your magic at the best of times. Can't you feel it, always a hair away from slipping out of your grasp?

She did feel it. Death often chided Scarlet for nearly losing hold of her flames, and always giving them too much energy instead of modulating her flow of power.

You think you know more than you do. You get ahead of yourself. And you push against our bond, Scarlet. I can feel your resistance. I compelled you only once, and my power over you scares you. But you must understand: you are one of my tools, now. Accept it and let me guide you.

I'm a person, not a tool.

One doesn't negate the other. You took the emissary pact in exchange for your life. And now, you need to prove you can hold up to your end of the bargain.

The bond Scarlet could sense between her and Death widened, and suddenly she could feel a well of power on the other end. Death's energy was offered up to her.

Go on, Death urged. *Draw on my power. You're going to need it.*

It was breathtakingly tantalizing, a vast pool of energy that had been beyond her imagining before meeting the god. Feeling Death's power once again was overwhelming, even more now that it was available for her taking.

But Death was right. Ever since she had used their bond to force her to stand in the library, Scarlet had fought against the idea that even the simplest of her actions could be controlled by Death. Her body moving against her will felt viscerally *wrong*. She thought that when she learned magic, she would finally be free. But if Death decided to control her actions, she would remain powerless.

And if Scarlet had learned anything, it was that she had to be able to take care of herself alone. Her mother, father, sister—all gone. The only constant was herself. How could she relinquish control and rely on the power of a god whose motivations she didn't fully understand?

Scarlet had only hesitated for a few moments before something hit her hard from behind. She stumbled forward but managed to keep her footing. Her lower back stung where the magic bolt had made contact.

It's in your best interests to obey me. Do I need to compel you? I thought you wanted power.

Yes, Scarlet thought to herself. She didn't dare project her words toward the god, *but not like this. Is this what Mom meant when she said power doesn't keep you safe?*

You want to keep living, don't you? Death's voice echoed within the confines of Scarlet's mind.

Scarlet's heart pounded louder until it felt like it was the only thing that existed in this place where most of her senses had been torn away from her. *I'm not learning fast enough. If I just get better, maybe I can rely on myself, and not Death.* She braced herself, hoping to sense the next of Death's energy bolts before it hit her.

She didn't. The magic collided with the back of her thigh, and she staggered forward.

So that's how it is? Then **get down.**

Scarlet found herself lying on the floor, face down, before she even processed Death's words. Her head spun from the sudden movement and the panic that rose in her chest from losing control of her own body.

Do you think you'll survive when he comes for you?

Death didn't have to say his name. The black starburst scar on Scarlet's back would never let her forget.

He wants what you want, Death continued. *Power. Control. Except, unlike you, he has it.*

The floor was cold and hard on her forehead. Scarlet couldn't move an inch.

He doesn't just have it. He's the god *of it. And he hates everyone who seeks power for themselves. Why do you think he condemns all the mages in his territory?*

All the heat from Scarlet's body seemed to sink into the stone floor. She was left frozen but too weak to shiver.

You think I'm going to control you. Use you. And you're right. It's why Kiera kept you from me for so long. But in return, I can give you one of the things you want.

In sharp contrast to her body of ice, Scarlet felt something hot press on her. Through the emissary bond poured a searing energy, no longer waiting for her to take it. Like lava through her veins, the power surged.

Scarlet's body was molten. She was awake for the first time, aware of every humming particle and subtle emotion. Her presence reached beyond her.

As fast as she'd gone down, she was back on her feet. The room was still shrouded in impenetrable darkness, but her enhanced senses kept her alert. Another bolt was coming from behind, but she sidestepped it.

Death's orders came. They weren't compulsions, but Scarlet felt herself following them regardless. *Turn left. Spot-shield now. Go forward. Faster. Two more steps. Stop, stop. Use your fire now, it will be enough to disable part of the system.*

Scarlet released a blast of flames. It was effortless. The resulting inferno bloomed largely, and she could feel it devouring a magic field before her. It must be what she had stumbled through earlier.

Don't let those flames get away from you. Okay. Good.

As the field gave way, Scarlet's ears popped. Suddenly, she could hear her own labored breath.

Bolts are incoming from the right. Spot-shield now.... and... now.

Following Death's directions, Scarlet navigated through the room, avoiding attacks and taking down traps that Death had set up to fire magic bolts at her. After she disabled the last energy field, the darkness lessened. She summoned a flame into her hand, and finally, it lit the room.

Death stood on the other side of the room, in front of the door. Her arms were crossed, and the expression on her face seemed hard and soft all at once. After giving Scarlet a curt nod, she exited.

Scarlet's blood cooled and the euphoria of wielding Death's strength faded, leaving her raw. She was full. She was empty.

Was this a victory, or a defeat?

CHAPTER 7

Dante knew he was dreaming, and it filled him with dread.

He was inside. The building was massive. With his extended dream-sense, he could feel it stretch out around him. It was spiraling, twisting, ever-changing. The floor was stone, so very cold and hard beneath his bare feet. There was magic in the core of each stone and crevice of this place, pulsating.

There was a long red carpet in front of him that stretched from the room's entrance all the way across to the dais to Dante's right. A large chair sat at the far end. It looked to be a throne, though it was simple, hewn from dark stone, with armrests and a tall back.

A woman with wine-red hair stood atop the dais in front of the throne. She outshone the muted tones she was wearing. A certain tension ran through her, coiled. She pulsed to the same beat as the magic beneath his feet. She belonged here.

To the left, closer to the entrance to this room, was a fair-skinned man with brown hair that gently cascaded to his shoulders. The aura of magic that surrounded him was dissonant. Sharp. Cold, like metal. He was the intruder, *the one who wasn't supposed to be here. He grinned; his teeth just a little too white.*

Suddenly, his perspective shifted. He was standing on the dais now. He looked down at his hands. They were slender and had long, pointed nails, along with skin darker than his own. These weren't his hands, they were the woman's. Somehow, he was her. He felt himself melding into her, his own identity falling to the wayside.

The world spun for a moment. Eva looked up from her hands. Riordan strode across the carpet toward her. She focused her power within herself, careful not to let anything leak out toward him, lest he steal even more of her energy.

"It's time for you to join me, isn't it?" Riordan asked. "I promise, this is everything you've wanted, all along—"

"I will never, *ever* come with you." The mere thought of it made her stomach churn. "Get that through your thick skull and go back to your own realm."

"Deianira could be home to both of us if you would come to your senses."

Her rage lit up like dry leaves in a forest fire. "Don't you dare say that name. *Ever.* You took her from me. You took everything. How could you think I would even consider your ridiculous propositions?" She was losing control, summoning her latent power to her fingertips, some of it spilling out to form an aura around her that would be visible to any mage. He was playing her, and she was being a fool.

The other god's expression turned grim. He held out his hand and the magic surrounding Eva was drawn toward him, twisting into a vortex that terminated at his palm as he absorbed her energy. Stripped of strength, she dropped to her knees.

Eva spat at him, defiant. "Curse you." Yet, she bowed her head in defeat. Despair. Between heaving breaths, she declared, "You can't do this to me forever. I *will* find a way to end you."

"You will reconsider, or you will continue to suffer." Riordan shrugged. "Your choice." He turned to walk out of the throne room.

"Not much of a choice."

His cold shoulder was the only reply she got before he disappeared from sight.

As the man made his exit, Dante was shunted back into his own body within the dream. The woman looked up, seemingly at the very spot Dante was standing. He couldn't be sure though, because as he saw the flash of her green irises, he jolted awake in his bed, released from the dream.

Dante opened his eyes and saw nothing.

He could feel his worn blanket around him, he could hear the rain pattering down onto the tin roof—and though it was warm enough to rain, he could still smell the sharp chill of the night, drifting in through the cracks in his window that would not seal. But he could not see.

Instead of the darkness and shadows cast across his room, his vision was overtaken by solid white. Panic rolled through Dante as he became more and more sure that he was, in fact, awake, not trapped in another nightmare. He tried not to hyperventilate while he sought for what to do.

He immediately discarded any thought of calling for his parents. This was too strange, too... magical to risk their involvement. Zandra wouldn't be a problem in that regard, but she might try something with magic to help him. Even though the soldiers had left, he still couldn't put her at risk. Already he was putting them in enough danger, with that godforsaken crystal orb he still hid under his bed.

Zandra was right: he needed a better hiding place, but something made him want it close. He wanted to get rid of it altogether, but he just... couldn't. He was unnaturally drawn to it, despite all his reservations. At least Dante couldn't sense any magic coming from it once he had finished putting it together. It laid dormant, haunting him from below each night.

For now, he was still blind, and no solutions sprung to mind. *I'll just have to wait and hope my vision returns.* He shut his eyes, and though it had no effect on the strange brightness, it made it slightly less disturbing. He adjusted his blankets and made himself comfortable, wondering what his life would be like if he remained blind. Could he still work for Ferrick at the clinic, or would he be doomed to accomplish whatever farm tasks his parents thought safe enough to assign him?

He pooled in his misery until a few minutes passed and the light began fading into the darkness of his true surroundings. His sight slowly returned. Dante had never imagined he'd be relieved to see the back of his eyelids.

So everything was okay. For now. *But if this happened once, it could happen again... will my vision always come back?*

The dream he woke from had felt so real—just like the ones he had of Zandra falling. There had been other dreams like this, too. Most of them had been disorienting, the images not quite fitting together. But even in those, he could sense the weight, the reality of them. Others had been images of his past, things he'd rather forget but was instead forced to relive in excruciating detail.

Tonight's dream was a new variety. He had become the woman—Eva?—and felt and thought what she did. *Why would I dream of these two mages... these two... gods? Was that really King Riordan? I've never even heard of a god named Eva, if she was one as well.*

These were visions. He couldn't keep denying that it was what they were. Visions of the unchangeable past, the permutable future, and whatever that last one had been.

Magic kept drawing him in, even as he tried to escape it. A simple life, to be a healer and herbalist, was all he wanted. He shivered beneath his woolen blanket. If he tried hard enough, maybe he could finally turn off the powers he'd never sought out. He shut his eyes tight and wished it was so.

He couldn't sleep. He knew what lingered beyond his consciousness, the images that would come to him if he gave in to exhaustion, the recurring dream that haunted his nights more and more often. It was too vivid to be a regular nightmare. Too clear and detailed, every moment was exactly how it had happened.

The flames. The stench of burning flesh. The screams of the girl's pain and terror. His father, whispering into his ear: "You are not a mage. This is what happens to mages."

Dante could almost feel the flames licking his skin as he spent the night awake, afraid of what he was becoming.

Dante woke once more, not from a nightmare, but from the morning light shining in through his window. Somehow, he had managed to sleep for at least a couple of hours.

He rolled out of bed and worked through his stretching routine. Though his work with Ferrick was less physically active than farm work, he'd never grown out of the habit of stretching first thing in the morning. Even if he wasn't spending his days toiling in the fields, he still had chores.

Knowing his mother would want him to fetch water, he dressed and gathered the buckets from out back. He hummed merrily as he made his way down the path to the well and hauled clean water up from its depths.

The soldiers had moved on two weeks ago. Perhaps he could accept that he and Zandra were safe. Ferrick seemed to have gotten through to his parents—enough that they had dropped the talk of sending him off to the army.

Dante, encumbered with full buckets, made his way back to the house. As he got near, he spotted his father standing on the porch, waiting for him, his face white and stern.

Dante put the buckets down as his father approached him. "Dad? What's wrong?"

His father didn't respond at first. The soldiers were gone. Zandra had been more focused on her chores than seeking out opportunities to practice magic, for once. Everything should be good. But the stiffness in his father made panic rise from Dante's gut.

He wouldn't make eye contact with Dante. "Milo saw you. The other day."

"Milo?" *What does he have to do with anything?*

"He came to me last night. Told me that he saw you." He finally turned to look straight at Dante. "He saw you using magic."

Dante's stomach churned. He was sure that he and Zandra had been alone when she had fallen, and he hadn't used magic since. Milo had headed back home after they'd spoken that day—there was no reason he'd be anywhere near the forest. "That's impossible."

"Why would Milo come to me, if he wasn't sure about what he saw?"

"I don't know, but Dad—"

"You are no longer my son."

"Please, just listen—"

"No!" His father kicked over one of the buckets. Water pooled out around Dante's feet, soaking through the holes in his ratty boots. "There are no excuses. You will leave Briarglen by noon. If I see you again, I'll bring you to Kingsmount and hand you over myself as I should have in the first place. You're lucky I don't magebrand you here and now."

With that, his father stormed away toward the barn, leaving Dante shattered. His world was ripping apart. He felt like the crystal orb before he'd mended it. Fractured, scattered. But there was no fixing this. Magic had been the hammer, it wouldn't be the glue.

This can't be happening. How did Milo see him save Zandra from the fall, and how could he betray him like this? It had been over a fortnight since the incident and Milo had given no indication that there was anything wrong in the meantime.

"What was that about?"

Dante returned to the present and looked up at Zandra. She stood in the doorway, rubbing the sleep out of her eyes.

"Dad banished me from Briarglen."

"What?"

"Milo saw me save you with magic, back in the forest."

Zandra leaped down the porch stairs, wide-eyed. "He followed us?"

"I don't know."

"Well if he saw anything, he saw you save my *life*, Dante!"

"It doesn't matter. I'm... I'm done."

Dante had never seen such a serious look plastered on his little sister's face. "Look. I'll tell him it wasn't you using magic, it was me," she said. "I was the one messing around, you only used your gift to save me."

"No! No. He must not have seen you doing magic, or he wanted to spare you. I know I'd rather it be me than you."

"But—"

"Zandra. You'd probably get both of us thrown out, and what good would that do? You should stay here and be safe, for as long as you can."

"I'm coming with you." Zandra's fists were clenched tight. "We can make it on our own, the two of us."

Dante knew it would be hard to fight her on this, but he had to. "I promise I'll be alright. I know you'd make it out there if you had to. But I don't want you to have to. If I'm fending for myself, I can get by, as long as I know you're okay."

"But I won't be okay! I don't want you to be banished and gone, and I want to use magic, and I want—"

"Spend the next few years figuring out a plan to get out of here. And then, *then* leave this place."

"But it's my fault!" Tears welled up in her eyes. "I got you into this mess. I didn't listen, I just wanted to practice magic, I never thought... I never thought something like this would really happen."

"I'll forgive you. If you stay."

"Dante—"

"That's the only way." He gave her a sad smile. "Deal?"

Zandra sniffled and nodded.

Together, they packed what useful items they could into a travel bag, as much of the non-perishable food as they could find and fit. Warm clothes. A hunting knife. He fetched the crystal orb from under his bed, too. The extra weight was unwelcome, but he couldn't leave it behind.

His last moments with his sister went by too fast. She clung to him as they skirted the edge of town, avoiding the townsfolk who would be bustling about by now. They made it to the eastern road that led to Thornsbury, the next town over.

Zandra pulled him into an embrace. "Stay a little longer. Please."

"Even if I could, I should go while there's still light. I have to find somewhere to camp."

It was early enough that he could reach Thornsbury by nightfall if he tried, but he didn't want to rent a room there. Dante had a bit of coin, though that was going to be for emergencies, food and shelter when he couldn't make his own, or when the weather took a turn for the worse. In Saridian, that was bound to happen sooner or later. Today was warm enough. Hopefully, it would hold.

He didn't know if he wanted to stop in Thornsbury at all. Sometimes he went to the market there with Ferrick. Dante didn't want to be recognized, to have people ask why he was there alone, and not on a market day.

"Do you know where you'll go?" Zandra asked, echoing his line of thought.

"Nowhere near here," Dante said. He didn't know much of the land-scape beyond his hometown. He knew there was a city, maybe a week's walk away. But being around even more people was the last thing he wanted right now. He could head to a port, or a border, and get out of Saridian altogether—go elsewhere, where mages were accepted. Travel across the border was heavily restricted, and if they found him out as a mage, that would be the end. "I don't know. I'll have to figure it out."

"I have to be able to find you one day, but if I don't even know where to begin..."

"I'll find you," Dante said. "I'll come back for you. I promise."

Tears streamed down Zandra's face. Dante knew he had to leave now, or he never would. As he walked away, tears fell from his eyes as well.

All he had wanted was a quiet life. He didn't need magic or adventure. It should have been an easy thing to accomplish. But instead, he'd been born a mage, and now he walked down the path to the unknown.

CHAPTER 8

Jarrett calculated how long it would take before Morgane discovered his questionable escapades from the previous night. He flipped a mental hourglass in his head: the countdown between that moment and the one where Morgane would burst through the door of his cottage to question him.

I should have enough time to eat breakfast, at least.

As he rummaged through his pantry, there was a knock at the front door: insistent, furious knocking that didn't cease when he called out, "Coming!"

He opened the door to see Morgane, who immediately pushed past him to enter the house.

"So?" was all she said. The angrier Morgane was, the fewer words she used.

He might have miscalculated on several counts.

"Ravens? Alone?" Despite her short stature, Morgane filled the whole sitting room with her rage. "What were you thinking?"

"It's something I had to do."

"*Elaborate.*"

"You know better than to pry."

Jarrett was well aware that Morgane believed everyone was entitled to their past. Such was the way in the Vanguard. You couldn't be picky about who you included in your secret rebellion against a kingdom that had far greater resources.

"You've been my second-in-command for what, two seconds? And already, you're running off, consorting with *Ravens.*" Though the disapproval in her tone was clear, she didn't raise her voice. Morgane was good at keeping herself in check—something she and Jarrett didn't have in common. "I need to trust you. So if I must pry, I will."

"I can't tell you why I went, but trust me when I say I'm sorry that I did."

Morgane sank into a cushioned chair, deflated. Her eyes were bloodshot, and her skin was sickly pale. Her brown hair was frazzled, which was out of character for the ever-organized and put-together leader of the Vanguard.

"You're responsible for these people, Jarrett, as much as I am. All of their lives are in our hands. Not just the lives of the Vanguard, but every mage in Saridian, every person who suffers under the Tyrant's rule. You can't take risks like this. You can't run off to see the Ravens—*alone*—both because it's dangerous and because it doesn't look good to our soldiers to see you consorting with *death cultists.*"

Jarrett took a deep breath so he could give her a level response. "It won't happen again."

"What won't happen again? Speaking to the Ravens, or having a lapse in judgment?"

Suddenly, Jarrett wasn't hungry for breakfast anymore. After his soul-crushing meeting with the Ravens, he had hoped to be numb to Morgane's rebuffing. As awful as he felt, he wasn't immune to sinking even lower.

"The recruits are settling in, training across the Vanguard is going great, everything is calm and well-organized, and you know I've had a hand in that." Jarrett's voice grew louder, despite attempting restraint. "I know I made a bad decision. But nothing's been ruined, and it won't happen again—I swear to you. So please, let me have this one mistake."

In the following silence, the wear on Morgane's face struck him again. She looked far too exhausted for someone who wasn't even out late at the celebration last night.

"Morgane. What's going on? Are you still sick, or is this about something else?"

Morgane stood and pointed a finger at him forcefully. "I *am* pissed at you. And don't you forget that. But there is more." She stopped to clear her throat. "One of our informants came back last night. Soldiers are making some visits, and are going to be heading our way. They could be coming on a routine mage-hunt or evaluation, or maybe for recruiting—none of which would be great—but worse, they may have picked up that Rosewood is our base."

"What?!"

"It's a risk we've always run, you know that well enough."

It was true; more people knew of the Vanguard than was ideal. Rosewood hadn't always been theirs. Morgane took over the village's leadership around the time Jarrett arrived. She had carefully selected Rosewood as the ideal place to convert to a base of operations for the rebellion she was forming. It was far enough from Kingsmount that there weren't constant scrutinizing eyes—plus, an abnormally high amount of mages were born in this area. This made it a more sympathetic place to convert people into rebel agents, and thus, the Vanguard was born.

Of course, not all of Rosewood's original residents were amenable to their cause. While Riordan's reach this far south was weaker than near the capital, the punishment for treason was still death. Thankfully, most of those who didn't support the Vanguard simply left Rosewood, not wanting to incur the wrath of either side. Others, the Vanguard had been forced to pay off, intimidate into silence, or otherwise remove from the equation. While unpleasant, it'd been necessary. They had to think of the greater good.

Three years passed, miraculously, without incident. Well, not without *incident*, there had been close calls. More people who had to be silenced, one way or another. But somehow, they had evaded the notice of Kingsmount beyond routine check-ups and tax collection.

Still, it would be all too easy for someone to betray them, or for a soldier or tax collector to see something they shouldn't have. A peek into a training facility or an armory. A single whiff of the Vanguard's recruitment of mages and all others who strained against the Tyrant's reign.

If they had come so far, only to be discovered now...

Jarrett ground his teeth together. If he wasn't sure of it before, he was now: his luck had run out.

"One way or another, a small contingent of soldiers is heading this way," Morgane said. "I need you focused, more than ever. If people start to think you're a Raven sympathizer, that isn't going to do us any favors in holding this together."

Morgane was right. While she was bold enough to start a secret rebellion, she was also cautious enough to *run* a secret rebellion.

"I'll be more careful. I promise. The Vanguard is my life, and I won't put it at risk again."

"Good," Morgane said. She sat back down and motioned for Jarrett to do the same. He took a seat on the loveseat across from her. She eyed him appraisingly. "You're my second and I have to trust you. I *do* trust you. So I won't push you to tell me what your deal with the Ravens is. But, as your friend, if you want to tell me... I won't judge, whatever it is."

"I'm just... I'm looking for something. That's all."

Morgane raised an inquisitive eyebrow at him. "Ah. Well then."

"Morgane—" Jarrett started, but cut himself short. He hadn't told anyone about his missing memories. It was difficult to explain his situation since he didn't fully understand it himself. He also worried that the tattoo implicated him as being involved with the Ravens, which would foster distrust among the ranks. But mostly, it just hurt too much to say aloud.

Morgane had been his friend long enough that he could have told her. He trusted her with his life. Truly, she was the only person who he'd allowed himself to get close to. When his memories had been ripped away, he'd found himself alone. His memories of his early life seemed intact, and he knew his family was long gone.

His adult life, on the other hand, was foggy at best. He'd found himself with no friends, at least none that he could remember. He feared that if he got close to anyone now, he would simply forget them. Lose them. He couldn't shake off that trepidation.

Morgane watched him, her head tilted. "You know I'm here for you, Jarrett." Her voice was soft, kind.

"I know." Jarrett swallowed, feeling the lump in his throat. Part of him wanted to tell her. "If soldiers are coming, we need to prepare."

"That we do. We should disassemble our training facilities first. Hide all of our equipment, our arms and armor. Then we'll set up as many defenses as we can without it being suspicious, in case it does come down to a fight." She stood and paced the room. Her eyes flashed with a ferocity that reminded Jarrett that this woman was best to have on your side. "We'll go over the plan together and find some way through this. And the Ravens—we have to make sure they leave. Do you know what they want?"

"No. They'll speak only with you."

"Then you start the preparations and I'll arrange a meeting with the Ravens."

Morgane sent word to the Ravens that she would meet with them, and by noon, the Ravens had come to Rosewood. Jarrett was glad Morgane wasn't going to their camp. Even though he was fairly sure the Ravens didn't intend harm, he couldn't stand the idea of Morgane being surrounded by them. It wasn't worth the risk.

"Yeah, I'm a huge hypocrite, aren't I?" Jarrett muttered to himself as he hurriedly strode through town. *But I am less important than her... and I did have reasons I needed to be alone with them.*

He steered far clear of the town hall, where the meeting was taking place. He had declined to join them in favor of directing the obfuscation of rebellion activities—a necessary task and an excellent excuse to avoid having to see Leandra again. In case the Saridi soldiers began poking around, they had to make barns seem like barns once more, instead of the training facilities they had become. Weapons, armor, and training dummies needed to be dispersed into people's cellars and sheds, out of sight.

Word was spread to the Vanguard mages to lie low—no magic use was permitted until the danger had passed. Though the soldiers were still days away, the Vanguard had to take as many precautions as they could. Some mage hunters were uncannily good at identifying mages.

Jarrett just finished shoving a couple of training dummies into his pantry when he heard knocking at his door for the second time that day. Was Morgane's meeting over already? He rushed to his door and opened it to see not Morgane, but Fae. He stopped short at the sight of the Raven.

"Your presence at our meeting has been requested," Fae informed him coolly. Much as she had done upon their initial meeting, she turned to lead him onwards without another word. She strode confidently away, clearly expecting Jarrett to follow. He had to jog to keep pace with her.

"Requested by who?"

"Your leader."

Jarrett's blood ran cold, but he couldn't think of a way to weasel out of the situation if Morgane had a hand in summoning him. He had to prove his trustworthiness all over again and disobeying her summons wouldn't help.

He was led down the familiar cobblestone roads to the main square, then into the town hall. Off in a side room, where the Vanguard's council usually convened, Morgane and Leandra sat at opposite ends of the dark wooden table. The rest of the eight chairs were empty. Jarrett wondered if Morgane had wanted to meet with the Vanguard council present, or if Leandra had insisted on a private meeting.

Morgane's eyebrows furrowed as she stared at the older woman. It was enough for Jarrett to know that she was displeased. Leandra's face was a blank sheet of paper for all he could ascertain from her neutral expression.

As he and Fae took seats at the table, Jarrett caught a whiff of lavender, just strong enough to revive his memories of the previous night in Leandra's tent. He scooched his chair away from Leandra and wished he was much, much farther.

"We came with a proposal for Morgane." Leandra's cold eyes bore into Jarrett once again, even as he tried to avoid it. "But she insisted on conferring with you before giving us an answer."

"What's the proposal?" he asked.

Morgane glanced over to Jarrett. "They think that the soldiers are being sent here to search for a magical artifact that may be hidden underneath the village. They want to stay here, to protect the artifact... and us."

Over a century ago, as a part of the truce that ended the territory wars between the gods, magical artifacts created by talented mortals or the gods themselves were banned altogether. Not all of the artifacts were dangerous weapons used in the wars, some were simply delightful oddities—regardless, the existing artifacts were destroyed and the creation of new ones was prohibited.

"Wait, there's an artifact here, in Rosewood, that survived the Magus War?"

Morgane tilted her head. "You already know what artifacts are?"

Jarrett shrugged. Strangely, he didn't know where he'd learned about artifacts and the details of the treaty. Saridian wasn't rich with the history of magic and he couldn't think of anything he had read or anyone who had told him about this aspect of the Magus War truce. Leandra must have explained it to Morgane before he got there, but the question stood—how did *he* know? Was this a sliver of knowledge left behind from his previous life?

His tattoo prickled, just a little.

"This artifact didn't survive the war," Leandra said. "It was created more recently, to be used against Riordan."

"How do you know about it?" Jarrett asked. "If they're here, why don't *we* know about them?"

"We know because of our god."

"Death," Morgane clarified, an eyebrow raised. "Apparently."

"Death has a vested interest in removing Riordan from the throne—as much, if not more so, than you do," said Leandra "Riordan is terrorizing her. He may very well disrupt the cycle of souls and perhaps reignite the Magus War, if he has his way."

Fae spoke next, quiet yet confident. "Only recently has this artifact come to our attention. We don't know why it was stashed away instead of used, but regardless, we intend to use it now."

"But now," Leandra said, "Death and Riordan both know it exists, and we have to get to it before Riordan does. Rosewood, according to our information, is one of the possible hiding spots. If this weapon is what we think it is, it's the key to defeating Riordan and securing safety for the oppressed of Saridian, for Death, and for our whole World."

There was silence while everyone processed this momentous news.

Jarrett cleared his throat. "Why should we trust you?" This was the question he needed answered more than any other.

"We have a common goal," Fae said. "We all want Riordan to fall. Protecting this artifact and keeping you from being discovered when the soldiers come to investigate is in our best interest. We want to help you. No strings attached."

"We will consider this offer," Morgane said. "Once we discuss this matter, we will send a messenger."

"What's there to discuss?" Leandra asked. "You either want our help, or you don't."

Morgane looked to Jarrett, expectant. He realized suddenly why she had summoned him to this meeting. She didn't know what transpired between him and the Ravens but was sharp enough to pick up that his late-night visit hadn't gone well.

So, Morgane still trusted his judgment. But it was impossible to know if the Ravens would be reliable, plus there were complications that would come from allying with them. Many of the Vanguard wouldn't be fond of the risk of working with the brash cult. And of course, he himself was consumed by last night's failure.

But soldiers were coming to scour Rosewood. And if the Ravens were telling the truth, the Vanguard would need as much help as they could get, regardless of his gripes or anyone else's.

Jarrett swallowed and took a breath. "Some of our mages are here because Ravens directed them to the Vanguard. We have no reason not to accept help and knowledge where it is needed."

That seemed to be what Morgane needed to hear from him. "Then," she said, "we have a deal."

Leandra smiled and shook Morgane's hand. "We look forward to working with you

Jarrett met with Morgane once more that evening to debrief. It had been a hectic day, but they'd made decent progress toward preparing for the soldiers' arrival. Morgane picked up some pastries from the bakery on her way to Jarrett's house, which they now shared as they sat at his kitchen table.

Morgane licked some powdered sugar off her fingers. "We're going to make it through this."

Jarrett nodded absently. He took a small bite of the jelly-filled treat sitting in front of him. What he'd already eaten sat sourly in his stomach.

"It's nice to have allies for once," Morgane added, giving him a sidelong glance, as if daring him to speak his true thoughts regarding the Ravens.

Jarrett put the pastry back down. "I think you might have been wrong."

Morgane scowled. "About what? You told me the Ravens were trustworthy enough to work with, so don't—"

"Not that."

"Then what?"

"Making me your second. It should have been Rohan or Korene—"

"Jarrett—"

"—but not me."

Morgane glared at Jarrett as he shoved a bite of pastry into his mouth. He chewed slowly, giving himself time before having to defend his opinion.

"This isn't like you," Morgane said, angry and concerned. "You don't second guess anything, least of all yourself."

Jarrett's tattoo itched, but he resisted scratching at it. It'd been bothering him since he'd met with Leandra, and he'd nearly rubbed it raw since then. Reluctantly, he finished chewing and swallowed. "Maybe it's time I started."

"I picked you for a reason. It wasn't on a whim, and you can't change your mind on one either."

"Whims are all I have. It's not going to do us any good."

Morgane shook her head. "You have instinct. Decisiveness. The confidence that a true leader needs." She flashed a grin. "Most of the time, anyway. So get over whatever crisis of faith you've been having and give me back the swaggering, uncompromising, frustratingly determined attitude that we need to get the Vanguard through this." She raised an eyebrow at him as she lifted the pastry to her mouth. "Got it?"

Jarrett held up his hands in surrender. "Fine, fine. I'll snap myself out of it. You'll have swaggering Jarrett back tomorrow, I promise."

"Good," Morgane said, her mouth full. Then, spraying crumbs, "I don't know what I'd do without him."

Jarrett snorted. "I don't know what I'd do without *you*. What any of us would do."

Morgane waved her pastry in the air dramatically. "Run amok, most like. Good thing you're stuck with me."

"It is, indeed."

For a short time, they spoke of only light, inconsequential things. Jarrett began to enjoy his dessert in truth. Morgane was the best at distracting him from his darker thoughts, his fears, and the weight of his lost memories. With her, it was easiest to forget the forgotten and the dangers they'd soon have to face. The relief never stayed long, but still; it was nice while it lasted.

As Morgane stood at his door, ready to leave, Jarrett saw her demeanor visibly dampen.

"There are two more things before I go." Morgane let out a sigh. "Both of which I should have brought up earlier, but—ah, I suppose it is what it is."

It wasn't like Morgane to hedge, or to avoid difficult topics. Jarrett furrowed his brows. "What is it?"

"Okay. Well, the first thing is that there have been reports that Riordan is recruiting. But this isn't just the regular spring recruitment. He's offering coin to recruits... a lot of it."

Jarrett paused. "Why would he need more recruits than normal? Is he taking Saridian to war?"

The gods drew up a treaty decades before Jarrett was born in order to end the Magus War, in which they fought over how much of the continent belonged under each of their control. If Riordan was planning on violating that treaty, Saridian might have to worry about more than just the Tyrant. A war against the other regions, against the other *gods*.

"Or, he's planning on cracking down on dissenters in the farther reaches of Saridian that have escaped scrutiny so far. Like us. Either way, it's bad. I think we need to move up our timeline."

"Morgane. We aren't ready to take on the capital yet—"

"We might not have a choice. They might come to us before we can get to them. Or if Riordan *does* want a war, it's not just about us anymore. He's ready for this and the other gods aren't. He could expand Saridian."

A grim hope blossomed in Jarrett's mind. "If he breaks the treaty, the other gods will put him down. Maybe they can free us."

"Or they decide they *all* want more territory and power. The Magus War begins anew. There will never be a decisive victory between them all, and once again, us mortals will suffer for it."

Jarrett pinched the bridge of his nose. "You're right. The risks of a war are too great. But sometimes..."

"I know that what we have to accomplish seems impossible. But it's all we have. So it's what we'll do."

Covert operations were their only real option, no matter how many recruits they gathered. They'd never be able to take on the full military force of the Saridi army. They needed a strike on Riordan himself.

But killing him once wasn't enough. The Tyrant had a backup, a mortal in waiting that would become his next vessel. If they could wipe out his next incarnate, too, they'd have a real chance having the time they needed to change things.

Morgane had discovered a piece of knowledge that was not well known in Saridian: the amount of territory a god had under their control, and the amount of mortals that believed in their aspects and cause, was directly correlated to how much power that god wielded. The core of the Vanguard's plans rested on this. They had to convince enough of Riordan's loyal citizens to turn on him. It was the only way to strip him of his powers and gain independent control of the region.

But enlightening the masses and convincing them to release their fear or reverence of Riordan and instead take power for themselves—well, it wasn't going to be easy. But Morgane was right. It was the only option. And so the Vanguard prepared to make their stand.

Jarrett sighed. "We haven't even discovered the identity of Riordan's next incarnate yet. But if we have to move forward, then we must."

Morgane fished out a folded piece of paper from her pocket. She held it out to Jarrett. "That brings me to the second thing. Leandra gave me this."

Jarrett plucked the paper from her hand. He unfolded it to find a single word scrawled in ink: Calder. "A name? The name of—"

"Yes. That's him."

Jarrett's tattoo tingled, furiously this time. Until now, he wondered if it was just his imagination. *What's going on? Is Leandra helping me circle closer to the truth after all?*

"Jarrett? Is something wrong?"

He was sure Morgane had noticed the blood drain from his face. "Just... surprised. We finally have a lead. Did Leandra say anything else?"

"Not really. Just that it was a thank you for placing our trust in the Ravens."

Morgane left, and Jarrett was left wondering. As Riordan's replacement, was Calder a mage? And if so, could he be the man who had taken his memories?

CHAPTER 9

A jolt through Scarlet's chest woke her from her restless slumber.

Abruptly, she found herself sitting up in her bed. *Her* bed? Nothing felt hers in this room, in this castle, in this World.

Her heart raced. What had woken her? Was something wrong?

The dark walls closed in.

Something was wrong. Her heart? Something in her chest. It was crushing, sinking, burning. Wrong wrong *wrong*.

Was her heart still her own? Not while she was linked with Death; her actions beyond her control.

Her lungs were collapsing.

Why wasn't her mother here? That too, was *wrong*.

She's dead, she has to be dead, or she'd be here.

The moonlit room was spinning. Scarlet's fingers were interlocked with her tangled curls. She pulled her hair; the sensation was the only thing that kept her from falling out of her own body.

Am I dying?

She had to do something. Get help. Scarlet pulled herself out of bed, but her vision faltered, followed closely by her body. Her knees clashed into the stone floor. Everything spun.

I'm not going to make it.

Her mother wasn't here to save her. She was alone. Bronwen? Too far. She'd never get to his quarters before passing out, not like this.

I'm going to die.

Her vision faded to black.

Consciousness dawned. Sunlight bit at Scarlet's eyes. She pulled her covers over her head to block the light. *What happened when I woke earlier? A panic attack? I thought... I thought I was dying.*

She still felt unwell. Breathing hurt. Training yesterday had yielded some blows from Death's magic. *Maybe my ribs are broken.* She would have to make another trip to Bronwen's quarters for healing. *I probably should have gone yesterday...* But somehow, it almost seemed pointless. Though Bronwen's healing did significantly shorten her recovery time, it wasn't instantaneous. It taxed her body in its own way, as well. Her magic felt even more shaky after a healing session. She would only get injured again shortly, especially if she wasn't at full capacity to keep up with Death's brutal training regimen.

It's.... bright out. That meant she was late for training. They always began right at sunrise. She'd never been late before. *I'll be in trouble, won't I?* Yet, the thought failed to rouse her.

A voice echoed in her head. *Scarlet.*

"Viridian?" Scarlet whispered. "Are you back?"

I think so. For now. I don't know why, but it's easier to reach you when you're weak.

Scarlet let out a shuddering breath. *So I didn't imagine her.* "Gods, I miss you so much. I wish you were here. Like... for real here."

Me too. I want to be able to help more.

"What were you saying before? That I had to find Mom... do you know where she is? Is she okay?"

No... no.

Scarlet's heart stopped. She grasped her twisted covers in her hands as hard as she could. "Viridian! Is she dead?"

Not dead. But... weak. She's being tortured, Scarlet. I don't know where. Somewhere... dark. Beneath the earth, I think. Somewhere in the World. Beyond that, I don't know.

"So... so Riordan got her." Scarlet's heart sank. "What does he want from her?"

There's something she's protecting from him, but I don't know what either. If she's willing to give her life for it, it must be important to keep it from him.

"You're right. I have to find her, help her. I just... don't know how."

A series of knocks resounded on Scarlet's door, making her jump up in bed. Before she had a chance to respond, the door flew open. Death stormed in, brows furrowed. "Get up."

"Why should I?" Scarlet snapped. Her own anger surprised her. After her near-death experience, or her panic attack, or whatever it was, alongside Viridian's news of their mother, her emotions were unspooling. "You've been keeping things from me, haven't you? You know my mother was captured."

"I told you," Death said, "to **get out of bed.**"

Scarlet started to rise. Catching herself, she tensed her body to resist the compulsion, but the magic ran through her and it was impossible to resist for more than a couple of seconds. She got to her feet and stood face to face with Death and her razor-sharp gaze.

"Is that how this is going to be then?" Scarlet asked. "I'm forced to obey you, and you won't even tell me the truth?"

Death scowled. "It is time to train. I'll tell you what you need to know when it's time."

"The time is now!" Scarlet spat. "My mother needs help. You know where she is through the emissary bond, don't you? Send me there."

Death let out a sardonic laugh. "You aren't half ready to take on Riordan's forces."

"My fighting isn't perfect but I'm *capable* now," Scarlet growled. "I've thrown everything I have into training. You've torn me to bits and honed me into a tool, and I'm telling, asking, begging of you now, to use me. That's what you want out of me, isn't it?"

A more serious look dawned on the god's face. "You're weaker than you think. I can't send you to the World."

"But you admit my mother is in trouble?"

Death stood in stony silence.

"Why can't you just say it?" Scarlet's anger began to condense, and subconsciously, she started to gather energy at her fingertips.

Scarlet, what are you doing? Viridian snapped. *She's a god.*

"Kiera will be alright. And if you want to get stronger, you'd best come for training." With that, Death turned to head out the door.

Ignoring her sister's cautioning, Scarlet concentrated her energy into a dense magic bolt that she shot at Death's back. At the final moment before impact, Death spun and swiped her hand to spot-shield the bolt.

"This will not go well for you," Death warned.

Scarlet could feel the power in the air as the god focused her energy. "I don't care." She took a fighting stance and awaited whatever Death would throw at her, but she didn't even see the blow coming.

A rope-like length of pure magic swiped at her feet, knocking her to the floor. Scarlet scrambled back up, grabbing her dagger from her boot sheath. She couldn't beat Death with magic, but maybe she could catch her off-guard with a different tactic.

Scarlet charged at Death, but the god snatched her wrists and dug her sharp nails into Scarlet's skin. She pulled Scarlet into a hold, twisting her hand behind her back. Death ripped the dagger from her clutch and threw it onto the stone floor. It clanged as it made contact, making Scarlet wince. She hoped it wasn't damaged.

"What are you hoping to accomplish, Scarlet?" Death admonished. "To make a fool of yourself?"

Scarlet said nothing. *I just picked a fight with a god.* She knew what power her master held; she'd felt it firsthand, wielded it for Death's bidding. Of course it was idiotic. But her rage was all-consuming. She couldn't lose her mother. She'd claw and scrape for the slightest chance at saving the last of her family.

"Silence? Wise."

There was a yank on the emissary bond. Like a plug was pulled, all Scarlet's energy rushed out of her body. She slumped to the floor like a ragdoll. She was barely conscious as Death picked up her dead weight, slung her over her shoulder, and carried her through Deianira.

In vain, Scarlet tried to follow the turns despite her blurred vision and spinning head. Where was Death taking her? Down stairs. More turns. More stairs. She lost track of what floor they were on. It was so cold as they went down further; had they ventured below ground level? Scarlet had never found a way beneath the castle, despite Death's hint about there being a floor she hadn't discovered.

Scarlet blinked rapidly, trying to focus her eyes. Her vision cleared enough to see a set of bars before Death tossed her onto the floor. Scarlet hit the stone hard, her breath knocked out of her. Her entire chest rang with pain, the impact jostling her damaged ribs. Tears bit at her eyes; she tried her best to hold them back. Sobbing would only increase her agony.

"Stay here for a while." Death said. She slammed the cell door shut. The grating sound of metal on metal echoed down the hall. "Perhaps it will help you appreciate the privileges I grant you."

Freezing air refilled Scarlet's lungs, sending her into an immensely tortuous coughing fit. When she recovered, Death was already gone, leaving her alone in a bare cell.

Deianira did, in fact, have a basement. It was a dungeon.

CHAPTER 10

The mild weather didn't hold.

It'd been storming since the hour after Dante left home.

Home. He had to stop thinking about it like that. He would never go back, except hopefully one day to get Zandra, once he had established somewhere safe for them to go.

In the meantime, the storm was making Dante's journey arduous. Instead of making it to Thornsbury on the first day, he was forced to seek shelter from the hail beneath a copse of trees. His clothes had been soaked through, as well as his spare set—and everything else in his bag, for that matter.

He slept miserably and woke to the same weather he had fallen asleep to. Frozen to his core, he knew he had to get back on the road. There was no chance of lighting a fire to dry himself and his things, so moving was his only way to create warmth.

The rain and hail barely eased as the sun rose, and he finally arrived at Thornsbury. He waited until midday to go into town, around when he would get there normally if he had come with Ferrick on horseback. He hadn't wanted to stop in town, nor spend any coin. But, thoroughly soaked and chilled, he felt he had no choice but to get a hot meal at the inn.

He was approached by a couple of villagers he knew in passing, who were surprised to see him. Dante laughed it off as best as he could, telling them that Ferrick had sent him to get supplies, and made him go despite the weather to get back at him for slacking off last week. They all nodded in commiseration and told stories about times with their own masters and their various punishments for the crimes of youth.

Dante spent more of his precious little coin on supplies, not only to uphold his deception but also because if he did injure himself on the road, it would come in handy to have some disinfectant and gauze. He could find herbs well enough on his own, and he made a mental note to actively look for some on the next leg of his journey.

His journey to... nowhere, in particular. He had no plan. He could go far enough away that no one from his old life would ever find him. Try to find a new master. Build a new life.

It felt pointless to do so, so far away from everyone he cared about.

He hadn't even gotten to say goodbye to his mother. Still, it was better than his parting with his father. He shook his head as if he could shake off his family's rejection. He was born a mage, and because of that, he'd lost everything. He still couldn't wrap his head around Milo's betrayal. At least Zandra was safe, but for how long? *I have to find somewhere to take her.*

If he was leaving his whole life behind, perhaps he should head north. Leaving Saridian meant he wouldn't have to worry about hiding his magic. Getting out was the hard part, though. The border between Saridian and Celeigh was heavily patrolled, as were the ports. If he wanted to come back for Zandra, he'd have to risk the journey multiple times. Perhaps he should have let her come with him now. Everything seemed like a mistake; he couldn't stop second-guessing himself.

Eventually, he finished his meal and shopping, and couldn't delay any longer. He'd head north and see if he thought of anything better along the way.

He spent what was left of his coins on a simple map. It wasn't very detailed, but at least it would allow him to stay on the main roads, where he might be able to beg for some food from passing travelers and shelter in towns along the way if he needed to. Perhaps his expertise with herbs could earn him lodging.

It was still raining, but he couldn't justify waiting out the storm any longer. He left down the southern route towards Briarglen, in case anyone was paying attention to his departure, and then looped around Thornsbury to head north.

The storm got worse. Dante traveled through the rain and hail, flinching at each rumble of thunder overhead. When night fell he was scared to camp in the trees again, lest they were struck by lightning. He spent the night in the ditch, freezing and wet.

He slept little. At least that meant his visions couldn't disturb him. Wide awake and frozen to his core, he spent a lot of time thinking. Even though he tried to shun his magic, he'd used it. Maybe Milo wasn't the traitor. Dante was. The crystal orb in his pack was a testament to his failure. A different kind of chill seeped through him.

He had gotten himself into this. Magic lured him into using it, but he should have resisted. He couldn't regret saving Zandra, but if she had stayed away from magic too, he wouldn't have had to save her. The king had been right all along. Mortals shouldn't be entrusted with magic. *I'll never use it again.*

On the third night of his banished life, he ran across a group of travelers who were kind enough to take him in, letting him sleep on the floor of their wagon. He was grateful for the chance to dry out. The group consisted of four young men, ranging from around his age to a handful of years older. When he asked where they were heading, they said they were going northeast, to Kingsguard. The four of them were heading there to join the army.

One of them was especially keen on becoming a mage hunter. Dante stiffened at this revelation and did his best to smile and nod throughout their late-night conversations, trying not to show his discomfort.

He reappropriated his earlier lie about his master sending him through the storm as a punishment. They laughed at him.

"If your master is that bad," the oldest of the boys, Keenan, said, "you should join the army with us. Not that they'll go easy on you there either, but at least you'd be in good company."

"Oh, I couldn't," Dante said. "I would make a horrible soldier. I've lost every fight I've ever been in."

"Ah, well," Keenan said, "that's what boot camp is for. They'll whip you into shape in no time." He clapped Dante on the back. "Sleep on it, alright?"

Dante mumbled a noncommittal answer. He was grateful to not sleep on the ground, but he couldn't be more eager to part ways with the soon-to-be soldiers.

In the morning, things were looking up. It was only drizzling now, and the sun peeked out from behind the clouds. Dante shook hands with the travelers and wished them a safe journey. They were all turning to leave, and Dante sighed with relief.

"Hey, what's your village called anyway?" Keenan turned around to ask. "Maybe we'll come to visit if we're on duty in this part of the kingdom. You know, badger you a little, in case you change your mind about joining us in the army."

"Uh, it's a little place called..." Dante sputtered trying to spit out a random name from his map. It took him a second but a name trickled out. "Called graystone."

One of the others glanced over his shoulder. His name was Gideon if Dante remembered correctly. "Wait. Did you say graystone?"

"Isn't that where you were from?" Keenan asked. "Before your family came to Airedale."

"Yeah, it is," Gideon said. "And I've never seen him before."

"I moved there recently," Dante said, mouth dry. Why had he even lied? His nerves were getting the best of him.

"Yeah? From where?" Keenan asked as he and Gideon moved to surround Dante from the other side.

Dante froze, brain going blank.

"Doesn't matter," Gideon said. "I'm not sure I would believe him anyway. graystone doesn't even have an herbalist for him to be apprenticing under. Ours died a year ago, right before I left. Why are you lying?"

Dante didn't know what else to do other than continue trying to weasel his way out of this mess. "My... my master and I both came from Thornsbury. That's why he sent me there for supplies."

"Oh come on." Gideon shoved Dante to the ground. He landed hard, knocking the air out of his lungs. "Your master made you walk *three days* in a storm from graystone to Thornsbury? Seems a little extreme."

"We don't like being lied to," Keenan said. Dante tried to sit up, but the older boy put a boot to his chest, pinning him back down to the ground. "So what's your deal?"

"My parents were tired of me slacking off, so they turned me out. I'm actually from Briarglen. I was embarrassed and I didn't want to get into it. I'm sorry."

There was a long pause where the pair of boys standing over Dante considered his excuse. The other two, Wren and Barek, observed from the sidelines.

"If you guys believe that, you're the ones who are an embarrassment," Wren said. "Think about it. What would be a good reason to lie to us? A good reason to be expelled from your village, to boot."

There was a long pause.

"If he were a mage," said Wren. "He would definitely lie to us. Don't you think?" He looked over to Barek, his younger brother, who shrugged in response.

"It's not like that—" Dante started.

"Shut up." Keenan ground his boot down on Dante's chest, pressing the air out of his lungs. "Is he right? You're a mage?"

"No," Dante choked out.

"Did you see the way he froze up when I told him I'm making a run at becoming a mage hunter?" asked Wren.

"Because I know how dangerous mages are to fight," Dante said. "It's a crazy thing to do—"

"And I bet you know that because you are one," Keenan said. He lifted his foot off Dante. "Get up."

Dante stood cautiously, glancing in turn at each of the young men surrounding him. His body was tender from the fall and Keenan's boot driving into his ribs.

Barek finally spoke up. "I don't know if he's being honest with us, but we don't have any proof."

"That's why I'm planning to get some," Keenan said. "Show us what you're made of, mage." He threw a punch at Dante, who managed to flinch out of arm's reach. "Fight me."

Dante's heart pounded like it was about to explode, and his vision narrowed. Keenan rained down an onslaught of jabs, which Dante did his best to dodge and deflect. But the older boy had almost a foot of height on him, not to mention more muscle and actual fighting prowess. It didn't take long for the blows to start connecting. Fist to shoulder, ribs, stomach. Dante lost track of how many hits he took.

As a last resort, Dante tried to kick Keenan between the legs. If he could take him out for a moment, perhaps he could get away. But he wasn't fast enough. Before Dante could strike, Keenan landed a blow directly to Dante's face. Dante's eyes stung as pain blossomed from his nose. He stumbled to his knees.

Keenan took the opening and leaped onto Dante, easily wrestling him into submission. The larger boy's superior strength made it impossible for Dante to struggle free. Unless he used magic. But that was Keenan's plan—to put Dante in a fight he couldn't win, to force him into revealing himself as a mage.

If Dante didn't give in to the temptation, it was possible to get out of this. He had to prove himself, to let himself be beaten to a pulp without magical retaliation. He could do that. It wouldn't be the first time. He'd been bullied his whole life for being the runt. Who knew that withstanding being beaten up would someday become a skill that would save his life?

Then, Keenan wrapped both of his hands around Dante's neck and squeezed hard, like he meant it. Dante gasped and squirmed, trying to loosen the grip, to get any amount of air into his lungs. Keenan just pressed harder, cutting off his breath completely. Black spots started to fill out Dante's vision, terror taking over as he fought uselessly to fill his lungs. He scratched and tore at the hands that were strangling his life away, to no avail.

Keenan was going to kill him. Dante would be choked to death, or burnt at the stake for being a mage. *There's no way out.*

"Stop it! You've gone far enough," yelled one of the others. In his panic, Dante couldn't tell whose voice it was. "He hasn't used a lick of magic, and even if he is a mage, we aren't actually *in* the army yet. We can't just—"

"He's a mage and I know it," Keenan said. He stared straight into Dante's eyes. "He's not getting away."

"So magebrand him and turn him in," said another voice. "Barek's right, even if he is a mage, we don't have the authority to execute him."

"The proper way is to burn them anyway."

Dante's vision had faded almost entirely to black, but at these words, he flashed back to the execution. His father took him to Kingsmount to watch one after he'd been caught doing magic. That poor girl, she'd burned right in front of him. The pain on her face. The life leaving her eyes. The smell of scorched flesh. He'd never forget it.

And he'd never let that be him, either.

With a shockwave of magic rolling out of his body, Dante threw his attacker off of him. Keenan went flying several feet and skidded across the muddy ground. Dante took a couple of breaths, heaving to refill his lungs with precious air. The others stared at him in surprise. Their slight delay was all Dante needed. He scrambled up and took off.

He ran toward the nearby brush. He knew he wouldn't outrun the other boys while he was still trying to catch his breath. His best chance was to lose them in the trees.

He made it into the cover and wove his way through. The soldiers-to-be had to be close behind him. Dante risked a look back, but it was a mistake. His foot caught a root, and he tumbled forward.

That was it, they were going to catch him.

"Here," a voice said. It was too soft and kind to be one of the boys. "Take my hand."

Dante looked up. A cloaked man stood before him, hand outstretched. His hood was up, leaving his face shadowed.

"Quickly," the man urged. His eyes flickered behind Dante, where the sounds of yelling boys came from close by.

Dante, half-stunned, accepted the man's help. The man kept hold of Dante's hand and used his free one to draw a large circle in the air next to them. Dante felt the rippling of magic as he did so, and watched as the world distorted and fell away within the circle, leaving an image of a field within its borders instead of the trees that surrounded them.

The man stepped through the portal and tugged Dante through behind him. Dante spun around as soon as the man released him, just in time to see the window back to the forest shrink and disappear.

They were in a field now. Thick teal grass came up nearly to his knees, swaying gently in the wind. It was a wide and open plain, though there were patches of trees with similarly colored foliage in the distance. It wouldn't have looked so different from the parts of Saridian that he'd been traveling through, if not for the discolorations. Above him, the purple sky was filled with voluminous clouds.

The boys were nowhere in sight. They'd been left behind, and now Dante was... somewhere else. Dante looked back at the cloaked man, who'd taken his hood down. He had shaggy brown hair and looked a few years older than Dante.

"What just happened?" Dante wiped his forehead with a shaky hand. "Who are you? Where am I?"

The cloaked man smiled. "My name is Bronwen. Welcome to the Crossworld."

CHAPTER 11

Perhaps Death had left her to die.

Scarlet couldn't keep track of the days inside her prison cell. Her sleep had become irregular as she attempted to forego consciousness as often as possible. Doing so got harder as time stretched on and her discomfort grew. Her body was sore from lying on the hard stone, especially with her broken ribs, and with only the scant amount of loose straw she had for bedding.

Perhaps it had been a week. It could have been a month. At first, she'd tried to escape, but Death had created a barrier that protected the cell's bars. She'd touched the wall of magic once. It sent a painful shock through her body, like lightning through her veins. She stayed far away from the bars after that, though she wore herself out a few times trying to blast through the barrier with magic until she collapsed. Eventually, she gave up.

She wondered if the barrier kept Viridian away as well. The first days, she cried out for her sister often, to no avail. It was no use. She was alone.

Her body and mind were both battered. Broken, sore, hopeless. Each day that passed was another that she knew her mother was suffering through as well. Each minute that passed was a step closer to the possibility of Riordan leaching whatever it was he wanted from her and killing her. And Scarlet could do nothing.

I'm a mage, a proper one now, and I'm still useless.

Someone was bringing her meals, but only when she slept. She hoped it was Death. It was too painful to think of Bronwen coming down to the depths of Deianira to leave her food, but not to speak with or free her. It was hard to motivate herself to consume the offerings.

It had been some time since the last delivery of food. But, it had also been some time since she'd slept. She'd have to fall asleep to see if Death was purposefully starving her. She left her mind blank, open, ready to accept the embrace of nothingness. But it rejected her. It left her awake, mind and body void of everything except pain, and the slow creep of fire that built up beneath her skin.

Anger. Anger was the beast lurking in her blood, her stomach, her brain—anywhere it could fit, it squeezed its way in. It smoldered. Burned. Bided its time. *Why couldn't Death just use me like she said she wanted to? Am I really so weak that I'm worth nothing to her? She's spent so much time training me, and I'm better every day... meanwhile, my mother is suffering, and she won't even admit it.*

She couldn't do it anymore. Hungry, tired, aching, empty—how could she last like this? Was her mother's suffering even worse? *No. I can't... I can't just give up. I have to find a way to save her, even if Death thinks I'm worthless. I'll save her, and then one day I'll burn this whole castle to the ground if I can.*

Her resolution granted her a deep calmness. Her anger still twisted underneath, a smoldering ember of resolve. She didn't know how she would see this through, but somehow, repeating her plan over and over in her head was a mantra that instilled peace. *I won't let anyone stop me. There has to be a way. My mother evaded Riordan long enough to get me to safety. Despite their raw strength, the gods aren't infallible.*

This kept her going until footsteps resounded down the passageway of the prison. There was a flash of magic and Scarlet sensed the barrier around her cell dissolving. Then came the jingling of keys. She summoned enough strength to look up.

Death unlocked the cell door and threw it open. The screech of metal on metal made Scarlet flinch. She had become accustomed to the heavy silence of the prison.

"Come on," Death said, beckoning her.

Scarlet almost thought to remain on the cold floor of her cell in an act of defiance. Then she remembered the comforts of a real bed. Of sunlight, and fresh clear air. Plus Viridian, and their mother. She needed as much freedom as she could to enact her unlikely rescue plans. So, she pulled herself up despite the excruciating pain of movement and followed Death out of the dungeon. Once they reached ground level, Death simply disappeared around a corner, leaving Scarlet alone in the hall without another word.

So Scarlet was free, and yet not. She couldn't be, with the emissary marks emblazoned on her hand. *If I can find a way to break the emissary bond, then she'd have no more control over me, and wouldn't be able to track me if I ran away.* More trips to the library would be necessary to determine if this was possible, and how. *The other thing I need to do is learn how to open a portal to the World. Then, I can go look for Mom.*

For now, she took her time getting back upstairs to her room. As she hobbled up the stairs, she extended her consciousness, searching for Viridian. Now that she was free, would she be able to communicate with her sister again? But she heard nothing, felt nothing.

A spike of fear ran through her. *Did I lose my connection to her?* She took a deep breath as she made it to her room. She flung open the door and promptly collapsed into bed.

She'll be back. She has to be.

The warmth and softness of a real mattress nearly brought her to tears. Sleep overtook her instantly.

When Scarlet woke, bright midday light shone into her room and she found herself unbearably hungry. With a modicum of autonomy returned, her appetite had made a comeback. She rolled out of bed stiffly, her body not yet adjusted back to movement. Most of her body ached terribly. It would take her some time to recover.

Death better not want me to train today. Not that she could decline if the god requested it. The idea of getting tossed back into the dungeon outweighed her will to disobey. *Which was probably the whole point of that experience,* she thought bitterly.

She replaced her soiled clothes with clean ones from her wardrobe, then made her way downstairs to raid the pantry. Bronwen had kept it well-stocked. There was an abundance of fresh fruits and bread, and many other delights that she piled into her arms.

She usually ate at the small table in the kitchen, where the cooks and other kitchen staff of a properly staffed castle would have eaten. But after her time in the dungeon, the walls of the smaller room pressed in around her. Instead, she carried her food out to the great hall, a room that in any other castle would be meant for merriment, dancing, and dozens if not hundreds of diners. Of course in Deianira, it was large and empty, other than a great long table and now, Scarlet. She took a seat at the middle of the table and began to savor her own personal feast.

"Ah, Scarlet."

She jumped at the sound of Bronwen's voice, nearly inhaling a grape.

Bronwen took a seat next to her. "How are you doing?"

"I'm fine." She stuffed a chunk of bread in her mouth. She didn't much feel like conversing with the other emissary. It was Death that threw her in the cell, yet bitterness toward Bronwen flooded out from her. He could have helped her, but he hadn't.

"I... I can sense your pain. We will have to do some healing sessions. Whenever you are ready, I can start."

"You could have started days ago."

"Death is too hard on you. I'm sorry for that, Scarlet, I truly am."

"Yet," Scarlet said, mouth still full, "you work for her."

"I do," Bronwen said. Scarlet couldn't tell if he was resigned, or resolute.

She said nothing in return, instead chomping down on a juicy fruit that she didn't know the name of. Its sweet, exotic flavor was the best thing she'd ever tasted.

Bronwen's words were offered softly, like a peace offering, "I have someone to introduce you to."

Introduce meant it wasn't her mother. "Not interested."

"I think you will be."

Scarlet scrunched her brow. "An emissary?"

"No. A new arrival."

Who would be here other than an emissary? Despite her exhaustion, Scarlet's curiosity was piqued.

"I'll bring him here," Bronwen said.

Scarlet was unwilling to admit her interest to him. "Fine. Whatever."

Bronwen left and returned a few minutes later, once Scarlet had finished eating. He had in tow a boy who looked to be around Scarlet's age. His hair was shaggy and blond.

As they got closer Scarlet noticed the boy had dark circles under his eyes that gave him a haunted look. He looked up and their eyes locked. His irises were bright green, like Death's, but warmer, and more curious.

"Scarlet," Bronwen said, "this is Dante."

Scarlet glanced at Bronwen, then looked at the boy again. She avoided his sharp, inquisitive gaze this time. Dante. A boy. Not an emissary. He held himself stiffly and didn't seem to know what was going on any more than she did.

"Dante will be staying at Deianira from now on and joining some of your lessons. Scarlet, why don't you show him the way to his quarters? He'll be staying in the room across from yours."

The last thing Scarlet wanted was to be left with this new boy. She had barely begun to recover from her imprisonment and had no idea what Death had in store for her next. This new arrival, this stranger invading what little space she had was too much.

Her tongue felt like lead. She said nothing and took another bite of her feast, which suddenly tasted bland. She had to force herself to swallow.

Bronwen cleared his throat. "Scarlet?"

She glowered at him. How could he ask anything of her, right after what she'd been through? Even something as simple as this. She was exhausted both mentally and physically.

Dante caught her eye again. This time, she saw her own weariness and pain reflected in his posture.

Ugh. Is he getting pulled into all of this, too? What does he have to do with Death, with any of this madness?

"Okay," Scarlet said, quietly, before she could retreat back into the thorny recesses of her mind.

Bronwen scooped up her now empty plate. "Well then, I'll take care of the dishes, so you can take Dante straight to his room."

As Bronwen left, he insisted she report to his quarters for healing later, then left the great hall, leaving her alone with Dante.

What could she even say to this boy? It had been days, if not weeks since she'd had a proper conversation with anyone, let alone a stranger.

"So." Dante stuffed his hands in his trouser pockets. "I should come with you?"

Scarlet gave him a nod before taking off.

She stole glances at him as they made their way through Deianira. The way he held himself slightly hunched betrayed his timidness, and he worriedly picked at his fingernails. But his apprehension didn't stop him from observing every detail of the castle. He seemed to take particular interest with the light orbs that lit the halls of Deianira. He was small; they were about the same height. His hands were calloused and his fingertips were stained green. He had freckles.

"This place is like a maze," Dante observed. "Do you know why it was built like this?"

That was something she knew how to answer, at least, after all of her reading. "Everything in the Crossworld is malleable. A reflection of the World combined with the will of the gods. It's this way because that's how Death wants it."

"Death…" Dante let out a deep breath. "So this is *Death's* castle? Bronwen told me that she's… a god?"

Scarlet gave him an affirmative grunt.

"Aren't you afraid of her?"

The prison, the brutality of her training, and the lack of information—Death's treatment of her was maddening. But fear wasn't the emotion boiling in Scarlet's gut. Her fear was reserved for Riordan. She ascended a full flight of stairs before her anger simmered down enough that she could speak. "No. I'm not… *afraid* of her."

"Should… should *I* be? I haven't met her yet."

"Bronwen said you aren't an emissary."

"I don't even know what an emissary *is*, so—"

"Then I don't think you have to worry." *At least, not as much.* But he seemed scared enough already, so she kept that to herself. "And if you have a choice, I would keep it that way."

Dante held his silence for the rest of the walk. Scarlet was grateful for that—she was anxious about navigating more of his questions when they both seemed decidedly overwhelmed. She wasn't sure how best to protect him from Death, but saying something that could send him into a panic was probably unhelpful.

When they arrived, Scarlet gestured to the door across from her own. "According to Bronwen, that's your room."

"Thanks."

Scarlet was eager to retreat to her room, yet, her curiosity begged to be sated. "So if you aren't an emissary... why are you here?"

"My family exiled me. I had to leave my home, and then I got into trouble on the road... Bronwen saved me by bringing me here. I can't say I know why... but here I am."

"Why did they exile you?" Scarlet asked, but she knew the answer to her question as soon as she'd asked it. This boy looked Saridi. There was an obvious explanation.

Dante looked away and cleared his throat. His voice came out scratchy. "I got caught using magic."

Scarlet paused. "You know Riordan is in the wrong, don't you? Magic belongs to mortals just as much as the gods. It's not *bad*."

"Isn't it?" There was an edge to his voice that hadn't been there before. "I lost my home, my friends, my family. My whole life is gone because of magic. How is that *not* bad?"

"You didn't lose your life because of magic. You lost it because Riordan is the king, and he wants all the power for himself."

Dante tensed. Maybe that hadn't been the right thing to say. She should have followed her initial instinct to keep her mouth shut. But magic was the only thing that gave her any hope, and she didn't want Dante to reject the one tool he had to protect himself.

"I don't know what to think," Dante said. "But I'm going to get settled in because there isn't anything I can do about it now." He entered his room and shut the door firmly behind him.

Scarlet went to her room. She wanted to rest for a while before going to Bronwen for healing. The magical assistance would be a relief, yet she wasn't ready to face more conversations with the other emissary yet.

She lay in bed face up, staring at the ceiling, tracing the patterns in the stone with her eyes. Taking pity on anyone without compensation didn't seem like Death's style, and she doubted Bronwen could have brought Dante here without Death's permission. Dante was a mage, so perhaps he was meant to become an emissary, too.

She hoped for his sake that he wasn't.

CHAPTER 12

At noon, two dozen Saridi soldiers rode into Rosewood atop fine horses. Swords swung from their belts, and they wore the colors of the Tyrant—blue and gold. At the back of the group, two white horses pulled a large wagon crafted from splendid redwood. It might have been a grand sight, had they not been the Vanguard's enemies.

They were as ready as they could be for this moment. Jarrett had gone over plans with Morgane and the Ravens meticulously. It hadn't been easy to convince everyone that working with the Ravens was their best chance of survival, but he and Morgane eventually convinced the dissenters. It'd been a week since they struck up their partnership, and now it was time to put it to the test.

Jarrett, attempting to be unassuming, shadowed the soldiers as they rode through town. They stopped to ask about the town's leader. Everyone in the village had been briefed on the plan and told to act normally. Dutifully, the Vanguard members that were approached told the soldiers it was a market day, and that Morgane could likely be found in the town square.

Jarrett followed them down the brick road to the square and strategically chose a market booth to pretend to browse at, keeping an eye on the soldiers all the while. The market quieted as people stopped to observe the newcomers. In the center of the square, a larger-than-life statue of Riordan towered over them. Jarrett hated how the stone statue's eyes seemed to watch them.

According to the Ravens' information, if the artifact was here, it was likely hidden in a vault beneath the statue. Ironic, that a weapon to be used against the Tyrant was stored beneath a statue meant to honor him. Neither the Vanguard nor the Ravens had found an entrance to the potential vault, and they couldn't attempt to brute force their way in yet. If they could maintain secrecy until the soldiers passed, it would serve them well.

The head of the Saridi troops dismounted to greet Morgane, who had approached the soldiers. It was her job to see how much they knew.

Morgane extended a hand to the man. "Lieutenant. Welcome to our humble village. To what do we owe the honor of your visit?" Morgane was always unfailingly polite where Jarrett knew that a hint of passive-aggression would leak into his own voice. He was envious of her control.

"You're in charge of this settlement? Nice to know someone in the smallest of villages still recognizes rank symbology these days." The lieutenant barely looked at Morgane and ignored her outstretched hand. "I am Lieutenant Jonathan. We're here on the orders of King Riordan to retrieve an illegal magical artifact, so it can be disposed of."

Morgane remained cool despite the lieutenant's rudeness. "A magical artifact? I'm sure we have nothing like that here in Rosewood."

"You'd be surprised what a group of mages can get up to."

"There are no mages here, I assure you."

"Oh, of course not. Our king dealt with the perpetrators already."

"I see. Do you know where to find this artifact?"

"We're told it may be underground, beneath the village." The lieutenant looked up at the statue of Riordan. "Right around here, in fact. We may need to use explosives to break into the cache. You'll have to clear this market out so we can get to work."

"*Explosives?*" Morgane looked concerned. "If you're going to be blowing up parts of our village I—"

The lieutenant waved a hand dismissively. "We have the situation under control."

Jarrett wished he could punch the lieutenant, but violence wasn't his mission today.

The lieutenant ordered Morgane to clear the square, and then began organizing his soldiers. They pulled out an assortment of shovels and pickaxes as well as a few barrels.

After Jarrett had a good overview of the situation, he finished his feigned browsing and headed to the rendezvous point, a nearby inn. A group of Ravens, including Fae, as well as some rebels dressed up as Ravens, surrounded Jarrett as he began his report.

"Twenty-five soldiers. They're armed, mostly swords, plus other equipment they might use in a pinch. They brought explosives—watch out for the barrels. They might repurpose them to attack us when provoked. If they're aware of the rebellion, they aren't letting on. They're getting right to business so this needs to happen fast. Get to your positions."

Jarrett held fast as the Ravens and their impersonators surged out of the inn. He could feel the blood rushing in his ears. He wanted to go with them, to take action, but if everything went right, his work was done.

Not everyone could go undercover as a Raven. Since the cult's numbers were generally small, pumping them up too much could raise suspicions. The plan was to let the Ravens take the blame for the attack since they were already known enemies of the kingdom.

Despite any concerns he and the others had, the Ravens appeared to truly be aiding them. They would be bringing down more heat on themselves to protect the Vanguard from being revealed and to guard the artifact—if it was even here.

After a minute, Jarrett hurried back toward the square. If things did go wrong today, it was his job to protect his people, to defend noncombatants caught in the crossfire of this battle. Although everyone left in Rosewood was supportive of the cause, not everyone was a fighter. He didn't know how well the Ravens fought, but with the Vanguard members they disguised as such, they outnumbered the soldiers. Their chances were good, but he wouldn't say that he was optimistic—not with the nosedive his luck had taken, and not with the lives of his friends on the line.

A throng of people were heading in the opposite direction as him, away from the square. Morgane must be clearing the market out, as ordered. He searched each face as he passed them, looking for his leader. She was probably still at the square, but Jarrett wanted her either out of there or to have eyes on her when the battle began.

The town square was nearly empty when he arrived, save for the soldiers. Jarrett peeked around a corner to watch them. They were rolling the barrels over to the base of the statue. Whatever intel the Ravens had on the artifacts, it seemed Riordan's soldiers did as well.

As two soldiers rolled a third barrel up to the statue, an arrow struck one of them in the neck. The victim collapsed to the ground, sputtering briefly before death claimed him. Confusion erupted, the soldiers furiously looking around for their attacker, drawing their weapons and a few frantically gathering their shields.

"What the f—" Another arrow pierced through a soldier's breastplate to strike her shoulder, interrupting her expletive.

The soldiers, while surprised, were also well-trained. They fell into formation, creating a wall of shields to shelter them from the oncoming volley of arrows.

"Ravens! On the rooftops!" one of their numbers yelled. Some soldiers rushed back to their horses to fetch bows to return fire.

Meanwhile, more rebels began to close in from all sides, with mages among their numbers. Flashes of light and flames flew by, all aimed at the enemy—the fact that they had magic on their side was a definite advantage.

It wasn't easy to combat mages without magic, even if you were prepared for them. Jarrett learned this the hard way while helping the Vanguard mages train.

A couple of soldiers worked in tandem to light a fuse on one of the barrels, then rolled it toward a group of rebels on the far side of the square. Jarrett bit his tongue, hard. He hated being on the sidelines. Fortunately, a mage thought fast and exploded the barrel from a distance with a bolt of fire. Jarrett sighed in relief. He didn't want anyone on their side to get hurt, but it was especially important that their small number of mages stayed safe.

Jarrett skirted the edge of the square, but couldn't spot Morgane in the ensuing chaos. At least the battle was playing out in their favor. Surprise and numbers were on their side. As the rebel forces continued to prevail, Jarrett expected the remaining Saridi soldiers would flee, or possibly surrender.

There was a tap on Jarrett's shoulder. He swung around and had half drawn his sword when he realized it was Morgane standing behind him.

"Gods, woman. I thought you were a soldier," he said. "Would it kill you to warn me before I accidentally run you through?"

"No time," Morgane said between panted breaths. "There are more soldiers than we thought. Another group is headed into town right now."

"What? How many?"

"Didn't get a count. But... too many. The Ravens were right. This is important. The Tyrant is taking this seriously. What's the situation like here?"

"It's going well. There are some explosives—we might be able to use them against the reinforcements."

Morgane nodded. Her lips were pulled into a thin, determined line. "It's worth a shot."

Most of the soldiers at the square had been dismantled. Morgane yelled to the archers on the rooftops to spread the word of more troops incoming. Together, Morgane and Jarrett organized a ground crew with some of the explosive barrels, ready to light and roll them at the new combatants heading their way.

Morgane dragged him into an alleyway. Both of them were breathing heavily by the time they were shrouded in the shadows.

Jarrett clawed at his hair in frustration. "I feel so useless. I should be out there."

"What's wrong, Jarrett?"

"What's *wrong*? I want to help our people. Our friends could die out there."

"No, I know that. Trust me. But we're doing our part. It's just... look, I know you don't want to talk about it, but is everything okay, Jarrett?"

"Is this really the time to talk about this?"

"It's not *ideal*. But my adrenaline is pumping. So, a good time to ask those prying questions, I guess," Morgane said. Despite his best efforts to avoid her gaze, he couldn't help but notice her looking at him very seriously. "You've said we can trust the Ravens. But I don't know what's going on with you. With them. Is there something else I should know? Because we're going to keep needing the Ravens to survive this, and whatever else Riordan throws at us after today."

"We'll talk after the battle."

"Our friends' lives are in the hands of the Ravens. We should have spoken sooner. But we will, *now*."

There was vulnerability beneath Morgane's composure. Jarrett realized she wasn't asking for information so much as for reassurance.

"Morgane. Whatever issues I have with the Ravens, it's personal. But as I've told you, I trust that they will work with us as long as our goals align. Our missions are one and the same here."

Morgane nodded, seeming somewhat placated, but Jarrett could see her lingering concern.

He answered the question she was trying not to ask, "Does it matter what's going on with me? The past is the past, isn't it?"

"This isn't about the past anymore. This is affecting right here and now. You're miserable, which, knowing you, means your self-control is shot and that puts us at risk. And beyond that, you're my *friend*." She whispered the last word.

There was silence between the two of them, which was filled with distant sounds of combat echoing down the streets and into their alley hideaway. The reinforcements must be arriving. There was yelling and clashing, general clamoring and chaos. Jarrett felt a constant, anxious pull toward it, hating that he didn't know what was happening.

"I can't remember," Jarrett said. The words felt tight in his throat. "My memories were tampered with. Sealed with magic. I haven't figured out why. Big parts of my life are missing, just... torn away from me."

"Since when?"

"About five years ago."

"And what do the Ravens have to do with it?"

"Whoever took my memories left a mark. A tattoo of a raven, imbued with magic. I think an emissary did this to me. An emissary of Death."

"So Death *is* a god?" Morgane asked. "So, the Ravens may not be as strange as they seem."

"I'm fairly convinced," Jarrett said. "But... Leandra told me that I won't find answers. Or that I shouldn't find them. But I can't accept that."

"I'm so sorry Jarrett," she said softly. "You really have no idea who did this to you, or why?"

Their conversation ended with an abrupt boom in the distance. A series of explosions echoed down the streets.

"We'll have to finish this later," Morgane said, turning to run. "Let's make sure everything is going alright."

Adrenaline brought Jarrett back into focus. Together, they took off down the streets, toward the sounds of combat.

If the square had been chaos, Jarrett didn't even know what to call this. The streets were a gruesome sight—bodies littered the ground, some of them burnt from magic or explosives, Jarrett wasn't sure which. He only knew the stench of burnt hair and flesh was horrifying. Other bodies had arrows pierced deep into their flesh or had been slashed open with blades.

Though the scene was awful, Jarrett was grateful that most of the bodies were uniformed soldiers, and not Ravens or his people. His heart dropped every time he saw one of his own fallen. They would have to take account of who had been lost after the battle concluded. Now was not the time for mourning.

"Come on," Morgane said. "I hear people at the square. We have to make sure the statue is defended."

"Don't blow our cover after all this!" Jarrett yelled at her as she grabbed his hand and pulled him down the street.

"Only if we must."

Jarrett growled but hustled to the square alongside her.

What used to be a cheery and bustling market was now the most grisly scene they had ever seen. Bodies, fires, and fighting surrounded them. The lieutenant appeared to have survived the initial onslaught, and a group of new arrivals were defending him. The other soldiers were setting up one of the few remaining explosives at the base of the statue. Vanguard and Raven mages blasted magic bolts at them, but the guards effectively absorbed the volleys with large shields that Jarrett suspected were reinforced specifically for this purpose.

"We have to help stop them," Morgane said.

"How? We're dead meat in the long run if they think the village is involved."

"We're dead meat now if the Ravens are right about that artifact being here."

"I want to be in there as much as you, Morgane, but—"

"Stay here." Morgane strode towards the fray.

"*Morgane!*"

Morgane spoke over her shoulder, not slowing down, "Stay here. I've got this."

Jarrett swore under his breath. He was caught between obeying his leader and defending her in a dangerous situation. He steeled himself, pushing against his instincts. As much as he wanted to protect Morgane, she wouldn't forgive him for disobeying a direct order because of his hot-headedness. He could only hope that she, in typical Morgane fashion, had thought things out more than he had.

Morgane forced herself through the chaos, making a run for the statue. Sweat dripped from Jarrett's palms as soldiers began to light the fuses. A deadly blast was imminent. His friends would be caught in the explosion. He had spent the whole battle sitting back and watching the violence unfold around him, restraining himself at every turn. He couldn't hold back any longer.

Jarrett drew his sword and leaped into the square. A Raven mage had been backed against a market stand by a soldier and was desperately defending herself against his sword swings with shimmering shields of magic. Jarrett tackled the soldier from behind, throwing him onto the ground. The soldier's head hit the stone pavement hard, and Jarrett thrust his sword into his neck before he regained his faculties.

The mage that Jarrett rescued flashed him a smile. It was Fae. Most mages could only create short-lived spot-shields, but Fae had been using long-lasting ones that surrounded large portions of her body. She was a protection mage, attuned to Meyrin.

"Nice assist," Fae commented. She glanced at the statue. "Those explosives will go off any second. We have to stop them."

Jarrett nodded and followed her toward the center of the square. Between Fae's magical blasts and Jarrett slicing through any soldier who got in their path, they cut their way forward to the pile of explosives. The fuses were running short.

Jarrett grabbed a barrel and heaved it over onto its side so he could roll it away. Fae was using her magic to blast the barrels towards the Saridi soldiers attempting to clear the area. One by one they began to combust.

A concussive blast almost knocked Jarrett off his feet. *It's time to get out of here.*

Dazed and ears ringing, he reoriented himself and stumbled away from the blast zone, grabbing Fae's arm to drag her out with him.

Wait—where did Morgane go? Jarrett turned back just in time for another explosion to nearly blind him in its destructive luminescence. Acrid fumes from the newly born flames and noxious explosive powders filled his lungs and made his eyes sting.

He coughed as smoke filled his lungs, but he wasn't about to leave without finding Morgane. He scanned the area frantically before spotting a familiar silhouette. Morgane was on the ground, laid out face up right next to an explosive, its fuse burning perilously short. He was too far to get there in time.

"Fae," Jarrett choked out as loudly as he could, knowing her ears would be ringing too. "Morgane is in trouble. Get that barrel away, or shield her—now!"

"Hold on." Fae was focused back towards the statue. She had noticed one last barrel within range of the statue. She blasted magic at it, trying to push it out of range.

"Forget the vault, Morgane is about to *die*! Save her."

"I can't. Not until—"

"*Fae!*"

A series of explosions rocked the ground beneath them. The buzzing in Jarrett's ears became too loud to hear over, the smoke too thick to see or breathe through. He heaved, desperate to find oxygen in the air around him.

This couldn't be the end. Not for him, for Morgane, for the Vanguard. They were the only hope for the kingdom, they had to survive. He choked on the smoke, there was no reprieve for his lungs. The last of his vision blotted out into darkness.

CHAPTER 13

Scarlet gazed out her window. The sun was beginning to peek over the horizon, but the first morning's light did little to bring warmth to the swamplands that stretched out below. The violet sky of the Crossworld had become familiar by now, yet it was still a reminder of how far she was from Saridian.

Scarlet had risen early, dressed, and did her best to tame her wild curls, and tried to center herself in preparation for her return to training. She'd had a full day off after being released from her cell and she couldn't imagine that she would get a second. Bronwen had healed her twice since her release, and she could move somewhat more freely now, but not entirely without pain.

Though it would be good to eat and replenish more of the strength she had lost while imprisoned, her stomach churned, so she paced her room instead. Her emissary mark prickled as it neared time for her to meet with Death.

Then, the prickle grew into an uncomfortable pulse. Scarlet braced herself for a compulsion to arise, but no urges came. She ran her fingers over the emissary mark, pondering. If not a compulsion, then what? Something wasn't right; she didn't know what it was, but it was urgent. As she focused on her mark, she could feel the trail of her emissary bond more acutely.

Time to investigate. Scarlet threw open her door a moment before Dante did the same with his, emerging from the opposite side of the hall. They stared at each other blankly.

Dante released a deep breath. "I thought that I... I don't know. Felt something. Is that weird?"

"No. I feel it too."

"Something's happening?"

The pulsing from Scarlet's mark became more intense by the second, her discomfort morphing into pain. "Yeah."

"What is it?"

"Not sure."

Dante wasn't an emissary, but somehow even he was sensing whatever was going on. She needed to figure out what was happening. She traced the origin of the tug of her bond and began following its trail through the halls. Dante's footsteps pattered behind. She couldn't worry about him right now. She had to figure this out before she was incapacitated by the pain, which grew stronger with each step, seeping deeper into her body.

Scarlet was shaking by the time she got to the obsidian door that she now knew led to the throne room—though she'd still never been inside. Right now, the door was wide open. Scarlet peered inside the room and froze. Dante stopped close behind her. Death was stiffly seated on a throne, which was on a small dais on the far side of the room, with an elegant red carpet leading up to it. Bronwen stood next to her on the dais, his eyebrows furrowed. But what made Scarlet pause was the man in front of the throne.

The man turned to Scarlet and Dante, smiling. It was the toothy grin of an animal who had cornered his prey. "Good, I see we've all arrived."

For the briefest of moments, Scarlet was relieved that it wasn't Riordan. She knew it wasn't Riordan for two reasons. Firstly, he didn't have a god-like aura. The second reason was also why her relief was so short-lived: she recognized him.

"Calder." The name slipped from her lips. He was Riordan's concealed second-in-command, his only emissary, and the one who had been in charge of hunting down Scarlet and her mother, until Riordan took the task into his own hands.

Calder and his team of mage hunters had circled close to them, but Scarlet's mother had always managed to spirit them away to safety using her obfuscation magic, or in rarer cases, fight them off. She had nearly killed Calder once. He ripped open a portal to the Crossworld just in time to avoid Kiera's fatal blow of magic. Scarlet had advocated for her mother to follow and finish him off, which, frustratingly, she had refused to do, worrying there was an ambush waiting in the Crossworld.

In retrospect, Scarlet really, *really* wished her mother had killed him. Then he wouldn't be standing here now, staring at her from across the throne room with his piercing blue eyes. His shoulder-length hair was, as always, opposite of hers: so blond that it was nearly white, and dead straight. The air around him wobbled and distorted from the waves of energy radiating from him—or maybe into him? She didn't know what this magical effect was, exactly, but she was sure it was the source of the discomfort that was affecting Death and leaking into Scarlet through the emissary bond. From the strained look on Bronwen's face, he was experiencing the same.

"Good to see you again, Scarlet." Calder's voice was even and sickeningly sweet. "Please, let's all gather closer. I know not who the boy is, but all of Deianira's residents should be present."

It may as well have been a compulsion, as Scarlet found her feet moving without her conscious control. Her throat tightened with each step. Calder directed her to take a place next to Bronwen on the dais, and Dante followed suit, the color sucked out of his face.

Death hissed. "Keep her name out of your mouth."

Scarlet was puzzled at this. *My name, or the castle's?*

Calder's only response was a continued smirk, depriving her of any further context.

Death shifted in her throne. "Tell me why you're here."

"We'll get there. But first, I've been curious to see this one up close." With that, Calder closed the distance between himself and Scarlet. He took her chin between his thumb and forefinger.

Everything in Scarlet screamed at her to flinch away, but her body was unresponsive. She felt her strength draining into his fingertips, leaving her face cold. Was this what he was doing to Death—draining her energy?

"She's strong. Maybe even worth her keep." Calder released his insidious hold on her. His eyes flicked over to Dante. "That one's not even an emissary. Are you simply rescuing orphans these days? I know you're desperate, but if you're lining up children to defend you then we're even closer to victory than we thought."

Scarlet started to breathe again. She'd been unaware that she had even stopped. Terror held her in place now, instead of Calder.

"Are you done with the needless banter?" Death snapped. "Get to the *point.*"

Calder shrugged casually. "I'm here because I can be. Your defenses are so specifically tuned to Riordan that I could slip by them. Oh, and he wanted me to deliver a message. He wants you to know that you are a fruit almost ripe enough to pluck, and there's no way to stop him."

Death's pointed nails were digging into the throne's wooden arm. "You're wrong."

"Oh, but I'm not." Calder's sugarcoated tone grew more serious now. "Your bulwarks are failing, one by one. The Ravens and rebels are falling. Your last emissaries are spread thin. Your magical defenses are good—but not good enough. Riordan can still drain your power from afar, as you well know. And of course, not enough to keep me from coming here to ensure your energy has run dry."

Calder loomed over Death's throne now. He reached toward Death; Scarlet thought that he would take the god's chin the way he had hers.

Instead, Death spat in his face.

Calder recoiled and his grin reversed into a snarl. He wiped the spittle from his cheek. "You—" Calder grabbed Death by the collar of her shirt and ripped her off her throne, heaving her off the dais, onto her knees. He towered over her from above. "You're done. And soon, Riordan and I will have everything we want."

Scarlet was shocked back into control of her body. Dante was visibly shaking next to her, and on her other side, Bronwen's face dripped with sweat.

Three of us, and one of him, thought Scarlet. She couldn't count Dante; she didn't know what he was capable of yet. *Maybe we can take him.*

"Leave, you bastard," Bronwen growled. He began to lunge toward Calder but froze mid-movement. Calder had held up a hand and Bronwen stopped in his tracks. With a forceful downward gesture, Calder made Bronwen crumple to the ground.

Scarlet shuddered. She'd never seen manipulation magic used before. That was Riordan's "gift" to the mages attuned to him. Her mother's magic could be used to shroud them from such effects.

"You may have the upper hand," Death said as she stood back up. "But I will fight you to the bitter end."

"Fight us with *what*? You can't even trust your own. What ever happened to Angelise, anyway? She and Kiera were the only ones that ever had a chance of stopping Riordan. And of course, I'm sure you've noticed Kiera is gone."

Death stared at him, expressionless.

"*Gone*?" Scarlet asked. It took every nerve she had to force the word out, but she needed to know what he meant. Had they killed her now, or was he speaking of her capture? Calder turned back to her, his gaze making her skin crawl.

"Gone," he repeated, lightheartedly. "She got a good strike in against Riordan. After the audacity of that, killing her was off the table. It would be like giving her back to Death, after all. Sure, she wouldn't be *useful* anymore, but it's the principle of the matter."

Scarlet's rising anger made the next words come easier. "Where is she?"

"You'll never know. Your god can't even find her through the emissary bond—"

Flushed with fury, Scarlet raised a hand to summon a blast of fire. Before she could strike, Calder bound her in place. She strained against the magic with everything she had, but his power was ironclad. Neither her physical strength nor her magic could break through.

She wanted to scream, but her words came out closer to grunts. "What did you do to her?"

"Nothing nice."

Bronwen's hoarse voice cut in. "Stop goading the child."

"If she wants to be coddled she'll have to go elsewhere." Calder's toothy grin returned. "Or maybe we'd spare Kiera in exchange for Scarlet becoming a turncloak. A mage with her power and inside knowledge would be valuable."

If she hadn't been bound in place, Scarlet might have followed Death's example and spat at him. "I would never help Riordan."

"How could he work with mages?" Dante said, barely above a whisper. "He kills them. But they work for him?"

"Riordan needs Calder. If we kill Riordan in his current mortal form, he'll need another to join with if he wants to be a physical incarnate. Any other mages he keeps... well, Riordan will do whatever gives him the most power, ultimately," Death told him. "Scarlet, do not play into his games."

Calder huffed. "Most mortals don't even know what to do with their powers. And to think, some would turn their divine powers against the gods their magic comes from? Horrendous. Pathetic. You, Scarlet... you have potential. But, alas, such passion burning within. You need breaking before you are of use. I'm surprised Death kept you at all; she isn't a fan of wildcards." Calder turned to address Death once more. "Or is it that you see her more like a *daughter*?"

Death's voice was flat, "It's time for you to go." She raised an arm. A streak of energy flashed from her hand and crackled through the air toward Calder.

With near-impossible reflexes, he caught the energy bolt in midair. Somehow, it didn't hurt him. Calder observed the sphere of condensed magic floating in his grasp for a moment before he absorbed it into his hand, his grin widening. "You make this too easy."

Energy crackled and gathered around Death as she focused her strength. The majority of Death's power was being siphoned into Calder. He was draining her magic from her, just as he had absorbed her energy bolt.

Anything Death threw at him would only feed him, make him more powerful. Calder gathered a dense ball of energy in his hand, while Death struggled to scrape together any amount of magic.

Abruptly, all of the warmth in Scarlet's body was drawn into her emissary mark. The tattoo burned hot as her energy reserves were sucked dry. She collapsed to the floor. Calder must have drained her energy, too.

A sudden blast of light filled the throne room, with an accompanying *crack*. Scarlet's head spun. With tremendous effort, she pulled herself up enough to take account of the room. Bronwen had dropped down next to her. Dante was still on his feet, eyes wide. Death had her index finger pointed directly at Calder. A single wisp of smoke dispersed from her fingertip.

Calder had been brought down to his knees, his hand held over a smoldering spot on his chest. In Scarlet's estimation, just above his heart. He growled. "Soon you won't have anyone left to draw on. And then it will be the end of this."

Suddenly, Scarlet understood. Calder hadn't drained her. Death had been gathering her own magic as a decoy, then instead drew power through the emissary bonds to direct a blast of energy at Calder while he thought he had the advantage.

Calder rose. "Because you don't have enough power left to kill me now, do you?"

Death barred her teeth but said nothing.

"That's what I thought." Calder's hand pressed over his wound. His grin had melted into a grimace. "And one day soon, you won't have enough power to keep Riordan out."

With that, he turned and left the throne room.

Bronwen scrambled to his feet. Dante reached down to offer a hand up to Scarlet. She took his hand, then quickly let go as she stood on her own two feet again. All three turned to the god, who was standing still as stone as she stared at the door Calder just exited through.

"This is not over," Death whispered. "Not yet."

CHAPTER 14

The morning after Calder's harrowing visit, Dante was to start training with Death. Scarlet fetched him at sunrise. He tried to make conversation with her the whole way out of the castle and through the swamp, but she would only give him curt answers to his questions about where they were going and what to expect.

Though Dante was grateful that Bronwen rescued him, he wasn't exactly excited to be here. Once he'd met Death, he realized that she was one of the mages from his dream. A god. The other mage he had seen must have been Riordan. Suddenly, Dante was caught up in a conflict out of his league, in a place even more dangerous than Saridian.

Dante's boots became soaked with water as they trudged through the swamp toward where he and Scarlet were to meet Death. "So, I told you how I got here. How about you? Did Bronwen bring you here, too?"

"No."

He was about to follow up with another question, but he stopped when he saw the stern look plastered on her face. Scarlet didn't seem keen on discussing, well, *anything*—but Dante sensed that this would be a particularly poor subject to probe her about.

He sighed. Guessing at her past was the best he could do. She didn't look Saridi—her eyes were angular and sharp, unlike his own rounded eyes, and he'd never seen hair as dark as hers. With Saridian's borders being as tight as they were and Briarglen being both small and remote, he'd had little chance to meet anyone outside of his home region, so he couldn't even take a stab at guessing her heritage.

They reached a part of the swamp that was less wet and mostly clear of trees and brush. Death was there, waiting for them. *This isn't a dream,* he had to remind himself.

"We will start at the beginning, to get Dante caught up," Death said.

Dante thought he caught Scarlet grimacing.

"Dante," Death said, "What do you know of your magic? Do you know what god you are attuned to?"

He tried not to let his voice shake. "I'm not a mage."

He had told Zandra that magic was dangerous, and now he believed it more than ever. Scarlet and Bronwen were both emissaries of Death, whatever that meant—so far, he had discovered that Death could draw energy from them to the point where they were incapacitated. It wasn't a good first impression.

"You're not a mage," Death repeated dryly. "You were exiled because you got caught doing magic, were you not?"

"I have magic. But it's brought nothing but pain into my life, so I'm not going to use it. Therefore, I'm not a mage."

"You are from Saridian." Death sighed. "I suppose you have spent your life being brainwashed by Riordan and the like."

"Sure, but—"

Scarlet broke in. "Magic gives you the chance to fight back." A flame sparked to life in her hand.

Dante jumped away from the fire. "Get that away from me. I don't—I don't want to *fight* anyone."

Scarlet stared at him. The light of her fire cast an orange glow onto her face. She was so nonchalant about using magic. It was easy to tell she was comfortable with it. She didn't get it.

Scarlet glanced at her flame, then back to Dante. "I'm not going to hurt you. I'm attuned to Kajiem, so I have immolation magic. Do you know what your gifts are?"

"It doesn't matter," he said, "because I don't want them."

"You may observe today," Death said. "Tomorrow, you will participate in the lesson. If not, you will go."

Dante glanced around the swamp. "Go where?"

"You must leave the Crossworld. Beyond that, I care little."

Dante bit his lip. *Maybe Bronwen could portal me back somewhere other than Saridian.* It would still be tough to make it with no resources, but at least he wouldn't be murdered for being a mage. He'd be no worse off than before.

"Fine," he said. He sat down with his back to a twisting, leafless tree.

Death started the lesson by leading Scarlet through a series of exercises based on focus and meditation. Scarlet struggled with these tasks. She fidgeted and sighed as time wore on, and Death rebuked her every time she grew distracted.

Once they moved on to a more active lesson, Scarlet was in her element. Dante saw her light up as she moved through a combat drill. While Scarlet was turned away, Death would set up a series of target dummies. Once the set-up was complete, Scarlet would turn and immediately shoot controlled balls of fire at each one, aiming for an area on each dummy that had been circled with red paint. Both her speed and accuracy were tested by this exercise, and she did well at it. It was like watching a dance.

As the morning melted into noon, they started the final chapter of training before taking a break for lunch. There were a number of stones set up in a circle to denote an arena. Death and Scarlet stepped into the ring, each took a deep breath, then began to spar.

Death sent out round after round of energy bolts at Scarlet, which Scarlet dodged or dissipated with flames. Scarlet weaved lithely around the makeshift arena, careful to stay within the boundary lines. She held her own against the intense barrage that Death sent at her, but lacked an opening to force an offensive strike.

"Is that all you have in you today?" Death goaded.

Scarlet's eyes hardened. Fire sprang into being around her, swirling until it formed a long whip of flames held in her hand, which she lashed at Death with a fluid motion.

Death grinned as she sidestepped out of danger. "Better."

Scarlet kept swiping her improvised weapon at Death. Her brow was furrowed, she was more serious than before. More reckless, too. After her whip proved to be ineffective against Death's speed, she began to blast large spheres of flame at the spots she predicted that Death would leap to.

As fireballs began to sizzle through the air, Dante suddenly felt much too close. He stood up just in time for a blaze to strike inches from his feet, causing him to fall right back down in his attempt to skitter away from it. He yelped and his heart hammered as the fire sputtered out against the damp ground.

He stood back up, making brief eye contact with Scarlet as she glanced over at him. Death took advantage of the diversion by zapping Scarlet in the shoulder with a quick jolt of magic. Scarlet cried out and grabbed her shoulder.

"No distractions," Death said.

"No distractions," Scarlet repeated. She was breathing heavily. Through her curtain of dense curls, she watched Death.

Death smirked. She circled Scarlet. The space of a few breaths was all the time Scarlet got to recover before Death renewed her assault. With vigor, she released a volley of energy bolts that Scarlet struggled to evade. Scarlet had lost her rhythm, and Death wasn't cutting her any slack. Scarlet dodged each blow, though each leap away was a closer and closer call.

Sweat dripped from Scarlet's face. She looked like she was about to collapse. Then, she took a deep, long breath, and appeared to gain a second wind. Fire danced around her, moving as one with her body. Jets of flame shot at Death, sustained blasts of heat and fire more powerful than before. Death swiped her attacks away easily with well-timed shields, similar to the one Dante had used to save Zandra. Scarlet's face grew tight with frustration as she increased the intensity of her bombardment against Death.

Dante felt something go wrong before he saw it. Scarlet flung an arm out to release another stream of flames, but instead, there was a flash of light and a crack. Dante, momentarily blinded by the burst of magic, blinked away the bright spots in his eyes. When his sight returned, Scarlet was face up on the ground. Death loomed over her, her expression unreadable.

Dante tentatively stepped forward. "Is… is she alright?"

"I'm fine," Scarlet said. She rolled to her side, which revealed that the sleeve of her shirt had disintegrated, leaving only tatters of fabric. Almost the entirety of her arm was rippled red with burns. Dante smelled the burnt flesh.

"Her magic backfired. That is what happens if you are not in control. If you are distracted or overcome by your emotions," Death said. "We are finished until tomorrow. I will see you both then." She gave Dante a meaningful glance. "Or, not."

Death headed back towards the castle, leaving Dante alone with Scarlet.

"I—you're burned badly. I'm an herbalist. I can try to help—"

"There's a healer. Bronwen." Scarlet wobbled up onto her knees. Her face was drained of all color.

So the man who'd brought him here was a healer, too. "Are you getting Bronwen?" Dante called after Death. There was no response, and she disappeared over a ridge.

"It's fine," Scarlet said.

"You need to cool the burn, or else it'll get worse." Dante surveyed his surroundings. There was the grungy swamp water—not exactly ideal. He scanned the area for familiar plants as well, but the flora was foreign to him. "Let's get inside, so we can get some clean water."

"I can manage on my own."

"I'm trained for this. Please, let me help."

"Bronwen will heal me. Let me be."

Dante was confused at her refusal to let him help, but he stayed quiet. The last thing she needed was him continuing to pester her while she was in pain.

Cradling her burnt arm, Scarlet stumbled back toward the castle. Dante kept his distance, as she clearly wanted, but followed behind her. Even if he couldn't help directly, he was going to make sure she got to Bronwen.

There really is nothing here for me, though, is there? Death was intimidating and wanted him to be a mage, possibly an emissary which would no doubt put him in more danger, which was the opposite of what he wanted. Scarlet was distant, at best. He was only an apprentice so no doubt Bronwen was a better healer than him. Bronwen was the only one who wanted him here, and Dante didn't even understand *why* the man had bothered to rescue him.

At least he'd been saved from the grasp of some Saridi soldiers-to-be, and now he could, hopefully, build a life somewhere safe. He would leave magic behind him. As much as his visions would let him, anyway.

Once back inside, Scarlet wound her way through the halls. It still amazed Dante that she knew her way around this maze of a castle at all. She never looked back at him. He wondered if she even noticed him trailing her, since she was evidently in a lot of pain.

After a couple of flights of stairs, they reached a door that Scarlet knocked on. It looked identical to every other door in the seemingly endless series of hallways.

Bronwen swung the door open, his posture stiffening as he saw Scarlet's condition. "What happened?"

"Training."

"Come in," Bronwen said. Bronwen glanced at Dante as Scarlet moved past him. "Him too?"

Dante cleared his throat. "Oh, I was just making sure she got here, I don't want to intrude—"

"I'd like for you to see this, actually, if it's alright with Scarlet."

"I don't care," Scarlet said, her voice thin.

Dante hesitated, but Bronwen's eagerness for him to stay was apparent. Besides, he'd be gone soon, and then Scarlet wouldn't have to put up with him anymore. He stepped into Bronwen's quarters.

He couldn't have imagined that a place this bright and airy existed within Deianira. It was much larger than his own room. They were nestled in the corner of the castle, with large windows on both outer walls. Natural light streamed in, giving life to the multitude of plants and herbs growing out of a variety of pots scattered around. Some hung from the ceiling, others littered the floor and tables. Luxurious couches and cushions were spread across the room, draped with colorful fabrics. A curtain of similar vividity hung in a doorway to an adjacent room, which Dante assumed was Bronwen's bedroom.

Scarlet collapsed onto one of the sofas and wiped her sweaty brow. Dante stood at a respectful distance as Bronwen got to work. He opened a kit full of salves and examined Scarlet's burn.

"Anywhere else? Or just the arm?" he asked.

"Mm. My shoulder too. Not a burn, but—" She pulled the collar of her shirt down to show where Death had struck her. The mark had turned black.

Bronwen muttered something that Dante couldn't hear, but the words sounded harsh. He pulled out a crisp white cloth, doused it with a liquid, and wiped both of her injuries clean. Then, he laid his hands over Scarlet's arm and a shimmering flow of magic streamed from his palms into her skin.

Dante watched in fascination as the marks grew less severe before his eyes. After a few minutes of flowing energy into her burns, Bronwen moved on to her shoulder. The strained look on Scarlet's face gradually eased, though it didn't disappear completely.

Bronwen turned to Dante. "You were training as an herbalist, right? Do you know what aloe looks like?"

"I don't know that one."

"Ah, I shouldn't be surprised. It doesn't grow in your part of the World. It's up high in the corner, in the red pot. It's a succulent. Thick and fleshy. Cut a piece off for me, would you?" Bronwen handed him a small pair of clippers from his kit.

Dante found the correct pot and stood on his tiptoes to slice a plump leaf off the aloe, noticing the stringy goo that oozed slightly where it had been cut. He'd never seen another plant like it and was slightly less disappointed in himself for not knowing what it was offhand. He gave the clipping to Bronwen and watched as he sliced it open with a small blade to reveal a gel-like substance. He scored the leaves to loosen the insides, then scraped it into a dish.

"The pulp of the aloe vera plant aids in the healing of burns," said Bronwen as he began to gently spread the gel onto Scarlet's arm. Dante quickly realized that he would need a lot more aloe to cover the whole burn, and fetched some more. Bronwen nodded his approval and handed him the knife. Dante began to process the aloe in the same way he had observed, as Bronwen continued to apply it. "You don't want to use this on a burn if it's any worse than this one. If the skin is burned enough that there are open wounds, the aloe won't allow it to dry properly."

Once Bronwen finished with the aloe, he bandaged Scarlet's arm with gauze. "Come back tonight," he told her. "I'll re-apply the aloe. Perhaps another healing session as well, if I have the energy."

Scarlet nodded. Her eyes were still closed. "What was the point of Death saving me if she's just going to tear me apart?" Her voice sounded smaller than Dante had ever heard it.

"Death has gone through a lot of her own pain. Though that's no excuse for how... severe she can be. She often forgets basic kindness."

"And yet you've chosen to work for her."

"Death isn't perfect. Sometimes, she is downright cruel. I would say she's only human, but that isn't fully true. Even so, I don't believe the gods to be infallible." Bronwen paused. "You think I've put all of my faith in her, but I haven't, as hard as it might be to see. And sure, I understand the burdens she carries. But that still doesn't excuse the horrendous things she does.

"I've dedicated my life to fighting the same injustices as her. Fighting Riordan, trying to keep the World safe, as well as trying to protect Death herself. Along the way, I try to remind Death of compassion. I'm not always successful. But I do my best. And that's why I'm still here. In my official capacity, I am the caretaker of the castle. In my own eyes, I see myself as Death's caretaker as well."

Silence permeated the room for a few heartbeats. Scarlet's eyes opened. Dante realized for the first time how blue they were. They were dark and hard. Exhaustion and passion swirled equally in their depths. "And what about my mother?"

"Calder was telling the truth," Bronwen said. "We haven't been able to find her."

"Neither of you told me *anything*."

"It would have worried you more if we had. We were hoping we could find her and then—"

"I'm an emissary, too, aren't I? I can help."

"You aren't ready for those dangers."

"So what, you want to *protect* me? You've already proved that you can't do that, Bronwen. You help clean me up, but you can't stop Death from breaking me in the first place." Scarlet stood and made for the door.

"Scarlet—"

"And there *is* something I can do," she added, standing in the doorway. "If you and Death stop *protecting* me for long enough, I can find my mother." She slammed the door behind her as she left.

Bronwen ran his fingers through his hair. He cleared his throat. "May I offer you some tea, Dante?"

"I... suppose."

Dante tried to process what he just witnessed as Bronwen lit his wood-burning stove and heated water, then steeped a blend of tea when it boiled. Dante wondered if the mix Bronwen used was of herbs that he grew himself. The tension hanging in the room from Scarlet's outburst began to dissipate.

"I know magic has brought a lot of hardship into your life," Bronwen said, setting a cup down for Dante on the side table nearest him. "But, I wanted you to watch me healing Scarlet so you could see for yourself that there's more to it than suffering. Magic can do good, in the right hands. It can do good in *your* hands."

It was captivating to watch Scarlet's wounds heal at such an unimaginable rate. Many of the herbs he had learned about in his apprenticeship aided healing, and that was the part of the work that he enjoyed the most. Magical healing was on a whole different level.

"So some people can do good things with magic. But maybe... maybe not just anyone should be allowed to use it," Dante said.

Bronwen shrugged and took a sip of his tea. "But who gets to make that decision? Riordan banned his whole region from using magic, and many people could be using it for good. Many people get punished for even having the ability to use magic. That isn't fair. I think the only thing we can do is to use our gifts in the best way we can and hope others follow suit."

Dante picked up his mug and stared into his tea, but didn't drink any.

Using magic for the greater good. And letting people be who they were. He thought about Zandra, so insistent on using magic despite all the risks. It was a part of herself that she refused to deny. He didn't feel the same way that she did. Was it possible for him to accept the dubious "gift" of magic?

"If I were going to use magic, I'd like to use it for something like that. Healing. But my gifts are... something else."

"I believe you are somewhat mistaken," Bronwen said. "We are both attuned to Io. My skills lie more in healing, but I have a small gift of insight. Enough to see that we are similar. I believe you are a healer."

"I mean, I was training as a healer. But not with *magic*, just the, uh, regular kind. Are you sure your insight isn't seeing that?"

Bronwen chuckled. "No, I'm sure."

"What is Io, anyway?"

"Ah. I forget how hard it is to learn about the world when one grows up in Saridian. Io is not a what, but a *who*. They are the Sage, the god of knowledge and restoration, among other things."

"They? Are there more than one of them?"

"Io is a single being—at least, if they are not bonded with a human incarnate so that they may roam the World—rather, they have no strong gender identification, and choose neutrality instead."

Dante paused for a moment and took a sip of his tea. Though he couldn't quite place the flavors, they were familiar. "Okay, so. I am 'attuned' to this god. And I might be able to heal."

"Healing is a rare art, but I believe I sense it within you. That's part of the reason I brought you here."

"What's the rest of the reason?" Dante wondered if Bronwen knew about his visions as well. Were those also from Io?

"Ah. The truth is, Scarlet must stay here. And she needs a friend. A peer. I can't be that for her for a number of reasons, including the fact that my duties often take me elsewhere."

"I'm not sure how well I can do at that either. She doesn't seem to like me."

"Give her time. Like Death, she's been through a lot," Bronwen said. "I realize living in the Crossworld and becoming a mage wasn't what you wanted. But now that you're here, I hope you will stay."

"Should I be worried?" Dante asked. "About Death."

"I can see how what you've seen so far could give you pause. But, what I will say is that Death has more of an investment in Scarlet than she does in you. You aren't an emissary. And if you have healing abilities, your combat abilities are less vital. You would also be training with me for half of the time, rather than with her."

Dante bit his lip. *Could I do it? Could I really stay?*

"Take the night to consider it, alright?"

"Okay. I will. Thank you, Bronwen."

"Of course."

"I have one more question."

"What is it?"

"My sister." Dante swallowed, finding a lump in his throat. "She's a mage. Would it be possible to bring her here, too?"

Bronwen looked down. "I wish I could say yes. However, it was hard enough to convince Death to allow me to bring you here. I don't think she would take in another. I'm sorry."

Dante was both relieved and distressed. After what had happened to Scarlet today, perhaps Zandra would be safer at home. Then again, much worse could happen in Saridian; he knew that well enough.

As they drank the rest of their tea, Dante almost asked Bronwen to look at the crystal orb he'd dragged here all the way from Saridian. With Bronwen's insight, perhaps he could tell Dante what it did. But somehow, the orb felt like something private. Something he shouldn't share, even though a magical object shouldn't get him in trouble here. His visions felt personal as well, so if Bronwen couldn't sense that as a part of Dante's powers, he wasn't going to bring it up.

When Dante left Bronwen's quarters, he let out a deep sigh. He was surprised at his resolve, but he'd already decided what he was going to do.

Staying, leaving—either was a risk. But if he left, how would he help Zandra? Trying to smuggle them both out of Saridian was a death sentence, as much as he wanted it to be viable. But if he stayed... if he learned, to fight, to heal... then maybe he could actually *do* something. Something... good. Maybe he could have hope. Maybe he could help the people who were fighting the god that made his, his sister's, and every Saridi mage's lives miserable, if they even got to live.

And so, regardless of the pit of dread brewing in his gut, his warnings to his sister, and every promise he'd made to give up magic, he had decided.

I'm going to be a mage after all.

CHAPTER 15

Scarlet longed for the days to flow off her like heavy rain running down a pane of glass. If she could only stand still, and let time wash away her pain—

But no. Time moved on at a crawl, and so did she, slogging through each second of it.

Her body still ached from her days in the prison cell. It had been a week since her release and her memories of the experience were still fresh. It felt as if she had been alone in the cell for an eternity. And then, of course, there was the burn from her backfire and her shoulder wound from Death's energy bolt.

Training had slowed since Dante had joined her lessons. They had, indeed, started from the beginning. Dante fumbled through forming bolts of energy, spot shields, and meditations to focus or detect energy.

It might have been a relief if it wasn't so frustrating. Death's expectations of her were minimal compared to before. It let her rest while she was still recovering. It was the opposite of what she wanted.

I have to be stronger.

Viridian's presence had returned a few days ago. Reforging that connection was an immense relief. Their minds touched as Scarlet lay in bed, nearly asleep. It jolted her awake, and she didn't fall back asleep until it was nearly time for training. Her rest that night was holding her sister close and sharing all of her pain. Viridian's anger at Death and fear at the thought of their mother's fate reflected her own. She was Scarlet's only true ally.

It seemed that Scarlet's assumption about Death's energy barrier in the cell blocking their connection held true. Neither of them knew why it took so long to regain their contact with one another after Scarlet's release, but now that they had regained it, it was stronger than before. Their connection was now constant, unlike before.

After the first day, they had scarcely exchanged words with one another. They didn't need to when they could feel each other's emotions so readily. They shared a continual anxiety, knowing that Scarlet had to find a way to save their mother before it was too late, as impossible as it seemed.

As the days went on, Scarlet felt herself shrinking. At the end of a tedious day of drilling through basics at training, she crawled into bed and curled herself into a tight ball.

Viridian, she called out to her sister.

I'm here, Viridian said back. The words were a bittersweet comfort. She was there, but not there. While grateful for her sister's presence, to share the bond they now did... it was a deep connection, but it wasn't the same as her being alive.

What do I do? Scarlet asked.

There was a pause. Scarlet imagined her sister's face scrunching and contorting as she thought. *Just... keep going. We'll figure something out.*

Scarlet bit her lip and tried to force her tears to stay locked within her. She was falling apart, but she had to hold it together. Viridian couldn't help her, not really. No one could. As much as she loved her sister, as much as she cherished connecting with her again, Viridian was still dead. And Scarlet was still alone.

Scarlet woke. She soaked in the precious, infinitesimally small moment during awakening when she didn't quite feel her aching body and didn't quite remember that the fate of her mother rested in her hands.

Before the weight of these things locked her in her bed, she dragged herself up. She got dressed. She brushed her hair. She stared at her own tired eyes in her mirror. She noticed the pile of fruit she had squirreled away from the pantry, meant for easy breakfasts before going to training. Her stomach twisted. She ignored the food.

She cracked open her door. Dante wasn't out of his room yet. It had become her habit to sneak out early enough that she could make her way to training alone. It was impossible to relax with him around, especially when it was just the two of them. When he directed his unending stream of questions at her, she found herself either freezing or snapping at him. Neither felt great. Dante appeared determined to befriend her regardless. But like she had told him, she couldn't lose focus. His presence both slowed her training and distracted her from it, and she was too exhausted to figure out how to interact with him.

Due to her avoidance of Dante, she would be early for training. She took a winding route through the castle to kill some time, and to attempt to clear her head and loosen her stiff muscles. As she passed Bronwen's quarters, she heard Death and Bronwen arguing. Curiosity prompted her to creep closer to his door, trying to make out the words.

"—can't keep going like this." Scarlet caught the end of Bronwen's sentence. Footsteps punctuated his words like he was pacing the room.

It was Death that responded. "You are being stubborn."

"You're the one being stubborn!" Bronwen's voice was raised. It caught Scarlet by surprise. He was usually mild-mannered and deferent to the god.

"You hold everyone at arm's length. Ever since Kiera, you're too afraid to care about anything or anyone."

"I have done enough caring and enough losing for this lifetime—don't you think?" Death spoke like she was spitting acid. Neither the god nor the emissary were pulling any punches in this quarrel.

Bronwen grunted, loud enough that Scarlet could hear from outside the room, in apparent frustration. "That doesn't mean you can just *stop*."

"That's *exactly* what it means."

"And what about Scarlet?" Bronwen snapped back. "She isn't going to last at this rate."

Wait—he's talking about me? Scarlet was so close now that her ear nearly touched the door.

"We found her a companion as you wanted," Death said. "She hasn't taken to him. It certainly hasn't helped her at all. So now what, what would you have me do?"

"Let her come with us. I think she's ready, and being more or less alone here isn't—"

"Absolutely not."

"Send her to the Ravens then. Or the Vanguard. She can learn from someone other than you, and the rebellion desperately needs more mages."

"No."

"You really don't think she's prepared enough for that, at least?"

"It's... it's *complicated*." Death sounded flustered. That facet of the god was stranger to observe than Bronwen being aggressive.

"You promised Kiera you'd keep her safe? Is that it? Because it isn't much safer here, not unless these missions are successful. She could *help*."

"Bronwen," Death said. It sounded like a plea for him to stop.

"You can see her deteriorating day by day, can't you? You've put her through too much. You have to—"

Death seemed to get a second wind, her words becoming sharp once more. "No, I do not *have* to, and I question your abilities if you can't see why I am holding her back, and—hold on."

Scarlet heard footsteps. It only took her a moment to realize that Death was walking right toward the door where she was listening.

She turned and ran, skidding on the stone as she slid around the corner. Once out of eyeshot, she held very, very still, and held her breath. If Death discovered her—

Death rounded the corner. "Scarlet."

Scarlet swallowed hard. Eavesdropping had been a horrible idea. She was too tired to be in trouble right now.

"You should know better than to spy on me."

"I'm sorry." Scarlet looked at her feet, trying to be as small as possible. "I didn't…"

She had been about to say that she hadn't meant to, but she had. Scarlet felt like her patron god would be able to see straight through her lie.

Death stared at her for an uncomfortable amount of time. Then, she simply said, "Do not do it again."

"I won't."

Death started to walk away. Scarlet was about to let her go, and escape this whole situation without incurring more of her god's wrath. But her impulsive and relentless nature prevented her from doing so. "What can I do?"

Death froze in her tracks.

"I'm an emissary, aren't I? I can help. What can I do to prove that I'm ready?"

The god spared her a glance over her shoulder. Her eyes looked… dull, for once, instead of piercing. "Nothing. There's nothing." She resumed her retreat with an air of finality.

Scarlet leaned against the wall. The cool stone against her skin was the only thing that grounded her, keeping her from shutting down and letting the anxiety take over.

"Are you alright?" Bronwen was peeking out from his doorway. Scarlet couldn't find her voice to respond and instead found him taking her hand and leading her into his quarters.

It was one of her favorite places in Deianira. Normally it brought her peace to be surrounded by Bronwen's plants and bathing in the light filtering in through the wide windows, but not today. The last time she had been here was after she had been injured in training, and those memories were uncomfortable.

The burns from her magical backfire had since healed over, quickly and without scarring thanks to his careful ministrations, but the wound on her shoulder from Death's energy bolt had turned into a black starburst, matching the one on her back. The previous blows she had taken from Death had faded away, but that strike from the spar had had more heft behind it than usual, and Scarlet doubted this one would fully disappear.

Bronwen made them a pot of lavender tea and they settled on a couch. "So, how much of that did you catch?"

"Enough." Scarlet sipped the tea. It burned her lips. "Where are you going?"

Bronwen grimaced, reluctant.

"Just tell me," she pleaded softly. "Please."

Bronwen hesitated once more before responding. "I, along with most of the remaining emissaries... we're going to fight Calder. We have reason to believe that in a few weeks, he will be residing in Riordan's realm. His presence in the Crossworld is a good opportunity for us, as he won't be protected by Riordan's soldiers."

A thousand thoughts sparked in Scarlet's head. "He'll be undefended? Are you... sure?"

"It could be a setup," Bronwen admitted. He blew on his tea, the steam rising out of his cup to swirl wildly around his face. "It's not often we get much intelligence on the movement of either Riordan or Calder. But we're... desperate, to be honest. We have to take a gamble. Taking out Riordan's second-in-command could buy us a lot of breathing room for Death to recover her power and for us to grow our own forces."

Scarlet looked down into her cup and swirled it around, watching the flow of remnant tea leaves. "Take me with you."

"I can't do that."

"Did she compel you?"

"No."

"So you *can* take me. You just... won't."

Scarlet's words seemed to puncture Bronwen. He slouched a bit, deflated. "You know it doesn't work that way. Even without a compulsion, I won't go against Death's wishes. And even if I would, she would just compel you to stay or return."

Scarlet slammed her cup on a side table. Tea splashed out wildly. "Why is there *nothing*? Nothing I can do. Why is Death holding me back, while sending everyone else into danger? Am I really that weak?"

"You are... an exceptional mage. Truly. I have seen you grow over these months. But Death has her reasons and I must respect her judgment, regardless of my own opinion."

"Whatever her reasons are, they're *wrong*."

"Please, Scarlet, trust me. I know that Death doesn't deserve it, but trust her, too. We're working so hard to fight Riordan, to bring your mother back—"

Scarlet got up and headed for the door. *I can't do this, I can't take this.*

Bronwen hopped up and moved to block Scarlet's path to the exit. "I wish I could give you answers. But please, if you're just patient—"

"*No.*" Her sharpness made Bronwen freeze. For a quiet moment, while Scarlet composed herself, time seemed suspended. "I've always been pushed to the sideline. First, I was too young to learn magic. Then, it was too 'dangerous' for me to learn, because the mage hunters might sense me... but *really* it was more that my mother wanted to keep me from being able to insert myself into a dangerous situation. She never wanted me to fight, only to run. And so she left me helpless, to give me no choice in the matter. But if I had learned how to fight sooner, maybe... maybe my sister wouldn't have been killed. And perhaps, if she had lived, my father wouldn't have left us. And maybe I wouldn't have been injured by Riordan, and I wouldn't have had to bind myself to Death to save myself—"

Bronwen tried to cut her off, noticing she was spiraling. "Scarlet—"

"I've lost most of my family and my freedom. And now I refuse to stand by while my mother, the last of my family, suffers alone. Riordan could take her life at any moment. I could never live with myself if I stood by and did nothing. I can fight now, and so I will."

Bronwen let Scarlet push her way past him, back out to the hall. Once she had stormed out, she couldn't make herself stop, she weaved through the halls aimlessly, heart hammering.

It occurred to her that Bronwen could be injured or killed by Calder on this mission Death was sending the emissaries on. She didn't want her harsh words to be the last thing she ever said to him if the worst was to happen. Yet she couldn't make herself turn around, to go back and leave things on a better note. Her momentum pushed her forward, only forward.

Why am I never allowed to protect anyone? I need a plan. I have to figure out how to get out of here without Death stopping me.

Her hands were shaking. She ran her fingers through her hair over and over, pulling hairs out as she did so, as if pulling out the tangles would unravel the knot of anxiety in her chest. Viridian pressed up against her mind. Scarlet walled herself up against her sister's concern. The well of guilt was too deep right now. *I couldn't save you. I couldn't do anything. You died to get me and Dad out safe. I'm sorry, Viridian. I'm sorry.*

Scarlet kept wandering the halls, unable to find peace. *How early is it? Could I go back and lay in bed, for a while?* Regardless of the answer, she found herself heading to her room.

As Scarlet reached for the handle to open her bedroom door, the door behind her creaked open.

"Scarlet?"

She turned. Dante was peering out of his room.

"Are you okay?" he asked. His forehead was wrinkled, and he had circles under his eyes, even deeper than when she had first met him.

She gathered herself, changing her posture with a sharp intake of breath to appear casual and failing to do so. "I'm fine," she said, opening the door and stepping into the small sanctuary of her room. "Just fine."

CHAPTER 16

Dante was breathing hard as he carefully sidestepped around the edge of the sparring circle. He knew he should be closer to the inside of the circle. It would be a more aggressive position and take him farther away from being pushed outside the ring—which would net him a loss. But he was no stranger to losing sparring matches against Scarlet. He had yet to eke out a single win in the couple of months since he had started learning magic.

Scarlet watched him with the eyes of a hawk as she planned her next volley of attacks. He should have been scheming his own strategy to overcome her, but instead, he mentally rehearsed the quick flick of his wrist and release of magic he would have to let out to create a spot shield to block her next attack. The magic that he had instinctively used to save Zandra from her fall was similar to this.

Death had granted him a reprieve and an advantage by not allowing Scarlet to use her fire against him in this match. Dante was grateful for this for a couple of reasons. Scarlet was unrelenting when she had full reign to use her fire magic. Fighting came naturally to her, especially when using her flames. Dante hated fire and all the associated memories seared into his brain.

Dry-mouthed, Dante swallowed uncomfortably. *Okay, I have to attack. I can't just let her trample me. There's no fire right now, don't be afraid, don't be afraid—*

Dante jumped forward into a widened stance and punched out a triad of energy bolts. Scarlet deftly lunged away from the one projectile that was on target, then used her momentum to launch a forceful wall of magic toward him. Dante tried to summon the largest spot shield he could, but it was no match for the blast of energy. It knocked the wind out of his lungs as it crashed against his body, knocking him down and just barely out of the sparring ring.

"Scarlet is the victor," Death announced needlessly. "Again. And that will be all for today."

Dante pulled himself up from the damp ground, head spinning. Death was already on her way back to the castle. Scarlet was brushing some dirt and twigs from her clothing, and he had no doubt that she would leave him behind in the swamp shortly. It was clear she put effort into avoiding him. At least she was less chilly toward him since he started doing half his lessons with Bronwen, away from her and Death.

As predicted, Scarlet walked away. Then, he found himself jogging after her. Assertiveness wasn't his strength, but he was frustrated at her constant dismissal of him; aggravated enough to be bold.

"Hey," Dante called out. "Wait up."

Scarlet didn't slow. He trudged after her through the murky swamp, nearly slipping and embarrassing himself further.

"Hey," Dante said again, as he managed to catch up to her. She didn't turn, so he grabbed her shoulder.

Scarlet swung around and swatted his hand away. Her look was fierce. "Don't touch me."

"I'm sorry." He clasped his hands together behind his back. "I just... I wanted to talk to you."

"Look, I'm sorry if you're offended that I keep trouncing you at the whole 'being a mage' thing but I can't hold back just to—"

"That's not it. That's not it at all."

That appeared to catch her off-guard. Her frozen exterior seemed to crack. "So what do you want?"

"To be friends."

Scarlet crossed her arms and stared up at the gnarled branches of the trees around them. Her body was held tense like she was about to spring away. "I don't... know how to do that."

"What, have you never had a friend before?" He tried to say it jokingly, but Scarlet's face remained as serious as ever. "Not really. Not since I was a kid." She closed her eyes as if lost in past memories. "My mom was—*is*—an emissary. We lived life on the run from Riordan and his soldiers while she did work for Death."

"I... sorry. That sounds like it was hard."

Scarlet's eyes blinked open and locked onto Dante. Her dark blue eyes bored into him now that she was looking directly at him. "Bronwen brought you here so that I could have a friend. I don't... I don't need a pity friend. I need to get stronger, and I have to do this alone."

Dante considered that for a moment. "Bronwen saved me. I'm not sure... that I care *why* he brought me here. I'm just grateful to be alive. I never thought I could be stronger, but now I have the opportunity to be. But I lost my family, my friends. And I'm not like you, I *can't* do this alone."

Scarlet diverted her gaze again and ran a hand through her tangled hair. "I haven't been nice to you. And, you have Bronwen. Why would you still want to be friends with me?"

It was a good question. It wasn't like Scarlet had shown him any sort of kindness—quite the opposite. But Dante didn't buy that her rough exterior was all that there was to her. Beneath her aggression and sharpness, he sensed something else. Hurt. Fear, maybe. Loneliness? She was angry, but not at him. She was suffering.

"Bronwen is a good mentor but... he's busy, and focused on his own work. I don't know your story, and you don't know mine. But it's clear that we're both going through a lot. Maybe, together... we could get through it better."

Scarlet wrapped her arms around herself, as if she were holding herself in, or maybe just trying to keep warm. In the long silence that followed, Dante had convinced himself that Scarlet was going to turn and walk away once more; his breathing went from short and tense to long and resigned. But she didn't budge this time.

She cleared her throat. "Like I said, I just... I don't know how to be friends. There's so much right now, with training, and Death, and... it's just..." she trailed off.

"Well, I don't know how to be a mage. Maybe we can help each other."

Scarlet laughed. It startled him—he had never seen her be anything but serious. *If that's her reaction, I may be worse at magic than I thought.*

"Yeah." Scarlet flashed a sly smile. It made him feel more accomplished than anything else ever had. "Maybe we can."

While Dante's lessons with Death were harrowing, he enjoyed his time learning from Bronwen. Training under Bronwen was much like his apprenticeship with Ferrick, but with a few key differences.

Firstly, Bronwen's personality and instruction were much different than his former master's. Ferrick was erratic, somewhat disorganized, and often left Dante with little oversight when he had to run off to do other tasks. Dante had learned a lot from Ferrick, but it hadn't always been a smooth process.

Meanwhile, Bronwen was careful, purposeful and didn't leave Dante to do anything alone until he was sure it would be done properly—even things as simple as caring for the various plants housed in his room, though Dante was familiar with tending many of the species already.

Secondly, there was no one here to disapprove of his training. While Dante missed his family, it was a relief not to worry about his parents pulling him back to the farm. He no longer lived under the constant fear of being caught using magic—though his thoughts often drifted to Zandra. He hoped that she was keeping herself in check and that Milo was keeping his mouth shut about anything else he might have seen that ill-fated day in the forest. His friend's betrayal and his father's rejection weighed heavily on him.

Lastly, and most significantly: Dante was learning about magic, of course. While Bronwen continued Dante's education in the more mundane aspects of healing—how to set bones, the uses of various herbs, and a million other things—he also began to teach Dante the basics of magical healing, though he had yet to allow Dante to try it out firsthand.

Whenever Scarlet or Dante got scrapes or bruises in their training with Death—which was often—Bronwen would heal them, and talk Dante through the process as he did so. Dante continued to be captivated by how quickly their wounds faded. It was—well, it was magical.

"Why even bother with all of the non-magical stuff?" Dante asked him one day, as they were mixing a salve meant to disinfect wounds. It smelled like feet. "Healing with magic seems... more effective."

Bronwen gave him a wry grin. "Ah, a question each young mage asks at some point: why not use magic for everything? It's an elegant solution to many problems. Important things too, like healing. An easy ticket to save someone's life." Bronwen lowered his voice, serious now. "Except, it's not as simple as it seems. Magic can go wrong in all sorts of ways. You've seen it already, with Scarlet, and I'm sure Death has lectured you on end about the dangers of magic. But, these warnings are required tenfold for healing. It's too easy to pour yourself into trying to save someone who's beyond saving. That is a mistake that will end with two losing their lives, instead of one."

Dante shivered as he recalled Scarlet's magic backfiring on her, the burns that had stretched across her skin. "That makes sense," he said. "You try to minimize the magic, do as much as you can without it, to conserve your energy."

"Precisely. Plus, knowing all the mundane techniques makes you a better magical healer as well."

Dante nodded. He was done stirring together the components of the salve and began to spoon it into a glass jar. "So," he said carefully, "do I get to try it soon?"

"The salve? Well, I hope you won't need it, though that's probably a bit too optimistic—"

"I don't mean that, I mean healing. With magic."

Dante had been in the Crossworld for weeks now, and Bronwen had yet to let him attempt to heal even the smallest of scratches. All of their lessons had been theory, demonstrations, or more general magic exercises. Healing was the one part of magic that he was actually interested in learning, so if he was going to be a mage, he wanted to find out if he was even capable of healing. Bronwen continued to assure him he did, but Dante wouldn't believe it until it was put to the test.

"Right. Of course. I have been a little hesitant, but I do think you have a solid enough base to work from, now." Bronwen held up a finger. "I nicked my finger while clipping herbs this morning, if you want to give it a go."

"N-now?" Dante hadn't expected Bronwen to meet his request so easily.

"If you feel ready."

Bronwen held his hand out to Dante. Dante took it into his and examined the tip of his mentor's finger. It was indeed a small cut, shallow—something that magic could instantly repair. If done right. If Dante *could* heal. He wiped the nervous sweat from his brow.

Bronwen nodded. "Go ahead. It's okay. I know you remember what I've told you."

A vote of confidence from Bronwen was almost enough to overwhelm Dante all by itself. He had to do this. He took a long breath as he called forth his power. Energy pooled in his hand, and carefully, he tried to coax it to flow into Bronwen's wound.

The magic trickled slowly at first, but Dante could feel it—it was working. In his excitement, he let the flow increase. He saw Bronwen tense.

"Too fast," his mentor warned. "Keep it controlled."

Dante panicked, jumping back from Bronwen and cutting the flow completely. "I... did it?"

Bronwen glanced at his fingertip, then held it up, grinning. Dante couldn't even see where the cut had been.

He'd done it.

He could *heal*.

In that moment, he was filled with bittersweet relief. Magic had taken so much from him. It was about time it gave something back.

CHAPTER 17

The door to the office swung open. Jarrett looked up from a blank leaf of paper. It took a moment to force his eyes to focus on the figure who had entered: a woman with brunette hair pulled back into a warrior's tail, lean and muscular frame, sharply dressed. It was Hera.

"Jarrett," she began. Her voice seemed far away. "The vault is open. We need to make some decisions."

Jarrett leaned back in the chair.

"I'm sorry to pull you out while you're still recovering, but—"

"It must be done."

Hera nodded. "I've gathered all the other council members."

"We won't keep them waiting, then."

Jarrett's head spun as he got up. He stumbled across the room and grudgingly accepted Hera's arm. She supported him out of the house and across the town square, where a group of Vanguard fighters gathered around a hole in the ground at the base of the now-broken statue. Jarrett wanted to investigate, but he couldn't keep the council waiting.

They made their way to the town hall, at the edge of the square. Rosewood used to be governed by a different council before the Vanguard took leadership of the town. They still met in the same place, but things worked much differently now. It wasn't all small-town drama and harvest celebrations. They had military decisions to make, first and foremost. They entered the council room, and three council members were already seated, as Hera promised.

On one side were two men. There was Rohan, who was big and bald, a sturdy presence in the Vanguard. He was often silent and always watching. He was the only mage on the council. Jarrett often wished there were more mages in the Vanguard in general—magic was their main advantage over Riordan's forces. Unfortunately, it was difficult to recruit mages before they were uncovered by soldiers, or good enough at hiding that the Vanguard couldn't find them either.

Next to Rohan was Leon, a boisterous fellow, at least in the good times. Currently, his face was pulled into a scowl. His beard was uncharacteristically unkempt. His sister had been one of the many to fall during the battle.

Opposite them sat Korene. She was small compared to the other council members. Her strength came not from physical prowess, but from her intelligence. She had chopped her hair short since the last time he'd seen her. Her expression was neutral but she avoided his gaze. Maybe she was still angry at him for agreeing to work with the Ravens. If so, he couldn't blame her.

Hera took her place next to Korene. Of the four, Hera was the youngest. She was eighteen; Jarrett had watched her grow up the last few years. When she first came to the Vanguard, she was a timid girl, recently orphaned. The young woman she had grown into had some teeth. Sharp ones.

Jarrett's eyes landed on the empty chair at the head of the table. It should have been Morgane's spot. Now, it was his. Emotion welled up in his chest. He'd spent the last two weeks licking his wounds and mourning the fallen, including their beloved leader. His best friend. Now it was time for him to be strong, for the Vanguard. Jarrett straightened his back and took his seat.

"So," he said. "The vault?"

"We finished what the soldiers started," Leon said. "All those layers of the crystal under that statue... those explosives would have come in handy. It wasn't easy, and I'm not sure we should have done it but, it's open."

"Has anyone gone in yet?" Jarrett asked.

"No," Hera said. "We were waiting for you."

"We're giving the Ravens exactly what they want." Korene's hands were clenched tightly in front of her. "I still think we should have left it be. But now that it's open, we can't just hand over whatever's inside."

"If they take away the artifact," Rohan said, "then the Tyrant won't have any reason to send more soldiers here. They'll be busy chasing the Ravens instead. Wasn't the whole point to pin everything on them anyway? We can continue gathering strength until we're ready to launch our strike."

"From what little the Ravens have told us, the artifact is meant to combat Riordan," Hera said. She spoke confidently, but Jarrett thought he heard a slight tremor underneath. "They want to take him down too. With this weapon and our forces combined, maybe we have a chance. It might be our only chance. We have to take it."

"You want to keep working with them?" Korene slammed a fist down. "You're naive if you think they can be trusted. They've proved they can't be—"

"Morgane knew the risks," Hera said. "I wish we had her back, Korene. I really do. But the Ravens believe that these artifacts, these weapons, whatever they are—they're our path to defeating the Tyrant. *Bringing down a god.* If they're right, it could change everything. We can't let her death be in vain."

Korene slumped back in her chair. Her face was red. Rohan and Leon exchanged worried glances.

Hera leaned in toward the other woman. "It was Riordan's soldiers that killed Morgane. Remember that. My revenge will be killing *them*, not taking it out on the Ravens."

"Jarrett," Leon said. "You're quiet. What do you think of all this?"

Jarrett took a deep breath, held it for a moment, then exhaled it forceful-ly. "This argument is pointless until we know what is actually in the vault. That was the whole reason for opening it in the first place. It's important enough that Riordan wants this artifact, either to use or destroy. We can't just take what the Ravens tell us at face value. So." He stood. Vertigo was still taking him off-kilter, but he managed to force himself into balance as he left the council room.

The others filtered out behind him. Hera caught up to him, obviously keeping an eye on him in case he stumbled. He was grateful that she didn't offer more active assistance in front of the others.

The town square was empty of the normal hustle and bustle. Jarrett had avoided coming here since the battle, and it seemed he wasn't the only one. Normally, they'd be throwing all sorts of summer celebrations, making the best of the few warm months they had. No one was in the mood for that sort of cheer right now.

He did his best to avert his gaze from the bloodstains on the stone pave-ment. The darkened blotches grew more numerous as they approached the center of the square, where the statue of Riordan lay face-down, an arm broken off. The small crowd was still there, guarding the vault and eager to see what they'd sacrificed so much for.

Where the statue had once stood there was now a gaping hole, sur-rounded by stones that had been stripped away from beneath the sculpture, as well as shards of clear crystal. From what Jarrett had been told, once the pavement had been lifted up, there was a thick crystal that was incredibly hard, making it difficult to excavate. The cavity that the Vanguard spent the last weeks creating was about four feet across. Jarrett peered down. The layer of crystal was a few feet thick, and after that, there was only darkness below, opening into a cavern of some sort.

"They were mining through the crystal and then suddenly, there was nothing left underneath," Hera explained. "Darren almost fell through. We don't know how deep it is, yet."

"How do we get down?" Jarrett asked.

Leon pointed out a rope ladder anchored to the fallen statue. "We climb."

"Who wants to go?" Hera asked.

"I'm going down," Korene said. Her face was still flushed.

"I'll go first," Rohan said.

"I think we're all going," Jarrett said. He was eager to be the first one down, but it made more sense for a mage to lead the way—and Jarrett wasn't exactly in top condition.

A voice came from behind them. "All of us? Good."

Jarrett spun around. He immediately regretted the sudden movement, the world kept spinning even after he'd stopped. Leandra had come up behind them.

It took Jarrett everything in him to keep his voice even vaguely civil. "You aren't welcome here."

Leandra crossed her arms. "We saved you from complete destruction, yet we're supposed to stand aside and let you take the spoils?"

"You told us there were no strings attached for your aid."

"But now you don't want our help. You want to do it all alone, don't you?"

Hera added softly, "Well, that hasn't exactly been decided yet—"

Leandra's eyes were locked on Jarrett. "He is easy to see through. Perhaps he hasn't laid it out for you yet, but he's made his decision."

Jarrett lost control of his measured tone. "Fae let our leader die. She could have shielded her, but she didn't. Morgane is *dead*. Gone. Now you want us to keep working with you? No."

"Fae prioritized under the heat of battle. You don't understand what is below our feet at this very moment. It can change the tide, and put us at an advantage against Riordan. Some of your compatriots can see that already. Your reason is clouded by your loss, Jarrett."

"You only care about your own interests, not ours."

Leandra's expression did not change. "You know nothing of the weapon below. Many of your forces were taken down. Many of your warriors were left injured. We have mages and knowledge. We're on the same side. You *need* us."

"We'll make it work. We always have." Jarrett was done with this. "Rohan, let's go. The rest of you—stay up here, and make sure the Raven does as well."

The atmosphere was tense as Jarrett's orders were obeyed. Rohan summoned an orb of light, which floated next to him as he took the rope and began to descend into the vault. Leandra stood by, arms crossed, her sharp eyes watching the proceedings closely. Korene, in turn, stood close to Leandra, keeping a close watch on her. Leon and Hera just looked concerned, along with the rest of the gathered Vanguard members.

Once Rohan made it partway down, Jarrett wiped his sweaty hands on his pants and began his descent. He didn't want to wait until Rohan's light was too far away. If he was being honest with himself, he shouldn't be exerting himself this much at all. His concussion had been severe and his vertigo was constant. But whatever was in the vault, he needed to see it firsthand.

Jarrett forced himself to breathe steadily, lowering himself to each successive rung on the ladder. He tried not to look anywhere. Especially not down. It was a long time before his foot reached a solid surface. It was unexpected, and he was shaking from both effort and nervous tension, so he almost lost his balance before Rohan grabbed his shoulders to steady him. Jarrett thanked him quietly. Rohan fed his light more energy so they could better assess their surroundings.

They were at the bottom of a deep, circular cavern. The jagged walls of the cavern consisted of clear crystal, shimmering and reflecting everywhere that Rohan's light hit it. The floor was crystal as well but was smooth and glass-like. Looking up at the hole that they had climbed down from, Jarrett estimated that they were around fifty feet below ground.

The crystal almost looked like ice, making the warmth of the cavern seem off-putting. Jarrett's skin tingled. The air around him felt heavy.

Though the cavern was deep, it was not wide—maybe three arm spans across. The rope dangled from approximately the center of it. There were a series of pedestals in a ring around where Jarrett and Rohan now stood. The pedestals were likewise made of crystal; jagged sides, and smooth tops. Jarrett counted six of them.

He circled the cave, inspecting each one. On each pedestal laid an identical longsword. Their hilts were wrapped with leather, but otherwise, from tip to pommel, the swords appeared to be made of the same crystal as everything else in the cavern. Circling around to the last pedestal, he realized that not all of them held a weapon—one was left bare.

"So there isn't just one," Rohan commented. "Five artifacts, if that's what these are."

Five potential weapons to fight Riordan with. Excitement rushed through Jarrett's veins. He stepped towards one of the pedestals that held a weapon and reached out to pick up the sword.

Rohan grabbed his wrist before he could. "Don't touch it."

Jarrett shook his hand free. "Why?"

"Magic. This whole cavern is steeped in it."

"Is that bad? Dangerous?"

"I don't know. Could be." Rohan looked around the cavern, a worried glint in his eye. "You aren't a mage but, can you feel it?"

Jarrett's skin was still prickling. It almost felt as if there was a breeze. Impossible, of course. "I feel... tingling."

"I think it's the crystal. I feel magic... flowing through it. *Rushing* through it." Rohan paused. "It's unnerving."

"Agreed. However, I'd like to see what Morgane died for."

This time, Rohan didn't stop him as he reached for the sword. A jolt ran through him as his fingers made contact with the hilt. He gripped the weapon tightly as he lifted it. It had some weight to it but was lighter than he expected—the crystal, while evidently quite strong from how long it took the Vanguard to break through the crust into the vault, lacked the heft of metal. He took some tentative swings with it while Rohan watched stiffly.

Jarrett shrugged. "It's a sword. I'm not sure what magical properties it may have, though I assume it has some."

"I'm not sure either. Should we take it back up with us?"

"Seems safer down here. Especially with Ravens above."

"Then let's go back up. I'll assemble a team of mages to come down and see what we can figure out."

Jarrett grunted his approval. Rohan motioned for Jarrett to ascend first and he obliged. He would be happy to get out of this hole. The climb back up was harder than down, though. Halfway up, darkness started to creep in on the edges of Jarrett's vision. Pausing, he closed his eyes and took a deep breath. For once he wished he wasn't so stubborn. It hadn't been a great idea for him to come down here.

Rohan called from below, "You alright?"

Before Jarrett could respond, he heard commotion above—yelling from a few voices. His eyes snapped open, but he couldn't see anything but the bright hole he had climbed down from. One more breath, then he resumed his scramble up the ladder. He powered through the rest of the climb. The uproar subsided by the time he reached the top.

"A little help here," he called. Someone obliged, a hand reaching down to help pull him over the edge of the hole and back up to safety. He had expected a friendly face to greet him, but as his vision cleared, it was Leandra whose hands aided him. He let go and stumbled back, narrowly avoiding falling back down into the cavern, a plummet that would surely kill him.

Around him, his comrades were all prone, most of them unmoving, though a couple were conscious and heaving for air. A primal rage surged through him. "What have you done?"

"Don't worry. I didn't kill any of them." Leandra said calmly as if that would placate him.

"Do you think *attacking* us will convince us to work with you?" Jarrett reached for the sword at his waist. Leandra flicked her wrist and a small bolt of energy, flying so fast as to be almost imperceptible, struck Jarrett's wrist. His sword hand turned heavy and numb.

"Desperate times, desperate measures, and all that. You have to understand that the Vanguard cannot do this alone. Without us, you have no idea what that artifact does, or what you're up against."

"We're done with you."

"That is unfortunate."

"So what then, you're taking the artifact by force?" Jarrett wasn't about to let her know that there was more than one sword in the vault. It did cross his mind that he could give one to her and hoard the rest. *And maybe I would have if she hadn't just hurt my people.*

"I don't *want* to force anything. I want to continue being allies."

Rohan reached the top of the chasm. Jarrett helped him over the edge with the hand that still worked. The one Leandra had struck with magic was still numb.

"Jarrett. Rohan. Please. I know the loss of Morgane struck deep. But we must work together to ensure her life wasn't given in vain."

Rohan's brow was creased in uncertainty. Jarrett had no such hesitations. He had already lost his whole life once. *Working with the Ravens feels like... forgetting about Morgane. And I never want to forget anything important, never again.*

"The Ravens value this artifact more than they value our lives," Jarrett said. "I know the weapon is valuable. But there also needs to be someone left alive to use it. My people aren't expendable, and we won't work with those who see us as such."

"Many more will die throughout Saridian if we don't act swiftly," snapped Leandra. "But still. I see you are in mourning, and I see there will only continue to be strife between the Vanguard and the Ravens if I take the weapon now. I will give you some time. *Some.* We can't wait forever for you to come around. And in the meantime, we cannot let you act alone."

Leandra sauntered off. Jarrett and Rohan set to work checking on their fallen comrades. They were all alive, as Leandra promised, but they were decently battered by her onslaught.

Jarrett wondered if Leandra planned on stopping them from confronting Riordan by using such force. A fight with the Ravens on their way to fight a god seemed less than ideal.

That night, a dense fog rolled in to surround Rosewood from all sides.

Jarrett didn't need to ask a mage to know that it wasn't an ordinary fog. The Ravens had devised a way to imprison the Vanguard in their own homes.

CHAPTER 18

Scarlet was less flighty after they agreed to help each other. She still didn't seek Dante out, but she also didn't immediately turn on her heel as soon as she saw him. On the days they shared lessons, they engaged in small talk on the way to and from the training grounds. Occasionally, when they came across one another in the afternoon, she would coach him on some of the finer details of magic. Sometimes, she would smile. Even rarer, he would elicit another laugh from her. That too, seemed like a kind of magic.

It was nice.

But as the days drew on, Dante knew he was reaching a breaking point. Though his loneliness had dulled, his exhaustion was a monster that was fed each day. Every hour he could feel himself fading, overshadowed by fatigue. His nights continued to be disturbed.

Each time he would drift into a deep slumber, a vision began. He would see an inferno scouring the world around him. He wasn't sure where he was in these dreams. There was only smoke and flame. *The flames, the flames, the smell of flesh burning*—he couldn't take it. It was too much, and he forced himself awake. Like before, his eyesight was gone upon awakening. Every time it happened, it took longer to return. It was a terrifying few minutes, wondering if he'd lost his sight permanently.

So he'd been doing his best to avoid sleep altogether. He'd pace his room, read a book Bronwen recommended or that he'd seen Scarlet pick up in the library, and go through what he had learned in his magic lessons.

As he learned more, he'd examined his crystal orb once again. It had seemed inert to him after completing its repair, but now that he had honed his senses, he could feel something resonating from it. It was a subtle magic. Across the room, he felt nothing from it. Held in his hands, it had something resembling a heartbeat, as tiny as it was. It tickled something in the back of his mind. It took a long time for him to realize it, but eventually, it clicked.

It was intensifying his visions. Back home, his dreams had become much more vivid after he'd repaired the sphere. Only then had he begun to make sense of anything he saw in them, and they'd gotten stronger since.

Maybe he could finally rest if he got rid of the crystal orb.

But somehow, he couldn't part with the orb. There was a force connecting him to it. He was bonded to it, with magic. He couldn't figure out how it had happened, or how to break it, but it was there, and the thought of ridding himself of it was unbearable.

And so it stayed, the bogeyman under his bed. And Dante stayed awake.

Now it had been too long. He would break if he kept avoiding slumber. Magic took energy, and his lessons were draining him more and more each day. From what he had learned from Bronwen, he was beginning to understand how dangerous overuse of energy could be. He had to be careful not to overstep the threshold that could put his very life in danger.

There was a vision determined to be seen, he could feel it bubbling out of him. He had to sleep. He needed to see it through, no matter what he saw. He knew deep in his gut that he didn't want to know what his subconscious—or the mysterious orb—was begging to show him.

After a particularly tiring day of training, he settled into bed. He hugged one of his pillows tight into his chest, where his heart pounded ferociously. It felt entirely wrong to be letting himself sleep after avoiding it for so long. Regardless, his exhaustion ran so deep that he couldn't fight it.

Dream with me, a voice said. *It was raspy and soft. So familiar, and yet Dante knew he had never heard it before.*

Dante smelled the flames before he saw them. Billowing smoke surrounded him. Embers licked at his heels. Fire can't hurt me here, *he tried to remind himself. But between the smoke and the panic racing through his veins, he couldn't breathe. He had to see whatever he needed to see and get out of here as fast as possible. Coughing, he began to fight his way through the inferno.*

A gust of wind cleared the smoke in front of him, and Dante stopped to take the sight in. Before him, burnt nearly to the ground, was his house. It was nearly unrecognizable, but in the way that you know things in dreams, Dante knew this was his home. All around him, destruction reigned. The farm was being ravaged by flames.

A scream pierced through his shock. This was a voice he recognized instantly. He dashed towards it, around the back of his razed home.

Two figures stood behind the house, and a third, smaller one was on the ground at their feet. The two men were outfitted soldiers. The girl knocked onto her stomach was his sister. Zandra pulled her head up, and as her eyes met Dante's, a wave of dizziness washed over him. He blinked, and when he opened his eyes he was the one on the ground, looking up at the two soldiers.

Zandra barred her teeth at the mage hunters towering over her. She had been so close to getting away. She'd left the other two hunters far behind after she enhanced her legs, magic powering her muscles and enabling her to outrun them easily. Her mistake was heading toward the farmhouse, closer to the part of the woods she was more familiar with. When she got there, the house was aflame. She ran up to try to see if her parents had escaped, only to be ambushed by the hunters before her now.

Her voice shook as she spoke. "Why are you doing this?" She glanced at the inferno consuming her house, spreading to the rest of the farm. "What are you *doing?*"

"Punishing those who would shelter a mage," said the hunter on the right. His voice was deep and stern. "Fire is useful when it comes to mages. It is tradition, after all." He looked at his partner. "Cedric, get the brand."

"You mean... you mean they're in there? My parents?"

"We made sure of it."

The other hunter, Cedric, had gone over to the flames and retrieved a metal rod. *Wait, he said brand. They mean to magebrand me—*

Zandra tried to skitter up but the hunter caught her arm. She barely felt the pain of his fingernails biting into her skin. *I have to use magic, I'm not strong enough to pull free...*

Her eyes locked on to the red-hot brand Cedric was bringing closer and closer. The hunter's grip on her tightened, and her grasp on magic loosened. She was frozen, she couldn't summon her power, and it was all happening too fast.

She began to scream before the metal even touched her face.

Someone was shaking him.

"Dante, wake up. You're dreaming. It's just a dream."

Dante opened his eyes back to reality. Everything was white. He pulled himself up, blinking and rubbing his eyes, uselessly trying to clear the blindness from them. "Who... who's there?"

"It's... Scarlet." She sounded puzzled. "You... you were screaming. Are you okay?"

I'm not, but how can I possibly explain that right now? His whole body trembled. Struggling to find a start, he realized she probably had conjured an orb of light to wash away the darkness, and there was no reason for him to not know who was there, hence her confusion. He tried to push out a few words. "I can't see."

"What?"

"I'm blind for a while. After this happens."

"After dreaming?"

"Yes... no, it's more than that, but—" But he had never told anyone. Not even Bronwen. Though he had accepted much of his magic, this piece of it always seemed separate. Private.

He buried his face in his hands. Zandra, they had gotten to Zandra. His parents as well. How long ago had it happened? He'd been pushing back the vision for days, but could it have happened even before that? Or was this a premonition of what was still to come?

There's more, the familiar-yet-not voice said to him. Dante was startled to hear it while awake.

"I don't understand," Scarlet said.

"Did you hear that?" Dante asked. "That other voice just now?"

A pause. Dante imagined Scarlet's face scrunched in bewilderment. "No," she said.

"It said that there's more," Dante said. "There's... more. Then I have to... I have to go back to sleep."

"Sleep... is good?"

"It is but it's not. It's... not." Dante stopped. He tucked his knees close to his chest. Everything was pouring out and he needed to hold it in, somehow. "But I have to know what happens next. If she's okay."

Scarlet put a hand on his knee. Somehow, her touch was calming. Her worry seeped into him, and it grounded him into the space around him that he could not see. "If who is okay?"

"My sister."

Scarlet's grip on his knee tightened. "Then you should sleep, if that's what you need to do."

"It is. But…"

"…You're afraid. Of what you might see."

Dante was relieved that she understood enough, despite his poor explanations. "Yes. I don't know that I'm brave enough to face it… or even to fall asleep again."

Scarlet removed her hand. The room suddenly felt much colder. "Lay back down."

Dante took a breath, then did as she said. Scarlet pulled his blanket back over him. Then he felt his mattress shift with the weight of her sitting down next to him. "Sleep. I will watch over you."

Dante wondered if her kindness was genuine. It was a stark change from her prickliness when they'd first met, and even the careful friendship they'd been cultivating. "Th-thank you."

"If you scream again… should I wake you?"

"No. I need to see the whole thing through."

"Okay." She rested a hand on his shoulder. Somehow, her touch felt like armor. Her power smoldered within her, as if fire was working on Dante's side for once.

Dante's heart hammered. He didn't know how to face what he would see next if his worst fears came to fruition. But he had to know. And at least he wouldn't be alone. He tried to steady his breath and his heart and slipped back into unconsciousness.

CHAPTER 19

*D*ante stood in the darkness. He was alone. The air felt heavy, and it almost seemed to hum. He was in a tunnel.

The sound of footsteps echoed in the distance. Dante looked toward them. A faint light appeared from around a corner. Someone was walking toward him, holding a lantern that lit the curved walls around him. The passageway was made of clear crystal that held a faint blue hue.

Dante was locked in place as the person approached him. It was a soldier, wearing armor made of leather and metal. His tabard was blue, striped with gold. Riordan's colors. He didn't seem to see Dante. Dante realized that his inability to move meant that the soldier would march right into him. As he got closer and closer, Dante began to make out the soldier's face. He looked... familiar.

As the soldier was about to collide with Dante's incorporeal dream body, he realized that he was one of the soldiers-to-be that Bronwen had rescued him from. He tried to flinch away from the soldier, but he couldn't move, there was no time—

Barek was tense. Each muscle in his body was coiled tight as he followed the tunnel, which sloped shallowly upward as he made his way back to ground level. He felt dizzy as he made it to the room carved out of crystal that was used as a guardpost. Gideon was already sitting at a table, playing a solitary card game while waiting for Barek to arrive to trade off guard duty.

Gideon brushed a blond lock of hair out of his eye and flashed Barek a smile. "How was your shift?"

"Fine," Barek said. It came out more bluntly than intended.

Gideon immediately dropped his smile, picking up on Barek's mood. "Hey. What's wrong?"

Barek didn't know how to organize his thoughts. He took a seat across from Gideon.

Gideon reached out and took one of Barek's hands. "Is it about Wren? I know I've been pushing to tell him about us, but—"

"It's not that." Barek closed his eyes for a moment, trying to recenter himself. While he wasn't looking forward to telling his older brother that he was dating his best friend, Barek had another vital crossroad to pass first. "I just... I'm still not sure I made the right choice about enlisting."

Gideon's mouth twisted in concern. "I know I was more excited about this than you, but I'm glad you're here, and... you can't exactly change your mind at this point. And it's good coin to send home, too."

"What use is coin if we get *killed*?" This too, came out sharper than Barek meant it to.

"We aren't going to get killed. Who's going to kill us, the mages?"

"The ones *here*, no. But beyond that, look at the signs. King Riordan has been offering more and more coin to enlist, and the army has grown so much... it can't be for nothing."

That made Gideon pause. "I know... I know there's danger. At least if there *is* war, we're mage hunters. There's not that many of us, and we're valuable. We won't get thrown to the front lines."

It took Barek a moment to force out the next thing he needed to say. "I'm... not sure I want to be a mage hunter anymore. I know I can't leave the army completely, but..."

"Barek, come on. Please." Gideon squeezed his hand tighter. "This is an important assignment, and it also means we get to spend time together."

"But it's *wrong.*" Barek pulled his hand out of Gideon's grasp. "Can't you see that?"

Gideon's voice was low. "They're blasphemers. They are wielding power that should only be our god's. It is outlawed by the king himself, and they *chose* to do it anyway."

"And what about the girl?" Barek snapped. "The newest mage they brought in. She's... just a kid. You think she deserves this?"

"It's unfortunate. But everyone knows the law, and the consequences for breaking it."

"They were all just... born with access to these powers. They didn't *choose* this! And we know, Gideon, we know what it's like to be born different than most anyone else. Do you really have no compassion for them, for their suffering?"

Gideon averted his gaze. "Compassion... yes. The consequences are extreme. But so are their trespasses. I can't absolve them of their crimes. This is bigger than me, or you. This is the decree of our *god.*"

Barek's heart dropped. He wanted to scream, to argue. They were complicit in this, in the torture of mages, their neighbors, their families. For the crime of having any power at all. *This is it, this is the end, it's the end. There's no convincing him.* There was concern on Gideon's face, but that was it, and it wasn't enough. Barek had made his decision.

"Why don't you get some rest?" Gideon suggested. "Just... take it easy. We can talk more about this later, after my shift."

"Could you do me a favor, actually?"

"Of course."

"Let me take your shift."

Gideon furrowed his brow. "You want to work a double shift? Why—"

"I only had a half-shift. And I need… I just need to be doing something right now. Even if it's pacing back and forth."

Gideon stared at him for a few moments, evaluating. "Okay," he said. "If that's really what you need right now."

They both got up. Before leaving, Gideon pulled Barek into an embrace. Barek hugged him back, hard. He knew it might be his last chance to hold him.

"Come talk to me when you're ready, okay?" Gideon whispered as he let Barek go.

"Yeah. I will." Barek wondered if his words sounded as hollow as he felt.

Gideon left, heading back above ground. It took a while for Barek to regain his bearings and steel his resolve. After a few minutes, he headed back down the tunnel, into the mage prison.

The prison only had one guard on duty at a time, despite holding the highest valued prisoners. The guard was always a mage hunter. In fact, anyone who was not a mage hunter didn't even know about the prison. It was highly secretive, and the king himself had promised that it was secure despite the minimal presence of guards. He had told them that he would be able to sense if something went wrong and deal with the problem himself if it came to that.

Barek doubted it would, though. He didn't entirely understand the mechanics of the prison, but just like he could sense when people were mages, he could also feel the presence of magic in the crystal that the cave was carved from. The captured mages were… sufficiently subdued. It was probably unnecessary to have them behind metal bars. In each cell, there was a set of crystal spikes protruding from the back wall. The mages were pressed against them, the spikes penetrating their skin. Barek wasn't sure how, but the crystal absorbed all their magic. All of their energy. As he walked further, deeper into the prison, each mage he passed was slumped over in some fashion, nearly catatonic.

It was uncomfortable and disturbing to witness, to say the least. Barek had been drifting away from the acceptance of King Riordan's strict laws for some time. After Gideon and his brother, along with the rest of his family, pressured him to enlist, which caused him to see the suffering the king caused firsthand... it accelerated his departure from seeing their ruler god as an infallible being.

He hurried through the prison, doing his best to avoid looking into the cells, at seeing the dozens of unresponsive mages. He wished there was more he could do, but his impact could only be small. Anything he did was risky, and most of the prisoners would need too long to recover before they would be able to even stand up. His plan couldn't work with them.

But there was one prisoner who should have more energy left than the others. Their newest addition. She had arrived close to a fortnight ago. While her magic was drained quickly, like all the others, this prisoner seemed more resilient than most. She also had the benefit of her imprisonment being short, so far. Her muscles hadn't had the chance to atrophy like the others that had been here for months.

When Barek arrived at her cell, her head was hanging downward, limp. Her matted blonde hair hung down, hiding what little of her face he might have been able to see. Barek stood silently in front of her cell, figuring out his approach.

The girl's head jerked up. He saw her flinch a little, the light of his lantern searing her eyes that were accustomed to the darkness that pervaded her existence now. "What do you want?" she said, her tone cold and acidic.

He stared at her, unable to stop looking at the angry red flesh, the vertical burns from the bottom of her eye down her cheek. Her magebrand hadn't fully healed yet. "I want to get you out of here."

The girl pressed her lips together. "A cruel joke you have there. Leave me alone." She turned her head down again.

"I mean it," Barek said, trying to pour his emotion and sincerity into his voice. "Please, trust me. I can't be a part of all this anymore. I'm leaving, and I want to take you with me."

She snorted. "The joke's on you if you think I will ever trust someone wearing that uniform. You wear the god's colors."

"From this moment on, I wear these colors only to avoid suspicion. I swear to you."

The girl only shook her head. "If you must take me, I have no doubt you can force me. But I will not wade into whatever this is with open arms."

Barek felt stumped. He didn't expect her to reject a chance at freedom. "What's your name?"

"...Zandra."

"My name is Barek." He paused. He bit his lip. "Zandra. Tell me. What do you have to lose? This prison is horrendous. Inhumane. I'll be the first to admit it. I'm risking my life by deserting the army. But if I can save someone from these horrors... I have to do it."

"And what of the others? I'm one of many."

"It would be impossible to sneak out a large group, even if they were in any condition to leave. Everyone else has been here too long. But... I think I can get the two of us out. Maybe we can find a way to save the rest later. I've heard rumors of a rebellion. If they exist, it's my goal to find them."

At hearing the word 'rebellion', Barek saw something flash in her eyes. Perhaps it was hope.

"Okay. Get me out of here."

Barek scrambled to unlock her cell. He winced when the cell door creaked as he opened it. The sound echoed down the crystal cave. He glanced over his shoulder. The mage in the cell opposite Zandra's hadn't even looked up.

There's no one here, it's okay, it's okay. Barek kept repeating this mantra as he stepped into the girl's cell.

Zandra's green eyes stared up at him. "I need help up."

"Y-yeah, of course." He took her hands and tried to gently pull her away from the spikes embedded into her back. She gasped and almost fell forward as she was released from the crystal's grasp, but Barek held her steady. "Do you think you can stand?"

Zandra shivered, then pulled herself up with Barek's aid. "I think I can walk." She took a tentative step, wobbling slightly.

"Here. Lean on me."

Together, they slowly began their way out of the tunnel.

"Is there another mage you've captured recently... that's close to my age?" Zandra asked. "A bit older. A boy."

"No," said Barek. He thought back to the boy he and his friends ran into on the way to the capital. His group had been convinced he was a mage, with their suspicions being confirmed when he used magic to free himself from Keenan's grasp. He'd escaped, though they spent a decent chunk of time attempting to find him before giving up and continuing on their journey. *Who knows what happened to him?* Barek wondered if he should mention him, but was distracted by the tap of footsteps further up the tunnel.

Barek swore under his breath.

Zandra looked up at him with wide eyes. "What do we do?"

Barek fumbled to get ahold of the keys attached to his belt while still supporting part of Zandra's weight. He unlocked the nearest cell. "Get in, get in. We just have to wait for him to pass." He helped her down close enough to the spikes at the back wall so that she could pretend they were once again protruding into her back. He got back out and relocked the door, grateful that this cell door wasn't as creaky as the last one was. These tasks were finished just in time for Barek to pretend he was strolling through the caves on his regular patrol.

His body froze against his will. His head was pushed down, forcing him to look only at the ground. It wasn't the first time the king had toyed with controlling his body, preventing Barek from ever seeing him... but it was always disturbing.

Riordan continued toward him. Barek saw a drop of sweat drip off his forehead as he stared at his feet. He almost thought he would get away with it, that the god would pass by without word or incident, as was standard on his visits to the prison. But then he stopped next to Barek. He could see the god's bare feet out of the corner of his eye.

The king's voice was both honey and tar. "Everything operating as normal, soldier?"

"Yes, your Majesty."

"Good. It's... Barek, is it?"

Barek thought his heart stopped beating for a moment. "That's correct, your Majesty." Did the god take care to know all of the mage hunters' names, or had Barek been singled out for some reason?

"I look forward to your continued service." With that unsettling line, the god left Barek behind.

After a few moments, he could move his own body again. He took a few shaking breaths while waiting for the king to be sufficiently distant from them. Then he unlocked the cell door to release Zandra once more. He helped her up and noticed that she looked even paler than before, if that was even possible. "I know this is a ridiculous question, but are you alright?"

"I can make it," Zandra responded, though her voice was thin. "I thought... I thought I was far enough from the spikes, but one jabbed me."

Barek glanced at her back. The back of her shirt was almost entirely stained with blood, both old and new. The sight made him nauseated, but he pushed the feeling down. *There's time to feel guilt later, right now I just need to get her out.*

"Why does he come here?" Zandra asked.

It was known among the guards that Riordan visited the prison every day or two. Notably, he was always barefooted, for some reason. He went to the deep underground, where no guards were permitted. No one knew exactly what was beyond that point, though Barek suspected that it may be a particularly high-value prisoner. Once, he heard screaming echo through the tunnels while Riordan was there.

"I don't know," Barek said. It was the technical truth, plus he didn't want to traumatize the girl any further with his suspicions. "But we're getting out and you *never* have to come back."

Dante opened his eyes to the white void of nothingness. He was drenched in sweat, but he wasn't screaming this time. Though he couldn't see her, he felt Scarlet's hand still resting on his shoulder and the weight of her body on his bed.

"Is everything okay?" Scarlet asked. Her words were soft, small, and much different from the sharp edges they usually had.

His mind flipped through everything he had seen, his stomach churned, and he wanted to throw up. He was feverish, drained, unsettled by the horrors his sister and other mages were subjected to. He was blind, lost, alone—

Scarlet squeezed his shoulder tighter. A wave of calm washed over him. He was hopeful. Zandra was alive. She could have made it out. And his parents... could they have survived the burning house?

"I don't know," he answered. "But... it might be."

"Should I go now?"

"Could... could you stay until my vision comes back?"

Despite his blindness, it felt like she nodded. Regardless, she stayed.

He'd never had someone with him in the aftermath of his visions before. It felt... vulnerable, but having a point of contact with someone helped ground him back into reality. He could feel her prodding worry, but she didn't ask him anything more.

As the whiteness eventually faded, Scarlet came into sight. She was perched on the edge of his bed. A summoned blue glowing sphere floating gently above her free hand. Once his vision was fully restored, he was suddenly self-conscious about touching her. Now that he was less in need of immediate comfort, it seemed much more awkward and intimate.

Scarlet must have felt the same way because when they made eye contact and she realized his vision was back, her hand flinched away. "I should go back to bed. If... if you're okay now."

"Yeah. I'm alright."

Scarlet got up.

"Thank you," Dante managed to call out before she was gone.

Scarlet paused in the doorway. She looked back at him. "Yeah," she said softly, before slipping out of his room.

CHAPTER 20

Scarlet wandered the library with little purpose. The pacing helped bring her adrenaline back down after a harrowing day of training. Dante, having started his lessons with Bronwen a few weeks ago, was only with her and Death roughly half of the time. His progress was slow. Scarlet renewed her focus, drilling the basics with little complaint. She'd perfect her techniques and give Death nothing to scold her about. On days like today, when she had lessons alone, she would go full force.

Her free time was split between training on her own out in the swamp, and studying in the library when she was too tired for magic. Or, when she was too exhausted even for that, like today, she would try to settle herself into some semblance of relaxation.

The solo practice that she did whenever she could kept her sane amid the slower days with Dante. Scarlet could drill as hard as she wanted to, and get more creative with her techniques. No interferences, no interruptions.

But also, despite her frustrations, she was beginning to enjoy Dante's presence now that the ice between them had broken. As much as she hated to admit it, Bronwen was right. She did need a friend. There was always a tension between herself and Death, and to an extent, Bronwen as well. They were the gatekeepers, standing between her and her mother's rescue.

Dante, however, seemed not to have any particular plans at all—apart from his fascination with the magic of healing. *But to what end?* Scarlet wondered. Death seemed uninterested in gaining him as an emissary. Perhaps the god feared he would take up the offer to be portaled back to the World if such a thing was otherwise forced on him. Given his initial unease at staying in the first place, it didn't seem unlikely. But even then, he wouldn't be able to return to Saridian. Not unless he was committed to forgoing his powers once more.

They both pointedly avoided talking about plans for the future. She helped him with magic but felt that she had little to offer beyond that. Often, she struggled to say something relatable about their experiences in training or about the strangeness of the castle and its layout. Dante told her about the town he came from and some stories from living there. He chronicled his journey from being a farmer to an apprentice herbalist. Certain details were skirted, though. He never spoke of his family, and Scarlet offered nothing about hers, either. But that had changed last night when Dante brought up his sister.

She'd been frantic when she heard him screaming across the hall. Her first thoughts were of Riordan and Calder, fearing that one or both of them had made their way into the castle. Even though she knew Dante would be the least interesting target for the god, the fear still cropped up.

Dante had been... she couldn't say *just* dreaming, as it seemed to be more than that. Anxiety had spiraled through her as she watched him go back to sleep. It felt strange to touch him, to rest her hand on his shoulder. It had been so long since she had experienced any sort of comforting touch or physical affection. But she felt deeply that he needed an anchor, something to hold him steady while he experienced whatever it was that he did. While she didn't know what was happening, she knew it was real and important.

She wasn't sure if she should pry, or if perhaps Dante would offer more of an explanation on his own. *I wish all the answers were here, in the library. It would be so much simpler.*

While they had become closer, Dante also gave her space. When he first arrived, he tried to ask her so many questions. It had been overwhelming. He asked less, now, and gave her room to approach him instead. His presence didn't make her so tense anymore.

The one place he had always let her be, even from the beginning, was the library. He seemed to understand the sacred silence that books required. He would often join her there, and at first, she had taken books back to her room to avoid him, but she had stopped such a practice after realizing he would keep his distance.

Dante would walk the stacks quietly as Scarlet read, or pick a book and read it a respectable distance away from her. Sometimes, in the before-friendship days, she caught him eyeing her as if she were a wild animal he was considering how to approach. Once, as she flamescribed a note, he snuck up on her to watch. When she startled, he scampered off, not to be seen again that day.

She was surprised at first to find that Dante could read, though she supposed it made sense if he had been an herbalist's apprentice. Scarlet could see how reading and writing would be useful in that sort of profession.

Scarlet wove her way through the library and took a seat at one of the desks sitting on the far end. It was her favorite desk out of the few in the library. It was in the corner, which felt sheltered, and she had moved all the blank paper she had scrounged from all the desks to use for flamescribing when she was drawn to doing such a thing. She absently ran her fingers over the desk's surface, a dark wood that had been sanded flat into a smooth veneer. She closed her eyes, trying to sort through her chaotic thoughts.

There was the whole thing with Dante last night, of course, but there was another topic weighing heavily on her mind. It wasn't long now until Bronwen and the other emissaries would leave for Riordan's realm. She had no idea how many emissaries would come, or when exactly the mission would begin... but Bronwen had been either cagey or absent lately, and the storeroom had much more food in it than usual.

When she thought about them leaving without her, she felt sick.

Scarlet sensed something, and her eyes flew open. Dante was right next to her, having snuck up to her without her noticing.

"Sorry. Did I startle you?" he asked.

"No. Yes. It's... fine."

He looked at the papers she had left out on the desk. On top of the pile was the map she had drawn of the Crossworld, its edge singed from her previous outburst. Dante gestured to it. "So is that what you do? When I see you working with your flame?"

"Yeah." Scarlet reached for the pile of papers, self-conscious. She almost moved to put them away into one of the desk's drawers, but paused. She handed the map to Dante.

He took a moment to study the map. Scarlet had put a lot of work into detailing the different landscapes of each realm. Tall mountains for Meyrin's realm, plains and foothills in Riordan's, the desert of Kajiem's realm, scattered islands for Cascara, and the dense jungle of Io's. "How do you do this? How do you keep the whole page from catching fire?"

"It's called flamescribing," Scarlet said. "The flame has to be small and cool enough. It takes a lot of practice."

"Is it easier than pen and ink?"

Scarlet couldn't remember the last time she'd picked up a quill. It seemed like an unwieldy thing to do now, to have a device in her hand, that she had to dip into ink constantly and try not to get blots. "It is for me."

Dante kept inspecting the map. Scarlet became fidgety as he continued to examine her work. "You can keep it," she said. Then he could look at it without her around, feeling awkward.

Dante looked up at her, a funny silent expression on his face. "Thank you." The moment dragged out. There was tension running between them like they both had more to say. "And about last night... thank you for that, too."

Scarlet nodded curtly. Her curiosity about his dreams burned, but she finally decided it wasn't her place to ask. She would leave him room, as he had done for her.

After a few long moments, Dante spoke again. "I haven't talked to anyone. About my dreams. Not even Bronwen. It's always felt... private, for some reason."

"I understand," Scarlet said. After all, she felt much the same about hearing Viridian since she'd come to the Crossworld.

"You do, don't you?" Dante stared at her, unblinking, suddenly very serious. "If I tell you my secret, will you tell me yours?"

Scarlet tried to swallow but found her mouth dry. "Why do you think I have a secret?"

"I just... do." Dante shrugged. "There's a lot of things I can't explain... and not because I don't want to, but because I don't know how."

Scarlet considered for a moment. She reached out to Viridian. Her sister drew closer.

You can tell him if you want.

How do I know if I even want to? Scarlet wondered, half to herself and half to her sister.

Go with your gut. I trust him if you do.

Scarlet took a breath, her shoulders tense. "Okay." She was immediately unsure of her decision, but she'd made it.

Dante pulled up a chair from another nearby desk so he could sit near Scarlet. "Okay. So. I... have visions, I guess? I see things that haven't happened yet, and different ways they could turn out. Or sometimes I see the past, I think. Sometimes it's not even from my own perspective... I had a dream that I was Death. I saw her and Riordan speaking."

Scarlet's eyes widened. "Is that what you saw last night?"

"No. I saw that before I even came here. Last night... I saw my family. My sister." His face scrunched and he turned away.

Scarlet's heart sped up. "Are they okay?"

"I don't know. Soldiers burnt down my house. My parents were inside… I'm not sure if they would have been able to escape. And I don't know when this happened, or if this happened, or will happen."

"I'm sorry." Those words felt insufficient, but what else could she say?

"It was always complicated with them, but…"

"They were still family."

Dante shrugged helplessly. Scarlet knew how deep her own mixed feelings about her parents went. She wasn't about to push him on it more.

"And what about your sister?"

"They… magebranded her." Hatred was laced into his voice. "But they didn't kill her. They put her in a prison for mages, and they were draining the energy out of them… Someone was helping her escape, but I woke up before they made it all the way out."

"A mage prison?" Scarlet nearly jumped out of her chair. She'd never heard of Riordan doing anything with mages other than outright killing them. "Do you know where it is?"

"It must be in Kingsmount. Riordan visits the prison often. I think to visit a particular prisoner?"

Scarlet's heart was racing now, to the point where she felt a bit dizzy. "My mother. It could be my mother."

Dante nodded. "I thought about that too. That's why I wanted you to know."

Knowledge was power, and Scarlet finally had a piece of power that she needed. "Thank you." She felt a surprising gratitude, unlike anything she'd experienced before. She thought for a moment. "Riordan being at the prison often doesn't necessarily mean it's in the capital. He can travel quickly around Saridian using his realm as a shortcut."

"How does that work?"

"Each of the god's realms here in the Crossworld is a manifestation of the land they control in the World." Scarlet got Dante to hold out the map she'd given him. "The form of their realms, the landscape, is a reflection of their territory in the World. When you portal from the Crossworld to the

World, or vice versa, you travel from a corresponding location from one place to another. But, the thing is, the Crossworld is much smaller than the World. So Riordan, or any emissary, can portal from the World to the Crossworld, take a stroll, and then pop back into the World much farther away."

"Wow. Okay, that's crazy. And only emissaries can do it, it's not something I could do?"

"Before the end of the Magus War, any mage could open portals. But as part of the treaty that ended the war, mortals were banned from living in the Crossworld, and the gods were able to block non-emissaries from getting in and out. Uh, we are living in the Crossworld, obviously, but Death is an exception to many things since she wasn't a part of the treaty."

Dante bit his lip, taking in this information.

"Is there anything about the prison that you saw that might give us a clue about where it is?" Scarlet asked.

"It was underground," said Dante. "There were all of these tunnels, carved out of crystal."

Scarlet thought for a moment. "I wonder... I wonder if it's magus crystal. In which case, it is definitely in the World." She got up from her seat. "Dante, we have to find it, we have to. For my mother and your sister if she's still there."

"But... but how? The two of us can't do it alone."

She sat back down, deflated. "I don't know. But we have to. I can't sit around and wait for Death to let me do something anymore."

"...Okay," said Dante, "so if we *do* decide to go find this place... you would open a portal for us?"

Scarlet grimaced. "I've never made a portal. But... I can try to figure it out. The bigger problem is that I can't even attempt it from here. Death's realm isn't connected to the World the same way the other realms are."

"So we'd have to escape from the castle without Death noticing, and get across the river..."

"Yes."

"Scarlet—"

"We have to. We have to figure it out."

They locked eyes. Dante's green eyes held uncertainty and fear. *Do this with me. Please, do this with me.*

Dante took a slow, slow breath. "Okay." He didn't sound convinced, but Scarlet was intent on having enough conviction for the both of them.

"Get together whatever medical supplies you think will be useful. I'll pack us food. I... I still want to try to convince Death to let us go on the mission Bronwen is leading into Riordan's realm. It would be the easiest way to get out of here."

"Wait, mission?"

"Bronwen hasn't told you? Ugh. Okay, I will explain more later. I need... I need to think, to make some plans." Scarlet's mind was overwhelmed with the possibility of finally being able to *act.* "I have a book in my room that explains a bit about portals. I'm going to go read it again and see how much I can figure out."

Scarlet was out of her seat and about to beeline out of the library when Dante stopped her.

"Wait," he said. "I told you my secret. What's yours?"

This broke Scarlet's momentum. "Oh. I... ever since I got to the Crossworld... I can hear my sister."

"You can hear her? ...Where is she?"

"She's dead."

Horror appeared on Dante's face instantly. Scarlet knew he was thinking about his own sister and the loss he may have to face himself. Tears bit at her eyes and she spun away before he could see them. She couldn't bear to tell him any more right now.

We'll save his sister, Scarlet swore to herself as she left the library. *We'll save what's left of our families.*

CHAPTER 21

The next day, Scarlet and Dante had a joint training session with Death. Scarlet felt herself stumbling through the drills. Even her spars with Dante were a closer call than usual, though she pulled a victory in each. Her clothes were soaked through; a consequence of tripping over a root and floundering in the mud.

She was preoccupied with trying to figure out the best way to convince Death to let her and Dante go on the mission into Riordan's realm. Swimming across the stream of souls seemed like a treacherous proposition, and she had never seen a boat on the river's shore, so whatever way Death would get Bronwen and the other emissaries across to Riordan's realm would be the best option. *But getting Death to send me with them might be futile.*

Viridian touched her mind. *You have to try.*

I know, I know.

The both of them had wallowed together over the idea of having a lead to follow to find their mother but with potentially no way to investigate it.

"That's all for today," Death said, snapping Scarlet out of her thoughts. "There will be no training tomorrow. I will need to keep my energy and focus reserved for if the other emissaries call upon my power. While I cannot leave this realm, I must provide what support that I can."

Scarlet's heart skipped a beat. She shared a quick glance with Dante. "Wait. The mission—"

"Yes. The emissaries will arrive this evening, and I trust you will **not disturb them** before they set out in the morning."

Scarlet flinched as Death wove the command with magic. It had been some time since the god had last compelled her. The control over her felt like a noose tightening around her neck. *She really does not want me to speak with the other emissaries. Why? Does she think I'll convince them to let me help?*

Scarlet opened her mouth to speak, but Death cut her off before she could even begin. "No, you may not join them. It is already decided."

Death flipped her red braid over her shoulder and left Scarlet and Dante behind in the swamp. Scarlet looked over to Dante. He was chewing his lip.

"What now?" he asked.

She thought for a moment. *Of course. I knew it would be useless to even ask.* Death had held her back at every turn. Whatever the god's reasons were, she would never let Scarlet join the mission.

"Scarlet?"

"We stop asking permission," Scarlet told him. She turned to look toward the path to the river. "We go anyway."

Scarlet did as she was told, and avoided the other emissaries by holing up in her room—not that she had a choice, with Death's compulsion. Dante joined her but was driving her mad. He had spent the last hour pacing back and forth across the small room. She watched him from her bed, where she sat leaning back against the headboard, her stillness offsetting his frenetic energy.

"What happens if she catches us?" Dante asked for what felt like the billionth time.

Scarlet sighed. She had already answered this repeated query in various ways, more flippantly with each iteration. "Then she'll throw us in a caldron and make a nice stew."

Dante threw his hands up in frustration. "Scarlet! Are you not worried at *all*?"

She was. She kept thinking back to Death locking her in the dungeon. It was a strange turning point in her time at Deianira. It was the peak of her conflict with her imposed patron god, and of her helplessness. She still didn't know exactly how long Death had kept her down there. It felt like an eternity of pain and wallowing. And then... then Death gave her an olive branch. Dante. Her assigned friend. It was a patronizing gesture. But ultimately, she had become grateful for it, though she loathed to attribute any amount of kindness to the god's actions.

If Death caught them disobeying her, she could easily throw Scarlet back into the dungeon. Dante could be punished as well. Somehow that was more scary than risking consequences for herself. *I will protect him however I can*, she swore to herself vehemently.

Instead of answering his question, she asked one of her own. "Are you thinking of staying behind?"

That finally stopped him from pacing. He pivoted toward her and ran his fingers through his shaggy hair. "I... no. I have to find Zandra."

"I can look for her. If she's still in the prison, that's where I'm hoping to head anyway. If not, hopefully I can figure out if she's safe somewhere."

"It just... it all seems so impossible. Even if we get back to the World, what could the two of us possibly accomplish that all of Death's other emissaries can't?"

Now that he wasn't walking, Scarlet could see him shaking. She swung her legs off the bed and leaned to grab one of his trembling hands. "I know.

But I also know... I could never forgive myself for just standing by. I spent all of my life feeling incapable of doing anything meaningful, and maybe I still can't, but now... I know how to fight. So I'm going to. I have to. Even if in the end, it was all pointless, I can either live or die knowing that I tried."

Dante closed his eyes and gripped her hand tight.

"You don't have to do this," Scarlet whispered. "You don't have to come with me."

Dante drew a breath in and out, long and shaky. His eyes opened, a new clarity set deep in his green irises as he met Scarlet's gaze. "When are we leaving?"

"Tomorrow at nightfall. We'll try to follow in the other emissaries' footsteps. And we'll pray that Death will be too preoccupied with them to notice us leave."

Scarlet shivered as the brisk air met her skin. She'd never left Deianira at night before. The swampland outside the castle felt like a forbidden land after the twin moons of the Crossworld rose. There was no reason for this beyond her intuition. Death had never banned her from leaving the castle. *I suppose she has taken for granted that the stream of souls traps me here.* She could only hope that the god's confidence was misplaced.

Still, she found herself surprised when she touched the grand doors that guarded the way out of the castle, and they readily opened themselves for her and Dante, veins of silver running across the surface of the obsidian door as they used her magic to open.

She and Dante were burdened with supplies; though not heavily so. They had some food, scavenged from what remained in the pantry after the emissaries' departure. They had spent much of the day prowling around the castle for anything else that could be of use. This had yielded some mismatched pieces of leather armor in various states of disrepair. Scarlet found a chain shirt as well, which Dante had almost taken before he realized how much it weighed. In the end, they made do with their patchwork leather, some musty sleeping bags, and not much else.

Scarlet longed for her mother's obfuscation magic as they lurked through the darkness toward the river. It had always made her feel safe. As much as Scarlet had wished to be self-sufficient, her mother had always shielded her the best she could.

The Crossworld was quiet. It lacked the sounds of wildlife, which she found easily forgotten when out in the swamp for training, her mind otherwise occupied. But in the night, scampering across the landscape with Dante by her side with only a summoned orb of light brightening their path, the silence was stark.

Does the rest of the Crossworld have wildlife? Is it only because Death's realm is less connected to the World that nothing else lives here? She could only hope that she would have an answer to this question soon. They still didn't have a plan to get across the stream of souls, other than simply to swim and pray that the current wasn't too strong and that contact with the stream didn't have any ill effects.

Throughout the day, they had discussed building a raft. However, the idea was scrapped due to their worry that being away from the castle for a long period would signal trouble to Death, and their inexperience in building anything at all, there was no guarantee their efforts would yield a useful watercraft.

Scarlet tensed as they approached the river, the sound of rushing water meeting her ears. There were so many impossibilities to overcome in their journey, and this was only the first. In her grand scheme of things, it was such a small step—compared to her ultimate goal of finding and freeing her mother. But all of that rested on securing her freedom from the god that had kept her bound in this plane.

Dante stopped and threw Scarlet a wide-eyed look. "Do you see that?"

Scarlet looked more carefully into the distance, toward the moonlit water, and spotted a dark, bobbing shape. "A boat?" she whispered back. A chill ran down her spine. *It can't be.* "Did... did Bronwen leave it for us?"

Dante shrugged. Scarlet wiped her sweaty hands on her dark cloak. *This is really happening. We're going to get out.* Unable to contain herself, she began to jog toward the small vessel. Dante was slightly more restrained but followed behind.

As she approached, a figure on the boat moved. Startled, Scarlet hopped back and prepared to summon flames.

"Scarlet." The utterance of her name cut through the night. It was Death's voice that spoke the syllables, that gave an edge to the knife that slashed through Scarlet's hope. "Dante," the god added as the boy arrived at Scarlet's side. "Come. Let us speak."

Why, why *did she have to be here? All I want is a chance!*

Viridian touched her mind. *Don't lose hope yet. There's something odd in her voice.*

Scarlet and Dante closed the distance between themselves and the god. Death sat in one seat of a boat just big enough for two. Her blood-red hair was loose instead of the usual long braid. It swept down to the boat's seat, swaying with the gentle breeze. Death didn't look at them as they arrived. Instead, she continued staring out across the stream.

"I should be mad that you're here," Death said. She stopped, swallowed, then continued. "I could punish you for disobeying my wishes, but..."

The god trailed off. Viridian was right, there was something different in the god's tone. It was soft instead of sharp and blunt. Out of the corner of her eye, Scarlet could see Dante staring at her, then at Death, then back at her. Scarlet, as if she were made of stone, could not move a muscle in the anticipation that had overcome her.

Death's gaze snapped over to them. Her eyes, strangely bright in the relative darkness, caught Scarlet off-guard. "I've made a horrible mistake."

Death is admitting she was wrong about something?

"What do you mean?" Dante asked.

Scarlet cut in, recalling what Bronwen had told her. "You think Riordan set a trap."

"Yes. That's exactly it." Death ran her hands through her loose hair. Somehow, with her hair down, and her less confident tone, she felt more human to Scarlet. "I always knew that it was a risk... a too convenient piece of intel meant to bring my emissaries right into the claws of Riordan's forces... but I felt we had to take the chance. The odds are against us. If we can take advantage of a chip in Riordan's armor, it could mean all the difference."

"So what now?" Dante asked. "Are you calling them back?"

Death shook her head. "I can't reach them. Riordan is shielding me from being able to communicate through the emissary bonds."

Scarlet's eyes widened. "He knows they're coming."

"Yes."

The pieces clicked together in Scarlet's head. "And you can't leave your realm to go after them, because he still has you trapped here."

"Yes."

"And..." Scarlet paused. She was on a precipice and wasn't sure if she was about to fall. "And you want us to try to save them?"

Death stood, causing the boat to rock. She stepped out onto the shore and then reached back into the boat. She pulled out an oar and held it out to Scarlet.

"Yes."

CHAPTER 22

This doesn't feel real.

Scarlet took a wobbly step into the boat. She nearly lost her balance as she tried to step her other foot into the vessel, but Dante caught her hand and steadied her. Her instinct was to let go of his hand as soon as possible, but then she realized he probably needed help stepping into the boat as well. With her help, Dante got into the boat and took the seat across from her.

We're really doing it. Going to Riordan's realm, with Death's permission and all.

Death watched the two of them from the shoreline. "Try not to drift too far downstream, or you'll end up in the wrong realm," she advised. "There is a post on the other side that you can tie the boat to. You want to keep traveling straight through from there. You should reach a path that will take you to Riordan's fortress, which is where Calder was supposed to be."

"Do we have any hope of catching up with the emissaries before they get there?" Dante asked.

"I don't know," Death said. "They would be traveling swiftly, and I'm not sure if Riordan planned to let them get all the way to his fortress. I must admit this is a futile effort, in all likelihood, but..."

"But we have to do something," Scarlet filled in.

Death pursed her lips. "Indeed. Even if the worst has happened, perhaps some survivors could be helped."

Dante nodded. "We'll do what we can."

Death bobbed her head in acknowledgment, then looked to Scarlet. "One more thing," she said. Her voice was coarser again now, having lost her uncertain tone. "Scarlet. **You are not permitted to leave the Crossworld under any circumstances.**"

Scarlet's emissary marks began to burn. It was an order. She clenched her jaw and resisted the urge to let out a scream. *I was so close... I can see if I can help Bronwen, but I'm still kept from saving Mom.* She felt Viridian's frustration echo alongside her own.

"Fine," Scarlet said. She waited for Death to untie the rope that tethered the boat to a wooden post, then used her oar to push them further into the stream.

Scarlet looked over across the water as they began to paddle. The opposite bank looked much the same as their side. Gloomy, barren trees ringed the edge of the river. It was all mushy swampland for as far as she could see.

"So..." Dante started. "What happens if you disobey Death?"

"I can't."

"You're giving up on going to the World, then?" Dante sounded perplexed at how easily Death had quenched her stubbornness.

"No. But... Death used a compulsion on me. It's something she can do because I'm an emissary. I literally *can't* defy her order."

They kept paddling. Scarlet was glad her training had bulked her muscles up, otherwise this crossing would be much more difficult. Dante seemed to struggle as they reached about halfway across.

She was glad that Death hadn't made Dante an emissary, though she often wondered why she hadn't. Regardless of the reason, Scarlet was glad Dante hadn't been subjected to Death's controlling side.

Dante exhaled a big breath. "So then... what now?"

"We try to save Bronwen and the others," Scarlet replied. She knew it wasn't an answer to the question he was asking.

"If we manage to do that... afterward, we can't go to the World."

The following silence between them was filled with the sound of rushing water. Scarlet worried they were drifting too far downstream. She switched what side she was paddling on, hoping to steer them straighter across toward the post Death had mentioned, which was now in sight.

"Death barred me from leaving the Crossworld. But she didn't say that I couldn't open a portal. You can still go."

Scarlet's stomach twisted into knots waiting for Dante's reply, but he took a minute to think. They were making good progress, not even drifting too far downstream anymore. She finally broke her gaze from the opposite bank to look at Dante. His blond eyebrows were scrunched down.

"No. I can't go alone."

"Why not?"

"I... I don't know what I'm doing!" Dante stopped paddling and his body seemed to crumple in on itself. "I'm a horrible mage, I can't fight anyone, I don't know how I could find Zandra alone, let alone save her if she didn't manage to escape."

"Do you know anything about the Vanguard?"

"No. What's that?"

"I think they're a group working against Riordan. I overheard Bronwen and Death talking about them once. Bronwen wanted Death to send me to them. But of course..." *Of course, she won't let me go anywhere.* Scarlet could feel Viridian seething in the background, likewise frustrated at their plans being thwarted at the last moment.

"How would I find them?"

"I don't know. But we never had a solid plan on how to do any of this. We were always going to have to figure it out. The Vanguard isn't your only option either. There are the Ravens as well."

"The Ravens...? Wait, I think my dad spoke about them once. They're some sort of cult, aren't they?" He sounded concerned.

"Most of Death's emissaries are Ravens. There are other mages with them as well. They're the only surviving group that is openly hostile toward Riordan. They would help you too, I think."

The rest of their journey across the river was spent in silence. When they reached shore, Scarlet disembarked first, giving Dante a hand out of the boat afterward. They hitched the boat to the post. Scarlet glanced back to Deianira, protruding from the trees in the center of Death's realm. She couldn't see Death back on the other side. Perhaps the god had returned to her castle already.

"You think I could do it by myself?" Dante asked. "Find other help, look for Zandra... and hopefully your mother as well?"

"Our chances of success have always been low. But it's... it's not about that. At least for me. Like I said before, I could never forgive myself for not trying. I know you have your fears, but I think you feel the same way."

Dante closed his eyes and steadied himself by grasping the post they had tethered the boat to. "Maybe," Dante said, "After we rescue whoever we can. If... if you can figure out how to open a portal. Then, maybe—"

"Then you'll go."

And she'd still be stuck here. Alone.

The swampland faded into plains, making Scarlet and Dante now undeniably in Riordan's realm. They found a stone pathway and began to follow it.

"So what," said Dante, "we just follow this all the way to Riordan's lair?"

Scarlet shrugged. "That's what Death said."

They continued down the road, which led them in a fairly straight direction across the plains. Even after a couple of hours, the path didn't split off in any other directions.

"We're so out in the open," Scarlet commented. "If any of Riordan's forces are out and about, they'll spot us immediately."

Dante grunted in agreement. "But look," he said, pointing toward the horizon. "I think I see trees."

Eventually, a forest came into full view. The path led into it, giving them some cover at last. *I suppose it helps a bit, but if anyone is patrolling this path, they're still going to come across us.*

In her anxiety, Scarlet reached out to Viridian for comfort, only to immediately realize her connection to her sister was gone.

"Scarlet? Are you okay?"

Scarlet hadn't noticed that she had stopped dead in her tracks. "Viridian," she said. "Viridian is gone."

I can't lose her again, I can't, I can't. Not right now, I need her. And if Dante's leaving too, then I really will be alone. Alone, alone. Nothing. No one.

"Viridian?"

"My... my sister."

"Right," Dante said. "The one... you can hear, you said?"

"Yes." Scarlet glanced over her shoulder as if she would find her sister, just lagging behind them. "I can't reach her now. I don't know—she can't be gone—"

It felt like she was drowning. She couldn't breathe. She brought her hands to her hair and started tugging. *All of my family, all of them...* Dante gently took her hands, untangling them from her hair.

"It's okay," Dante said, tentative. "She's... maybe you just have to be at Deianira. Death's realm. You only started hearing her when you got there, right?"

"R-right." That was true. Plus, Scarlet had felt Viridian right before they had crossed the river. *It would make sense that I can connect with her only in Death's realm. Although, that means if I do make it back to the World, I wouldn't have her anymore...* Scarlet shivered. That wasn't helpful to think about right now. She needed to focus on the task at hand, and hopefully, she would be able to reach Viridian again soon.

"Okay," Scarlet said, steadying herself. "Okay. Let's keep going. Sorry."

"We could take a break, if you need—"

"No. We have to keep going. I couldn't do anything about Viridian, and I might not be able to help my mom, but by the gods, I will not risk losing the chance to save Bronwen."

Dante nodded, echoing her feelings. They forged onward. Hours passed. After a while, they emerged from the forest, the land opening up into a field of wildflowers.

"It's strange," Dante said. "This place is so much like Saridian, but also... not."

Scarlet glanced around. Her wary mind was set more on looking and listening for danger than paying attention to the landscape around them. It was indeed a bizarre version of her homeland. Like in Death's realm, the greens of leaves and grass were shifted into a teal color. The field of wildflowers contained an assortment of colors, shapes, and sizes of petals, all close to what she was familiar with but also... not.

It was beautiful in a way. But it also set her on edge. Saridian had been dangerous enough for her and her mother, and now, the creeping feeling that someone was sneaking up on them was only growing. Her curiosity about animals living in other parts of the Crossworld was satisfied when a deer startled her in the woods an hour ago. She'd nearly sent a firebolt at it but recognized the creature for what it was just in time to hold back. Bees, striped orange and red, buzzed around and carried pollen from flower to flower in the field.

Soon they were led by the path back into a forest. This time, the woods seemed more foreboding than protective. Her last memories of Saridian, of being in a forest had been with Riordan. He would have ended her, if not for the deal she made with Death.

Am I... grateful to her? It was a strange thought, with mixed emotions. She was glad to be alive. But what was a life if her decisions were not her own? What was *anything* worth if she continued to be separated from everyone she cared about? *Is this why Death is as bitter as she is? Riordan has had her trapped here for much longer than I've been here...*

Scarlet grew tired, but she knew they had to keep pushing. They didn't stop for proper meals, instead snacking on the fruits and bread they had packed while making their way closer and closer to Riordan's fortress. Eventually, the sky began to grow dark. Long shadows were cast by the trees surrounding them.

"Should we stop?" Dante asked. "I know we want to get there as fast as possible, but we also need to keep our energy up."

"I don't know if I could even sleep right now anyway."

"I—" Dante started, and then abruptly stopped.

"What?"

Dante shushed her, grabbed her arm, and pulled her into the cover of trees. Scarlet grunted as branches scraped across her face. "Don't you hear that?" His voice was gruff.

She hadn't, but now that adrenaline coursed through her veins, all of her senses seemed heightened. Holding her breath, she heard voices coming from farther down the path.

They crouched in the brush, hidden from the road. Scarlet felt for the dagger clipped to her boots. The sheath was still strapped on tightly. It was unlikely she would use the dagger—magic was much more effective—but having the weapon her mother gave her grounded and focused her attention.

The voices drew near. Scarlet readjusted so she could peek at the oncoming passersby. Two men marched down the road, toward Death's realm. They were armored and wore blue and gold tabards. Each had a circular shield, blue with Riordan's sigil emblazoned on them in gold. She couldn't see their weapons, but she could only assume they had swords or something else suitably blunt or pointy sheathed on their hips. They were close enough now that Scarlet began to understand their words.

"...don't think that she has any reinforcements to send."

"Can't underestimate a god, though."

"True. But—" the soldier stopped cold. "Hm. I sense something. You feel that?"

Scarlet realized that Dante was still holding her hand when his grip became painfully tight. "Mage hunters," he whispered. His face was white. "We have to run." The soldiers began to bushwhack toward them. It would be mere seconds until they spotted them in their hiding spot.

Scarlet almost nodded, nearly letting him drag her along once more, deeper into the woods. But a pang ran through her, remembering when she and her mother were hunted by Riordan, the headlong dive through the nighttime woods as they ran for their lives. Instead, she released his hand and called forth flame.

"Scarlet—"

"I'm staying." *No more hiding.* It hadn't worked that night with her mother, and it wouldn't work now. She had to be decisive.

Scarlet stepped out of the bushes to face the hunters. She fired a bolt of flame at each of them, causing them to squawk in surprise. One of her shots went wide of its mark, and the other was blocked by the soldier's shield, thrown up in quick response.

The soldiers drew their swords, one charged toward her while the other closed in on Dante. Scarlet let more flames flow from her hands and spun the fire into a ring to surround the man rushing at her. Pouring more energy into the fire, she grew the ring into a whole wall of fire separating them.

Glancing at Dante, she realized that he was struggling with the soldier who had targeted him. He jumped back to avoid a swing of the man's sword, then fired a few energy bolts that only made contact with his enemy's shield. Scarlet focused her powers once more and blasted a fireball at the soldier before he could take another jab at Dante. The fire hit him squarely in the chest, staggering him and singeing his tabard.

Scarlet thought she had a moment to breathe and take account of their situation, but a shield burst through the wall of fire. The flames dissipated with the shield's touch, and the soldier emerged, continuing his charge.

She swiveled back to her original attacker, caught off-guard. He blocked her panicked volley of energy darts and forced her to tumble backward with a swing of his sword. He managed to slice the front of her leg. She yelled out in frustration as her flesh was torn open. She wasn't sure how bad the cut was, only that it hurt with a white-hot pain.

Meanwhile, Dante was doing his best to hold off the other soldier, who had gotten back on his feet. She watched him in her peripheral vision as her own opponent stared her down, grinning.

"Come on now," he said to her. "Why don't you just come with us nicely? No one has to get hurt here."

His condescending tone made Scarlet's blood run as hot as her new wound did. She spat at him. "Never."

The soldier leveled his sword at her. "Hah. You give 'spitfire' a whole new meaning don't you?" He glanced at his partner, who tackled Dante into a tree. "Careful. I'm sure Riordan would want these two little mages alive."

"Yeah, yeah. Just got him pinned now. You getting the girl, or what?"

"No," said Scarlet. "He's not." She shot a series of energy bolts at her attacker, but something felt off. Her control was slipping. None of her shots landed.

"Oh, shush," the soldier said. He bashed her with his shield. She stumbled back, barely able to keep her balance with her injured leg.

"Scarlet!" Dante yelled out.

She had to focus. She had to get them out of here.

Focus, and breathe.

The next burst of flames Scarlet emitted overtook the soldier, coiling around his shield and scorching him. She sent two energy bolts into his chest as he fell, ensuring he was in no shape to pursue her further.

She formed a fire whip and swung it at the soldier pinning Dante. It lashed across his back, he grunted and released Dante. Another well-placed bolt stuck him in the head. He dropped to the ground, limp.

For good measure, she let flames flood from her hands, engulfing the bushes around them in fire.

"Okay," Scarlet said. "Now run?"

Dante stared at her, nodded, and together they fled.

They made it to the edge of the woods before setting up camp. It was fully dark now. They didn't make a campfire. No one had come after them, and they didn't want to change that. Scarlet summoned the tiniest light orb she could muster so that they could see enough to set up camp.

"Do you think they're dead?" Scarlet asked. She was sitting on her laid-out bedroll, her back to a tree. Dante sat across from her, cross-legged.

He opened his mouth, then closed it, hesitating to answer her. The bread and fruit they had eaten sat uneasily in Scarlet's stomach. "You... you did what you had to do."

Scarlet leaned back into the tree, letting the bark prickle through her shirt and into her skin. The discomfort was nothing compared to the pain of the gash the soldier had given her. "Should we have just run?"

"No. You did the right thing. They were onto us. We couldn't have gotten away from them. Even if we did, they'd just track us. But I... froze. They had mage hunter shields."

Scarlet nodded. Every mage in Saridian had a healthy fear of the mage hunters and their ability to both track and defeat mages with their specialized tools. It was kill or be killed. She should know that well enough by now.

It eased her discomfort, though only incrementally. *It's different, being the one to do the killing.*

"How do their shields even deflect magic like that?" Dante asked.

"Part of Riordan's skillset."

"Riordan would have to be nearby for that, wouldn't he?"

"If he was the one who cast the enchantment, yes."

"Wait." Dante's brows furrowed. "Are you saying that mage hunters are... also mages?"

"They have to be. They track mages by sensing magic."

"But... that... goes against everything we're taught. Riordan doesn't allow mortals to use magic. I don't know how mage hunters would even *agree* to it."

Scarlet shrugged. "They don't know. They just do what they're taught to do by Riordan, not understanding that it's *magic* that they're using to do these things. They think anyone could sense magic if someone showed them how. But that's not true unless maybe there is a *lot* of magic. You have to be a mage if you're going to follow trace quantities of magic back to its source."

Dante pondered for a long moment. "I don't understand how they could not know. I was just... so aware of magic as soon as it came to me. How could anyone possibly be so in denial?"

"So my mother was... is... a scholar of sorts. She knows a lot about magic and other things that Riordan doesn't want anyone in Saridian to know. She told me that Riordan's kingdom has the least amount of mages born into it. To be able to use magic, you have to be born with a connection to the veins of magus crystal that run underneath the ground. These veins contain the power of the gods. Primarily, the god that controls the region has the most power there. So, mages are most often attuned to the god of their land. But not always, there are still many anomalous mages who are attuned to one of the others. Anyway, Riordan does his best to cut off any flow of magic throughout the magus crystal in Saridian, since he wants to limit anyone else's connection to those powers.

"This means Saridian has relatively few mages in comparison to other places since Riordan makes it so difficult to connect to the magus grid. But many people, who probably would have been proper mages if born elsewhere, have a sort of... half connection. This is what my mother theorizes, anyway. Riordan tolerates them because they're less of a threat than full mages, and he can use their abilities in his favor to wipe out other mages, without them even realizing that they're using magic."

They sat in the dark silence for a time.

"I want to find Zandra. But also, this rebellion you mentioned... I think I need to find them, for reasons even beyond that. I hate everything that Riordan does. To mages, to all of us. What he's done to Death. The army he is building, and whatever he intends to do with that. He has to be stopped."

This was the first time Scarlet had heard fire in his voice. The will to take action, to push back. She smiled, despite the dire circumstances. *We need this, more people like this.*

They lapsed into silence again. Scarlet wished they could have a campfire. The warmth would be nice, the cold was biting through her clothes, and the crackle of wood burning would fill the gaps in their conversation.

"Your leg," Dante said.

"Yeah." Scarlet had been doing her best to not think about the searing pain radiating from her leg. The wound ran from her hip bone diagonally down to nearly her knee. It wasn't that deep, but it was deep enough. Fleeing had hurt horribly, and she'd barely endured their search for a suitable place to camp. After their harrowing encounter, rest was no longer something they could go without.

"You need to let me bandage it properly. And I could try healing you."

After they were relatively sure they'd lost the mage hunters, Scarlet had stopped the bleeding with a strip of her bloodstained clothing. She hadn't wanted to stop moving for too long until it was darker, in case the hunters had managed to escape their fate.

"Give me the gauze. I can do it," Scarlet said.

Dante dug through his bag, seeming reluctant. Scarlet wondered if she hurt his feelings by rejecting his help. He was better trained for it, but she could bandage a wound well enough on her own.

Once he'd found it, Dante handed her a roll of gauze. "What about healing?"

Scarlet used her waterskin to clean her leg, cringing as the cool water ran over her wound and soaked the thin layer of leather that had protected her from a deeper cut. "No healing."

"We have a long way to travel still. And we might come across more reasons to run. With your leg wounded—"

"If we come across Bronwen or one of the other emissaries, and they're on the verge of death, and you used up a bunch of your energy healing my *leg* and can't save them..." Scarlet shook her head. "That's not happening."

Dante sat up a bit straighter. "Scarlet. Sure, you don't have a mortal wound. But if you're injured tomorrow, it could easily cost you your life. Or mine, if you aren't able to keep me out of danger—I'm no good at fighting, you know this. I'm the support, so let me play my part."

Scarlet was hesitant, but couldn't think of a reasonable argument. "Alright. Fine." She leaned her head back against the tree, bark prickling into her scalp now, and closed her eyes. Hopefully not looking would make the process more bearable. "Only enough to get me through tomorrow."

Dante cleaned her wound more thoroughly and used a cloth to pat it dry. Scarlet grimaced the whole time. Her entire leg was lit up with pain. Then, the familiar tingling of healing magic washed away some of the sensations.

It wasn't the first time he had healed her—Bronwen had supervised him in healing some of Scarlet's scrapes and bruises from training—but it was always an uncomfortable experience. It just felt so... *intimate*. And right now, she was worried about him using up too much energy.

From her understanding, healing was more or less shoving a bunch of energy into a wound—feeding it the energy that it would normally use to mend itself over a matter of days or weeks in a few minutes instead. With a decent healing session, some of the progress happened nearly instantly and the rest of the mending process would be sped up considerably. It was all probably a bit more complicated than that, given the amount of time Dante spent with Bronwen. She had learned that even small amounts of healing could take a lot out of a mage.

"Not too much," Scarlet said after a couple of minutes.

"I know what I'm doing," Dante insisted, but he stopped. As soon as the stream of magic ended, much of the pain returned. It was a little duller than before, but even that was a relief. Dante bandaged her leg. She didn't protest this time, she was too exhausted.

When he was finished, she said softly, "Thanks."

"Of course."

Scarlet slumped into her bedroll, taking cover in its warmth. Dante didn't settle into his own bedroll.

"You sleep," he told her. "I'll keep watch."

"You need rest too."

Dante shook his head. Scarlet's pinprick light orb floated next to him. He reached out and gently enclosed it in his hands, dissipating it. There was only darkness now. Scarlet shivered.

"I can't sleep," he said. "I can't risk it. If I dream, I'll wake blind. You know this."

She did. But he still needed energy for tomorrow. "Dante—"

"It's okay. You keep me safe in the day. Let me keep you safe at night."

His words made the darkness lighten slightly. Scarlet, exhausted, was quickly claimed by her fatigue.

The next morning was filled with tension. Scarlet was sure that Dante felt the same urgency she did. Each moment they wasted could mean the difference between life and death for Death's emissaries.

Scarlet's leg still pained her as they continued down the path through Riordan's realm, though it had mended a fair bit overnight. She grudgingly admitted to herself that Dante was right to heal her. Today's journey would have been unbearable otherwise.

They traveled through the sparse landscape with its open plains and smattering of trees. As the sun rose, the snowy peaks of a mountain started to appear on the horizon. By the time the sun was about to hit its apex, the spires of a tower came into sight. *There it is. Riordan's fortress.*

The road led them through a copse of tall pines that sheltered them from the brunt of the biting wind. Scarlet suddenly realized that Dante had stopped a few paces behind her. He was staring toward the side of the path, into the trees.

"What is it?" she asked. Dante didn't answer, but he didn't need to. The moment after she spoke, Scarlet saw it for herself: a lifeless body, strewn at the base of a tree, a dark pool of blood beneath.

CHAPTER 23

O ver the past couple of weeks, Jarrett's concussion symptoms had more or less subsided, only to be replaced by a constant, gnawing anxiety.

The mist the Ravens had conjured to keep the Vanguard stuck in Rosewood was... effective. One could only walk for fifteen minutes in any direction out of town before hitting it. Anyone who went into the mist stumbled back out an hour or two later, unable to orient themselves well enough to escape through to the other side. Presumably, it worked the same way for anyone trying to get into Rosewood, as no one had come to town—or maybe all the travelers just had the good sense to avoid entering the mist in the first place.

And so as intended, they had been cut off from the rest of the world. They had to be self-sufficient now more than ever. No outside food or supplies. Thankfully, the farms just outside Rosewood had been included in the accessible perimeter. They were also free from attack by more soldiers for the time being, though Jarrett had no doubts that Riordan himself could come for them if he wanted to.

Not everyone was happy with his decision to oust the Ravens. It'd left them in a tight spot. Sure, they had the weapons to use against Riordan, but they couldn't take action until the Ravens stopped their tantrum and dispelled the mist. They could no longer recruit, which was a problem after losing both the support of the Ravens and a number of their troops in the battle over the artifact cache. All they could do was keep training the forces they had, and hope to find some way out of this mess.

In the meantime, Rohan was heading the research on the artifact swords, working with a few other Vanguard mages to try to determine what they did. The intensity of the magic field inside the vault spooked everyone who went into it, so they had carefully extracted one of the swords out of it and left the other four inside for safekeeping. Jarrett still wondered why there had been an empty plinth, but he was far more curious about what the swords could do for them.

I just hope these weapons were worth the sacrifices we made. Morgane's death still weighed heavily on him, and the Vanguard as a whole. She had kept Jarrett steady, and he'd been able to open up to her more than anyone else since he lost his memories. There were days when Jarrett wasn't sure how to go on without both her friendship and leadership. But giving up would be an insult to everything Morgane had built, so he kept on.

So far, there had been no breakthroughs with Rohan's experiments. Jarrett tried to be optimistic about his daily meeting with him as he strolled down the street. Perhaps today there would be some illumination.

Hera and Korene rushed to interrupt his path to Rohan's house. Jarrett's heart jumped to his throat as he wondered what emergency he'd have to deal with next. The two women weren't a common pair. They disagreed immensely on how to handle almost every situation and were clashing more intensely than usual since the battle over the vault. The looks on their faces as they approached gave him no comfort.

"What now?" he asked them.

Hera had to catch her breath before answering. "Someone made it through the mist."

"Two 'someones'," Korene corrected.

"Ravens?"

"No," Hera said. "Well... Leandra escorted them through the mist, but she left after. She said they were recruits for us—one is a mage. The other..."

Korene crossed her arms. "The other is a mage hunter."

Hera cleared her throat. "I don't think he's actually—"

"You're just gullible."

Jarrett waved his hands as if it could wipe away their bickering. "Where are they?"

"Town hall," Korene said. "Leon and a couple of the others are keeping an eye on them."

"I was on my way to meet Rohan. Can you let him know I'll be delayed?"

The women agreed to do so, and Jarrett turned around to head to the town center instead. His mind ran wild, theorizing about who had shown up on their doorstep, and why the Ravens had let them through.

When he got to the town hall, he found Leon and the newcomers in the council room. Leon stood near the door, and the newcomers were seated at the council table. They weren't what Jarrett was expecting. They were young: a teen girl and a boy on the cusp of manhood—not an experienced mage and a hardened soldier like he had originally imagined.

The girl's hair was tawny blonde, cut short and unevenly. Her eyes looked glazed over, disengaged with the world around her. Two vertical scars marred her cheeks. *They magebranded the poor girl.* She looked tiny next to the boy, who was bulky with muscle. His head was shorn close to his scalp, and he wore blue and gold. Both looked near to collapse, covered in scratches and bruises, with clear signs of exhaustion written across their sagging forms.

"So," Jarrett folded his arms, "who are you two, exactly?"

The newcomers glanced at each other. After the hesitation, the girl was the one to speak. "I'm Zandra. And this is Barek."

"Why did you come here?"

Zandra continued to answer for them. "We were told that this is the home of the resistance."

"And you wanted to find the resistance because...?"

"I'm a mage."

"And?"

Zandra shrugged. "Isn't that reason enough? I want to fight the king. The Tyrant."

Jarrett gestured towards Barek. "And him?"

"I'm a defector," he said.

"You had a change of heart?"

Barek scrunched his eyebrows. "I'm not sure I ever wanted to be there."

Jarrett had to pause to think. The Vanguard had gained recruits with many different backgrounds, but never had an ex-mage hunter come to them. They were usually among the most loyal to Riordan and known to be the most cruel among the Tyrant's soldiers. "How can we trust you?" Jarrett asked.

"He saved me," Zandra said. "The mage hunters discovered me and..." She pointed to the brand marks on her face. Jarrett thought she was about to say more, but she turned away.

"You don't hear much about mages breaking free once they've been caught," Leon said from behind Jarrett.

The mage hunters were effective at their jobs. Fae was one of the few mages he'd met before this that had survived after being branded. Once a mage's face was marred, it was nearly impossible to find refuge if they managed to escape the grasp of the soldiers who'd discovered them.

"Well, we're here," Zandra said. "And if this is the rebellion, we want to join. We risked our lives to find you, and we were barely lucky enough to come across—what are they called, the Ravens?—before we were caught. We have information and we want to help. Please." Her voice was desperate, and it scratched in a way that sounded painful.

"We are indeed the rebellion—we call ourselves the Vanguard." Jarrett took a seat at the table across from the newcomers. "What information do you have?"

The newcomers locked eyes again, and this time Barek spoke. "There was a reason we were able to find you. The king knows about you, and that this is your base of operations."

Leon swore. Jarrett's head spun, processing this dire news. *I was a fool to think the Tyrant still had no idea about us.*

"If you have any other bases, he doesn't know of them," Barek continued. "Or, at least not that he has told his soldiers about. He interrogates every mage his soldiers capture, prying them for information about any kind of opposition."

"Wait," Leon said, "Riordan is imprisoning mages?"

"Yes," Zandra said. Her voice was soft but still carried a great weight. "There's a whole prison just for mages. Barek broke me free."

"A mage prison?" Leon was aghast. "I've never heard of anything like that." He glanced at Jarret and the two locked eyes, silently sharing their horror.

Jarrett pressed the strangers for more information. "Where? How many mages are imprisoned there?"

"I'd never heard of it either until I was assigned there as a guard. It's deep in a tunnel beneath Riordan's castle. There were maybe... around thirty mages, when we left."

Thirty mages that Riordan was keeping, instead of executing. Jarrett couldn't wrap his mind around it. He'd imprisoned more mages than they had in the Vanguard. "How could he keep that many mages imprisoned? I would think that they would be able to break free, especially as none of the guards would have magic."

Barek opened his mouth to speak, but Zandra interrupted. "That's not true. Mage hunters have magic."

"I—what?" Barek's eyebrows furrowed.

"They have magic. *You* have magic. At least to some extent. How else would hunters be able to sense us?"

The room was quiet for a few moments as Jarrett and the others considered this.

"The way the king reviles mages..." Leon said, "I never really thought to look at it that way. I assumed there was some other technique non-mages used. Are you certain about this?"

Zandra shrugged. "I don't have any training, but it makes sense to me."

Jarrett looked over to Barek, whose pale face had gone even whiter in his apparent bewilderment. *I suppose it would come as a shock to suddenly learn you're a member of the group you had been subjugating.* "As much of an interesting revelation as this is, it doesn't my question. The mage hunters aren't even aware of their magic. So how were they able to keep mages under control?"

Barek cleared his throat. "The mages are drained of all their energy. The only reason I was able to escape with Zandra was that she was still relatively new to the prison. The other mages... I would have been surprised if any could even walk still, much less use magic."

Riordan is... draining them somehow? Curious. Jarrett wanted to ask more about how Riordan was accomplishing this, along with *why* the Tyrant would now choose to capture mages instead of executing them. Or, certain mages at least. He did not doubt that the king would still sacrifice mages to the flame to serve as a lesson to all others about disobeying his law. He held back his questions after looking at Zandra's haunted face. The last thing he wanted to do was to emphasize how close to death she had come. Anger made his throat tight. *She's so young. Riordan's cruelty truly has no bounds.*

"And the Ravens, they were amenable to simply guiding you through the mist?" Leon asked.

"Yes. They were likewise interested in our story and brought us through to be of use to you." Barek looked to Zandra, whose face fell. It was clear that the two had no more energy for questioning. "We've been through a lot, though. Could we rest before we continue?"

"Of course. We have lots of time to talk." Jarrett stood. "After all, you're stuck here with us now."

Jarrett decided the best place to board the newcomers was at his own house, at least until more permanent arrangements were made. He could keep an eye on them that way. The rest of the council was wary of this decision. He couldn't blame them. Accepting two strangers into his home in these uncertain times was probably not his brightest idea.

In the end, he agreed to have Rohan stay with him too for extra security. Jarrett took pity on the exhausted newcomers and let Zandra have his bedroom, and Barek the spare room. Jarrett and Rohan would sleep on the couches in the main living area. He wasn't about to make the poor kids sleep on the floor after everything they'd gone through.

After getting the two settled into their respective rooms, Jarrett finally got a chance to confer with Rohan about the progress on the weapon research.

"There's not much to tell, unfortunately," Rohan told him as he searched through a pile of Jarrett's spare blankets. "All we've figured out is that somehow, magic flows through the crystal. In the vault, this much is obvious. Even you could feel it down there. So, this week's experiment was trying to store magic in the sword, to be used later by a mage."

Rohan found the thickest woolen blanket and laid it on the couch he'd be sleeping on. Jarrett raised an eyebrow. As miserable as the Saridi weather usually was, it was actually warm out for once. Rohan was a strange man.

"And?" Jarrett prodded.

"And, nothing. We can't figure out how to get magic into it."

"So that isn't what it's meant for."

"It doesn't seem so."

"And you haven't tried drawing blood with it yet?"

Rohan took a seat on the couch. "No. Too dangerous." He sighed. "That's probably the key to figuring these swords out, but who knows what it could do? If these are god-slaying weapons, I imagine a single cut could kill a mortal."

"Right." Jarrett took a seat opposite Rohan and dropped his head into his hands. "We really need a win, you know? We're just sitting here, waiting for Riordan to come get us. He knows. He knows we're here. The mist may keep out his troops, but they won't keep out a god."

"I know. These swords, this crystal, it's stumped us, but we won't give up."

"You'll figure it out. There's still time, for now."

"Pardon me—" The voice came from Jarrett's room, startling him. Zandra stood in the doorway, dressed in oversized clothes Jarrett had loaned her, as her own were filthy. "I didn't mean to overhear. But I heard you say something about crystal. Are you talking about magus crystal?"

"Magus crystal?" Rohan asked. "What's that?"

"It's clear, colorless crystal," Zandra said. "It, uh, drains magic. It can be used for other things too. But I don't know much."

"That might be what we're talking about," Jarrett said. He gestured for her to come sit with them, and she obliged, sinking into an armchair next to him. "Is there anything else you know about it?"

Zandra's eyes flickered back and forth uneasily. "Not really. But they used it." Zandra shivered. "In the mage prison."

Rohan leaned forward. "Used it how?"

"The prison was underground. It was in a cave of magus crystal. And, um..." She took a shuddering breath. "I'm sorry. I didn't know how hard it would be to talk about it. I just don't want to think about it anymore."

Jarrett felt a pang of sympathy. "It's alright. We don't have to talk about it right now." He got up to pour her a cup from the teapot. She gave him a weak smile as she accepted the mug.

"No. If it could be important, I want you to know as much as I know." Zandra took a deep breath and stared straight ahead of her as she spoke. "They used spikes of magus crystal to pierce our skin. And it drained us, not just of our magic but of any energy. The mages... the other ones, who had been there for longer than me... they're alive, but they nearly looked like corpses."

She seemed so small. She was neither a child nor an adult but wavered between the two. Fragile one moment, confident the next. The more Jarrett heard, the more his rage grew. *Damn Riordan for throwing this girl into a torturous prison, her only "crime" being that she is a mage.*

"That's awful," Rohan said. "But it is useful to know what our swords might accomplish."

"Zandra. I am very sorry that all of this happened to you," Jarrett said. He tried to speak steadily, though he wasn't sure he accomplished it. "We are doing our best to stop Riordan. The Tyrant *must* fall." He nearly snarled the last four words.

It dawned on Jarrett suddenly that she was someone's daughter. She had come from somewhere before all this happened. He almost asked her if she had family before he remembered that she was a mage. And if her family hadn't known she was a mage before, they would when they saw her scarred face.

"I want to help," she said. She clutched her teacup, her knuckles white. "In any way I can. But I... I need to sleep now, if that's okay."

"Yes, of course. Please, rest," Rohan said. "And, you are helping. Really. Learning anything we can about this magus crystal is of utmost importance. If you can think of anything else, please let us know."

Zandra paused. "The Ravens know about magus crystal. They're how I know what it's called now. Are you not working with them?"

Shame ran through Jarrett's veins. Was he failing the Vanguard by refusing the Ravens' help? *Perhaps we would be farther ahead with them. But, if we can't trust them, how can we work together?* "It's... a complicated matter,"

Jarrett replied. "We can speak more of it in the morning. For now, I hope you can get a good night's rest."

Zandra nodded. "I hope so too." She set her teacup down and retired to Jarrett's room.

"More information than we've been able to come up with in weeks just dropped onto our lap," Rohan commented when she was gone.

Jarrett considered this. "It's lucky," he said. Zandra's situation pulled heavily on his heartstrings. *It couldn't all be a ruse, could it? Her pain seems so real.* "*Too* lucky?"

Rohan shrugged. "To just march in here, with some critical information, right when we need it... I don't know. I don't want to doubt them. They're just kids and it seems like they've had a harrowing experience. But I also can't help but wonder, and be a little paranoid. Am I crazy? Should I just go ahead and trust them?"

"Trust?" Jarrett shook his head. "That's always the tricky thing, isn't it? They might be young, but we can't afford to trust anyone who hasn't proven themselves. Not anymore."

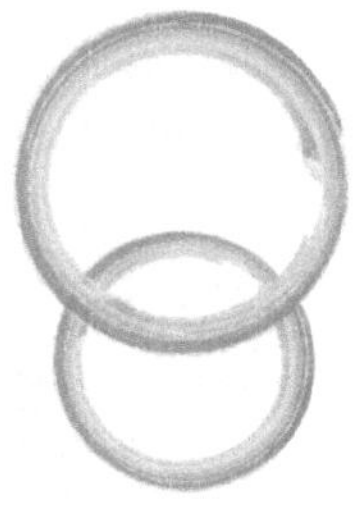

CHAPTER 24

T he body they found in the copse of trees wasn't Bronwen's; not that this discovery made Dante feel much better.

He knelt next to the corpse of the unknown man. He'd been an emissary, made evident by the markings on his hand. Dante had seen bodies before, back in Ferrick's clinic. Some patients were beyond saving. But it was different to know that this man had been killed. A fatal blow had been punched through the chainmail he wore under his cloak and had pierced deep into his chest.

He was dealing with the discovery better than Scarlet was. She had confirmed it wasn't Bronwen and otherwise kept her distance. She turned away and was staring at the path ahead of them, arms crossed. He wondered if this hadn't been her first time seeing someone dead. *Maybe she saw her sister. And... she did just kill those soldiers, in all likelihood.*

He didn't know if he should be thinking of death differently after training with the god of Death. She'd told him that souls move on to the Nextworld when they die in this one, and she didn't seem to think that it was a tragic thing. But, did she know what the Nextworld even was? Even if it was an alright place, people would still be separated from all of their friends and family. What if they weren't done in this World yet? Was that why Scarlet's sister was still present in Death's realm? There were so many questions left unanswered.

Scarlet broke him out of his thoughts. "I think there are more."

Dante used his waterskin to wash off the blood that had stained his hands during his inspection of the body, then went over to Scarlet.

She pointed out past the grove of trees they stood in. There were more bodies strewn out in the open plains.

"Okay. Let's... let's go see." Dante didn't want to take the lead, but Scarlet stood fast and obviously wasn't going to, so he headed up their journey out of the trees.

Scarlet snapped out of her brooding and caught up to him. "There could be more mage hunters, too."

"Yeah."

They investigated the closest one. Before they approached it, Dante turned to Scarlet. "Are you okay?"

"Why would I be okay?"

Her blunt words almost made Dante flinch. He supposed it hadn't been the greatest question he could've asked, under current circumstances. "I know that none of this is remotely okay. I just want to make sure..."

"I'm okay enough," she conceded.

"Alright."

Dante stepped up to the body. It was a woman this time, another emissary. Multiple wounds had been pierced into her, leaving a pool of blood to soak into the earth. Dante's stomach grew queasy. Another corpse. He could do nothing to help. They were too late.

"What are we going to do?" Scarlet asked quietly. "They're all... they're all dead, aren't they?"

"There could still be some alive, hiding out. Or captured." Dante tried to believe the words as he said them. "But the ones who are dead... we should bury them."

"We can't dig that many graves. The hunters would come after us long before we finished. It would make a lot of smoke, but maybe we could build a pyre—"

"No!" Dante felt like something snapped within him. "You don't... you don't *get* it, do you?"

Scarlet jumped back a little at his outburst. "What?"

"Burning is for mages."

Scarlet stared back at him blankly. "Well, they *are* mages."

"No. It's a *punishment* for mages." Dante stopped. His breaths were ragged. He stared at her, and she stared back, face to face. "You're from Saridian. You're a mage. Your mother is a mage. How can you not know this?"

"I... I don't know. My mother tried to protect me from a lot of things."

"That's how they execute mages, Scarlet. They burn them at the stake in the capital. They do it as a show, a spectacle. For entertainment, and more importantly, as a lesson. A promise. A *threat*."

Scarlet looked down at her feet. "I honestly didn't know. So that's... that's why you're afraid of my fire."

Dante didn't know if he should continue, but his thoughts kept tumbling out of his mouth. "When my father first caught me doing magic... he did a lot of things, but the worst of it was that he took me to Kingsmount. He brought me to a burning. So that I knew what would happen to me if I ever used it again."

"Dante, I'm sorry—"

"I'll never forget it. His plan worked, for a long time. I swore to never use magic again. But then the dreams started. The ones that were more than dreams. I couldn't escape it anymore." Dante stared down at his hands. Hands that had healed—both with and without magic. Hands that had fought, though never well. Hands that could kill with the bolts of magic he could summon. *I'm a mage. Bronwen tried to show me how magic could be good and yet... I still feel ashamed. Who am I, to wield these powers?*

"Dante. Dante!" Scarlet took him by the shoulders. He was sure she had said his name more times than he had heard it. Her anguish seemed to leak into him. She worried about him, about the fate of Bronwen. She was furious that Death had sent the emissaries to their deaths. There was sorrow, too, at the fact that she'd had to kill as well. It was necessary, but that didn't mean there wasn't remorse, too.

"I should have known," she told him. "My mother told me that in the Galapian Islands, they cremate the dead. But while she is from the islands, I was born in Saridian. I don't know if she hid it from me to protect me from the fear of Riordan's brutality, or if she didn't want me to feel ashamed of my abilities, the fire that runs in my blood. But still. I should have known."

To be free from the shame of one's own magic... The roaring boil of Dante's temper quieted to a simmer. He wasn't used to being angry. Usually, the only person who could get on his nerves was Zandra. He took a sharp breath at the thought of his sister.

"Are we okay?" Scarlet asked. The tension between them was palpable.

"We're okay enough."

They took account of the rest of the bodies. There were six in all, spread across the open field, each of them emissaries. If any of Riordan's soldiers had fallen, they had since been taken away.

The emissaries' corpses would stay here for now. As much as it pained Dante to leave them behind, they didn't have time for burials and he would rather see them rot in the open than go through the disrespect of burning.

As they moved farther down the path, more of Riordan's fortress became visible. No mage hunters appeared, but it was impossible to be at ease in the looming shadow of the enemy's lair.

"There's only open plains between here and the fortress, it looks like," Scarlet said. "I don't know that we should get much closer." She stared at the looming structure, almost longingly. Dante was sure she wished they could go and try to confront Calder or Riordan themselves, but even she wasn't foolish enough to think that was a real option. "We haven't found Bronwen. Do you think there's any chance..."

"I don't know. Maybe they captured him? Though I'm not sure if being thrown in the mage prison is a kinder fate than the alternative." Dante's heart ached at the thought of Bronwen, either imprisoned by Riordan, or dead somewhere, lying unburied. "But I guess we should search the last of the trees around here, and then..."

"And then we go back." Scarlet paused. "Or I guess, *I* go back. After I open a portal for you."

"Even if I go, I'm making sure you get back to Death's realm safely."

"If? I thought we decided."

Dante drew in deep breaths, trying to stop himself from hyperventilating over the thought of being thrust back into Saridian. *It didn't exactly go well for me the last time I wandered alone.* "I feel like... I'll just get myself killed. When we ran into the mage hunters, you saw what happened. I froze."

"No. You wanted to run. Which, if you're alone... is probably the smarter option, to be honest."

Not exactly a ringing endorsement. "Can you even open a portal?"

The corner of Scarlet's mouth twisted. "Don't know 'til I try."

"Plus, if I go, you'll be alone."

Scarlet got sharp. "I can be alone."

"The only way to stop this, for real, is to stop Riordan. So maybe I should focus on that. You could be the last of Death's emissaries. Maybe now, Death will let us help. If we can work with her, then at least we aren't just a couple of mortals trying to defeat a god alone."

"She also might not! Enough excuses. This is a way to take action. Don't be too afraid to take that chance while you have it."

Dante bristled. "I would do anything for my sister. But right now, if she's alive, I have to believe that she can handle things on her own. I never thought I'd say this, but I have to stay and keep learning magic. The situation is dire, Death is going to need us."

Scarlet grabbed at his sleeve suddenly. "Dante—"

He almost ripped his arm away from her, but then he saw what she saw.

Calder had appeared in front of a nearby copse of trees in the direction that would lead them back out of Riordan's realm. He wore the same armor and tabard as the mage hunters had. At his feet was a slumped figure, wearing a black cloak. Dante's breath caught in his throat. "Do we run?" he whispered. "Or fight?"

Scarlet's eyes snapped between Dante, Calder, and the cloaked figure on the ground. Calder was too far to hear them, but close enough that Dante could see his grin. The man made no move toward them yet.

"That could be Bronwen," Scarlet said. "We fight."

"Calder is... out of our league. Are you sure?"

"Yes," Scarlet said, without hesitation. "If we run, he'll catch us anyway. You patched my leg up, but I'd still be slow. Plus, I still have some tricks up my sleeve."

Dante exhaled a breath he hadn't realized he'd been holding. *I wish she wasn't right.* Together, they approached Calder. When he saw their aggressive stances, he held up his hands in mock surrender.

Calder called out to them, "Settle down. I'm not here to fight you."

"Somehow I doubt that," Scarlet growled at him.

Calder shrugged. "Believe what you'd like. But listen carefully if you want your friend to live."

Dante felt as if daggers stabbed at his heart. *Does that mean that's Bronwen?* The cloak covered the head of whoever it was Calder loomed over, and they were faced away. He could, however, see them taking shallow breaths.

Scarlet's voice was steady, though Dante saw her trembling. "What do you want?"

Calder's grin widened. "Two things. First, a trade." He kicked the cloaked man, rolling him over. It was, in fact, Bronwen. He groaned, and let out a mouthful of blood. Dante's breath hitched at the sight of his mentor. Bronwen's face was unnaturally pale, and parts of his cloak were dark with blood. Dante's instincts fought with each other—half of him wanted to run up and immediately start tending to him, and the other half was too terrified to take a single step closer to Calder.

"You can have him back," Calder said. "But in exchange, I want *you.*" His eyes were locked onto Scarlet.

"What?" Dante took half a step back. *No, no he can't take Scarlet.*

Next to him, Scarlet was stiff, bracing herself. "You'd let Bronwen and Dante go?"

"Yes, they'd be free to tuck their tails and run back to Death."

"Scarlet—" Dante started, but Scarlet put her hand up in a motion for him to stop.

"What's the second thing?" she asked.

"For Dante to deliver a message to Death."

"Which is?"

"That Riordan spared her favorite: Bronwen. He wants her to consider it a bridal gift."

"Wait," Scarlet said. Though she hadn't summoned fire, Dante could feel the heat rolling off of her. "Riordan wants her to *marry* him? That's what this is all about?"

"Among other things, yes."

"I—" Scarlet shook her head, briefly at a loss for words. "He is terrorizing her in an attempt to *seduce* her? I suppose 'seduce' is not even the right word. That is insanity! It's disgusting!" She spat on the ground beside her.

"And you are simply a pest," Calder responded.

"So what do you want Scarlet for?" Dante cut back in. "She has nothing to do with any of this."

"Untrue. Because of her mother's involvement in this struggle, she is *immensely* relevant."

"I'm a bargaining chip," Scarlet stated flatly.

"A keen observation." Calder's sneer sent a shiver through Dante's body. "Your mother is quite the woman. I've never seen someone hold up to torture quite like her. And so dedicated to her secrets, as well as her family. It's a shame that she's going to have to choose which she'd like to keep."

"What do you want from her?" Scarlet managed to keep her voice steady, but Dante knew it must have taken significant effort to do so.

"She hid something from Riordan. Something he *dearly* wants. Not very nice of her to do something like that, don't you think? Ah, well. Nothing that a visit from her *remaining* daughter can't solve."

For a moment, Dante's vision doubled, then snapped back into place. Disoriented, he nearly toppled over but managed to widen his stance to steady himself. Next to him, Scarlet was vibrating. He could feel the embers of her rage, ready to ignite. He turned to her, and then somehow he was both looking at her, as well as looking at Calder, the two images superimposed on each other. Then the image of Calder took over and locked firmly into place.

He was looking out from Scarlet's perspective. Out of the corner of his eye, he could see his own body. It was immensely disorienting.

How is this happening while I'm awake? *he wondered.* Why is this happening?

The voice he had heard in his dreams once before spoke to him again. **Because you need to see what real power is. To *feel* real power.**

Dante was too dizzy to process what any of this could mean. He gave in and let himself meld fully into Scarlet's perspective.

"So," said Calder, "do we have a deal?"

Scarlet's hands were balled into fists, her fingernails digging into her palms. If she gave herself over to him, Dante and Bronwen would be safe, and she would be taken to where her mother was. But would she be in any position to free her? Dante had told her that they drained mages of their energy. If she had no magic, there wasn't any chance for her to prevail. She would simply be used against her mother.

The other option was to fight Calder. Her fingertips burned, wanting to release streams of fire at her enemy. She thought back to her extremely brief fight with Death, if it could even be classified as such. She'd been handily outmatched. Would a conflict with Calder be much the same? He wasn't a god, but he would be able to call upon Riordan's power.

"Time is ticking," Calder said. Scarlet hated his wolfish grin. "You'd better decide before your friend here bleeds out."

Scarlet, loathe to take her eyes off her enemy, spared a glance down toward Bronwen. He was so pale, and there was so much blood... *Will Dante be able to patch him up?*

Her mind spiraled in anxiety. She had to decide her path. The only way to save them all was to fight and win. The thread connecting her to Death was pulsing, a reminder that she, too, had a god to call upon for energy. The bond was weaker than normal, but she hadn't been cut off from Death the way the other emissaries had.

I have to accept Death's power. It's the only way.

As she resolved herself to this, she pulled upon Death's strength. Immediately, the god's power began pouring into her, like molten lava running through her veins. She unclenched her hands, and flames cascaded from her palms. An aura of inferno wrapped around her, surrounding her in its red-hot blaze. It didn't burn her; it *was* her.

Scarlet grinned back at Calder. "I decline your offer." She could feel him drawing upon his power, beginning his attempt to steal her energy to use as his own. *I have to end this, fast, or he'll bleed me dry.*

She drew her hands up to her chest and called in all the fire that encircled her. It wrapped around her body, her arms, then concentrated into a roaring blaze held in her hands. She pushed her hands out from her chest and sent the ball of fire speeding toward Calder. As it flew, she willed it to condense further, until it became a thin, molten arrow of flame.

Her aim was true, and the fire arrow struck Calder in the chest. The blow caused him to roar in pain as he stumbled back, and then collapsed. It had pierced through his armor, and a tendril of smoke rippled up from his wound. The bolt of flame carried so much energy that he wasn't able to absorb it fast enough to save himself.

Is that it? Did I do it, just like that? Her body felt empty, drained of the exhilarating power that had coursed through it only moments ago. She was so cold now, without it. Her head spun. She had nothing left. Her knees gave out, and she crumpled to the ground.

Dante snapped back to his own body. His vision was obscured by a blanket of white for a moment but cleared in the span of a few blinks. Scarlet had just collapsed next to him.

"Scarlet!" He dropped down to his knees to examine her. He froze when he saw Calder stir, rolling over from where he had fallen. Adrenaline rushed through his veins. *Am I going to have to finish what Scarlet started?*

Calder didn't get up all the way. He propped himself up with one arm, and with the other made a gesture that made the air around him ripple. *He's opening a portal,* Dante realized. Before he could gather himself to try to stop him, the man pushed himself through the hole into the World, and the portal promptly closed behind him.

Dante exhaled. *Well, I might need all my energy to take care of Bronwen and Scarlet anyway.*

With that, he gathered Scarlet's stiff body into his arms. Her skin was ice cold. A lump formed in his throat as he remembered Bronwen's warnings about using too much magic. *If you use all of your energy, it could result in* death. "Scarlet!" He tried to let some of his energy flow into her skin, not a true healing but a boost of vitality that he hoped would help stabilize her.

Scarlet's eyes fluttered open. She blinked a few times, dazed. "What happened?" she mumbled.

"Calder portaled away," Dante told her. "Are you okay?"

"Yeah. I think. Just... lightheaded." She pulled herself up out of his arms. She rubbed her hands on her arms as if trying to warm herself. "Bronwen! Go check Bronwen."

Dante nodded and rushed over to his mentor's side. Scarlet heaved herself up and followed behind more slowly. Dante was surprised to find that Bronwen was conscious.

"Ah," Bronwen croaked, "You two are a sight for sore... well, sore everything."

"We're here, we're going to help you. I'm going to heal you." Dante swallowed hard. Oozing wounds covered Bronwen. His face was slashed, and his shoulder was cleaved open, but what worried Dante the most was that Bronwen held his hand over a dark stain on his abdomen.

Bronwen shook his head. "Dante, you haven't done anything like this before... bruises, scrapes, yes... but this..."

"He healed me yesterday," Scarlet said. "It was more than a papercut."

"This is different," Bronwen insisted. "This could *kill* him."

"I can do this," Dante said. His hands shook as he helped Bronwen roll onto his back. Bronwen's face contorted with every movement. Calder had barely spared their dear friend; he wouldn't last much longer in this condition. *I have to do this. I have to heal him.*

Bronwen's words were labored, and perspiration dripped down his dirty brow as he resigned to Dante's decision. "Dante. Listen carefully. Don't... try to do it all. Just... stabilize me. Get me well enough... that we can return to Deianira. No more."

"I'm getting tired of people telling me not to heal them. You taught me well, Bronwen. Trust me now." Dante hoped he could fake confidence until he felt it. He and Scarlet cleaned Bronwen's wounds as gently and thoroughly as they could using their waterskins before he began the healing session. He clasped his hands together and called forth the energy he needed to mend what was broken.

The energy wouldn't come. Usually, after a few moments of focus, he would feel tingling, starting at his fingertips and then spreading into his hands and arms. Instead, his body was shaking, his heart fluttering as fast as a hummingbird's wings.

Then there was a hand on his back. "Take a deep breath," Scarlet told him. "In, and out. In... and out." She seemed to have recovered from her shock, and her steadiness permeated through her touch. It gave him courage to know his efforts had brought her that much strength. She coached him for a few more breaths before withdrawing her hand and taking a step back.

The magic coalesced this time, obeying his wishes. He allowed it to stream into Bronwen. He could feel so much of the wrongness in his mentor's body, so many aches and incisions. Not enough blood. Internal damage. Dante sussed out the worst of it, channeling the energy to those parts, coaxing organs into patching themselves, torn flesh to pull together once more.

Dante was lightheaded when Bronwen panted out, "Enough, enough." It was followed by a series of punctuating coughs, and he sat up. Dante ceased his flow of magic and sat back. Now that he stopped, he was frighteningly woozy. He closed his eyes to stop the trees from spinning around him.

Scarlet said from above them, "We can't linger here long, can we?"

"No," Bronwen said, his breathing still labored. "We've been here... been here too long already."

"Come on, then." Scarlet offered Dante a hand up, but he waved it away. "I need a second."

She helped Bronwen up first instead. He groaned as he rose, and still held his side, but some color had returned to his skin. "Come on," she said to Dante, insistently thrusting her hand at him. "Up."

He took her hand, wobbled to his feet, and they slowly began the journey back to Deianira.

CHAPTER 25

After a grueling expedition, an exhausted Dante, a remarkably sturdy Scarlet, and a gravely injured Bronwen arrived back at Deianira. Progress had been slow, it took them at least twice as long to get back than there in the first place.

Dante's head spun after he had used so much of his energy to heal his mentor. He would have asked to lean on Scarlet during the first leg of their journey had she not needed to support Bronwen. His light-headedness didn't leave him, even after they slept, but he was functional enough.

Bronwen, on the other hand, faded with each step. Dante offered to heal him more, but Bronwen refused, insisting he was well enough to get back to Deianira.

Dante was sure the whole way back that mage hunters or Riordan himself would appear behind them, ready to steal Scarlet away and finish off him and Bronwen. Scarlet said little on the way back, returning to her brooding ways. He didn't push her to talk.

It was night now as they returned to the stream of souls, the twin moons shining above them. After the two of them loaded the nearly unconscious Bronwen into the boat to cross back over to Death's realm, their eyes met. Even in the dim moonlight, Dante felt the sadness hidden behind her deep blue irises.

"He needs you, doesn't he?" Scarlet asked.

Dante dipped his head in a defeated nod. Bronwen wouldn't survive without his healing. If they followed through on their plan to send Dante to the World, they would be dooming his mentor. Their plan was truly dead.

They paddled across the river and found Death waiting for them at the opposite pier. She took account of Bronwen's condition solemnly. Together, they lugged him as gently as they could out of the boat. Death cradled him and pressed her fingertips against his pale forehead. "Was he... the only one?"

Dante and Scarlet looked at each other. Neither of them wanted to say it. Scarlet cleared her throat. "As far as we know... yes," she said. "Calder tried to trade Bronwen for me. To use against my mother. He wanted to spare Bronwen for you as a gift."

Death snarled at that. Then, they took Bronwen up to his quarters. His rooms seemed so luxurious, especially now, after the difficult days on the road. Bronwen finally stirred after they settled him into his bed.

"Let me finish healing you now," Dante insisted. He couldn't stand Bronwen being in this much pain any longer.

Bronwen spoke, with obvious effort. "I think it's over, Dante. I'm sorry."

"What are you talking about? I can heal you. You're going to be okay."

Bronwen shook his head. "I feel it. Infection. Internal damage. It's too much. You're a good healer, but your energy reserves aren't large enough to take this on. You'll go down with me if you try."

Scarlet spun toward Death. "You saved me. Can't you save him?"

Death shook her head. "Keeping you alive took some complicated magic on my part, as well as Bronwen's aid. While I can give him energy through our bond, I'm not a proper healer. I can sustain him for a time, but not long enough for his critical wounds to heal. If we had a team of healers, or someone as talented as Bronwen himself is at healing... there would be a chance. But a single, apprentice healer, and with my powers drained as they are... no, it won't be enough."

Dante felt numb. "There's nothing we can do?" he whispered.

Death took a moment to consider. "You are not a powerful mage, Dante. I am sure you know this. You are satisfactory, and competent in some areas, but you lack the capacity to draw energy from deep within yourself. You cannot heal Bronwen from this brink alone. But, if you could draw energy from another source, well—that could change everything."

"From another source?"

Scarlet gazed flatly at Death. "She wants you to become an emissary."

"Yes. If you bond with me, you can draw on my power, and you can use it to save Bronwen. I don't have much energy left, but what I do is better utilized by you rather than me, in this instance."

Dante's throat was dry. He had felt it. Death's power, flowing through Scarlet as she took down Calder. Even with her strength being drained, the god had more power than Dante could have imagined. *And that voice again... who is that? How are they making me have all these visions, asleep and now awake as well? Is this anything like Scarlet hearing her sister?*

"You can't do it," Scarlet stated.

Death glared at her, her sharp-nailed fingers coiling in frustration. "Are you arguing against saving Bronwen?"

"No," said Scarlet. Her words were acidic. "I'm arguing against Dante committing his life to you."

"It isn't your decision. Dante?"

Dante's emotions were tied into a knot he wasn't sure how to even begin untangling. "Do I have time to think about it?"

"One more healing session," Bronwen said, "and Death holding onto my soul... I believe I can last the night."

"Bronwen, I want to save you, I just..."

"Take the time. I understand."

Scarlet and Death left so that Dante could focus on healing. During the session, Dante paid close attention to the infections and internal damage that reigned within Bronwen's body, and he gave in to the fact that his healing wouldn't be able to outpace it. Death was right; he would need help if he was going to save his mentor.

After the healing, Dante retreated to his room. Before he went in, he knocked on Scarlet's door, but she didn't answer. Dante sighed. Some advice would be useful, but at the same time, Death was right. This was his decision. Maybe it was better he made it on his own.

The moment he lay down in his bed, he knew he wouldn't fall asleep. It was like the sleepless days when he was pushing back his dream of Zandra, though this restlessness had a different flavor to it. It was rare that he wanted to escape from his waking mind more than his sleeping one. The churning of his thoughts made him queasy.

What would my life be like as an emissary? If it weren't for the threat of Riordan, living in the Crossworld wouldn't be so bad. But after seeing Riordan in his vision, and Calder twice in the flesh, the danger this god and his minions posed was no theory.

At some point, he had to find out what happened to Zandra. The necessity of helping Bronwen had overridden the potential of Scarlet opening a portal for him. There was a chance they could carry out that plan later, but if he were to become an emissary, he wouldn't necessarily have the opportunity to sneak away.

Being here temporarily was one thing. But permanently? *Is this what I want my life to be?*

And yet, how could he leave? Scarlet would be alone again. While their friendship had been slow to develop initially, it was unbearable to think about abandoning her now. Maybe he should have held less affection for her, with how sharp she could still be sometimes. But there was a softness to her too when she was able to let down her defenses for a moment.

He'd never had a friend like her before. Back in Briarglen, he had friends, sure—it still hurt to think of his best friend, Milo, selling him out for using magic. Since he'd come to the Crossworld, he hadn't had to hide that part of himself. Nor had he had to fight to justify his interest in healing and herbalism over skills that he had no talent or interest in.

Adjusting to being a mage was a challenge. But for the first time in his life, he felt like he might... belong. And while he and Scarlet struggled with different aspects of their training and isolation in Deianira, he also felt like he had someone who was in this with him. Scarlet had his back. She worked on their friendship even though it was difficult for her. She saved him from the mage hunters in Riordan's realm. She was there for him after waking from his worst visions. She was the only one who he'd even *told* about his visions.

And then, of course, there was Bronwen. A man who had mentored Dante and accepted him more than his parents ever had. His old master, Ferrick, had supported Dante as well, but more for his own benefit than anything else. Dante could tell that Bronwen cared about him beyond his usefulness.

His parting with his father was awful, and he hadn't even gotten to say goodbye to his mother or anyone other than Zandra. He never would now. Riordan had convinced his parents that magic was wrong for mortals to have, and their whole relationship had been ruined because of that, and now... they were probably dead.

He couldn't save his parents, or maybe even Zandra, but he had the chance to save Bronwen. To have a shot at fighting Riordan and freeing his homeland from his rule. Or he could flee from the dangers of living in the crossfire between gods, have his freedom, and perhaps find the last of his family.

Dante was so wrapped up in this dilemma that when he ran out of thoughts for a moment, he realized his face was wet with tears. He wiped the dampness away and tried to steady his breathing.

His door creaked open a crack. An orb of blue light illuminated a block of his room. "Dante? Can I come in?"

Dante's chest felt so heavy that he couldn't even force a response out. Scarlet crept a bit farther into his room regardless. He wasn't sure if he wanted her to be there or not.

"I know you're awake," she said. The light she was gently carrying shone on him softly as she approached. "I mean. I felt like it was a pretty good guess, anyway." She sat down on the edge of his bed, where she had perched when she guarded him during his post-vision blindness. "I can't sleep either. I just... keep thinking. I'm worried." She cleared her throat. "About you. It's a big decision, an important one. There's just... a lot. There's a lot." Her dark curls guarded her face from him. "I hope it's okay that I'm here."

Dante sat up a little and took her hand. Though her hand was about the same size as his, it felt small. Too small to contain her fire and passion. "It's okay."

"Okay enough."

"You're more than okay."

Scarlet looked up, not at him, but across the room. Her hair fell away from her face, softly illuminated by her light. "I don't think you should do it. Don't become an emissary."

"Scarlet—"

"You *saw*. You saw their bodies out there. This is your chance to avoid that fate."

"But Bronwen would die."

"You can save him on your own. Don't give your soul to Death."

"Bronwen and Death both think I can't. And if they're right..." Dante choked back the rest of the sentence. He rolled away from Scarlet. Tears were stinging his eyes again.

He never wanted to be a mage. He never wanted to be a part of all this. Now his magic might not even be enough to save Bronwen.

Scarlet put a hand on Dante's shoulder. He jumped a little, surprised at the touch. "I'm sorry," she said. "Should I go?"

His heart dropped at the thought of her leaving. "No," he said. "Stay."

They remained like that for a while, Scarlet resting her hand on Dante as he lay in his bed facing away. Soothing warmth radiated from her.

Eventually, Scarlet said, "You should sleep."

He snorted. "I wish I could."

"Why can't you?"

"I'm afraid."

Scarlet ran her hand down his arm. Her touch was gentle. "What are you most afraid of?"

"When I have visions, I'm usually just watching a scene play out. I can't do anything, I'm helpless. I see horrible things, and I can't stop it. Then I wake up blind. I can't even bring myself back into a reality that feels safe when it's over. And now," Dante sighed. "Now, with Bronwen... I have to save him. This is one of those things that I have to do, or regret forever."

"I'll say it again: you don't have to become an emissary to save him."

"You're the only one that believes that."

"They're wrong. I'm right."

Dante smiled weakly at her insistence. His face dropped again. "I don't know if I can take that chance."

"Well... sleep on it."

"I'm not going to sleep. The last thing I want to do tonight is dream."

Scarlet stood up. Without her touch, he was suddenly cold.

"If you're going to heal Bronwen, you need all of the energy you can get. You have to try."

"I can't handle dreaming tonight. Not alone."

Scarlet slowly sat back down. Dante's face burned as they made eye contact for a brief moment. He saw her eyes flicker between sharp and gentle.

"Then I'll stay." She pulled her legs onto the bed and leaned back against the headboard.

"You... should sleep too."

"I can't guard you from dreams if I'm asleep. And I'm not the one who has to heal Bronwen." Scarlet snuffed out her light orb, leaving them in the dark. "You rest. I'll be here."

Dante wasn't sure what he'd been expecting, but it hadn't been for her to actually stay. He didn't want to be alone, but would he rest with her sitting beside him as he tried to sleep? He was lying face up next to her, so close they almost touched.

It was the wrong time to admit to himself how much he liked being close to her.

Dante could hear the pounding of his own heart. Fearing that Scarlet could hear it too, he forced steady breaths to calm his nerves. He couldn't process anything, his brain was full of twisting thoughts. Bronwen dying, unless he could save him. Riordan using them as game pieces in his conquest. Death wanting to bind him to her service. Zandra, captured, fate unknown and in the hands of some mage hunter who could have killed him. Scarlet sitting next to him.

She murmured something, but Dante couldn't hear her over the chaos of his mind.

"What was that?"

"Never mind."

"Say it again. Please."

He looked up at her, barely able to make her out against the darkness. She stared across at the wall, unblinking. He closed his eyes again, resigning himself to her silence. Just as he did, she said, "You aren't helpless. You can save Bronwen. And we're going to stop Riordan."

"He's a god. You keep talking like... like we can actually do something about any of this."

"Riordan tried to kill me, and I lived. Calder tried to take me, and I didn't let him. I'm not... I'm not going to stop trying. Even if it ends up getting me killed."

She means that, doesn't she? Dante paused for a few breaths. "When we got back... is Viridian still here?"

Scarlet let out a deep sigh. "Yes. Yes, I hear her again."

"What's it like?" Dante asked. "Dying. Being dead."

There was a pause while Scarlet conversed with Viridian in her head. "She says... dying hurt. More than she had ever felt. But only for a moment. Then the pain was gone. Her soul flowed into the stream of souls. It's both turbulent and peaceful. Most people, souls... unravel. Become one with the stream, and then flow through the planes into the Nextworld. But Viridian hasn't unraveled, she's still bundled together as herself. A bit because she wants to be, and a bit because... she's stuck. Death oversees this process of souls moving to the Nextworld. With Riordan interrupting her every move, it's causing disruptions. There are more like her who are trying to move on, but they can't."

Dante let this all sink in. *Wait, so if Riordan is defeated, she might lose her sister for good.* He could feel Scarlet trembling next to him. Maybe she had just realized the same thing.

"Scarlet, do you want to talk more about it? Viridian, or—"

"No." Her breathing was shaky, though she seemed to be making an effort to stabilize it.

"It's okay to be... upset. Hurting. You can open up to me, if—"

"I *can't.*"

"Why?"

She paused. "After Viridian died, my dad left. And now my mom left me here... she didn't even stay long enough for me to wake up. I might never see her again. And Viridian... she's gone. She will be gone, whether she wants to or not. So why, what's the point? The closer we get, the more it's going to hurt when you have to leave, too."

"I'm not—" Dante stopped himself. He already almost left her behind. He wasn't sure if he could have followed through on it, venturing to find Zandra on his own... but he had agreed to it. "So you're never going to be close to someone again, because you're afraid of losing them?"

"I'm not... afraid."

"It's okay to be."

"No."

"Scarlet."

"Dante," she said, although the way she said his name made it sound more like *shut up*. "I can't be distracted by... fears. Not now. Feelings aren't going to get me anywhere that I need to go."

Scarlet's words left Dante's chest hollow. Could she set all her emotions down by the wayside, just like that? He could feel it, her inner turmoil roiling around inside her. Yet somehow she was so distant. She was under too much pressure and she was cracking. He couldn't help but take it personally. *Even with everything that is happening... can she really just decide she doesn't care about me at all?*

"Just sleep," Scarlet said. "Please. Bronwen needs you."

If she could be this cold, maybe he'd been wrong about how he felt about her. Regardless, the emptiness he felt left him with nothing to fight off sleep any longer, and in the following silence, he drifted off.

He was standing on the outside of a cell. The air was moist and heavy. Water dripped somewhere down the dark hall. In front of him, metal bars separated him from a girl. Her chamber was small, and she had compacted herself into the corner, knees pulled up tight into her chest.

She looked up at him. The first thing he noticed, even in the dim light, was her eyes: one blue, one brown. Dante noticed her hair next. Blonde, sheared to a chin-length. She looked young, maybe twelve. He couldn't help but be reminded of his sister. Zandra had been that small and innocent only a couple of years ago.

This girl shouldn't be in a cell.

"Who are you?" he asked.

The girl blinked, and then her eyes focused on him. "I'm Ange." Her voice was too light and pretty for this place. "I'm glad you're here."

He wondered where *here* was, exactly. Dante felt off-balance, stuck between the unreality of a dream and the hyperreality of his visions. His mind did flip-flops like he was about to tumble out of this dream. His visions were so strange now. First, he had one while awake, and now, this... it was the first time he felt in control of his actions. Usually, he was just along for the ride, even if it was his own eyes that he saw through. He had to find out what he could while he was here. "Why are you locked up?"

"Eva put me here," the girl said. "You might know her better as Death. That's what she goes by now, isn't it?"

"You're just a child. Why would she put you in here?"

"It wasn't fair. Please, I can't keep you here long, but I can explain more if you come in person."

"You're in Deianira?"

"Yes. I need your help. Please come."

The ground was ripped away from under Dante's feet, vertigo taking over as he fell.

Dante's eyes shot open. It was dark. His sight hadn't been stolen, not even for a few moments.

Also to his surprise, Scarlet was still there, and not just next to him—at some point, she had rolled toward him and wrapped her arms around him. Her breathing was steady; he wondered if she was awake. Maybe she had drifted off and ended up wrapping herself around him by accident.

"Scarlet?" he whispered.

"Did you have a vision?" she mumbled, half awake. "Ugh. I fell asleep, I'm sorry."

"I... had a vision but... it's alright. I'll tell you about it later."

"But it's okay?" she asked. "Is... this okay?"

He wondered if she could hear his heart hammering in his chest. "It's okay."

"Sleep, then." She let out something that was between a sigh and a yawn as she pulled him just a little closer.

She was so cold sometimes. Prickly, harsh, distant. But then there was this: her being soft, her holding him, his face pressed into the crook of her neck, her hair tickling his cheek, the rise and fall of her breathing taking him to a place of calm. *She may claim she isn't afraid, but she is. I should know that by now.*

She was a girl of fire, and she made his heart burn.

Part of him wanted to kiss her, but he knew he couldn't. She was so close, so warm—this moment was too perfect. If he moved even an inch he risked breaking it. He couldn't do anything to scare her away, to break the magic of Scarlet's vulnerability. He even tried not to breathe too deep, lest his movement shake her out of her tenderness.

He didn't want to sleep away the moments of closeness with her, but eventually, he did. He had to. There was too much to do, and he needed every ounce of strength.

CHAPTER 26

S carlet didn't sleep much that night, at least not soundly. She intermittently flitted in and out of consciousness, her thoughts a constant, unintelligible stream in her state of exhaustion. The first time she woke, she found herself holding Dante. She panicked, she almost pulled herself away, and then—and then, she didn't.

When light started to peak in around the window's curtains, she disentangled herself from him and retreated across the hall to her room. She caught a glimpse of herself in the mirror. She looked as tired as she felt, with dark circles under her eyes and her hair a matted disaster. She grabbed the brush sitting on the vanity and began the frustrating process of untangling her hair.

At least it was something she could do without thinking. She wasn't ready to dig into her knot of emotions. It was too raw right now. Or sometimes, it was just dull, her feelings a monotonous tone that she couldn't interpret. It took a while to get through with her hair, cringing as she pulled the tangles apart. In the end, she looked in the mirror and realized the process had only made things worse. Her hair was frizzier and even wilder than usual. She sighed.

There was a tap on the door. It hadn't been closed all the way, so it swung open with the touch.

Dante stood, precariously, in the doorway. "You're up."

Scarlet put the brush down. "Yeah."

"I need to talk to you about something." He came in and sat across from her on the end of her bed.

The knot in her chest pulled tighter. Whatever he was going to say, she wasn't ready for it.

"That dream I had last night," he said. That wasn't what she expected. Her shoulders relaxed. She forgot he had dreamed. "I didn't lose my sight afterward, like I do after visions. But I don't think it was a normal dream, either."

"So what was it?"

"I'm not sure. But there was a girl. A young girl. She was in a dungeon, here in Deianira. She said Death put her there unfairly."

The dungeon? Scarlet tensed. "What did she look like?"

"Kind of like my sister, honestly. She looked Saridi. Blonde hair. Her eyes were two different colors."

"Well... if that was a vision, we need to find out what's going on. Or, uh, what will go on?"

"I think she's there right now. But what are we supposed to do, just ask Death about her?"

"What? Gods, no. We should go down to the dungeon."

Dante looked uncertain. "She did tell me to come find her. And while it does seem odd that Death would lock up a kid, there must be a reason."

"Doesn't mean it's a *good* reason. She did say she was unfairly impris-oned, right? Let's go find her, and we can decide for ourselves."

"I can't imagine Death would be happy about us poking around."

"She won't be." Scarlet scowled. "But what's she going to do about it? She needs us right now. And maybe this girl knows something useful. Even if she doesn't, we can't leave her imprisoned without finding out why she's there."

From the look in Dante's eyes, Scarlet was sure he'd say no. But he nodded. "Alright. Then we'd better go before Death comes looking for us."

They hurried through the halls. Bronwen couldn't wait forever, and Death would be impatient for Dante's answer. Anxiety ran high in Scarlet's nerves as she led Dante to a dark metal door on the first floor. She had barely been conscious when Death took her to the dungeon, but she thought this was the way down. Most of the doors in Deianira were simple wooden doors, but this one was heavily reinforced.

Dante tried the doorknob to no avail. It was locked. He turned to her. "This is it, for sure?"

"Pretty sure."

"How do we get in, then?"

"Unless you have a history of thievery that I don't know about, I'm going to melt the hinges off."

Dante's eyes snapped over to the bulky metal hinges. "What? How long will that take?"

Scarlet shrugged. "Have any better ideas?"

Dante shook his head and gestured for her to go forward. She took a breath and pulled her focus inward. She summoned a small, concentrated flame from her pinched fingertips, as hot and angry as she could make it, and set to work.

Her brow was soaked with sweat by the time she finished melting through the first hinge. She shook out her cramped hand before crouching down to get to work on the second. "How long did that take?"

"Don't worry about it," Dante said. His back was to her, watching the hall. "You're doing it as fast as you can."

It would be better to do it faster. She tried to power more energy into the flame as it slowly cut through the metal. After what seemed like an eternity later, the door fell from its hinges. Dante jumped in and caught the door before it fell onto her. Scarlet helped him lower it to the floor. Then, they stared down the steep steps leading into darkness.

Scarlet's head spun, both from the energy she had just burnt up and from dread. *I don't want to go down there again.*

Dante summoned a light orb for them. Its orange glow was a small source of comfort. "Are you ready?"

Scarlet took a breath. "Let's go."

The stairwell into the dungeon was narrow, so they took it single file, Dante leading with his light. Their footsteps echoed hollowly as they descended a couple of flights worth of stairs. The darkness and confined space pressed in on her. She stumbled slightly on a step and the sound of her feet reverberated off the stone walls.

Dante glanced back at her. "You're sure we should be doing this?"

"Yes."

She felt like puking. Her feet didn't want to keep heading deeper below the castle. But the idea of leaving someone down there was unconscionable.

The bottom of the stairs led into the narrow hall with cells on either side. They began to work their way through the dungeon, peering through the bars.

"Hello?" Dante called as they ventured further. "Is anyone here?"

There was no answer.

"Maybe it was just a dream," Scarlet said. "Like, a regular one." She shivered. Maybe they could leave.

"No." It was the first time Dante sounded at all confident since they had started this adventure. "This is the place I saw."

"Maybe you saw the future then. Or the past."

Then, further down the dungeon, a light blinked into existence. They rushed over to the cell it came from. Inside was a small blonde girl, sitting on a straw bed, a light mote in hand.

"Dante," she said. Her voice was small but bright like a bell. "You came." The girl's gaze flitted to Scarlet. Though Dante told her that the girl's eyes were mismatched, the stark difference between them caught Scarlet off-guard. "You brought a friend."

"This is Scarlet."

The girl nodded. "I know."

Scarlet stared at her. "Who… who are you? How do you know who we are?"

"I'm Ange." She stood and came up to meet them at the bars of the cell. "I see things, sometimes."

"Like me," Dante said.

"A bit like that, yes. That's why I could reach you in your dreams."

"How did this happen?" Dante asked. "Why did Death imprison you?"

"She hates me. She hates me for what I've seen. What I won't see. Don't see." The light of the motes made the tears welling in Ange's eyes glisten. "She was angry that I couldn't help her, so she threw me in the dungeon to rot. Please, you have to get me out of here."

"Don't worry," Scarlet said. "We're going to."

"You're an emissary," Dante said. Scarlet glanced at Ange's hand and spotted the two faint intertwined circles.

"I was." Ange held up her hand, so they could see the marks better. The tattoo was faded and broken in places.

Scarlet had to stifle a gasp. "Your emissary bond is… broken? How?"

"If you get me out of here, I can help you break yours."

"Of course," Scarlet said.

"Scarlet." Dante's voice sounded like a warning.

"What?"

"Just—come down the hall for a minute."

She followed him a few cells down, out of earshot of Ange. "What?" she repeated, harsher this time.

"I don't know if we can trust her," he whispered.

"Dante. She's a *child*. She can't be more than what, twelve? And Death has her locked away in a dungeon. She can't possibly have deserved this."

"Something doesn't feel right."

"What doesn't feel right is that Death is *cruel*," Scarlet snapped. "I don't care what you feel or what you think or what you do, I'm going to help her." Hurt spread across Dante's face. *Maybe that's harsh, but I'm not going to just walk away from this girl. He doesn't understand who Death is yet.*

"We don't know for sure that Death didn't have a good reason—"

"Death has no good reasons. She's petty and destructive. You can try to defend her, you can throw away your empathy in an attempt to convince yourself that becoming an emissary is a good idea—because you think you have to submit to her in order to save Bronwen. But if Ange is telling the truth, I'm not surprised."

Scarlet stomped past Dante, not caring if he was going to follow her. She was going to free this poor girl and find a way to free herself from Death.

"I'm going to cut through the lock with my fire," Scarlet told Ange. "It might get hot, so you'll want to take a step back."

"That won't work," Ange said. "The cell is warded with magic." To demonstrate, she sent a small bolt of energy towards Scarlet. She almost jumped back, but the bolt was absorbed by a field surrounding the cell that briefly became visible, a thin membrane of magic rippling as the energy hit it.

Dante had sheepishly followed Scarlet back to the cell. "I thought only protection mages could make long-lasting shields."

"This isn't the same as a force shield," Ange said. "Death manipulates pure energy. That's what that barrier is. Don't touch it, by the way. It'll give you a nasty shock."

Scarlet grimaced. She'd almost managed to forget the barrier that had been around her own cell.

"Is there a way to break it?" Dante asked.

Ange nodded. "If we all focus our magic on the barrier, we might be able to overload it."

"It'll have to be you and me," Scarlet told Ange. "Dante... he has to save his energy right now."

They staggered themselves so that if the barrier shattered, their magic wouldn't hit each other. Dante stood well out of the way and looked on with his mouth twisted into a worried frown. Ange powered bolts of energy at the barrier, while Scarlet poured a concentrated streak of flame at it. The barrier vibrated wildly with the assault.

Scarlet's rage grew and her flames became larger and wilder as her emotions intensified. *How dare Death do this, to Ange, to me?* Dante felt helpless, but he wasn't the one bound to a selfish god. Scarlet was a stronger mage than him, but what did that matter if she never got a chance to fight? She should have been sent to Riordan's realm with the rest of the emissaries. Maybe she could have made a difference, prevented or at least reduced the loss of life. But she was held back, protected from the dangers she wanted to face, and kept in the dark. Her mother had been traded away for her magical education and a new set of blinders. *Even though I'm a proper mage now, I'm still useless.*

Dante had to take an extra step farther away as the heat rolling off her flames became unbearable. Scarlet stood fast. The barrier became more visible, and it glowed brightly for a moment, then gave an audible *pop* as it broke. Scarlet's flames set fire to some of the straw from Ange's bed before she could reign in the stream of immolation.

"Free." Ange dropped to her knees, breathing heavily. "Free. Thank you."

"Not quite yet." Scarlet set to work cutting the lock with a precise blaze. She was getting even more lightheaded with the unrestrained amounts of energy she'd been outputting, but she was so close to freeing this girl. The lock clanked to the floor and Scarlet swung open the cell door.

Ange got up and smiled as she crossed the threshold of her prison.

"What now?" Dante asked. "I mean, Death—"

"Will know she's free?" All three of them spun to see Death standing in the hall. Red orbs of light danced around her, casting an angry glow across her face.

"You're... you're heinous," Scarlet spat out. "Why are you imprisoning a *child?*"

"You have no idea what you are talking about. **Sit**."

Scarlet's tattoo burned as she dropped to the stone floor. Unable to even form words in her frustration, a growl worked its way through her throat. Dante took a protective step in front of her.

"Eva," Ange said. "I would say it's good to see you, but..."

"I think it's time that *they* saw *you*." Death waved a hand. When Scarlet looked back to Ange, the girl that had been standing there was gone. Instead, a woman was before them. Blonde, with half of her hair sheared close to her scalp. The other half was about chin length, with the front strands reaching down lower. She had two mismatched eyes. It was Ange, but— "She isn't what she appears. She used an illusion to make herself seem more innocent, vulnerable, trustworthy. Angelise is none of those things."

Dante turned to Ange. "Wait—so..."

"I am sorry for lying to you," Ange said. "I did what I had to, to ensure my freedom. Regardless of my trespasses, Eva cannot be trusted. She really did throw me in here just because I couldn't help her as much as she wanted. I tried, you have to believe me."

Death snorted. "You're the traitor. A manipulator."

"You *hypocrite!*" Ange snarled. She pointed to Dante. "Why don't you tell him? Tell him what you did. Why he's here."

"He knows why he's here."

"But not how it *happened*. Dante. Eva—Death—told me she would set me free if I helped her with something. I didn't believe her, but I had nothing better to do, so," Ange shrugged. "So I did it. She told me Bronwen had scouted a mage that she wanted to bring here. But Death knew you would need a reason to leave home. So she had me disguise myself as your friend—Milo, is that right?—and tell your parents about the last time you did magic. That way, she could have Bronwen swoop in and save you. Of course, then you'd be grateful for having your life saved, and all that." Ange glanced at his hands. "You're not an emissary though. Good. One less bond to break."

Dante looked to Death. His voice wavered. "*You* had me banished?"

Death fidgeted with her braid. "I did what I had to."

"Does Bronwen know?"

"No."

"I thought my friend *betrayed* me." His voice was quiet, not in a calm way but in a deadly one. "I had to leave my sister behind to get captured by mage hunters. My parents will never forgive me, if they're even alive." Dante pressed his hands to his forehead and leaned against the stone wall.

A heavy silence fell over them. There was a bonfire of rage in Scarlet's chest. Death had ruined everything for Dante. But he responded with ice, not fire. He was frozen against the wall like he was hewn from the very same stone.

Ange clapped her hands together. The sound echoed down the dungeon. "Well, I'm leaving," she said. "You two should come with me. I can take you far away from Eva."

"**None of you are going anywhere**," Death said. Scarlet felt her feet lock to the floor.

Ange barred her teeth. "You can't *make* me stay. Not anymore." She held up her hand and pointed to her faded emissary tattoo. "I'm free of you. And I may have been rotting in this dungeon, but I see how weak you are now. You have nothing left. You want to stop me, to fight me? I'd like to see you *try*."

Scarlet could feel energy gathering around Death. Then suddenly, the tension faded. "Fine." Death waved a hand. "Then *go*, already."

"Scarlet. Meet me in Cascara's realm, if you ever can. You set me free, and I'll repay you in kind." Ange looked to Dante, still slouched against the wall. "Dante? Are you coming?"

"I can't." His voice broke. "I have to help Bronwen."

Ange shrugged. "Your choice. Thanks for the help." She pushed past Death on her way out. She looked over her shoulder at them before getting too far. "If you change your mind... I'll be waiting."

"What now, Dante?" Death asked once Ange had left. "Are you too proud now, to become an emissary? Are you going to let Bronwen die because I forced your father's hand? He was going to catch you, eventually. I may have sped the process, but it was always going to end the same for you."

Scarlet saw a spark of rage finally reach Dante. "That's enough!" Dante tried to storm past Death, but she caught him by the collar, choking him into stopping.

"You want to keep the rest of your friends alive? Then you had better listen to me."

"No," Dante said. "I'm done with you. Scarlet thinks I can save Bronwen without you, so that's what I'm going to do."

Death let out a bitter laugh. "Cute, how she believes in you." She gave Dante a little shove as she let him go. "Once Bronwen is gone, you will leave. No more dead weight is allowed in this castle."

CHAPTER 27

D ante was numb.

Milo. Milo didn't betray me. Death set it up. Thank the gods—no, not the gods, but something else—that Bronwen didn't know, at least.

It was a relief, but it also hurt. Things didn't have to be this way. He didn't have to spend all this time wondering how one of his only friends could have done this to him. And Zandra, his parents... if he had been there, could he have stopped them from meeting their horrific fates?

But he didn't have time to ponder. Not until after he healed Bronwen. He took a few moments pause after emerging from the dungeon staircase, then continued straight to Bronwen's quarters.

Gratefully, Scarlet didn't follow him. It was his turn to need time alone.

He threw all his energy into healing his mentor. Bronwen was unconscious and didn't wake. Little progress was made throughout the healing session. Dante's nudging struggled to convince Bronwen's weakened body to heal parts of the extensive damage.

Dante collapsed on the floor next to Bronwen's bed. He had no energy, physical nor emotional, to lift himself back up. He felt like he should cry, but he had no energy for that, either.

He closed his eyes. He slept. He dreamed.

His visions were disorienting and unclear. Lives hung in the balance... Bronwen's and... others, but he couldn't tell. Scarlet's? His own life? Zandra, if she was still out there? It could be any of them, or all.

He woke, blind, his body aching from laying on the floor. He sat himself up and stretched, waiting for his vision to return. The blindness lasted for longer than it used to. Other than with the two anomalous visions, where he hadn't lost his vision at all, it seemed to lengthen each time he dreamed.

"Bronwen?" Dante croaked. There was no reply. Bronwen was still unconscious. Or worse—

Dante curled into a ball, doing his best not to assume the worst before he even got his sight back. His insides felt like they were fracturing, every part of him was breaking.

Death had gotten him banished. Scarlet had been right, the god twisted everything she could to serve her purposes. He had been so grateful to have his life saved, slowly becoming accustomed to the idea that he might be able to get strong enough to do something to help fight Riordan... he wanted to believe that Death wasn't as bad as Scarlet seemed to think—he'd been a fool.

He'd lost everything because of Death.

Was he going to lose Bronwen now, too?

His vision returned, painfully slow. It was darker now, he'd slept until sunset. Dante stood, steadying himself against Bronwen's bed. His legs shook. He pressed his fingers against Bronwen's neck.

There was a pulse. Bronwen was still breathing, shallowly. Tears stung Dante's eyes. *He's alive for now.*

He settled in for another healing session. Dante let his magic flow into Bronwen's body, feeling around for the most critical damage. It was overwhelming, and he could feel infection creeping in deep within his mentor's body. The energy Dante provided was nothing, it was a drop when Bronwen needed an ocean to survive. Nevertheless, he didn't stop until his own body felt useless, and he dropped back to the floor, where he twitched and convulsed.

He'd gone too far. Bronwen's words cautioning him against overextending himself by healing a lost cause ran through his head. *I can't push myself any further.*

Scarlet was wrong. He wouldn't be able to save Bronwen on his own. She believed him to be stronger than he was. He admired her strength, her determination... but he wasn't her.

He fell unconscious. It wasn't quite sleep, it was too restless, but at least his visions didn't come for him. He faded in and out, it became dark and then light outside once more.

"Dante. Wake up."

"Scarlet?" he asked groggily, but as he came back to consciousness he realized it wasn't her, but Death.

"Get up," Death commanded. "Come with me."

Dante managed to push himself upright. His stomach ached to empty itself, not that it had much in it. He looked up at Bronwen's bed. "Wait, is he—"

"He's still alive."

Death's words were barely a relief. It was only a matter of time. Death held out a hand, taking pity on him, and Dante begrudgingly accepted her help to stand up. He almost toppled back over regardless, but was able to keep his footing and follow her out to the main area of Bronwen's quarters.

Death took a seat on one of Bronwen's couches, and Dante followed suit, collapsing onto one across from her. The light of the rising sun shining in through the copious windows warmed him.

"I can't become an emissary," he said, preempting her question while he still had the guts to say it. "I can't... I can't trust you."

Death's cold gaze was set firmly on him. "Perhaps not. But we both want Bronwen alive, and I'm sure you've seen by now that you cannot save him without my power. The only way for me to lend you my strength is to become an emissary. So maybe we can make a deal."

"A deal?" Dante snorted. "What kind of deal could you give me? You got me torn away from my family, from my sister, she needed me and I couldn't protect her—"

"What if you could protect her now?"

Dante tried to swallow, but his mouth was dry. "What do you mean?"

"I've kept track of Zandra. If you become my emissary, I'll send you to her once Bronwen is recovered."

"Is she safe?"

Death flashed her teeth at him. "For now."

Dante thought of Ange's illusion, a girl locked away in a cell. "Is that a threat?"

"She is a mage living in a land of mage hunters. I do not need to threaten her." Death leaned back in her seat. "Join me, save Bronwen, and then I'll send you on a mission that will also take you to your sister. Or choose to let Bronwen die, and I will not be kind in choosing where to leave you. *That* is a threat. For Scarlet's sake, I have let you stay, even though you are not an emissary. But no longer. The situation is too dire and I need every aid I can get."

Zandra. He could go to Zandra. "What about Scarlet? Would she come, too?"

"No. She must stay here."

Dante ground his teeth. Death was bewildering. "Why keep her here?"

"Become my emissary and I'll tell you whatever you want to know."

"How do I know that's true? That any of this is true?"

Death shrugged. "My word is all I can give you. You will have to decide for yourself if that means anything."

How could I do it? How could I bind myself to her, commit myself to being trapped in this crossfire between gods? She ruined my old life. He ran his fingers through his hair. *But if I don't, Bronwen will die, and how could*

I let that happen, either? How could I give up the opportunity to get back to Zandra, if there's even the slightest chance Death is telling the truth?

Hope and fear were tearing him in two. He didn't know what to do.

"I will hold vigil over Bronwen," said Death. "Your efforts have been enough that I can help hold him here, for now. But I doubt he will last another night, so you'd best decide by the end of the day."

Dante took a walk. He needed fresh air, even if it was murky swamp air. He needed to move, even if his body protested every step. He paced around until he found a relatively dry area shaded by a gnarled tree with low branches that were easy to climb onto. He perched on a branch, remembering Zandra and her reckless love of climbing trees much too high.

He missed her. How long had he been in the Crossworld, now? Months? It was hard to keep track here, no seasons came and went, each day passing in monotonous routine.

Bronwen would die if he didn't accept Death's offer, there was no question about it now. Plus Death would throw him out somewhere dangerous, and he'd be abandoning Scarlet. And, if he became an emissary, he would get to see his sister. If Death was telling the truth, anyway. He would find out why Death kept Scarlet here, and maybe he could use that knowledge to help Scarlet get out, sooner rather than later.

But he would be at risk of being controlled by Death. She'd already played puppet master with him. Two of her emissaries—well, an ex-emissary in Ange's case—had warned him against becoming one. Could he commit his life to serving Death? Could he come to terms that he would likely die fighting against Riordan? There would be no backing out, no changing his mind about leaving if he became an emissary unless he managed to break the bond, as Ange had.

His mind turned the conundrum over and over, like a rough stone that would become smooth with the erosion of his inner turmoil. He sat in the tree for so long that the sun rose to its full height above him. It didn't quite feel warm; they never seemed to get the full effect of the sun here, but it was still nicer than being in the stuffy castle. He didn't know how he would ever get up from his perch to go back inside and give Death his decision. It would be too final. He was hungry and uncomfortable, exhausted, and stuck.

As the sun began to descend, he saw someone coming towards him from Deianira. He thought it was Death at first. However, as she came closer, Dante saw curly black hair and not the red braid of the god. Scarlet had found him.

She came to him and leaned against the twisting tree. "Hey."

"Hey."

"So... Bronwen..." She bit her lip.

"I can't save him on my own."

"That's not true. You just have to dig deeper—"

"I don't have any deeper to dig into! You have this huge store of energy in you—I don't have that. I'm not like you."

Scarlet looked down at her feet. "Don't do it. Don't become an emissary. Even if Bronwen will die. Don't be trapped here. Please."

The way she said it, with such desperate sincerity, Dante was sure she wouldn't forgive him if he willingly chose the life that she had been forced into. His heart dropped. "I have to tell you something."

"So tell me."

"Death made me an offer."

"No." The word was soft but forceful.

"She said she would tell me anything I want. I can find out why she insists on keeping you here. And she'll let me go to the World, to help my sister—"

He had never heard Scarlet's voice falter as much as it did now. "She's telling you what you want to hear, then she'll use you however she wants to."

"Maybe. But I might have to take that chance."

"I was in that dungeon too, you know."

"What?"

"Where we found Ange. Death left me down there before."

"W-why? Why would she do that?"

"I tried to get her to tell me the truth. About my mother, about why I'm trapped here. I... attacked her. Not that I had any chance of hurting her. I needed answers, and she wouldn't give me answers. Not then, and not now."

Dante tried to think of Scarlet, locked away in the dungeon. Anger rose in his chest at the image. "How long were you there?"

"I don't know. Long enough. I got out the day we met."

No wonder she hadn't been chatty when he'd first arrived. No wonder she had no qualms about setting Ange free, with little question. "Scarlet. I'm so sorry."

Scarlet was still staring at the ground like she couldn't bear to look at him. "So don't do it," she repeated. "You don't know what she's capable of. She goes easy on you. She hasn't tested you like she's tested me, because you aren't an emissary."

"I don't know what to do. If I don't become an emissary, she'll make me leave. Who knows where she'll send me, or if I'll end up in the dungeon, or—"

"Death can't follow you out of this realm while Riordan is using his magic to confine her. Leave right now, on your own, go find Ange. Maybe she still has the ability to make portals. I'm sure Death will stop me if I try to cross the river, but you aren't tied to her like I am. So go, Dante, before you end up like me. Like Bronwen. Like all of the emissaries we had to leave rotting at Riordan's doorstep. Go find your sister. Fight Riordan on your own terms, if you want to. But once Death gets a hold of you, everything you do will be for her agenda."

There was a hard lump in his throat. "But I can't go."

"Bronwen isn't afraid to die. He'll forgive you."

"It's not just that."

"Then what?"

"I can't leave you."

Scarlet finally looked up to where Dante was perched in the tree. Her eyes were as hard as any wall he'd ever faced. "I'll be fine."

He knew it wasn't true. He'd be yet another person abandoning her. "You'll be alone. If I turn Death down, she'll send me away and I'll never find my way back. But if I become an emissary... even if I leave for a while, I'll still see you again."

"You don't know that for sure. You don't understand what you could be sacrificing. And... I don't want you to have this life." Suddenly, her toughness melted away, pain and sadness ringing clearly in her words. "Don't you *dare* become an emissary. Not because of me."

"Scarlet." As her walls fell, so did Dante's. Suddenly he felt too far away from her. He stumbled his way down from the branches to stand face-to-face with her. He reached for her hands and she let him take them.

Scarlet's fire, her intensity, pulsed through her hands to his. Dante's heart burned for her, and this was his last chance. Scraps of his dreams were piecing together, bit by bit. No matter what choice he made, he might never see her again. He had to say it before it was too late. "I could never leave you behind, Scarlet. I lo—"

"No." In that moment, every ounce of softness left her. He saw her tense, her eyes unlocked from his. She pulled her hands back. Suddenly, she was a thousand miles away. "Don't. Don't say what you're going to say."

"Scarlet—"

"Don't."

"But—"

"No."

Scarlet's rebuff struck him to the core. He felt every piece of his heart bursting open as her rejection set in.

"You can't feel that way about me," she said. "I'm... nothing. I'm just the one who's here. All we've had is each other. That just makes me a default, not anything real."

Dante's stomach dropped. "Scarlet, no. None of that is true. You're the opposite of nothing. You're strong. As a mage, sure, but more than that—as a person. It's impossible to not admire you. You try to keep everyone out, but I know... I know that you care. You care so deeply about everything, everyone that it tears you apart. But it doesn't have to be that way. You don't have to hide and you don't have to face any of this alone."

"You're wrong."

"About what?"

"All of it."

Scarlet cupped her hands together, face up, and for a brief moment summoned a roaring blaze into existence. Dante flinched back.

"You're afraid of me," Scarlet said.

"No, not you. Just... of fire. You know why, I told you why."

"But I'm fire, Dante. It's part of who I am."

"It's not you, it's just your magic."

"If that's what you think, you don't know me as well as you think you do."

All of this was going wrong, oh so wrong. Dante's whole body was vibrating now, threatening to fall apart. "I care about you. I like being with you. The other night, falling asleep together like that, I felt so safe. It felt right. It meant a lot to me, Scarlet."

Scarlet's eyes were closed and her face was strained.

"You don't have to feel the same way as I do," he said. "But... what do you feel? Just talk to me, please."

"Nothing. I feel nothing." Her voice was empty.

Dante felt a dot of cold land on his cheek, then another on his forehead. It was snowing. He didn't know that it snowed in Death's realm. Were there seasons here after all? It was so hard to keep track of the passage of time here, but he thought it had to be summer back in Saridian by now.

"I've never even had a friend, before you. I had my family, but no one outside of that," Scarlet said. Dante wasn't sure if the moisture on her face was from the snow melting as it hit her skin, or if tears were leaking from her closed eyes. "I don't know how to feel. So I can't. And I don't think you know me well enough to truly love me."

There was nothing left to say, nothing left to do, so Dante turned away As much as hurt to walk away, there wasn't anything he could think to do or say that would make either of them feel better. He had to do what he needed to do before he lost his nerve.

So he walked back to the castle, snowflakes kissing his skin the whole way back, he entered through the dark stone doors and weaved through the halls back to Bronwen's room, where Death sat next to Bronwen, tenderly holding his pale hand. She looked up as Dante entered, her face creased with worry.

He stood tall in front of the god. "I've made my decision."

CHAPTER 28

Jarrett's lungs burned as he and Barek circled one another. They'd only been sparring for a couple of minutes, but Jarrett was already regretting going up against the younger man. It might not have been so bad had mages been kept out of the mix, but right now Jarrett was teamed up with Lars and together they were facing both Barek and Zandra.

It had only taken a few days of rest before the newcomers had insisted on joining in on the Vanguard's training regimen. At first, everyone had gone easy on them. Now, Jarrett had learned that he needed to stop underestimating them.

Jarrett and Lars had strategized before this match, but their plan wasn't coming together. From watching the newcomers in their previous spars, they knew that Zandra used her enhancement magic to power up Barek, then stayed back to act as support, firing energy darts at her enemies from afar.

Jarrett had been sure he could take on Barek regardless of his magically increased speed and strength, but it turned out that he was harder to keep at bay than expected. He was used to the younger members of the Vanguard having the edge on him physically, but with Zandra's enhancements, Barek was outmatching him despite Jarrett's experience in swordsmanship.

Meanwhile, Lars was supposed to come around and flank Zandra, using his obfuscation magic to conceal his movements and gain the element of surprise. They'd thought Zandra would be the weak link, as her bolts weren't very accurate while she was focusing on her enhancements on Barek, and mostly relied on him to protect her.

But that plan wasn't working out either. Zandra was uncannily good at keeping track of Lars, despite his magic rendering him nearly invisible. She'd fire a volley of bolts at him, which even though they landed wide, alerted Barek to where his other opponent was and allowed him to intercept before Lars could reach her.

As the spar continued, the other training activities taking place in the converted barn ceased as curious onlookers gathered to size up the Vanguard's newest members: a couple of kids who were now walloping their leader and one of their most experienced mages.

Jarrett's frustration grew as the crowd did, the pressure to perform building. How was he supposed to lead the Vanguard into battle against a god if he couldn't even beat a couple of teenagers? He had to turn the tide of this fight, or he'd never ride out the embarrassment.

Barek beat back Lars once again, forcing him to block with a series of spot shields and retreat to Jarrett's side. Some of the crowd whooped and hollered in support of the newcomers.

"What now?" Lars hissed. "We're getting clobbered."

"I know." Jarrett kept his voice low. "Switch with me. Keep Barek occupied, I'll take the girl."

Jarrett's partner nodded, eyes narrowing as he refocused. Barek charged in, raising his dulled practice sword to take a swing at Jarrett. But Lars was ready to intercept the attack and sent a large orb of energy at Barek. Though the orb's force was blunt compared to a concentrated beam it was enough to bowl him over.

They wouldn't have another opportunity this good. Jarrett had to end this now.

Jarrett sidestepped the fallen Barek and rushed toward Zandra. Her eyes widened. She took a defensive posture, but it was obvious that she hadn't expected the tide of battle to turn so quickly. Jarrett tackled her to the ground before she could react, sparing her from the blow of even a dulled sword.

With the two newcomers downed, the crowd cheered at Jarrett and Lars' triumph. Jarrett wiped his brow. *That was too close.* Experience had won out in the end, but he barely deserved the victory.

Jarrett helped Zandra up and shook her hand, then Barek's. Lars followed suit. Zandra and Barek looked exhausted and a little disappointed. They moved off to the side, avidly discussing something, presumably debriefing. Jarrett dispersed the crowd, chiding them to get back to their own training instead of sticking their noses into his.

As the rabble thinned, Jarrett spotted Rohan. The man's arms were crossed, and he stared at Jarrett sternly.

"Ah," Jarrett said. "Sorry, Rohan. I forgot our meeting, didn't I?"

"You certainly did." Rohan's eyes flicked over to the newcomers. "Distracted by those ones, I see."

"I was. They're quite a pair."

"So they are." Rohan shifted on his feet. Jarrett got the sense he was holding something back.

"What is it, Rohan? Shall we head to the hall for our meeting?"

"No, I'll cut right to it." Rohan stopped, cleared his throat, and then blurted out, "We have to test the weapons."

"What? You insisted it was too dangerous. Plus, we know now from Zandra that they drain power. We can assume it'll do the same to Riordan."

"Maybe, but it's not safe to make assumptions. We need to know for certain how these weapons work before we face Riordan, because *that* would be truly dangerous. The only other option is backtracking and accepting the Ravens help, since they may know how they work."

Jarrett sighed. His stubborn decision to force the Ravens out continued to be controversial. Some members of the Vanguard stood by him, either because they had never trusted the Ravens in the first place, or they empathized with Jarrett's grief-driven resolution. Others were angry that Jarrett had thrown out allies that had aided them in their time of need.

Jarrett didn't regret his choice, although the godforsaken mist that the Ravens had conjured infuriated him to the point where he had nearly changed his mind. They couldn't exactly go attack Riordan with their newfound artifact weapons until they found a way out of their hideout.

"Alright," Jarrett said. "So, say we test the weapons. Who are we going to test them on?"

"Me," Rohan said. "I'll take the risk."

Jarrett shook his head. "Absolutely not. You're one of our best mages. If something were to happen—"

"My life isn't more important because I'm a mage."

"Come on, Rohan. You know that we need you."

"If I don't do it, then who? I'm not going to ask someone else to volunteer."

A voice came from behind them. "I'll do it."

Jarrett spun. It was Zandra. This girl had a knack for eavesdropping on him and Rohan. "What?"

"Test the weapons on me," she said. Her voice quavered, but she held her head high.

Barek came up next to Zandra, eyebrows furrowed. "That's not happening." He took her by the shoulders, as if about to drag her away, but she shook him off.

"I want to help," she said. Her green eyes bore into Jarrett. "I've been in contact with magus crystal before. I know what it's like. And I'm not afraid."

Silence held between the four of them for a few beats. Jarrett cleared his throat. "I think I have to agree with Barek, in this case."

"Why? Because I'm just a kid?" Zandra balled her hands into fists.

"Yes," Jarrett said. "I'm sorry but you're a child. I'm not letting you risk yourself."

"I want to be a part of the Vanguard," Zandra said. "So what if I'm a kid? I don't feel like one anymore, not after what I've been through. I'll put my life on the line, the same as everyone else here. Being young hasn't spared me from the Tyrant."

Rohan shook his head. "Zandra, I'm sorry for what you've had to bear, but I've already made up my mind. I'll be the test subject, if there is to be one."

Zandra was shaking now. "You don't trust us. I can see it. I get it, we're new, and one of us once swore fealty to your enemy. You have to be careful. But let us prove ourselves. I'll show you that I'm as committed to bringing Riordan down as you are."

Jarrett had to respect this girl. She had been through something horrible, but instead of hiding away, she wanted to fight. There was a tickling feeling at the back of his mind—she almost reminded him of someone, but the "who" of it kept slipping away like sand through his fingers.

"Zandra." Barek's voice rose as he went on. "We risked *everything* to get you out of that prison, away from magus crystal. Stop trying to subject yourself to more of this. It's done, we're free from that place, let's leave it behind."

"It's not over," Zandra bit back. "It's not done until Riordan is."

Zandra stormed away through the curious onlookers whose attention had sharpened as the conversation grew heated.

"Let's go somewhere more private to finish discussing this," Jarrett suggested to Rohan.

The next day, Jarrett, Rohan, and the three mages who had been analyzing the artifacts all met up outside the padlocked shed where the swords were being stored. Rohan would be the test subject after all. Jarrett still wasn't happy with the decision, but Rohan had continued to insist, and the rest of the council members had begrudgingly signed off on it.

Rohan unlocked the shed. Jarrett and the mages followed him in. It was a tight squeeze to fit all of them inside. The storage shed now contained the magus weapons and needed to be locked up securely. Some firewood was still stacked against the far wall. A sturdy table had been built against another, where the swords rested. Opposite that was a shelf full of various tools, axes, magnifying glasses, and some bottles of strange concoctions that the mages had been using to try to identify the weapons' uses.

"Are you sure about this?" asked one of the mages, Aribelle.

"For the thousandth time everyone, yes," Rohan said loudly, not concealing his frustration. "Zandra told us that the magus crystal in the mage prison drained her magic. These swords probably do the same thing, perhaps on a more powerful basis if they are meant to combat a god. As you have seen, Zandra's magic returned once she was freed, so hopefully the effects of these swords are also temporary."

"Hopefully." Jarrett rubbed his forehead. The thought of his friend losing his magic, or worse, his life, was too much for him to bear on top of everything else. His nerves were stretched tight; he could practically feel them humming.

"If these weapons can drain Riordan's power, we have a chance at facing him head-on," Rohan continued, voice still loud. "And, if we're lucky, they'll do what we really need them to—stop him from being able to choose a new incarnate. Even if they delay his return to physical form temporarily, we'll have a better shot at seizing Kingsmount and control of Saridian. This is what we're fighting for. Freedom for our people. So yes, I am sure about this."

Jarrett and the mages stood solemn as Rohan picked up one of the swords and took a deep breath as he leveled it over his hand, preparing to draw blood.

The door to the shed swung open. They all turned to see who the intruder was, but the light from outside was bright, only revealing a silhouette.

The intruder spoke, her voice pure and bright. "Oh good, I'm just in time."

The mages took fighting stances and Jarrett drew his sword. The woman took a step into the shed. She wasn't anyone Jarrett recognized, another newcomer. Her blonde hair covered half her head, and the other side was shaved. He squeezed by to stand between her and the mages.

"Whatever you're doing here, I would stop," the intruder said.

Jarrett took another step closer to her. She appeared utterly unconcerned at the bare steel facing her. They outnumbered her, so her lack of fear told him that she was either a mage or lacked a survival instinct. He and his people were trapped in tight quarters, but she probably wouldn't expect the majority of them to be mages, and that boded well for his side.

"And who in the gods' names are you?" Jarrett asked.

"Well, most importantly," the woman said, "I'm the one who made those swords. So, you should *really* take my advice and put that down."

He heard a clunk as Rohan placed the sword back down on the table, but Jarrett kept his eyes trained on the intruder. His tattoo stung sharply, which he did his best to ignore.

"How did you get here?" Rohan asked. "What do you want?"

"A little obfuscation magic isn't going to stop me," the woman said. "I mean no harm, I'm just here to reclaim what's mine."

Jarrett grunted. "I think you have some explaining to do."

"Whatever you want to know," she said, brushing a lock of hair out of her eye. Jarrett caught a glimpse of tattooed circles on her hand. It almost gave him hope, until he remembered that he had sworn off his search and anything to do with the Ravens.

"So you're a Raven?" he asked, grip tightening on his hilt.

She scoffed. "A Raven? No. I have better things to do than run around with that lot." Her eyes narrowed as she examined Jarrett's face. "Wait.

Jarrett? Dear gods, I didn't even recognize you with that beard. I didn't know you were in Rosewood."

"What?" Jarrett searched his mind for any trace of this woman. "How do you know my name?"

"It's Ange," she said, stepping closer. "Angelise? It's been a while but—you don't recognize me?"

She was very distinctive, from her bright and clear voice to her hair to the wildly mismatched eyes. Jarrett was certain he had never seen her in his life. He took a hand off his sword to rub his tattoo, his heart nearly beating out of his chest underneath. "I don't know who you are."

"Oh dear." Ange scrunched her face up. "What did she do to you?"

"I really—I don't know—"

"This changes everything. I think we should talk, privately."

Rohan stormed up next to Jarrett. "I don't think so. I don't care if you have the answer to all of our questions, you aren't dragging our leader off somewhere alone without a very good explanation of how you found us, how you got here, why we should trust you—"

Ange reached out, and pressed two fingers onto Jarrett's chest, right over where his raven tattoo was. The stinging on his chest expanded over his whole body and intensified tenfold. His head buzzed, like his brain itself was vibrating. He dropped his sword and stumbled backward, overwhelmed. Rohan caught him so that he didn't fall. The feeling faded after a moment but left Jarrett gasping for breath.

He was sure Rohan and the others were about to eviscerate Ange, so he quickly held his hand up and choked out, "Don't. It's fine." He took a few breaths, staring at the woman that he should remember, but didn't. "Let's talk."

Back in his home, Jarrett stared at Ange across the kitchen table. He was sitting, but she wasn't—instead, she loomed, examining each corner of his living quarters with prying eyes. He had waited for this moment, to meet someone from his past. Ached for it, every day since his memories had fled.

"So *who are you*?" he asked.

"I already told you. I'm Ange," she said, her eyes snapping back to him. "Angelise, if you prefer."

"But who are you to me?"

Ange planted her hands on the table and leaned toward him. "We used to know each other. We met not far from here, in a village called Kindlespire. You lived there for a while."

Jarrett searched his memories. He knew of Kindlespire but had no recollection of living there. "And you're an emissary of Death?"

Ange snapped her hands back and crossed her arms. He thought he caught the beginning of a scowl before she wiped the emotion from her face. "I used to be. My bond to her is broken."

"And you aren't a Raven?"

"I am not."

"Then how did you get here?"

Ange snorted. "Because of their mist? Please. I took a portal most of the way through it, directly from the Crossworld. Though I'm no longer an emissary, I still have enough connection to the gods to do so. Anyway, it wasn't hard to get through that last bit of mist."

"The Crossworld," he repeated. "What's that?"

"You forget that much? She did a good job concealing your memories. Very thorough." Ange sounded impressed.

She? So, it wasn't Calder who did this to me... if Ange can be trusted. "How do you know who did this to me?"

"The tattoo. The magic signature on it is unmistakable to me."

"Have you seen something like this before?"

Ange held up her hand, showing off her faded emissary mark. "It's like this, but also not. I've never seen anything quite like *that*, but the mage who did this is talented."

"Was it Death?"

"No, not Death." She smirked. "An obfuscation mage. Your tattoo—think of it like the mist that the Ravens made. It's a seal surrounding specific memories of yours, keeping them hidden."

"Can it be broken?"

"I broke my connection with Death. Your tattoo, it's similar to an emissary bond, in a sense. I believe I can break the seal..."

Jarrett's heart leapt. "Please."

"...and I will do so, on the condition that you and the Vanguard work with me on my plot against Riordan. Now that I have been reunited with the swords, it is time to move forward."

"Absolutely." Was Ange truly the answer to all of his problems? The creator of these weapons, here to fight Riordan with them, and also to solve the mystery that had haunted him for years. He was so hungry for answers. "The swords. You made them? What exactly do they do?"

"They're my life's work. They get around the whole problem of Riordan continually incarnating. If you land a good enough hit on him with one, it will draw his soul into the blade, trapping him so that he can't put his soul into another mortal's body. A surface wound isn't sufficient, but with a deep strike, the swords will do their job."

"That's... amazing." Jarrett shuddered as he thought of what could have happened to Rohan if Ange hadn't come in time to stop him. "So then, we wouldn't even have to worry about Calder first, we can go straight to Riordan."

"Yes. Although, I wouldn't mind tracking down Calder anyway. But that's less important, for now."

Jarrett was dumbstruck. They had a way to take care of Riordan, permanently. It was more than he ever could have dreamed of. Even with this revelation, he couldn't help but circle back to the other issue at hand. "Do you... do you know why my memories were taken?"

"Perhaps to protect you. Or to get rid of you. I'm not sure. You knew things that were dangerous to know." Finally, Ange sat, taking the place across from him at the table. She leveled a serious gaze at him. "As tragic as I'm sure all of this has been for you, there is also a potential benefit. This seal put upon you is powerful, and it holds the signature of the mage who put it on you. When it is broken, its magic will be released. When that happens, I believe the energy will be strong enough for Riordan to sense it from afar. I think he will come to us. We must use this to our advantage and lure Riordan into a trap."

Jarrett didn't fully understand, but he nodded. If they could prepare themselves, with Ange's help, and bring Riordan here on their terms instead of barreling into Kingsmount, maybe they would be able to get that one good strike they needed on him. He would get his memories back, on top of it all. But still, the question remained: "Who did this to me, Ange? I need to know."

"An emissary of Death. A woman named Kiera."

Jarrett didn't recognize the name. Of course, he wouldn't. It rang empty through his soul, an answer without being an answer.

The stealer of his memories.

The one who had ruined his life.

Kiera.

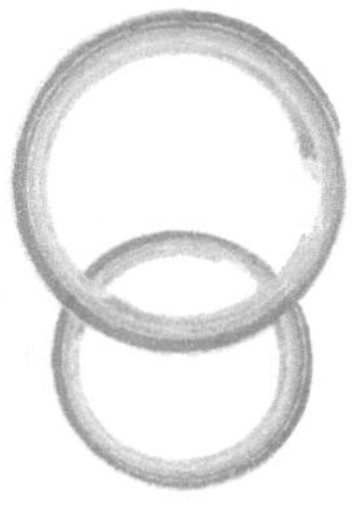

CHAPTER 29

The binding ritual was performed in the throne room.

Dante wasn't sure what to expect. He sat cross-legged in the middle of the room as Death placed lit incense in censers placed in a circle around him. In front of him, Death had placed a bowl containing a dark liquid, a small velvet bag, a knife, and a mortar and pestle.

As the incense burned and began to release its aroma, Dante inhaled the smoke. The scent was unique, yet blossomed deeply nostalgic feelings in his chest. *If magic had a smell, this would be it.*

A strange calm overtook Dante now that he had decided his path. His course was set, he would become an emissary, save Bronwen, go find Zandra, and Scarlet—well, she'd keep being Scarlet. His heart twisted. He didn't want to think about all that right now. "So, how does this work?" he asked.

Death lit one last stick of incense and sat down across from him. "Five censers surrounding us, representing the other gods," she said, placing the last censer in between them, "and one in the middle, representing me. Breathe deeply."

Dante took in a smoky breath. The feelings of nostalgia intensified. Memories ran through him. For a moment, he thought he was sitting at the kitchen table, back in Briarglen—then he remembered his house was gone. Burned to the ground. He exhaled, releasing the thought of home.

"We will make an ink," she said, loosening the drawstrings on the velvet pouch, "that I will embed into your hand. With it, I will make your emissary mark. It is the connection that will bind us." Death poured the contents of the bag, some crystalline shards, into the mortar.

"What's that?"

"Magus crystal. The only substance that can hold magic within it." Shimmering magic poured from Death's hand into the mortar, and the shards began to glow softly as the energy moved back and forth through them. "Veins of it run underground on your continent in the World, a network that the gods' energies flow through, allowing you gifted mortals to access magic." She held the mortar out for Dante. "Your turn."

He added his magic to the crystals, entranced by the energy running through them. Death took the pestle and began grinding the shards.

He remembered the first time he realized he had magic. One morning, when he was twelve, he had awoken feeling... full. Tingly. Something was bursting in his chest, wanting to leap out. He wasn't sure what it was until it overflowed, radiant ribbons of magic leaking from his palms. He'd tightened his hand, almost into a fist, and the magic condensed into a bolt much like the ones he had now practiced with for months. It had been equal parts exhilarating and terrifying to realize he was a mage. It had been amazing, at the time, despite the fact that he would be killed if anyone found out.

Death continued grinding until the shards had become fine, shimmering dust. Then she took up the knife. Dante cringed as she pulled it across her palm. Blood dripped from her closed fist into the mortar. She handed the knife to him, once again holding the mortar out.

Dante took the knife, reluctant, and braced himself. He winced as he drew the sharp blade across his skin. He squeezed his hand and allowed the blood to join with Death's. She mixed the concoction before adding it to the other bowl, which Dante realized was full of black ink, and then stirred that as well.

Death held out her bleeding palm to him. "Ready?"

Dante's calmness had been washed over with anxiety. "Yes." He gave her his hand.

She placed his hand bloody side down on the cold stone floor, firmly pinning it with her own. With her other hand, she dipped a finger into the ink. "This might hurt."

Dante took his last breaths before becoming an emissary. He hoped it wasn't his last breaths of freedom.

"You choose to bind yourself to me as an emissary, disciple of my tenants, agent of my cause," Death intoned. "Do you accept me as your patron god?"

"Yes."

Death touched her inked finger to the back of Dante's hand. He thought the liquid would be cool, but it burned on his skin, through his skin, soaking into his body. He gritted his teeth as Death drew the symbols that would bind them. The pain grew as she continued the process. Darkness crept in on his peripheral vision as the sensation grew to be too much.

This was it, the decision was made, and there was no turning back.

When Dante woke up, he was in his bed. His hand hurt and his whole body felt raw. He felt like he'd been struck by lightning, scorched through on the inside. He rolled over and was startled to see Death sitting in a chair next to his bed. There were dark circles under her eyes.

"Bronwen," was all she needed to say.

Dante hauled himself out of bed. He wasn't sure how long he'd been out after the ritual, but it didn't matter. Every moment counted while Bronwen's life was on the line. Together, he and Death hurried to Bronwen's quarters.

Bronwen was still unconscious. His face was jaundiced; he looked half-dead already. Dante tried to center himself in preparation for what was sure to be a difficult healing session.

He turned to Death. "So. How do I do this—drawing power from you?"

"Close your eyes."

He did so.

"Do you feel the bond? The connection between us?"

Dante searched within himself. It took a few breaths for him to sort through his energy stream, but he found it—it was like a thread running between them. "Yeah. I feel it."

"If I let you, you can pull some of my energy through it," she said. "I do not have a lot right now. So take what you need, but try to be efficient."

Dante began to pour healing energy into Bronwen, doing his best to guide his body's recovery process. As he did, he pulled gently at the bond, drawing energy from Death's pool. The power flowing through him was great, but it paled in comparison to what he had felt when he'd embodied Scarlet through his vision in Riordan's realm. The surge was turning into a trickle.

He could sense the infection running deep in Bronwen's veins. There was internal damage and bleeding, as well as his more obvious external wounds. Dante did his best to focus his energy on the infected cells and mending the worst of the damage.

When he felt both Death's and his own strength flag, Dante stopped.

As Dante pulled away, Bronwen's eyes fluttered open. "Dante?" he mumbled weakly.

"Save your strength," Dante told him. "I'm healing you. You're going to be okay."

"You became... an emissary?"

"Yes."

"I hope it wasn't just for... little old me," panted Bronwen.

"Not 'just', but... you've helped me so much, Bronwen."

Bronwen, moving lethargically, reached out and squeezed Dante's hand. "Thank you."

He smiled at Dante before closing his eyes, immediately drifting back into sleep. That was good. Rest was what his body needed the most now.

Death and Dante looked at each other. Her blood-red hair was flat, and the spark in her eyes had dulled. He wondered if she had any power left at all. He was sure that he looked as exhausted as she did.

Tired as Dante was, he wasn't about to forget their deal. "You owe me some answers."

"Back to the throne room, then," she said heavily.

When they arrived, Dante noticed the throne room was back to its pristine, austere, state—all evidence of the ritual had been wiped away. He wondered how many emissary bonds had been created in this room.

I'm an emissary. The words were still surreal.

Death didn't take her place on the throne. Instead, she stood in front of the dais, and looked at him, almost sadly. "What do you want to know?"

"Everything."

Death sighed. "Pick something."

"Ange. Why did you imprison her?"

"I was afraid she was working against me."

"Why?"

"She kept running off on her own, and she wasn't being honest with me. Even if I compelled her, she would find a way to dance around the full truth, if I didn't know the right questions to ask her. She is... wiley. And I wouldn't be the first god she's turned her back on. She used to be an emissary of Riordan."

Dante was dumbstruck. Ange had been on Riordan's side? "Does he have more emissaries?"

"Just Calder, I would think. Riordan purposely withholds his magic from the magus crystal grid and strangles the other gods' magic from flowing through as much as possible. That's why fewer mages are born in Saridian than in the other realms. And only very rarely is a mage attuned to Riordan. But the ones who are, he tracks down to recruit or eliminate. He chooses his future incarnate from his small number of emissaries and gets rid of the rest. He failed to kill Ange after Calder was chosen."

"So Ange is attuned to Riordan? I thought she was attuned to Io, like me. She reached me in my dreams."

"Ange is... an exceptional case. She is attuned to all of the gods' powers. I've never seen anyone like her."

This was growing stranger by the moment. "I suppose that explains her shapeshifting powers, too?"

"Illusion," Death corrected. "A facet of Cascara's power. Ange is a master of manipulation. She's dangerous, Dante. She's also an artificer. Do you know what that is?"

"Yes." Dante had flipped through enough of Scarlet's recommended books about the Magus War to know about artifacts. He also knew they were banned by the Magus Treaty. The creation of new artifacts was especially forbidden, as it depleted the magus crystal grid.

The use of magus crystal as a part of the binding ritual confirmed a couple of Dante's theories. The crystals they used looked the same as the crystal that hung around Death's neck. It was also the same as the crystal orb that was amplifying his visions. Perhaps his instinct to hide the orb had been the right one—who knows how Bronwen would feel about Dante having a banned artifact.

"She created artifact weapons to slay gods. Five of them. Perhaps six, actually. One for each god."

"Wait, Ange wants to kill *all* of the gods?"

"Perhaps. Or she wants six chances at killing Riordan. But the numbering is suspect."

Dante was suddenly very glad he hadn't chosen to go with Ange. Facing Riordan's forces was terrifying enough, he didn't need to get caught up in a campaign to kill *every* god.

"So that's Ange," Death said. "What else do you want to know?"

"Why is Riordan doing all this? What does he want?"

"That is a long story."

"When we spoke with Calder, it sounded like..."

"Like Riordan was obsessed with me?"

"Pretty much."

Dante stared her down, expectant, waiting for more. Death fidgeted with her crystal necklace.

"He got bored after the Magus War ended. I am the first incarnate of Death, and he found that... exotic. He fell in love with me, if you can even call it 'love', and I rejected him. He wouldn't take no for an answer. In his jealousy, he killed my partner and has been tormenting me ever since. He uses his powers to drain me of my own and to keep me locked in the Crossworld. Incarnates don't age here. I've been trapped for... years. Decades. I can barely rally forces to fight him from here, and slowly he gains ground on me while he continues his iron rule over Saridian."

"He's awful." It was putting it lightly, but Dante didn't even know what else he could say.

Death sat down on the edge of the dais, and let her head fall into her hands. "All I want to do is go to the Nextworld and search out my love. I miss her, Dante. I am exhausted."

She'd never looked so human to him. "I'm sorry."

Death cleared her throat and raised herself back up. "Next. Next question."

"When Bronwen is healed, what then? You'll let me go to my sister?"

"Yes. In fact, I will insist on it. She has joined a rebel faction in Saridian called the Vanguard. One of my last remaining emissaries is nearby, leading a group called the Ravens. They aren't currently working together, although I hope that will be resolved soon. The Vanguard has hold of the weapons Ange made. This is our final chance to defeat Riordan."

He would see Zandra again. Soon, even if it meant participating in a deadly battle between gods—he was going to have to accept that this was his life now. Regardless, relief flooded through him at the thought of being reunited with his sister, before another wave of dread hit. "And Scarlet?"

"She must stay in the Crossworld."

"Why?"

"Are you sure you want to know?" Death asked. "It might change things. And even though I am weakened, I will use some of my remaining energy to bind you against telling her."

"But—"

"I said I would tell *you* whatever you wanted. It doesn't mean you can tell Scarlet."

Dante's throat tightened. *She's already playing games with me.* "Why can't she know? It's cruel to trap her and not even tell her *why*."

"I made a promise to her mother that I would keep this from her. Kiera... has always tried to protect Scarlet from the things that will hurt. I doubt it is always the wisest course of action. Regardless, I've made the promise and I will honor it."

With his curiosity now sparked, Dante needed to know the answer, even if he had to keep it to himself. "Okay. Tell me."

"Riordan attacked Kiera and Scarlet. Scarlet was gravely injured. And then..." Death trailed off.

"And then you saved her." Dante had heard this story.

"No." Death played with the end of her braid, looking at her hair instead of Dante. "And then she died."

Dante's mouth opened and closed a few times. "But she's... she's *here*."

"Her energy had already merged into the stream of souls when Kiera brought her to me. Normally, when I save someone, I interrupt their energy before they join the stream. It's much easier that way.

"So I wasn't able to save her. Not completely. The emissary bond helped. I bought her more time, in hopes that I could figure out how to save her in truth. I tethered what I could of her soul back to her body and to the Crossworld. It's precarious at best. It's also part of the reason her powers are out of control. She isn't fully connected to her physical form."

Dante's heart dropped. "And if she goes to the World…"

"The connection she has to the Crossworld will snap and Scarlet will die. Even if she stays here, her soul will keep slowly leaking into the Nextworld. I've been feeding her energy through our emissary bond, enough that she hasn't noticed the transition yet. But I can't keep it up for much longer. She's slipping more quickly now, not just losing energy but parts of herself as well."

"There's nothing you can do to fix her?"

"If I had my full power, I may be able to find the pieces of her in the stream of souls but… in my current state, there is nothing more I can do."

Dante was frozen in place.

"I'm sorry, Dante. I can see the way you look at her. You care for her. But unless we defeat Riordan, it's only a matter of time until she dies."

CHAPTER 30

Scarlet thought that Dante had the sense to leave her to her misery. He left her alone for a week. Today, however, he had knocked on her door four different times throughout the day. It was dark out now, and he was pounding on her door once more.

She didn't answer. The last time she opened her door for him, she'd seen Death's mark on his hand and then slammed it closed in his face. They hadn't spoken since.

Presumably, he'd spent the last week healing Bronwen. In the meantime, Scarlet's maelstrom of emotions had settled into numbness. She wasn't sure if feeling nothing was better than the pain. She barely felt human anymore, she was a caged animal.

He'd had a way out. Dante could have left instead of becoming an emissary. But he threw away his chance to get away from here for good. For Bronwen and... hopefully not for her. She said everything she could to try to force him to leave.

"Come on, Scarlet." Dante's voice was muffled from the other side of the door. "I'm leaving. I don't know when I'll be back."

There was no lock on her door. He could have just come in instead of trying to convince her to answer him for the last half hour. At least he respected her that much.

"Please."

He's not going to go away this time, is he? Finally, Scarlet gave in. She rolled out of bed and flung the door open. The first thing her eyes darted to was the emissary mark on his hand. He noticed and clasped his hands behind his back.

"Death's sending me to Saridian," he said.

"Congratulations."

Scarlet started to close the door again, but Dante caught it with his foot. She was too tired to try to read the expression on his face.

"Scarlet. Can we just talk? I know you didn't want me to be an emissary but—"

"There's nothing else to talk about."

"Bronwen is going to live. My sister is with the Vanguard, and I'm going to go help them. I know it's complicated but I'm at peace with my decision—"

"Good for you."

He was still in the way of the door, so she left him in the threshold and went back to her bed.

"Scarlet." Dante's voice was forlorn. If Scarlet had any feeling left in her heart, this might have broken it.

She sat on her bed and stared out her window. It was impossible to look at him. "Can I come with you, to Saridian?"

Out of the corner of her eye, Scarlet saw his face drop. "No. I wish—"

"Have a good trip, Dante," she choked out. She turned fully away from him now, so he couldn't see the tears biting at her eyes. Those tears must have come up from her very depths, her last well of emotions. Everything hurt and felt like nothing, all at once.

She heard Dante exhale deeply and then leave, quietly closing the door behind him. She was alone again. She wanted to be. It was all she could stand. Even Viridian's presence felt like a knife pressing into her skin. She wanted her sister back, for real, in the flesh. But it was impossible. Her bittersweet contact was a tease, a taste of what she wanted but nothing more. It wasn't real. Scarlet didn't feel real. She was a shadow, barely a person.

If Scarlet hadn't lied to him, perhaps Dante wouldn't have become an emissary. But she had, and he did, and now he was gone.

Maybe being honest wouldn't have saved him either. The truth was messier, and no less cruel than her rejection. She didn't know how she felt. How was she supposed to know what love felt like when she barely knew friendship? He was her friend. The only friend she had ever had. To sort her feelings into romantic or platonic seemed insurmountable.

Maybe she hadn't lied to Dante. Maybe she did feel nothing. Her insides felt as cold as the snow that had been falling outside Deianira since that day.

She wrapped herself up in her blankets. Trying was useless. Death would send everyone else on missions, but not her. Scarlet was trapped, and there was nothing left to do about it.

Death came by shortly after. She didn't give the courtesy of knocking. Scarlet, in return, didn't give her the courtesy of standing up or even rolling over to face her.

"What do you want?" she asked her god.

There was a pause. "A favor."

Scarlet snorted.

Death cleared her throat. "I know you probably want to find Ange."

"You're here to compel me against going to her."

"I will be honest with you Scarlet, in hopes that you will take this seriously. I can't. I cannot compel you. After creating the bond with Dante, helping him heal Bronwen, and the amount of energy that Riordan has drained from me… I have nothing left."

"So I should just listen to you anyway, is that it?"

"I hope you will, for your safety."

Scarlet let out a sardonic laugh. "What's Ange going to do to me that you haven't?"

"Ange has no interest in keeping you alive. She'll use you for her purposes and throw you away."

"Ange knows how to free me from you and that *scares* you."

"Yes. But I'm afraid *for* you. The consequences of you leaving the Crossworld, or breaking your bond with me, are dire."

"What exactly are these consequences?"

"I can't tell you," Death said, "because of a promise I made to your mother."

That piqued Scarlet's curiosity enough that she rolled over to look at the god. Death's face was serious and sad. "What's my mother got to do with this?"

"I cannot explain more, because I told Kiera I wouldn't."

"That's a low blow. Bringing her into this. You just want to trap me, like Riordan has you trapped."

Death got so quiet that Scarlet could barely make out her next words. "That isn't true."

"I'm sure my mother is afraid of me facing Riordan. She always wanted to protect me from all this. But she's not here, and I'm a part of this fight too."

As Scarlet spoke, a spark of motivation reignited. The idea of running to Ange had been appealing but was impossible before. Now, Death herself admitted she didn't have the power to stop her. It was time. She'd find Ange, break her emissary bond, and be free to leave the Crossworld, to help fight Riordan, to finally save her mother.

"It is not so simple, Scarlet. Please. You and Bronwen must leave my realm now, though you must remain in the Crossworld. There are still tribes roaming among the other gods' realms, though it is against the Magus Treaty. Seek them out, or wander freely, but don't go to Angelise." Her red lips twisted into a grimace. "Riordan will come for me soon. I can't protect you here anymore."

"So what—you want me to feel sorry for you?"

Death looked like all the life had been sucked out of her. She looked mortal. Scarlet didn't let that temper her tirade. "I wanted to fight Riordan. But you were too busy trying to protect me or whatever it is you are really doing, instead of letting me look for my mother or do anything to help you."

"I did all I could, Scarlet. I know you do not believe me, but I did."

Scarlet didn't believe her. But she could disobey her. There was no point in wasting any time, in sticking around until Death could build up the energy to stop her. She rose and pushed past Death.

Death looked resigned. "Scarlet—"

"This is over," Scarlet told her. "I'm going to find Ange."

"I told Kiera I would keep you safe." Death's voice was small again. "It is not safe for you in the World."

Sparks crackled on Scarlet's fingertips. "I don't want to be kept safe." Each word was spoken like the crack of a whip. "And what an excuse that is—like you really care about your emissaries. You sent the rest to their deaths."

Scarlet thought Death would get angry, but she just looked defeated. "I know it is hard to believe that I care, given what you have seen, what I have done... and I am sorry for that."

Scarlet felt her magic overflowing, ready to explode. She had to reign herself in, lest she cause another backfire. "I'm going," she repeated.

"Do not leave the Crossworld," Death called after her. It wasn't a command; it was a plea.

The boat was still tethered to the dock, where they'd left it. Probably Dante was meant to take it when he left tomorrow. Scarlet untied it and hopped in.

Scarlet bit her lip. *Viridian?*

Her sister made her presence known, touching her mind softly. *I'm here.*

I'm leaving Death's realm, so... I don't know when I'll be able to talk to you again.

Viridian was quiet.

I know I haven't... been in contact much this past while, Scarlet continued. *I'm sorry. I miss you, but... it hurts so much. I don't want to have to say goodbye to you again.*

I'm sorry too, Viridian returned. *I know it's complicated. I'm still... dead. Even when we do not exchange words, I am glad to feel your presence again. I am glad to have a chance to have a proper goodbye.*

This isn't goodbye *goodbye yet, is it?*

Maybe. I don't know when I'll cross over, and I don't know when you'll be back.

Scarlet was sure she never wanted to come back to Deianira if she didn't have to. The only reason she would come back to Death's realm would be to talk to her sister again. She blinked and realized she was crying.

I don't know what happens next, either, Scarlet said. *But I guess if I end up getting myself killed, I'll see you again soon.*

Don't say that.

I'm finding Mom, no matter what.

I know. But Scarlet, you've grown so strong. I'm so proud of you. I think you have a chance. Pure strength will not win this battle alone, you'll need wit as well. I don't know if you can trust Ange but, one way or another... don't try to do this alone, okay?

Scarlet took an unsteady breath, her tears falling silently down her cheeks.

Even if this is goodbye for a while, Viridian continued, *we* will *see each other again. We will find each other in the Nextworld.*

Do you know that for sure?

I still don't know what awaits in the Nextworld but… I believe that we'll always be connected.

Scarlet pressed her palms into her eyes as if she could hold back the tears that were pouring out. *I love you, Viridian.*

I love you too, Scarlet.

Scarlet paddled across the river, alone.

The last time she'd been in this boat, she had faced the thought of losing Dante. She was going to open a portal for him and send him back to Saridian. She wished he could have gone then, instead of having to become an emissary to do so. She tried her best to put her thoughts of him out of her head as she let her boat drift downstream from Riordan's realm, toward Cascara's.

Cascara—the god her mother was attuned to. This thought only deepened the aching in her chest.

Once she reached the shore, Scarlet caught the branches of a tree overhanging the river and leveraged it to pull herself in. She hopped out onto the slick muddy bank, then tethered the boat to the tree. She'd never been to the Galapian Islands, but she would finally get a chance to see what her mother's homeland looked like once she got deeper into Cascara's realm.

Scarlet trekked through the swamp, and soon enough the trees changed from the gnarled and gray to luscious weeping willows. The ground became more solid as she went along, and slowly she became surrounded by more color. Plants of all sorts and teal moss covered the land around her.

It was breathtaking, coming out of Death's realm of gloom and into one of life. Scarlet drew in a deep breath, the freshness of the air filling her lungs, rejuvenating her. It was a balm for her raw feelings.

Large petals blew by on the breeze, carrying a sweet scent through the air, though Scarlet could not see anything blossoming. Curious to see where they came from, she headed upwind over a small hill covered with delicate grass which was tinged teal. She wondered if it was the same in the World, as everything in the Crossworld always seemed to be slightly off-color to their counterparts.

Scarlet crested the hill to see a stream flowing at the bottom. On the opposite side was a grove of trees covered in peach-colored blossoms. Her mother had told her about the cherry blossoms on the islands. She had promised to take Scarlet to see them, one day. In the World, they would be pink, not orange. Now her first time viewing the blossoms, she was alone. It soured the moment of beauty.

She came down the hill and realized she had miscalculated from above—it was not so much a stream as a river. *A river, in the middle of the realm?* She supposed it did make sense if this place was a mirror of the Galapian Islands. Perhaps here, the islands were split by rivers instead of the ocean. The water must feed back into the stream of souls.

The river stretched out into the distance, blocking her path forward. She'd have to cross it to continue her search for Ange. It had been a while since she had last swum, but with the months of training with Death, she was more fit than she ever had been.

Scarlet waded into the river as far as she could and took a few breaths to get her energy focused. She had no pack to get soaked through—in her rush to get out of Deianira, she had neglected to bring food or any other supplies. A critical oversight, yet she didn't care. Getting to Ange was the most important key to her survival. Everything else she would figure out later.

It would be a cold swim, so she heated herself from within. Learning to regulate her body heat with her magic was a skill that would come in handy.

She dove into the river, the freezing river quickly quenching the majority of the body heat she'd conjured and began to struggle through the current.

By kicking her legs and trying to remember how to stroke her arms through the water, she was making decent progress.

She was cold, but not nearly as much so as she would have been without her magic. Water splashed into her eyes, causing them to sting, but she pushed forward. About halfway across, Scarlet was confident that she would make it.

Then, something started to feel wrong. At first, she thought she'd hit a stronger current. Her movement slowed and she began to flounder. But it wasn't the flow of water pulling at her, it was the water itself, and it wasn't tugging her body, but something deeper... her energy? Was the stream of souls tugging on her very soul? She had no choice but to surrender to its grasp.

Her focus was lost and the water was free to rip away all her remaining warmth, leaving her frozen. The flow violently pulled both her body and soul along, submerging her in the stream.

Darkness encroached as icy water filled her lungs. At least, if this was the end, she perished in her own pursuits and not in Death's. What a strange comfort that was, as her vision faded to black.

CHAPTER 31

Dante's journey through Riordan's realm went smoothly up until the point where he had to open a portal to Saridian.

After a few days of healing, Bronwen had been properly stabilized, and Death told Dante it was time to go. He'd had his tense parting with Scarlet, then Death had brought him to the stream of souls, where a boat awaited—a different one than he and Scarlet had taken before, this one was larger—and gave him directions.

Though Scarlet had told him a bit, the intricacies of portaling didn't fully sink in until Death had explained it further. Certain points in the Crossworld corresponded with specific areas in the World, so if he wanted to end up in the right place, he'd have to travel within the Crossworld before opening a portal. Gods could freely portal around their realm of the Crossworld, but a mortal like him would have to walk.

He'd followed Death's instructions, traveling along the edge of the realm until he reached a forest. Then, he cut into the forest, heading deeper into the realm, until he found a large clearing. This part had been easy, and everything had been exactly as Death described.

There'd been one oddity along the way. At the point along his journey where he was to enter the forest, there was a boat shored up on the opposite side of the river. He wondered if it was Ange's, or if the Crossworld had other travelers. Regardless, he didn't want to linger and find out if the boat belonged to an enemy.

Now he was sitting in a clearing. Before him, a sharp black rock nearly as tall as he was jutted out of the ground. Emblazoned on the stone was Riordan's sigil. This was the waystone that Death directed him to, a landmark that emissaries used to navigate between the Crossworld and the World.

He was both so far and so close to his destination. Opening a portal here would take him to a place in Saridian near Rosewood, the home of the Vanguard. If Death was honest, the Ravens would be there too, including one of Death's last emissaries… and most importantly, Zandra.

All he had to do was cut through the fabric between Worlds.

This was his first task since becoming an emissary where he wouldn't be relying on Death's power to tide him through. Though he'd been trying for a couple of hours now, he hadn't managed to summon the amount of power he needed to open a portal.

Traveling to this point had taken him all day, and after his failed attempts at creating a portal, it was fully night. Only a sliver of one of the Crossworlds' moons shed light on him. The moonlight and the nearly colorless light emanating from the orb he had summoned glinted off the razor-sharp edges of the waystone.

His eyelids and limbs were heavy with exhaustion. He'd barely been sleeping this past week. Scarlet had been avoiding him, so there was no one to save him from his nightmares, but he had to sleep anyway for Bronwen's sake. Though Death loaned him energy, he needed as much of his own as well. Even with Death's added power, healing his mentor had been quite the ordeal.

For the first time, Dante felt like a real mage. In his previous life, he had been passive, never feeling like he made any real choices. Becoming an herbalist and healer was his one claim to individualism. He had things safe and only resorted to magic when he couldn't help himself.

Now, he had committed himself to being an emissary of Death. It was undeniably dangerous. It was a decision he'd been pressured into—but also against. *But in the end... I'm the one that chose this.*

It had gotten him answers, and power, and shunned by his best friend. The answers he had gotten from Death turned over and over in his mind as he tried to make sense of them all.

He did his best not to think of Scarlet, but that was impossible. Her determined spirit. The wry twist of her lips. Her sharpness, contrasted against her softness. Her warm body pressed against his the night they fell asleep together. That night meant everything to him. Falling asleep with her had been so intimate, even more than sharing a kiss could have been. But then, her utter rejection. It played over and over in his head.

And Scarlet was dying.

Dante's visions had intensified since becoming an emissary. Nightly, he dreamed of Scarlet's death, his own death, Bronwen's, Zandra's, anyone and everyone's. Riordan would come for them all.

He had to change the futures he saw, to get any of them out of this mess alive. But first, he had to open this portal.

Dante sighed as he released his skepticism and brought his focus back inward. He took in deep breaths, trying to recreate how he felt when Death's energy ran through him, trying to conjure strength of his own making. He was a mage. An emissary. *I can do this.*

A trickle of energy flowed through him, a pittance compared to what he had been using to heal Bronwen. Dante gnashed his teeth together. How could Scarlet do this? She seemingly wielded an endless store of energy when she fought. So what was different, between him and her?

He was timid where Scarlet dove in headfirst. She wasn't afraid of fighting or of getting hurt. Her flames danced around her, beautiful and deadly.

She let her magic run free, drive her, even to the point where it backfired. Dante had to think everything through. He held back, he resisted the call of magic.

But things were what they were, even if he didn't accept it at first. He was a mage. He didn't choose it, but he was. Even through becoming an emissary, using his newfound bond to heal Bronwen, he still hadn't accepted it, he realized. Not fully.

He was one of the gifted, able to access the power of the gods, to wield it for his own purpose. He was born with this talent that he had now honed into skill, and it was one he could no longer afford to waste—not if he wanted to protect those he cared for, to defend the powerless from abusers such as Riordan, or to turn his World into a better place: one where his sister could live safely without hiding her true self away.

I'm a mage. Magic is a part of me.

With this acceptance, something lifted. A block in the arteries that his energy flowed through loosened, and power ran through his veins. He was more whole. A few more breaths as he gathered this new strength and let it flow from his hands as it pooled in the air in front of him. The magic formed into a shimmering, mirror-like disk. He pressed his palms onto it, trying to push it open like a door, one that would cut through the barrier between Worlds. The disk shifted and suddenly there was nothing left against his hands.

The disk was shimmering, no longer solid. Through it, he could see another forest. This one was more green, the colors of the World he had grown up in. The World that Zandra was in.

He stepped through the portal. It smelled like home.

On the other side of the portal, Dante realized he was in another clearing. This one was smaller, and more enclosed than the one in the Crossworld.

He fed more magic to his light orb, but the brightness barely penetrated beyond the treeline. A thick mist hung among the trees, though it didn't encroach into the clearing. Next to him was another waystone, this one smaller and gray.

Death hadn't given him instructions from here, though she had assured him that the town of Rosewood was close. Dante picked the direction where the mist seemed the least thick and pushed his way through the brush. He stumbled out onto a game trail. The mist around him was too thick to see through in any direction except one, conveniently following the trail.

Even as the trail twisted and turned, the mist kept clear ahead of him. Dante's skin prickled, but he kept following the path laid out for him. Even when he emerged from the forest, perhaps out to an open plain, the mist was too thick to see in any direction except for forward, a straighter course now. Not long after, the mist gave way completely.

Dante could see the darkness of the sky arcing above him now, familiar constellations dotting the skies. In the distance, he spotted the dark shadows of buildings and scattered lights. It had to be Rosewood. He hurried toward it. The mist had left him damp and chilly, but now free of its grasp, he found the night's air pleasantly warm.

Dante dispelled his light as he got nearer to Rosewood. Using magic so close to people put him on edge. Even so, he was spotted as he approached. A half dozen or so figures, lit by torchlight, came from the town to surround him.

They came armed and armored. Hands were rested upon sword pommels, bow strings were drawn and aimed. They wore a mix of leather and chain mail. Dante's palms began to sweat as they formed a loose circle around him.

"Who are you?" a bearded man asked. "How did you get through?"

Dante tilted his head. "Get through?"

"The mist," the man clarified.

"Oh. It just seemed to... lead me through."

There was a silence, and some nervous glances between the crowd, then the man asked, "Where did you come from?"

How exactly do I answer that? His memories of being questioned by the soldiers-to-be when he'd left Briarglen flashed before his eyes. "The Crossworld," he said finally. He hoped the truth would either be welcome or only cause confusion. He certainly hadn't known what the Crossworld was before he had been taken there.

A woman spoke this time. "We'd better take him to Jarrett."

The man and the woman introduced themselves as Leon and Hera. The group led him into Rosewood and escorted him to a brick house in the middle of the town. Rosewood seemed a nice enough place, similar to Briarglen but a bit larger, and with more well-built houses.

The door opened, and a middle-aged man looked out at them. His hair was shaggy, dark brown but sprinkled with gray. He had a fair amount of scruff on his face, which couldn't quite hide a deep scar running across his cheek.

The man, which Dante could only assume was Jarrett, looked him up and down appraisingly, his eyebrows raised. "Another one?"

"Yeah," said Hera. "He said he didn't come through the mist."

"Portal?" Jarrett asked.

"Um," Dante stumbled. This was supposed to be the rebellion, but still, his heart hammered at the thought of admitting to being a mage. "Yeah."

"You'd better come in."

Dante shuffled into the house, alongside Hera and Leon. The others remained outside. "You're the leader of the Vanguard?" he asked.

"Everyone seems to know who we are now—I'm not sure if that's a blessing or a curse," Jarrett said and sighed as he reclined onto a large sofa.

"A blessing, I'd say," Hera said. "Especially if they keep being new allies. Who are you? Where are you from?"

"My name's Dante. I'm from... well, it's complicated. I was sent to help the Vanguard. And, my sister, Zandra, I heard she was here—"

Jarrett cut in. "Sent by who?"

"A god."

"Death." Jarrett gestured to Dante's hand when he saw his surprise. "I saw your emissary mark. That's Death's sigil, isn't it?"

Dante nodded. Jarrett was staring at him, a wary glint in his eye. None of these people seemed hostile, but Hera was the only one who appeared to be welcoming. He'd hoped the Vanguard would accept him easily, but Death had warned him that they'd been estranged from the Ravens, so their hesitation made sense. Reuniting their causes was part of his mission here.

"I know it must be hard to trust me," Dante said, "but I swear to you, I'm here to help."

Jarrett leaned forward in his seat. "Do you know a woman named Angelise?"

Dante hadn't expected that. "I met her once. Is she here?" He thought again of the boat, anchored on the river bordering Cascara's and Riordan's realms.

"She was, briefly." Jarrett's brow furrowed. "She offered to help us fight Riordan. She... has an interesting plan. She's left for now, promising to bring us more help. I'd like to know before she returns if she's trustworthy."

"Come on, Jarrett," Leon said. "How can we take his word any more than we can take hers? He's a stranger as well."

"If he has something to say," Jarrett snapped, "I'd like to hear it."

Dante cleared his throat. "I don't know. I have reasons to both trust and distrust her." Truthfully, his distrust rang louder, after his discussion with Death. But still, Ange appeared dedicated to eradicating Riordan, even if her reasons for doing so were unclear.

Jarrett leaned back again, his eyes searching the ceiling as if they held the answers he sought. "She's a strange one, isn't she?"

"She is. And, I would be happy to tell you all I know of her. But, I have to ask—is a girl named Zandra here? She's my sister, and it's been a long time since I've seen her. I'd like to know if she's safe."

"She's here," Jarrett said. "She's... okay."

Dante's heart leaped. "Can I see her?"

"Of course."

"I'll go find her," Leon said. "She's mentioned you. I'm sure she wants to see you, as well."

"Thank you." Some of the tension Dante held in his body was released as Leon took his leave.

"My apologies for jumping right into questions," Jarrett said. "There's just... so much going on."

Dante nodded. "I understand. And, I am here to help, so any information I have, you are welcome to."

"The Ravens," Hera said, Jarrett shooting her a dark look as she did so. "Have you had many dealings with them?"

"I haven't met with them personally, but I know they're on your side. Their leader is an emissary, like me. They want to take down Riordan as much as the Vanguard does."

"I'm trying to convince Jarrett that we need to work with them again." Hera gave Jarrett a sidelong glare. "Ange encouraged us to do so as well."

"Death told me you had a falling out with them," Dante said. "I'm not sure of the details, but I know we have a better chance of fighting Riordan if we're all working together."

Jarrett crossed his arms. "We have a better chance if we're working with people who can be trusted."

"I'm tired of your stubbornness, Jarrett," Hera snapped. "I'm sorry if you don't like it, but the Ravens have done the right thing. Your emotions are getting the better of you and endangering the Vanguard and our mission."

Jarrett turned red. He got up and stormed over to point a finger right at Hera's face. "They let Morgane *die*! You think that was the right decision?"

Hera stood her ground, looking up at Jarrett with fury plastered across her face. "We're the Vanguard. Have you forgotten? As hidden as we may be, we are at the forefront of the Saridi who stand against the Tyrant. That means we must be prepared to sacrifice ourselves for this cause. So yes, the Ravens saving the weapons over Morgane was the right thing to do. I'm certain she wouldn't have had it any other way. You know this too, deep down, but your hurt has made you stubborn. This isn't about you, or her, or *any* of us as individuals. It's about freeing our people from subjugation. So enough. Get your head out of your ass and remember what's important, or step out of the way as our leader and let someone else do what needs to be done."

Jarrett clenched his jaw, seething. He pulled at his hair and began to pace the room like a wild animal in a cage. "She was supposed to be here. She was supposed to be the one here, leading us—"

"But she's not!" Hera caught Jarrett by his shoulders and held him steady. She leveled another serious gaze at him as he breathed raggedly, his eyes darting around the room. "You need to decide, Jarrett. We've all been through a lot, no one would blame you for stepping back. But we need a leader who can hold all of this together."

Jarrett deflated. Dante didn't get a chance to figure out if this meant Jarrett would relinquish his leadership because the door to the house burst open. Everyone jumped back as the door slammed into the wall, and Zandra barreled in and practically tackled Dante.

"You're here," Zandra choked out through tears. "You're really here."

Dante held his sister tight. "I told you I'd come and find you, didn't I?"

After a long embrace, they released each other and Dante took a step back, evaluating Zandra. She was haggard, skinnier than before, and pale, as if her skin hadn't seen any of the sunlight of this year's summer. Her hair was chopped short and unevenly. Most shockingly, a long, gnarled scar ran down each of her cheeks. His sister had been magebranded. He'd seen it in his visions, but seeing it in person hit him even harder. Dante's stomach churned.

Though he had no physical injuries, the scrunched look of concern on Zandra's face told him that he didn't look great either. His lack of sleep had taken its toll.

"You made it here," Dante said, voice shaking. "I... I almost can't believe it."

"Yeah. Yeah, me too." The smile that had made its way to her lips suddenly faded. "Dante... I... Mom and Dad..."

"I know. I know what happened. I'll... explain how later but... you don't have to say it."

Zandra nodded and hugged Dante close again.

"What happened to your hair?" It was a silly question to ask, given everything else—like her magebrand—but it seemed like the easiest place to start.

"Oh." Zandra stepped back and ran a hand through what hair she did have left, perhaps self-consciously. "The mage hunters, they captured me and... I was put in a prison. My hair got so matted, I had to just cut them out."

Dante slumped. "Zandra. I'm so sorry, I should never have left you behind—"

"No. There was no way for you to know. It *should* have been safer for me at home. But I survived, I got out. A new friend helped me."

"Ah, and that friend has perfect timing, I see," commented Jarrett.

Dante turned to see the new figure standing at the door. It was Barek. Dante saw a note of recognition flash across the ex-mage hunter's face.

He had never fully processed the fact that his vision of Zandra in the prison was seen through Barek's eyes. Barek, who had been standing by as Dante was nearly killed by the other recruits, was the one who saved his sister. It hadn't seemed to matter much, as long as Zandra was safe. But seeing him in the flesh made his blood run cold.

"Dante, this is Barek," Zandra said. "He's the one who helped me escape the prison."

Barek's face had gone pale. "Dante?"

So, he remembers me.

"Barek, what's wrong?" Zandra asked.

"I... um..."

"We've met," Dante said.

"Y-yes," Barek said. "When my brother and our friends were first heading to Kingsmount to join the army, we traveled with him for a short time."

There was a pause as Zandra considered this. "That didn't go well, did it?"

The smart thing to do would be to sugar-coat this. He got Zandra out, he's on our side now. But something inside of him wouldn't let it slide. All the feelings rushed back, the pure terror he'd felt when he thought he might die. "No. They tried to kill me."

Zandra's brows furrowed severely. "*What?*"

Barek stared down at his feet. "Keenan thought that he might be a mage and attacked him. I tried to get him to stop—"

"But you didn't." Dante surprised himself with the amount of vitriol laced in his voice.

"I'm sorry," Barek said, and he genuinely looked it. "You're right. I should have done more. I've regretted that day ever since."

Zandra's safe, that's what matters, Dante reminded himself. His temper diffused a little. Zandra's did the opposite.

"But you must have known!" Zandra snapped. "I told you about him. You knew his name, and that he was a mage."

Barek drew in a deep breath. "Yes."

"And you said *nothing* about what had happened to him."

"I wasn't sure what *had* happened to him—he ran, and we couldn't find him, I didn't know if he was okay or not. I didn't know what to tell you."

"You could have told me you saw him." Zandra was practically crying with rage.

"I was ashamed." Barek turned fully to Dante now. "My family pressured me into enlisting along with my brother. I didn't want to go, but I went along with it. After running into you, Dante... it confirmed that joining the army was the last thing I wanted.

"But I couldn't just leave. Wren—my brother—along with my friends, wouldn't let me. So I went to Kingsmount, I enlisted like I was supposed to. They started to train me as a mage hunter and assigned me to the mage prison. It was awful there. I had to get out, and I managed to break Zandra free when I did."

Dante stared down Barek then turned to Zandra. "He was a mage hunter. You trust him?"

"He saved me." The look on Zandra's face was more serious than he'd ever seen on his little sister. "I'm not happy that he didn't tell me about meeting you. But without him..."

Dante bristled, more frustrations rising from the pit he'd shoved them into. Ange, Death, and Bronwen, all conspiring to get him banished, and to make him believe one of his best friends betrayed him. Scarlet's cold rejection still stung sharply. And now, a boy who'd almost helped get him murdered was his sister's savior, when he himself wasn't able to help her?

He shut his eyes, trapping the tears that threatened to fall. All of it just seemed like too much. *Zandra's safe,* he reminded himself again. *I'm so grateful for that.*

"He hasn't given us reason not to trust him," Jarrett said. "And, I assume you trust your sister, and she trusts him." Jarrett sighed deeply. "Hera... is right. We're going to need all the help we can gather. We have to keep sight of our ultimate goal."

Dante took a breath and opened his eyes. Hera was giving Jarrett a sidelong glance.

Jarrett sighed. "Yes, we need the Ravens, too. We have no choice but to trust the allies that have come forward. We've all taken risks, and to fight Riordan, we'll have to keep taking them. He's the one to blame for all the things—all the people—that we've lost.

"We have a common enemy. So now, let's unite against him."

Chapter 32

Scarlet didn't expect to wake up, but she did.

Branches full of orange blossoms greeted her when she opened her eyes. The sweet scent she had caught from the other side of the river was more potent now, mixed with the smell of damp grass that caressed her head. A pale petal gently floated down and landed on her cheek. It tickled. She brushed it away and found that the movement caused a flare of pain.

Something was deeply wrong, and it wasn't just her body. Her mind was clouded and slow. It took a monumental effort to coax her aching muscles to sit up. She was surrounded by a grove of cherry blossom trees. So, she had made it to the other side of the stream after all.

A voice startled her. "You're awake. Good."

Of course. It was impossible to have finished the river crossing without help. Scarlet swiveled to her right, where Ange was leaning against one of the trees. "I suppose I have you to thank for rescuing me."

"I suppose."

"I saved you and you saved me. So we're even now." Scarlet cleared her throat. It was scratchy and raw. She must have swallowed a lot of water in her near-drowning experience. "You told me you could help me. So, I came."

"Indeed." Ange crossed her arms as she eyed Scarlet up and down. Scarlet wasn't sure why Ange would be aloof now after she had invited her to meet here. Suddenly, she added, "I knew your mother, you know."

Scarlet prickled at Ange's use of past tense. "I didn't know."

"You look like her."

Scarlet ran her fingers through her hair. It was still wet and horribly knotted. She had inherited her dark curls from her mother who perhaps, being wiser, kept her hair chopped short.

"She never wanted you to meet me," Ange continued. "But we were friends, her and I. We worked together, developing weapons to use against Riordan." Ange paused. She plucked a blossom from an overhanging branch. "Eva didn't know that. Still doesn't, at least not about your mother. She—Kiera... changed her mind about the whole thing. The whole plan."

"If you were making weapons to use against Riordan, why would you hide that from Death?" The fact that her mother hid Ange didn't surprise Scarlet at all.

"The weapons are for more than fighting Riordan. A greater purpose that Kiera backed out of." Ange paused again as if gathering her thoughts, twirling the cherry blossom in her fingers. "She had one of the weapons. There's a chance she hid it somewhere else before Riordan got to her. Do you know anything about it? A broadsword, made of crystal."

Scarlet was sure she would remember a weapon of such description. "I've never seen anything like that."

"She may have disguised it with her magic. Did you transport anything of great importance?"

"Not that I know of."

"Ah, well." Ange shrugged and flicked the blossom away. "Your lack of knowledge is unfortunate."

It always is.

"Do you think my mother is still alive?" Scarlet thought that Calder threatening to use her against her mother was a sign that she still lived, but Ange put her on edge.

Ange looked at her for a long time. Scarlet fidgeted under her gaze. "I honestly don't know."

"Calder wanted to take me with him, to get her to give up... something."

Ange barred her teeth. "I don't trust him one way or another. He's a manipulator, just like Eva."

"And what about you?"

"Hm?"

Scarlet clenched her fists. "Will you help me? Or are you just going to manipulate me, too?"

"I'll help. There is one condition, but I'll make it clear." Ange came close, sitting down on the grass a couple of feet from Scarlet. Somehow, the woman was both soft and intense, which perturbed her. "You're set on freeing Kiera. I will help you sever your emissary bond so you may disobey Death. If your mother still lives, I'll help you save her, though she's done me wrong. But I want that sword back. Whether your mother hid, or if it fell into other hands, you will find that sword for me. Got it?"

"I don't want to do someone else's bidding any more," Scarlet said. "That's the whole point of breaking free from Death."

"Tough. That's the deal. One task, and then it's over, forever."

"Fine." Scarlet would take one mission over a life of being trapped. "So what's this greater purpose?"

"No, I can't tell you that yet. I don't want to let you in and have you run away like your mother did. Though, I think you may approve of my schemes." Ange flashed a grin. "For now, I will tell you this: I want Riordan dead. And I have a plan that will make that happen."

Scarlet was a moment away from agreeing when she noticed something: a mark on Ange's hand. But it wasn't the overlapping circles that composed Death's symbol, like she had seen on Ange's right hand in the dungeon. On Ange's left hand was yet another faded symbol, two "v" shapes with their tips interlocked.

"Wait," Scarlet said. "Is that... Riordan's symbol? You were an emissary of Riordan, too?"

Ange stiffened. "Yes. His was the first bond I had to break, many years ago. Back when I was a child, like how I first appeared to you."

"But... Riordan only takes a single emissary, the person who will serve as his next incarnate. So then, before Calder, that was meant to be you?"

"Not exactly. But I don't wish to speak about my past. Suffice it to say I hold only animosity toward both Riordan and Calder. My path for revenge led me to work for Death—and then, ultimately, to break that bond as well." Ange pushed a lock of hair out of her eyes. "So with all that, you need to decide. Are you in or are you out?"

"Alright," Scarlet said. "I'm in."

"And your friend, Dante," Ange said. "He isn't joining us?"

"No." A thousand icicles stabbed into her guts. "He isn't."

Scarlet had hoped that breaking the emissary bond would be simple, but of course, it wasn't. She began a whole new training regime under Ange, adjusting once again to a rigorous schedule. The tasks Ange gave her were mentally exhausting and relentless. Death had forced her into the practice of meditation, but those exercises were nothing compared to the hours on end spent clearing her mind for whatever came next.

The only things that gave Scarlet relief were Ange's other lessons. These ones were short, but more to Scarlet's liking. After Scarlet had recovered from her accidental underwater adventure—at least somewhat, her head was still foggy—Ange brought out two swords. They were simple, though their thin blades were curved in a way Scarlet had never seen before.

"These swords are from the Galapian Islands," Ange told her. "I popped through to the World to pick them up, since I thought you might be joining me."

Ange held out a sword to Scarlet. She accepted it, and turned it over in her hands, examining it. It was heavier than she thought it would be, but still lighter than the bulkier swords she'd seen before.

"What're they for?" Scarlet asked.

"For you. For training." Ange shrugged. "For *killing*."

"I understand what a sword does," Scarlet said, her annoyance leaking into her voice. "But I'm a mage, not a soldier."

"You're whatever you need to be. And if you want to kill Riordan, you're going to be a swordfighter. Magic itself isn't going to kill him. I mean, it could, but his divine self will live on and simply choose a new incarnate. You've had the dubious *pleasure* of meeting Calder, haven't you? We need a more permanent solution, and that's to cut him with one of the magus swords and trap his soul."

The magus swords. It was what Ange called the weapons she had forged—artificed—with magic. A real way to fight a god. Excitement tingled, and Scarlet gripped the sword by its hilt, assessing how it felt in her hand, its balance and weight. It was still too heavy for her, though she was stronger than she'd ever been. Her training had been rigorous, but not particularly focused on physical strength.

And so, a couple hours each day, she spent learning stances and how to parry, and having occasional spars with Ange. It was a relief from the mind-numbing meditation that filled the rest of her time.

Dimly, it brought back her memories of her mother teaching her to fight with a dagger, though with her head clouded as it was, it was harder for her to reach back that far into the recesses of her mind. She'd enjoyed that training, too.

She was grateful she had more useful methods of defending herself now, but she was glad her dagger hadn't come loose on her misadventures crossing the stream. Useful or not, it was still the last memento she had of her mother.

While Scarlet meditated, Ange foraged for fruit and other morsels for them to eat, but sometimes she would join Scarlet in her meditation.

"How is this helping?" Scarlet had snapped more than once when she hit a wall.

"You need complete mastery over your mind to break your bonds. When you have control of yourself, no one else can control you," Ange would explain. "Now, shut up. No talking. No thinking."

The days spent meditating must have added up to at least a week, maybe two. Ange encouraged her not to keep track of the time—too much thinking. Left alone with her mind, she couldn't stop the thoughts in her head at first. As much as she pushed them away, they battered at her, demanding to be acknowledged, examined, heard.

It was different from her days of isolation in Deianira. She had never felt so trapped in her head. Her meditation sessions as a part of Death's training were short in comparison, her magic training was more engaging, and in her downtime, she could read or talk to Dante. Now her days were solely filled with meditation and swordplay.

Her inner mind was distracted enough, back then. Now, trying so hard to not think at all, she couldn't help but scrutinize every thought and feeling that popped up. She imagined shooting each idea in her mind with a magic bolt, shattering it to pieces. That worked for a bit, but then the thoughts got more intrusive. Fighting them only made them more powerful. Her sluggish memories kept her thoughts narrowed to only the recent past, her time in the Crossworld. And, the less she wanted to think of something, the more often it haunted her supposed-to-be-empty mind.

Dante.

His name would float into her consciousness and she would immediately shoot it down. Three or four days into her forced meditation, she had eliminated all other thoughts, but his name still haunted her.

Dante. Dante. Dante. Dante. Dante. Dante.

It wore her down. She had to face it. Him. Herself.

Had she really told him that she didn't feel anything towards him? She had to tell him that. Because it was true. No, it wasn't. Yes, it had to be true, because she couldn't possibly love him, how could she love her first friend, she didn't even know what she was talking about, what she was feeling—she was being juvenile.

Even if she did like him, then what? They'd be in love, and he would become an emissary just so he could keep seeing her? She hated that he'd become an emissary, but he did it despite her, not because of her. If he'd given up his freedom *for* her... no, it was good she had turned him down, for that alone.

And still, it seemed he still had a life to live, even if she didn't. Death was willing to let him go to the World, for whatever reason. Why him? Why him and not her? Was Death's stubbornness really because of her mother?

She wanted to scream. How did she keep ending up alone? If Dante loved her enough, should he have cared enough to stay with her, instead of running off to the World without her?

No. Leaving had been the right thing to do. Scarlet couldn't hold him back. Especially not after she turned him down. Death probably hadn't given him a choice, anyway.

What if this worked and she could leave the Crossworld too?

She could join him in the World. Maybe they could save her mother and his sister. Maybe they could break his emissary bond, and they could get away from all this awfulness with Riordan and Death. If... if he really did care about her. *If.*

But Dante couldn't love her. She was a mess. She was nothing. She barely felt like a real person. She was flat, one-dimensional in her goals, unable to focus on anything else. Her past was a blur yet she was ensnared in it. She was exhausted, functioning only to do what she needed to. Become a better mage. Save her mother. She couldn't let herself want anything else.

Accomplishing that one thing was so far out of reach. Why even try? Why even keep trying, keep pushing forward, she couldn't fight a *god*, could she? Not with magic, not with a sword. It was ridiculous to think she could. She had lashed out at Death once, and sure it was back when she was weak, but even now… her, versus a god, she would be useless. Even with her talent, and all her training, she couldn't stand up to Riordan.

There's no point.

Even if she could disobey Death, even if Dante did love her, even if she knew how to save her mother, even if she had one of those magus weapons, even if she could drag herself out of this impossible hole she was in… she couldn't do it.

She was only mortal.

Death hadn't been able to defeat Riordan when she had a whole group of emissaries working for her, and now most of them were dead. Maybe Death keeping her in the Crossworld was protection, not against Riordan, but against realizing her hopes were worthless.

Scarlet cried. It was the first time in a long time she let herself sob instead of smothering her emotions. Under the protective canopy of the cherry blossoms, she wept until no more tears would come. If Ange saw her cry, she left her alone to it.

When her face finally dried, Scarlet was empty. Her mind was, too. She stopped asking Ange how much longer she had to do this for, and what use it was. She let it not matter. She let herself be hollow. Ange stopped interrupting her for sword training, and Scarlet barely noticed.

An indeterminate number of hours or days after that, Ange told her she was ready for the next step.

"And what, exactly, is that?" Scarlet asked. Her stomach growled. She hadn't eaten in… she wasn't sure how long. But it wasn't her body that was important right now, she had to focus on her soul.

"Go deep within yourself. Find your connection to Eva."

"I can already do that." At a whim, Scarlet could feel the magical link stretching between her emissary mark and Death.

"No. You can feel the superficial bond, the obvious parts of it. But not the core of it. It entwines through your whole body, your spirit, all of you. You have to find that, and then disentangle yourself from it."

Scarlet drew breath deep into her gut. She was so tired of all of this, but she had to keep pushing forward.

She closed her eyes and went back to the quiet place she had carved in her mind. Deep within her consciousness, she could envision this place: white, a field blanketed with snow, no footprints to be seen, the sky obscured with clumps of soft flakes falling. It smelled sterile, like the solutions Bronwen used to clean her wounds. And it was quiet, so quiet she could almost hear the snow as it fell. The silence was isolating. It could almost be peaceful; instead, she just felt alone.

She willed the wind to come into her mindscape, to blow away all the snow, to reveal what lay hidden beneath. With each breath, gusts tore through the quiet place and whisked the snow off to somewhere far away.

The winter scene was replaced by a feeling, rather than another visual representation. Scarlet felt tendrils running through her body, holding her tight. It was suddenly hard to breathe. She was weighted down, restricted. Bonds, grasping her, limiting her, spiked like barbed wire, all attached to Death.

The main one, the emissary bond itself, thrummed with power. It was power she could call on, if Death allowed. It would be hard to surrender that advantage if she were to face Riordan again, but she would never get that opportunity unless she broke free. The other bonds, the offshoots, were the compulsions Death had placed on her. They were smaller, but sharper, restraining her free will.

And then... there was one last bond, different from the rest. Though it was a thin wire, it clung to her desperately. It didn't cut her like the others did. It ran between her and Death, and then also... someone else. But who? Was it Viridian, was this how she could feel her sister's presence?

Scarlet felt like she was suffocating. She couldn't handle the feeling of each thorn, every compulsion, stabbing into her anymore. Her eyes flew open and she gasped her air. Ange took to her side as she breathed unsteadily.

"You feel them?" Ange asked.

Though the visceral intensity faded as her concentration broke, Scarlet doubted she could ignore the bonds, now that she had found them. "Yes. How do I break them?"

"Delve back into them, as you just did. It is painful, but you must take the time to disentangle yourself from your compulsions, and then from Eva if you can. Free yourself."

Scarlet took a deep breath to steel herself, then reached for the bonds once more. She could see parts of herself were intertwined with the magic that formed the bonds, as well as Death's energy. Examining how it twisted and turned, she realized Ange was right: it was like untying a knotted string, unraveling herself from Death's bindings.

With each knot untangled, each compulsion shrugged off, she was lighter. It was an immense relief to know that Death no longer limited her actions. Soon, only two bonds remained—the emissary bond itself, and the bond that connected to a third person. She had to figure out who that mystery person was before she broke that connection.

She traced that strange bond, and on the other end, there was... something familiar, but not her sister. It was an immediate relief to know that she didn't have to break her connection to Viridian to break free of Death's grasp. The bond connected to someone... more adjacent to Death. No, *it's not a person*, Scarlet realized after a moment. *It's a place.*

Somehow, Death had tethered her to the center of the Crossworld, where Deianira stood.

Perhaps it was a last-ditch effort by Death to keep her here, despite the god's faltering power. Best to disentangle this bond next, then she would tackle the emissary bond itself. Scarlet tried to grasp at it to begin the process, but it was solid, woven too tight to pull apart.

Did she come all this way just to fail? Was she too weak to break the bonds that mattered, the last that kept her from leaving the Crossworld?

No. If Ange could break her emissary bond, then Scarlet could break hers, along with the one tying her to this plane.

She sat in her empty place, the quiet place, now her place of power to work from, and began ripping the bond apart. It was thin, but dense. Tight like sinew, painful to claw at. Slowly, with effort, it loosened. It couldn't be untangled, this one needed to be ripped, cut clean.

Scarlet slashed at the bond, strands of it snapping as she did so. Suddenly, her emissary bond flared, and Death's words resounded loudly in her head.

Scarlet. You must stop.

Scarlet snorted. *Why would I do that? I'm freeing myself.*

Please, no. You do not understand what you are doing—

Scarlet swiped at the bond again, and Death's voice wavered with it. *Everything* wavered. She was so dizzy that her mind seemed like it was falling out of place.

A distant voice said, "Scarlet?" Not Death. Ange.

This life, these past few months, she couldn't do it anymore. Something had to break, and it was these bonds. She imagined cutting through the bond, sawing at it with her dagger, as she mentally thrust at it again. Another wave of dizziness washed over her.

YOU DO NOT UNDERSTAND.

The forcefulness of the words was overwhelming. In her vertigo and inner focus, Scarlet had all but lost sense of her physical self, but she felt her body crumple to the ground. She clawed at the dirt, bracing herself. *Of course I don't understand. You never explained* anything *to me!*

"Scarlet, what are you doing?" Ange, concerned, far away.

If you do this, you will die.

Scarlet laughed, perhaps out loud, but her body was distant right now. The fogginess was closing in on her, but she couldn't care. *Liar.*

It is true. I swear this to you. You must *stop.*

Waves of nausea swept over Scarlet. Was Death telling the truth, for once?

You must stop breaking the bond, and stay in the Crossworld.

No, she just wanted to keep her trapped here. Scarlet wasn't going to fall for that. She kept slicing.

Scarlet, I will explain everything to you, but stop. Please.

Never. Slice.

I only did this to save you. I saved you for Kiera, I promised her—

Slice.

I promised her to keep you safe. Just stop—

Slice.

Stop!

Slice.

And then, a snap.

And silence.

CHAPTER 33

The first night Dante spent with the Vanguard, he had a dreamless sleep. Reunited with his sister, his mind was at peace... at least for a moment.

In the morning he, Zandra, Jarrett, and Hera headed toward the wall of mist. It was time to make peace between the Ravens and the Vanguard.

As it came into view, Dante gestured toward the dense fog. "The mist let me through on my way here. But now, how will we find the Ravens in it?"

"It's more like they'll be finding us," Jarrett grumbled. "They're the ones who conjured it, after all. If they realize we're willing to speak, we're hoping they'll emerge. Or let us through, I suppose, like they did for Zandra and Barek."

They approached the mist, and it did not clear. Jarrett took a deep breath before leading the way in. "Stay close," he instructed, taking the lead.

Silence wrapped around as thickly as the fog did. It was eerie, only being able to see a few feet in any direction. Zandra clung to Dante, and Hera followed up in the rear, glancing behind them every few seconds.

"I can't believe you're an *emissary*," Zandra said to Dante as they continued through the mist. "You were so scared to use magic back home. What changed?"

"I left Saridian, first of all. Another emissary, Bronwen, took me to the Crossworld when I had to run from Barek and his... friends. He brought me to Death's castle and then... he showed me how to use magic to heal. He told me I could help people with magic."

Zandra nodded, solemn. "I want to help people too."

Dante stared at her for a moment. He had changed a lot in the months they'd been apart, but Zandra had changed too. She seemed older now. She'd been taken from home, magebranded, imprisoned... *It hurts my heart to think about all she's been through.*

"Everyone quiet," Hera said. "I think I heard something."

Listening closely, Dante could hear it now too. A gentle chiming, then the soft padding of footsteps on the damp grass. He turned to the sound and spotted a silhouette approaching them.

"Who is it?" Jarrett called out. Dante saw him reach for his sword's hilt, then purposefully move his hand away from it. "We're here in peace," he added.

A woman appeared out of the mist. The silver charms in her hair jingled as she moved. She wore black robes and layers of necklaces and bracelets.

"Fae," Jarrett greeted. His voice was steady but seemed forced. "You know Hera. This is Zandra and Dante."

Fae nodded. Her dark eyes flicked over the four of them. "I met the girl when she came through the mist. The boy is new, though, yes?"

Dante cleared his throat. "Fairly new."

"We'd like to speak with Leandra," Jarrett said. "Whether you'd like to take us to your camp, or if she'd like to come meet us—"

"Who says she'll speak with you at all?" Fae grinned, though her curled lips held no joy. "We sacrificed much to help you, and you treated us with contempt."

"And we'd like to apologize for that," Hera said. She looked pointedly over to Jarrett.

Jarrett held back a grimace. "Yes, we would. I know there's been... tension between the Ravens and the Vanguard, but we'd like to make things right, and work together against Riordan."

"And what makes this time different, Jarrett?" Fae asked. "You didn't trust us then, so why would you now?"

"We have to. Riordan is coming, and we can either be prepared or suffer the consequences of our hubris. *My* hubris. You know that, I know that, so stop with the games. Leandra will be happy to speak with us, won't she?"

Fae's lips twitched, a hint of a smile. "Yes. I just wanted to make sure your intentions were pure." Her face grew serious once more. "I'm sorry about Morgane. For what it's worth."

Jarrett nodded. His face was hard. Dante had heard a little last night about the conflict that had ended in the Vanguard's previous leader's death. Jarrett was clearly still grappling with grief.

Hera jumped in to spare Jarrett. "Would you like to meet on your turf, or ours?"

"Ours. Though soon it should be your turf as well." Fae's eyes darted to Dante and Zandra once more. "They're coming as well?"

"I wanted to see Leandra again," Zandra said. "She's the one who brought me and my friend through the mist."

"And you're an emissary of Death," Fae said to Dante. Her head tilted as she examined him.

Dante jumped a little. "I am. Death wanted me to assist the Vanguard in reuniting with the Ravens. She thinks it's within everyone's best interests."

"If you're a friend of Death's, you're a friend of ours."

Fae led the way and after a few minutes, they exited the mist at the Raven's camp. They still were not entirely clear of the mist. They were in a pocket of it that encompassed the Raven's home base. Fae led them through the spiraled layout to Leandra's tent at the center of the camp. The scent of lavender struck Dante as they all crowded into Leandra's tent. Fae left them, whether for privacy's sake or just to give them space to breathe, he wasn't sure.

Leandra sat cross-legged on a cushion, eyes closed. She left them in awkward silence for a few moments as she drew in a set of deep breaths. Then her bright eyes flashed open, and she took account of her guests.

"Jarrett. It is good to see you, once more."

Jarrett nodded stiffly in return. "We've come to make peace with you."

"You're ready to move past your anger?" Leandra asked.

There was a pause. Dante's hand began to sweat. He looked at Jarrett, expectantly.

"We're ready to move forward," Jarrett said, finally. "We hope you are, too."

"We have a new plan in place," Hera added. "We'd like to include you in it."

"A plan? Tell me about it."

"A woman named Angelise came to us," Jarrett began. Leandra's eyebrows shot up.

"Angelise is here?" Leandra hissed. "That woman—no, I'll let you finish first. What did she have to say to you?"

"She told me that I should recognize her." He paused a moment, but Leandra reacted no further, her face ironed back into nonchalance. "She offered to break the seal on my memories and told us that doing so would release a blast of magic that would draw Riordan to us, allowing us to ambush him. I don't know why he would take an interest in that, but I'm willing to place my trust in her if it will bring my memories back and give us a chance to face Riordan head-on without his soldiers."

Jarrett had also told them last night about his tattoo, and how it held some sort of magic. He had been reluctant to share any more than that.

"This seems a childish thing to say, as old as I am, but I'm a little hurt that you'd put so much trust in her, instead of us," Leandra said.

"We're sorry we didn't come to you sooner," Hera said. "It's difficult, knowing who to trust, and with all the pain we've experienced since our first fight to get the weapons. But you had our backs, and we're hoping we can restore your faith in us, and that you can trust us once again as well."

"I trust the Vanguard's sincerity in this matter," Leandra said. "Angelise, however..."

"You have something against her?" Jarrett asked. "Is it because she broke her bond with Death?"

"Among other reasons, yes. I don't think you can fathom how much danger and pain she's about to put you in. She'll have no consideration for your safety or well-being, as long as you're helping her move forward with her goals. Tell me, do you even know her true intentions?"

Jarrett dug his fingernails into his palms, attempting to restrain himself. "She wants me to have my answers, and to fight Riordan. To be blunt, that's good enough for me."

"I see that." Leandra frowned. "And I see there's no changing your mind."

Dante cleared his throat and spoke for the first time since entering the tent. "I know that Death has issues with Ange and that you probably do as well. Death sent me to help reunite the Ravens and the Vanguard, and while she may not have known that Ange would be a part of all this as well... the situation is dire."

"I regret that I must agree with you, but I do," Leandra said. "However, I must warn you that Angelise may not have our best interests in mind. But for now, we have little choice but to work alongside her. The Ravens will join forces with the Vanguard once again."

Dante exhaled a breath of relief and felt his companions all do the same. It had seemed fairly certain that the Ravens would work with the Vanguard again—it's what they, apparently, had been pushing for—but having it become official was the reassurance they all needed.

"What does our timeline look like?" Leandra asked.

"Ange has been gone for a few days," Jarrett said. "She said she needed some time to gather reinforcements. We expect her back any day now, and things should move forward quickly from there."

"Barek said that we need to act swiftly," Zandra added. "With the Tyrant's army growing as it has been, it's almost certain he is planning on breaking the truce with the other gods."

Jarrett nodded. "We'd like to welcome you to come to our planning sessions so we can discuss how to best combine our forces."

"Of course," Leandra said. "We'll arrange for that to happen shortly. For now, I would like to have a moment alone with the young mages here."

Jarrett glanced at Dante and Zandra. "You two are alright with that?"

Zandra nodded, her eyes locked on the older mage.

"That'd be fine," Dante said.

Jarrett and Hera shared a relieved look as they exited the tent.

It was strange to meet a new emissary, in Saridian of all places. He tried not to let the smoke from the burning incense make him cough. As far as Dante knew, she was the last emissary Death had left, other than him, Scarlet, and Bronwen.

Leandra didn't seem to be in a rush to speak after she sent Jarrett and Hera away.

Silence hung over them until Zandra broke it. "I wanted to thank you for bringing me and Barek to the Vanguard, even though you were feuding with them. We'd almost given up before we met you."

Leandra smiled softly. "The Vanguard is where you belong."

Dante wondered where he belonged. *Have I ever fully fit in anywhere?*

Leandra locked onto him as if his doubts drew her attention. "And you. A new emissary? It's a pleasure to meet you."

"This is Dante, my brother."

"It's good to meet you, too," Dante said.

"I hope we can end the struggle with Riordan," Leandra said. "Even now, I sense Death's power waning. Riordan will strike at her soon, and she has no defenses left." Though the woman's expression was stoic, Dante sensed the sadness beneath it. Surely she had known some, if not all, of the emissaries that fell during the Crossworld mission.

Worry brewed within him. If Riordan came for Death, Bronwen and Scarlet wouldn't be safe either. He doubted Bronwen would flee, even if he was well enough to do so. And Scarlet... he could only hope Death would force her to hide in another realm.

"What can we do to help?" Zandra asked.

"That all depends," Leandra said. "I never got a good reading of you when we first met."

Zandra tilted her head. "What do you mean?"

"I carry powers of insight." Leandra held out a hand to Zandra. "If you'd like, I'll tell you what I can."

As Zandra sat down and joined hands with Leandra, Dante realized that the woman must be attuned to Io. She was like him. He wondered what she could see as she stared into Zandra's eyes.

"You're strong," Leandra said after a few moments. "Stronger than you know. But, something is weighing you down. Many somethings."

Zandra's face twisted, displeased. "I won't let anything weigh me down. I'm going to help the Vanguard defeat Riordan."

"I think," Leandra said carefully, "that you should take a step back. Let yourself heal. You can't fight before you're ready to."

Zandra ripped her hand away. "Everyone keeps treating me like I'm a fragile little girl. But I'm *not*. No one can stop me from being a part of this."

His sister's words sounded so much like Scarlet's. "Zandra—" Dante tried to block her from fleeing the tent, but Zandra slipped past him. He looked to Leandra. "Sorry. I should go after—"

"Leave her be. She needs some time."

Dante bristled a little. This woman was a stranger, how could she possibly know what his sister needed?

"Trust me. Please." Leandra held out her hand. His turn.

Despite his reservations, he kneeled on the cushion in front of her table and took her hand. He had no idea what she could tell him, but if there was a chance it could help in the coming battle, he'd take it.

A calmness washed over him as their skin touched. Her gaze pierced into him, but he didn't feel the need to turn away from it. She wanted to help him.

"You carry Io's gifts as well," she noted. "Hm. They have an interesting hold on you."

"But... Death is my patron god. I'm attuned to Io, but they shouldn't be connected to me, should they?"

"It's true that gods usually do not have any particular claim on us mortals unless we become emissaries. But in this case... tell me, Dante—how have your powers manifested thus far?"

"I can heal."

"A rare art. I believe you have other affinities though, yes?"

He paused. Now that he'd told Scarlet, and fully accepted himself as a mage, it felt easier to say. "I have visions," he admitted. "In my dreams."

"You see the future?"

"And occasionally the past. Or... the present."

"Do you lose your eyesight afterward, for a time?"

"Y-yes. How do you know that?"

Leandra released his hands, and her mouth twisted, seemingly perplexed. Dante fidgeted anxiously. "You're a seer. So strange, for one like you to have been chosen at this time."

"What do you mean?"

Leandra leaned in closer to him. "Divination is not a regular gift. Your visions come not from your own power, but directly through Io's will. During the Magus War, Io would choose seers to help guide their followers—usually emissaries, or those who had otherwise joined their service. I don't know if there's been any since."

So Io had chosen him, for some reason. All of his visions had been caused by them. His skin prickled. He thought back to his first visions. They'd been so unclear at first. Then there was the crystal orb. His dreams had convinced him to find the pieces and taught him how to repair it.

That was a gift from Io too, wasn't it? His dreams had been more vivid and coherent since then, and they hadn't let him let go of it. It felt like a compulsion, akin to what Death did when she bound him from telling Scarlet the truth about why she was trapped in the Crossworld. Even now, the crystal orb was packed away with his things at Jarrett's house.

"Why would they make me a seer?"

"That is only for Io to know, I fear. Perhaps they will share with you one day. Though you are an emissary of Death, it seems Io has plans for you. But your talents, the ones you were born with, I believe there's more to those, too."

Dante grimaced. He had come a long way as a mage. He hoped it would be enough. It had to be.

"Along with your healing, you have powers of insight, too."

Dante was sure he couldn't look into people the way Leandra was reading him. Bronwen, too, had mentioned that he could sense people's gifts as he had with Dante's healing ability. "I don't think I can do that."

"Ah. Well. I feel that gift strongly within you. Perhaps you've been using it without ever realizing."

"Is that possible?" His head spun. Just as he gets comfortable with his current abilities, he finds out he could have even more?

Leandra shrugged. "What each person can sense with their insight is different. You could be reading people naturally, seeing through to some aspect of their true being without even realizing. Try to pay attention, especially when making skin-to-skin contact with someone, as that's when your powers will be the strongest."

When Leandra had let go of his hand, the sense of calmness he had been feeling receded. He wondered if that was something—her feelings, bleeding into his. "I'll try that," he said. "Thanks."

"Always happy to help a fellow emissary."

"Do you..." Dante paused, swallowing hard. "Do you think Zandra will be alright? There's so much that has happened to her, and I can't get her to talk about it with me."

Leandra's face darkened. "I'm sure you know she's been through a lot. The brand marks on her face tell a side of that story well enough. She will have some things to face inside herself. A great weight. I feel strongly that you should keep her far from Riordan. She needs to stabilize before she can face his darkness again."

"That may be difficult," Dante said. He knew how determined his sister was, and he could see how deadly serious she was about this matter. "But I'll do my best."

He and Leandra parted and he found his way out to the edge of the Ravens' camp, where Jarrett, Hera, and Zandra awaited him. He expected Zandra to be pouting, but she looked more angry than anything. It was strange to see her that way, so intense in her brooding. Jarrett was shifting from foot to foot as if he couldn't wait to leave. Hera was the only one who looked unequivocally pleased with the outcome of their meeting.

"What'd she say to you?" Jarrett asked.

"Probably nothing helpful," bit Zandra.

"She wanted to welcome me as an emissary," Dante told them. Though vague, it wasn't a lie. But he didn't want to get into a discussion about his powers. He didn't know how his insight even worked, and his visions—he hadn't even told Zandra about them yet.

Scarlet was the first person he'd ever shared his visions with. She'd protected him from them. He'd left her behind. He hoped, whatever was happening to Death right now, that Scarlet was safe from Riordan's grasp.

Days passed. Ange was taking her sweet time returning to the Vanguard, and Dante could sense how on edge that left everyone, particularly Jarrett. He wondered if that was a hint of the insight powers Leandra told him about. Could others not pick up on the emotions of others the way he did?

He was hyper-aware of his interactions with others over the next couple of days. Most of his time he spent with Zandra. His anxiety over her safety had only marginally lifted now that they were back together. He hated that she had gone through horrible experiences in his absence, and they weren't exactly safe yet. The magebrand that marred her face didn't help either, it was a constant reminder of the dangers that they still had to take on.

He offered to heal her scars. He wasn't sure that he could completely remove the puckered burns that stretched down most of her face, but he thought he could make them less noticeable.

But Zandra shook her head. "I'm a mage. I won't hide it anymore. Even if it means living with this." She held a finger up to one of the vertical marks. "I won't let them make me feel ashamed of who I am."

"You're sure?" Dante asked.

"I'm sure."

A darkness lurked inside Zandra that she never had before. Hatred rose in his gut as his insight touched her experience. Riordan had tortured her, had stolen his sister's innocence. Zandra was so different from only a few months ago; half the things that came from her mouth he couldn't imagine her saying back in Briarglen. She'd been so wild and carefree, once.

They avoided talking about home. It was gone, anyway, and they both knew it. Nothing they could say now would change how anything had gone with their parents, or bring them back. It was a pain that sat between them, shared but unspoken.

Dante supposed that he was different than he had been, too. He was a practicing mage, for one. That had been an unimaginable future before he left home. Now, he wasn't only a mage, but an emissary of a god. He'd summoned strength to do impossible things.

He was stronger than ever before. He didn't know if he was tough enough to help save the World from Riordan, but he was certainly tough enough to try. That, in itself, was a small victory.

CHAPTER 34

Scarlet was free, and everything was wrong. She was undefined, her senses bled outside of her body, not entirely attached. Waves of dizziness and nausea washed over her.

Ange brought her a waterskin to sip on. The sensation of drinking didn't feel right in her throat, in her stomach. It was like she watched her body from the outside as an observer.

Ange wouldn't stop staring at her. "Whatever you did," she said, "I don't think you should have done it."

Scarlet did her best to hold herself up off the ground as she struggled to remember how to breathe. It took a moment for her to figure out how to form words. "Too late now," she managed.

Energy flowed from her emissary bond to her. It didn't fill her with power to use, like when she had drawn on Death before, it simply gave her enough to energy sustain herself. She was leaking out, her energy dissipating nearly as fast as it was replenished. The god was saving her, for now.

Scarlet's heart hammered as she continued to gasp for air. *What have I done, what's happening?* Death had little energy left; if this problem was long-term, she wouldn't be able to help Scarlet for long. Scarlet definitely couldn't break the emissary bond now. It was the only thing keeping her alive.

The hemorrhaging of energy began to slow. She wasn't quite stable, but she also didn't feel the incapacitating vertigo as if she were floating out of her body... as much. She was able to sit upright. Ange sat down across from her.

"Death saved my life. Again." Scarlet swallowed. Bodily sensations were still weird. "I thought she saved me so she could have more emissaries. She needs mages, but she never used me for anything, even though I'm a good one. It never made sense to me. Why use so much of her power to save me, when she wasn't even going to use me as a tool to fight Riordan? Especially because I *want* to, I want to fight him, to find my mother, everything. Why save me, and keep me here? Why?"

"For Kiera," Ange said softly. There was an edge in her voice like she was holding something back.

"Death doesn't seem like the type to do favors."

"She has a soft spot for Kiera. They"—Ange gestured vaguely—"were involved."

"*Involved.* You mean, romantically?" Scarlet knew her mother liked women as well as men, but *Death* of all people? "You can't be serious."

"It's true."

"What about my father?"

"This was before Kiera met him. She and Eva had ended things quite explosively sometime before that. Things weren't the same after. Eva chose to call herself 'Death' as a tactic to intimidate her new emissaries. She didn't used to be as... aggressive."

Scarlet's memories had been clouded since plunging into the stream, and severing her connections only pushed them further away. Even before then, she had tried to distance herself from recollections of her father. She would never forgive him for leaving them. "Did you know him?"

"Only a little."

There was a mischievous glint in Ange's mismatched eyes. Scarlet was too dazed to try to interpret it. "So what, my mom broke up with Death, and then she turned into a monster?"

"Eva's transformation was a long time coming. She has lost a lot, and not dealt with any of it well. Do you know about Deia?"

"Like, Deianira? The castle?"

"The woman the castle is named after."

Scarlet shook her head.

"I'm not surprised. Eva does not speak of her easily. Deia was her first love, back when she was still a mortal. Perhaps all might have ended well, but then Eva became Death's first incarnate. This caught Riordan's attention. To him, she was something unique. Something wild that he wanted to control, just like he does with everything else. But of course, she spurned him. For revenge, he killed Deia. And as you know, he has not gone away since. He will wear her down until she has no power to hold him away."

Scarlet drank this information in. "I won't do it solely for Death's sake," she said, "But Riordan does have to be stopped."

"For many reasons, yes. If he has his way, he may also disrupt the cycle of souls, which would be disastrous for any souls entering or leaving the World. He wants more power, meaning the Magus War may begin anew. Mortals will be caught in the crossfire between gods once again, and I will not let that happen."

"So. When are we going to Saridian?" Scarlet asked.

"I'm not sure you should come to the World, given your condition."

"Oh, don't you pull this on me now." Sparks lived in Scarlet's fingertips, ready to break loose. "We had a deal. You want me to find your sword? You want to fight Riordan? Take me to the World. You said you had a plan, didn't you? No time to waste." Time might be limited, after all, if she kept leaking out her energy. If Death didn't have the power to keep sustaining her.

Ange shrugged. "Fine. Let's go."

As the afternoon drew on, Ange took Scarlet through Cascara's realm, using a boat to navigate the rivers crisscrossing through it. The sun lowered in the sky, and the twin moons of the Crossworld rose to take their place as they progressed into Riordan's realm.

They spent an hour or two trekking through a forest, eventually reaching a clearing. An obsidian pillar stood in the center of it. Something her mother once told her about something like this tickled the back of her mind, but she couldn't put together the thought. Ange stopped and slowly turned to Scarlet.

"This is the place?" Scarlet asked.

Ange seemed hesitant, her eyes flickering briefly over Scarlet as she scanned the area. "Yes."

"But?"

"I still don't think you should come."

"What? I'm coming. You already agreed. You took me all the way out here—"

"Yes, well." Ange huffed out a sharp breath. "It's unfortunate. I wasted a lot of time helping you free yourself from your bonds—"

"So, I'm coming."

"You can barely walk straight."

Scarlet grimaced. She had tried to hide the dizziness that plagued her their whole journey. She certainly wasn't in the best shape, but there was no way she could turn back now. "What other option is there?"

"Stay here and wait for me. I need to touch base with my contacts in the World, and then I'll come back and try to help you figure out... whatever's going on with you."

"Contacts?"

"Yes." Ange didn't elaborate. "I'll be as fast as I can."

"And in the meantime, you're leaving me alone in Riordan's realm?"

"Can you make it back to Cascara's realm? You'll probably be safe enough going back there yourself. Riordan should be pretty distracted shortly."

Just then, a new wrongness stirred in Scarlet's gut. "Riordan is coming for Death."

Ange nodded grimly. "She's been worn too thin and has no one left to defend her. He'll come soon if he hasn't already."

Death had sent Dante away, as well as Scarlet, and perhaps Bronwen too if she'd gotten her way. Death knew she was done for. Plus, on top of it all, she was feeding Scarlet energy now. Scarlet didn't know how to feel about her patron god keeping her alive because of her past relationship with Scarlet's mother. It was still too strange to wrap her mind around.

But if Riordan was coming for Death, her kindness, regardless of motivation, might not be able to last for long. Time was running out for them all.

Scarlet sighed. "How long will you be gone?"

"Give me a day."

A day. It seemed far too long.

Ange picked up on her hesitation. "I'm sorry. I need at least that much time to arrange everything. I'll meet you back at the river by sunset tomorrow."

"What exactly are you arranging?"

Ange pulled her lips tight.

"You're going to fight him."

Ange brushed a lock of golden hair out of her face but didn't answer.

"If you're fighting him, there's no way I'm staying—"

"I'm not taking you with me now," Ange snapped. "That's final. The plan has to go forward before we're out of time. We'll get you fixed up after and you can help me find that sword."

Scarlet snarled. Reflexively, she tried to draw energy to her fingertips, prepared to fight if she had to, but she couldn't coalesce enough power before it leaked out of her body and the effort to do so made her stagger.

Ange turned around and waved a hand, the air in front of her ripping open into a circular portal. Scarlet's heart dropped. That was Saridian, through there. Everything she wanted, only a few steps away, and yet she still couldn't go.

"You'd better start heading for the river," Ange looked back to tell her before she stepped through. "Riordan will come to us through the Crossworld, and you don't want to be caught here when he does."

CHAPTER 35

Jarrett barely felt like he could breathe for the days between the reunification with the Ravens and when Ange came back. The Ravens thought that Riordan wouldn't come for Rosewood quite yet, but that didn't put any of them at ease. Whatever he was up to was still no good for them, and if he did choose to come crush the rebellion, they'd lose their advantage.

The Ravens had moved their camp closer to Rosewood, now within the walls of the mist. They were extra protection, but loomed in a way that made Jarrett uncomfortable.

Jarrett was restless. Moreso than usual. He was on the cusp of having his memories back. He tried not to think about it, but that only made his anxiety more persistent. It was even worse when he ran out of things to organize. The Vanguard was ready, and so were the Ravens. They just needed the final piece: Ange, and whatever help she had mustered.

In the meantime, there was one other important thing to take care of.

He tracked down Hera. It took some time but as the sun was beginning to set, he found her at the edge of town, staring out beyond the path leading north in the direction of Kingsmount. Jarrett joined her on the ground, where she sat cross-legged. He was glad to find her alone.

"What are you doing out here?" he asked.

"Thinking." She didn't turn to look at him, but her tone wasn't dismissive, either.

"About what?"

He thought she'd respond with either something about their upcoming head-to-head battle with a god, or else something snarky. "My parents," she answered instead.

Jarrett didn't know how to respond to that. He knew that Hera's mother had been a mage. The mage hunters killed both of her parents when they found out. Hera escaped their wrath, left her town, and eventually stumbled upon the Vanguard. She'd only been fifteen, then.

"I always think about them before I do something stupid," she continued. "Eh, not *stupid* just... risky."

"Understandable," Jarrett said. "I can't promise we won't die, but I hope we can at least do enough to take down Riordan. Temporarily, if nothing else."

Hera picked a particularly long piece of grass and began to fiddle with it, twisting it and tying knots along its length.

"You were right, you know," Jarrett said.

"Hm?"

"I did have my head up my ass."

Hera snorted, and Jarrett saw a smile briefly flicker onto her face.

"I could have ruined your chance to get revenge for your parents' sake," Jarrett said. "I'm sorry for that."

Hera looked out at the setting sun, which illuminated her face with startling gold and red rays of light. "I'm not so sure this is even about revenge, for me. It *was* when I joined. But now... I mostly find myself hoping that they'd be proud of me. Who I've become."

"I never knew them, but I'm certain they would be. How could they not? You're only eighteen and you're already at the frontline of a mage rebellion, fighting against a tyrannical god."

She let out a deep sigh. "Thanks, Jarrett."

They lapsed into silence for a time. The sun was nearly below the horizon now; it was getting dark. Jarrett needed to say what he came to tell her. Though he was resolved, it was still difficult. He was sure Hera could feel the tension coiled within him, but she was patient, waiting for him to speak.

Jarrett swallowed. "I want you to lead the Vanguard."

"Jarrett!" Hera stood and looked down at him with consternation plastered on her face. "No. Why? And again: no."

"I'm getting to be an old man."

"You're not *that* old."

"No. But I've been realizing what the new generation has to offer. And while the Vanguard has been my life's purpose these past years... in some ways, I've also lost focus. I let my anger and grief nearly jeopardize the one chance we had to lash out at our enemy."

Hera held her hands out to him. He took them and let her help pull him up from the ground. His bones creaked. *Maybe I'm not old old, but my body isn't what it used to be.*

Hera clapped her hands on his shoulders. "You let Morgane's death get to you. I won't blame you for that. It's hard to lose the people you're closest to, those who you confide in when things get really hard. Plus, people have all sorts of reasons to mistrust the Ravens. They're *weird*. We don't understand them."

"But through it all, you saw what was important. The Ravens have been helping us... overall."

Hera crossed her arms and shrugged. "So, maybe I'm right this time. That doesn't mean I'm anywhere near ready to *lead* the Vanguard."

Jarrett sighed, releasing a breath into the chill night air. "I think you could be. Looking at you, as well as Barek and Zandra and now this Dante boy, too... you're all talented and determined. And so *level-headed,* as a team."

Hera took some time to consider this. "I say make me your second. You should have one before this battle anyway, in case something happens to you. But actually being the leader? I don't know. Not now, not right before we do the most important thing we've ever done."

"Yes, I was thinking it would be prudent to wait until after this confrontation with Riordan. I don't want to upend everything right before." Jarrett said. "But I also... don't know who I'll be after this battle."

He told her about his missing memories, and how Ange claimed that she could lure Riordan here when she broke the magic seal holding his past. The rest of the Vanguard had only heard a vague version of this plan, which excluded the particulars of Jarrett's personal connection in this plot. He hadn't realized how much he'd needed this, how much he'd missed having someone to talk to about all that was eating him up inside.

It became fully dark as Jarrett finished his explanation, so Hera lit a lantern she had brought along with her. By its light, Hera stared at Jarrett.

"Whatever you learn about yourself and your past, however the battle goes... if we both live, we will figure it out in the aftermath together."

He could only hope they'd be lucky enough to get that chance. "Thank you."

Ange returned a fortnight after she had left. When Jarrett received word of her arrival, he raced to the town hall where she awaited him. He burst through the doors, chest heaving. Leon and Rohan stood next to her.

"You're back," Jarrett said.

"So I am," Ange said. There was a glint of worry in her eyes.

Jarrett glanced around. "I thought you were bringing more recruits."

Ange grimaced. "That fell through. There were some... unfortunate circumstances."

"What? So you left us hanging for two weeks for nothing?"

"Jarrett," Leon broke in. "Take a breath. We have the Ravens back with us, and we needed the time anyway."

He's not the one waiting to get his whole life back.

"Trust me, I wish I could have been more successful," Ange said. "But regardless, we must move forward. How soon can you and the Ravens be ready?"

The sun would set soon. Fighting Riordan in the dark sounded like it would be inconvenient. "First thing in the morning?" Jarrett suggested.

"So be it," Ange said. "We'll break the seal then."

"I may be a mage myself," Rohan said, "but I still don't quite understand what you're going to do that will draw Riordan into our trap."

"There's a mage that Riordan has a particular interest in," Ange said. "This mage used her powers to leave a semi-permanent effect on Jarrett. I'm going to break that effect, and hope that the magic released from it is strong enough, and has enough of the mage's signature on it, that Riordan senses it. If he does, I know he will come to us. Probably quickly, using the Crossworld to take a shortcut to us."

"A semi-permanent effect?" Rohan asked. "How is that even possible?"

"She's a very good mage. And highly creative." Ange held up her hand, the one with the faded emissary marks. "Do you know much about the bond between a god and their emissaries? She figured out how to do something similar but for a different purpose."

Jarrett could feel Rohan and Leon's questioning gazes on him. "She clouded my memories," he told them. It was easier to say now. He was about to get them back. He cleared his throat. "Is there anything else we need to prepare?"

"From what Rohan and Leon have told me, you're quite well prepared," Ange said. "The only thing left to decide is who will wield the magus swords. I'll take one, so we'll have four left to distribute. Any suggestions?"

"Leon, of course," Jarrett said. "And myself."

"Oh." Ange twisted a strand of her hair, suddenly awkward. "No, you aren't a good pick."

"What?" Jarrett's knuckles turned white as he clenched his hands. Sure, he wasn't in his prime anymore, but he could still hold his own in a fight.

"You won't be in any shape to join the battle after I break the seal."

"I'm sure I can handle it. This battle is important—"

"Which is exactly why you're sitting out. Trust me, you won't be needing a weapon, especially not a magus sword."

Jarrett growled. "Fine."

"Leon, though, I'll agree with you on that."

"I appreciate the vote of confidence," Leon said, though his face looked grim. "I'd vote for Korene to have one as well. I might be the strong one, but she's quick as a serpent's strike."

Jarrett nodded his assent. He was grateful that Hera had a better tactical mind rather than being a great fighter. He didn't want them both to be a huge target for Riordan in this battle, now that she was to succeed him as leader. "The Ravens," he said with a sigh. "They'll want at least one."

"That they will," Ange said. "We'll let them decide who's best out of their own."

"Should we give them two, split the weapons evenly, after everything?" asked Rohan. "It would certainly be a gesture of goodwill."

"Waiting for me to arrive before beginning the meeting would have been a gesture of goodwill." The door swung shut loudly behind Leandra. "But I suppose that's beyond what I should expect, isn't it Angelise?"

"It is," Ange said, cold.

An emissary and ex-emissary of Death. Jarrett wondered what their history was. It didn't seem pretty.

"One sword is fine," Leandra said. "The Ravens focus more on magic than swordsmanship. I'll let you distribute the rest as you feel is best. Though I ask you to consider what Ange has in store for the remainder of these weapons if we are successful against Riordan."

"What do you mean?" Jarrett asked.

"Five swords, Jarrett. Do you think she doesn't mean to use the rest?"

"Enough," Ange snapped. "My intentions are the same as yours: to stop Riordan."

"But to what end?" Leandra's voice rose. "Why did you run away, Ange? What are you up to?"

"You think Death's rule is any better than Riordan's?" Ange asked. "I decided that I answer to no one. And yes, that includes you. So you can accept my help and the use of the artifacts I risked my life to create, or you can figure this out on your own."

"We have little choice," Leandra said. "All of us, we're stuck together for now."

Jarrett, Leon, and Rohan, all exchanged concerned glances. *Is everything slipping out of control in the final hours before facing Riordan?*

"We're all on the same side," Jarrett said. "Against Riordan, if nothing else. There's no moving forward until he is removed from the throne. There's one more sword. Let's decide together who should use it."

"What about Barek?" Ange suggested. "He's new enough to feel like a neutral pick, isn't he?"

"And talented enough," said Leon.

"He's..." *Young,* Jarrett wanted to say. But he continued to remind himself that he couldn't protect these young fighters. They came to fight and risk their lives just like everyone else and had seen just as much hardship as the others here. "He's a good fighter. If he wants to accept this offer, then he has my blessing. Leandra?"

"Only if the girl gets kept out of it. Zandra."

"I'm not sure anyone will be able to stop her from showing up," Rohan said. "Regardless of who wields the swords."

Jarrett's feelings were mixed. Zandra was young too, younger than Barek. And, obviously traumatized by her time in the mage prison. But still, she was a good mage, and she was determined to get her revenge on Riordan. Leandra tried to protect Jarrett from getting what he wanted, his memories. Something painful, and dangerous, especially when it meant drawing Riordan to them. He didn't want to be protected from doing what he needed to do, so would it be hypocritical for him to try to do that to someone else?

"Even if we could stop her," he said reluctantly, "I'm not sure we should. If she chooses to fight, that's her decision, ultimately."

Ange raised an eyebrow. "Good enough for you, Leandra?"

The older woman shrugged. "I suppose it will have to be."

CHAPTER 36

Dread tugged at Dante. Something was wrong. Catastrophically wrong. The sensation flowed through his emissary bond, overwhelming him. He slumped down onto one of the couches in Jarrett's sitting room.

"Are you okay?" Zandra asked. She took a seat next to him, hovering worriedly. "Your face went white."

"Something's happening." Dante tried to swallow, but his mouth was dry. "Death—" The inner turmoil was too much. He shuddered and doubled over.

"What's going on?" Dante could hear Barek asking. He sounded so distant, though he was only a few paces away.

"I don't know." Zandra's voice wavered. She placed a comforting hand on his back. "He said something about Death?"

More talking, but Dante couldn't hear anymore. Everything was wrong. He was lost. He wanted to puke, to escape his body. A boulder was weighing him down. He could feel rage, Death's rage. She had lost control. Something sinister was taking over. A sly grin. Riordan.

He'd come to get Death.

Dante couldn't let this overwhelm him. Riordan was draining the last of Death's energy, and Dante's energy would get sucked along with it if he didn't stop it. He found his emissary bond and pinched the flow. Suddenly, he could breathe again, the world slowly coming back into focus.

As he settled, he realized there were more people in the room. Jarrett had returned from the meeting he'd been called to, and Ange stood near the doorway, each of them holding a sword with a blade of crystal. They must be the god-slaying artifacts he'd been told about. Everyone was watching him, faces drawn with concern.

Most importantly, Ange had arrived. That must have been why Jarrett had run off in such a hurry.

"Do you feel it?" Dante asked her. "I know you aren't an emissary anymore, but..."

"Riordan got to her, did he?" Ange said quietly. "I wasn't sure, but I am now."

Dante lost himself for a few more moments before he was able to pinch off the emissary bond more firmly. "We have to stop him."

"Tomorrow," Ange said. "As soon as we can, at first light. There will be consequences that will be felt around both the World and Crossworld without Death performing her duties."

"What do you mean?" Zandra asked. "What kind of consequences?"

"This is unprecedented. So I can't say exactly," Ange said. "But I do have my theories, after spending time as an emissary of Death. Without her oversight, more souls crossing over to the Nextworld would become trapped either in the Crossworld or in the World. When souls become trapped like this, they're known as 'ghosts'. Too many ghosts will build up a large amount of unstable energy. It could wreak all sorts of havoc in both worlds. Natural disasters. Spontaneous combustion, maybe? Magic going haywire." Ange wavered. "And, it's possible that people could be born without souls. Or I suppose, not born at all."

A somber silence followed.

"So those are the stakes," Ange said. "Not to mention anything else that Riordan has planned. For example, a second Magus War. Any questions?"

Dante cleared his throat. "What about Scarlet?" he asked. "And Bronwen. Do you know if they made it out safe?"

When Ange didn't reply at first, Dante thought that he might be drifting out of reality again.

"I don't know where Bronwen is," she said after a long moment. "Knowing him, he probably stayed with Death."

Dante's heart dropped. He hoped his mentor had been wise enough to run. "And Scarlet?"

"She's not at Deianira. She came to me in Cascara's realm."

"So she's safe?"

Ange shrugged. "More or less."

That didn't give him comfort; she was clearly hiding something. "Where is she now?"

"Riordan's realm. Or, hopefully back in Cascara's by now."

"You left her *alone* in Riordan's realm?!" Dante shouted.

"I didn't have a choice." Ange's voice was growing sharp with impatience. "She couldn't come to the World, and she wouldn't let me leave her behind in Cascara's realm."

Wait, if Ange knows Scarlet can't come to the World... "Scarlet couldn't come with you because of Death's compulsion, or—"

"She... I helped her break her compulsions. Then, before she broke her bond to Death altogether... she broke her tether to the Crossworld. I didn't realize it was there, that it was helping to keep her alive..."

Dante went numb. Zandra still had a protective hand on him, but now he could barely feel it.

"She wanted to come to the World regardless," Ange said. "I thought that, maybe it would be okay, Death was feeding her energy to keep her stable but... I realized Scarlet was doing worse than I originally thought. So I told her to head back to the border between the realms and wait for me. If we can save Death, she might be able to save Scarlet still."

"You realize she's not going to do that, right?"

"Death will help her. We just have to—"

"No, not that." Dante's rising voice made Zandra flinch away. "Scarlet isn't going to walk away. Not if she can get here. At best, you left her there for Riordan to find on his way to us. At worst, she made a portal to come here, which would *kill* her."

"If she did anything other than go back to the border, that's ridiculous and wildly irresponsible—"

"You don't know Scarlet. Where'd you come through? At the waystone?"

Ange nodded and Dante bolted out of Jarrett's house. Ange followed him, leaving the others behind without another word. Dante hadn't spoken about Scarlet to any of them, but alleviating their confusion wasn't a priority.

The Ravens had dispelled the mist, which simplified his journey out of town and into the woods beyond. The brisk night air bit through his tunic as he ran through the plains and pushed his way through the narrow game trail, but it took seeing Scarlet slumped on the ground next to the waystone to turn his blood to ice. He shot an accusing glare back at Ange before rushing to Scarlet's side.

She was unconscious. He cursed under his breath when he felt her skin. *Cold, so cold.* He could feel her pulse, faint and slow. She was still alive, no thanks to Ange, who loomed over them both.

"How could you do this?" Dante started to gather his energy. He'd need to infuse Scarlet with it; she wouldn't make it otherwise. "You helped her break the bonds that kept her alive, then left her to *die.*"

"I told her to stay behind, where she would have been safe. And I wasn't the only one to leave her."

Guilt and bitter rage coursed through Dante. "I didn't leave her like *this*. And I had to, I had to come help—"

"So did I," Ange growled. "I made the same decision, Dante. What was I supposed to do, stay with her in the Crossworld until she dies? That would achieve nothing. We have to stop Riordan and we're running out of time."

Dante took a deep, shuddering breath. "*Go.* Just go back to Jarrett's. I'll take care of Scarlet." He had to heal Scarlet, and he couldn't concentrate while Ange was infuriating him.

Ange left the clearing without argument. Dante closed his eyes and gathered himself, letting Ange's vitriol wash away. He drew deeply from his well of energy and poured it into Scarlet. It wasn't a complicated healing; there were no problem areas to focus on. She just needed energy, pure and simple, to keep her soul from completely detaching and drifting into the Nextworld.

Scarlet stirred as he rejuvenated her. When he was done, her eyes flickered open. The blue of her irises was still captivating, although duller than before.

"Dante," she mumbled. She pulled herself up and took in their surroundings. "Where are we?"

"Saridian. We're near a village called Rosewood."

She gave him the slightest nod.

"How are you feeling?" he asked.

"Bad." She paused, running her hand through her hair. "I... did something I don't think I should have."

"Ange told me about breaking the bonds. You shouldn't be in the World—"

"It doesn't matter anymore." Scarlet sighed and laid back down on the grass. She looked up at the singular moon shining light upon them. "My bond to the Crossworld is broken. Being there won't help me. And Death can't help anymore. Our emissary bond remains, but I'm sure you've felt by now... Death has nothing left to give me." She shook her head, nearly imperceptibly. "I finally understand why she wouldn't let me leave. It's a death sentence."

Dante knew he couldn't sustain her with his magic for very long. Her need was constant, her energy being consumed from moment to moment. "So what do we do?" he whispered.

It was a long time before Scarlet spoke again. For a moment, Dante thought she had passed out again, but he saw her eyes flicker across the sky from star to star. There was still a distance between them, an awkwardness from her rejection. He wondered if anything would ever be the same as it was before.

"We fight," Scarlet said. "We *win*."

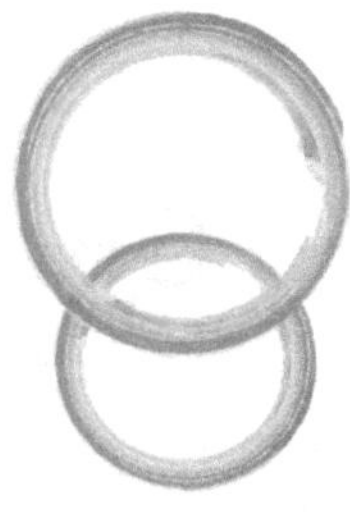

CHAPTER 37

Nightmares took over Dante's sleep that night. He wasn't surprised. Io must have a lot they want him to see before such a momentous fight. He still didn't know what the god's motivations were, but he'd use the knowledge to the best of his ability. Everything was about to change.

Dante shook himself from the dreams periodically. He got up each time he woke to check on Scarlet, who was sleeping on the couch opposite him. His companions were all jammed into various corners of Jarrett's house. Jarrett seemed too distracted to mind. Of course, they could have leaned on the hospitality of more of the townsfolk, but Dante and Barek both wanted to keep Zandra close, and Dante wasn't about to let Scarlet out of his sight either. She appeared to sleep soundly, conserving what little energy she had.

This could be their last night.pr

As dawn came closer, he pulled the crystal orb out of his pack. It was a solid weight in his hands, though always a bit lighter than he expected.

He knew now that Io had compelled him to repair this orb to help clarify the visions they gave him. He'd always kept it tucked away under his bed or in his bag. But if there was ever a time when he needed every drop of information from his dreams, it was now.

How could they win? How could they survive? He repeated these questions in his head as he fell back asleep, a prayer to Io, with the crystal orb clutched close to his chest.

Dante fell into whiteness as if he'd just woken blind from his dreams. Here, he was bodiless, a drifting spirit in a strange void.

So, you've finally come to me by choice. It was the same voice he had heard in his visions before. He had a hard time determining its tone. The voice resounded and echoed within his mind, gentle and harsh all at once.

Are you Io?

You figured it out, at last.

I had help from a friend. You're giving me these visions. Why now? Why me?

I see great potential in you. You can help me.

Help you... with what?

It isn't yet time to discuss that. You've come to dream with me, haven't you?

Dante's curiosity gnawed at him, but the god was right, he had other priorities. *I need to figure out how to do this. Defeat Riordan. And... save Scarlet. Help me save her like you helped me save Zandra.*

The odds are stacked against you.

That's why I need you, isn't it?

There was a pause. In the infinite white void, Dante lost focus for a moment until the god responded. *I can only help you with one of those requests.*

What?

Doing the right thing requires sacrifice. You can defeat Riordan, but you can't save Scarlet.

Dante's entire being churned. *That... no. If we defeat Riordan, Death will be able to help Scarlet again.*

It's not so simple. Keeping her alive in the meantime will consume too much of your energy. And as you know, Riordan has a particular interest in her, which will be useful. Let me show you.

Dante found himself packed in alongside armed and armored members of the Vanguard. They were grouped in a circle, surrounding a battle taking place at the center.

It had been a long time since he had seen Riordan, back when he'd had a vision of him and Death, before he even came to the Crossworld. Regardless, Dante recognized him instantly, even as a blurred figure in motion, his loose hair swinging to and fro as he deflected every attack the Vanguard and Ravens made at him. It was his energy that was the most recognizable, a palpable aura of malevolence and a thirst for power that Dante could almost taste.

The swordsmen he dodged, or blasted away with magic. The mages he drained with a quick flash of his hand, leaving them slumped over and useless. It was as simple to him as swatting flies. Merely annoyances he could almost ignore. Whenever his opposition left him a moment to breathe, he fired a series of magic bolts that ripped through the armor of anyone unlucky enough to be in range.

Dante flinched each time a warrior or mage fell. *This isn't real, not yet,* he told himself, trying to steady his focus so he could absorb what he could from this vision. He continued to watch Riordan, searching for anything that could be a weakness.

The god didn't seem too concerned about killing everyone immediately; Dante knew he could if he wished to. It wasn't that he was being merciful;

he took down his enemies whenever it was convenient, but otherwise, he seemed content to take his time with them. Why would he hold back?

He's waiting for something. Dante watched the god's eyes as he scanned the crowd around him. *No. For someone.*

A hand touched Dante's shoulder gently, and he jumped away, startled, before he realized it was Scarlet.

"Sorry," she said. "Dante, please. I know it might not make sense for me to fight but... I need to. I need the energy to do it."

Memories he didn't know he had flooded through him. Scarlet had wanted to be here for the battle, even if only to watch. Of course she did. But Dante had refused to infuse her with enough energy that she could fight. He'd only bestowed enough for her to continue to live, and observe the battle since she wouldn't agree to stay behind.

Was that the right decision? He opened his mouth to speak, but before he formed words, the Vanguard fighters in front of them were thrown aside with a decisive sweep of magic. Riordan swaggered toward them, a grin blossoming on his face. His eyes were locked onto Scarlet.

"Ah," said the god, "The second key. Yes, you will be coming with me." His slimy voice dripped into Dante's awareness like a foul infection.

Scarlet looked to Dante, her wild eyes begging him to give her energy so she could fight the god. He almost complied, but he was locked in place.

No. Io's voice echoed in his mind once more. *You can't help her.*

Dante's heart was pounding. *I have to do something!*

You do, but not this.

Io drew Dante's vision to the side, allowing him to spot Zandra and Barek. Zandra's body shimmered. She had enhanced her strength with magic so that she could drag Barek, unconscious, further away from where the battle had been taking place.

Go to her, Io urged.

Dante, frantic, glanced back to Scarlet once more before he obeyed and fled toward his sister. As he did, he listened as the fighters tried to stop

Riordan from getting any closer to Scarlet. "Is he alive?" he asked Zandra as he drew near.

"I... I think so," Zandra replied, her voice trembling. She pulled a crystal sword out of Barek's limp hand and held it out to Dante. "I don't... I don't know what to do with this. Someone needs to use it."

Dante automatically took the weapon, though he didn't know how to use it any more than his sister did. The sword, a crystal sword, able to draw out Riordan's very soul.

This isn't about skill, Io told him. *It's about timing.*

Dante adjusted his grip on the sword and tested out its weight. It was lighter than he expected. Something took over him—perhaps Io—and he turned around and began to rush toward Riordan and Scarlet. It was just the two of them now. The others trying to protect Scarlet had fallen. Riordan had his back to Dante, an opening that Io pressed him to take advantage of. His hands shook, his heart pounded. *I can't do this.* In his fear, he resisted the god's order.

Scarlet's face was white, and she was bowed over, not even able to hold herself up straight. *She's running out of energy, out of time.* She clapped her hands together and a blast of fire emerged from them, only to swirl around Riordan uselessly as he consumed her magic.

It was the last thing she had left in her. Scarlet fell to her knees, then collapsed fully.

"You insolent girl!" Riordan raged. "You would have lived if you had just come with me."

Dead? She's really dead? The fact that this wasn't yet a reality didn't spare Dante the shock. He was sure he would have tumbled over if not for Io forcing him onward. Only a handful of steps were between him and the god. Rage overtook his shock and sorrow. He gathered every bit of strength he had, leveled the sword, took one step, two steps—and plunged the blade deep into Riordan's back.

The feeling of the weapon slicing into this god's, this man's, body immediately sickened Dante. *I'm... I'm a healer. I'm not...this.* The hilt of the sword turned cold, then rapidly became blazing hot as the crystal ripped Riordan's soul out of the body. Dante let go before the body even began to tumble down.

I'm a killer. He killed Scarlet, he tortured Zandra, he deserved it but... I'm a killer.

He turned to retch.

Dante was pulled back into the white void. He was grateful for it. He wanted to cry, to scream, to throw up, but he had no body to do it with. Io let him be for a few moments, perhaps a few minutes, while he gathered himself.

That can't be the only way, Dante asserted. *There are better fighters and mages than me, there's no logical reason it* should *be me, and that Scarlet has to die—*

You're right. The future isn't set. There are paths to victory and to defeat... but most are to defeat. No matter what, not everyone can survive this encounter. This is the best way, because there are other stakes, too. This is not only about Riordan, but about all the gods, and what may become of us. If you take the lead, you get to keep the sword, afterward. Keep hold of Riordan's soul. This is important.

No. I can't do this. The only reason I even killed him in this vision is because you... helped me? Made me? I can't watch Scarlet die. And I'm not strong enough to truly kill Riordan. I'd lose my nerve.

Trust in yourself, Dante! You have come so far, but you have further to go yet. Don't stop now when we are on the cusp of victory over Riordan. This means freedom for your people, for your sister, and so much more. There is a price to pay, but it must be done. Some will die, but so many more will live because of it.

Dante found nothing more to say to the god. Perhaps Io was done as well, as they spoke no more to him either. Time passed and it was hard to tell how long—minutes, hours?—and yet he remained exiled in the void, unable to wake.

Even if he wanted to follow Io's plan, could he even do it? Did he have the conviction to let Scarlet die and to plunge a blade into a man's back? And if not, what else could he even do?

Maybe he didn't need Io. With his magic, as well as the crystal ball they had given him... maybe he could find another way.

Can I dream on my own?

He urged the dreams to come, the nebulous futures to unfurl before him, to give him the strength and knowledge he needed to protect everyone he loved. His parents were dead, his home was gone, and he couldn't let Zandra or Scarlet die too.

The dreams came. The rest of the night was long and arduous as Dante sorted through his visions, trying to piece together a path he could take, seeing all the possible defeats and victories lying before him, a lifetime of suffering and exalting in a single night's sleep. When he finally awoke at dawn, tears fell from his blind eyes.

CHAPTER 38

Dante wished he could rest more, but he only stayed in bed for long enough for his vision to return. It was time to prepare for the real thing.

Scarlet stirred as the sun began to peek around the curtains, and Jarrett's house bustled with a focused tenacity as everyone rose. Then everyone ran off to their respective posts—Jarrett and Ange went to organize their troops, and Barek was escorting Zandra to take shelter at the town hall, assuming she would oblige—and Scarlet and Dante were left alone.

Scarlet took a seat beside him at the kitchen table as he stirred a bowl of porridge that was sure to remain uneaten. "I want to fight today," she told him.

Dante nodded. She would be there, no matter what. He had seen it. Zandra would join them too. There was no point in trying to stop either one of them. "I'll give you as much energy as I can to get you through today." There it was. He was diverging from Io's wishes already.

Her face relaxed with his easy approval. "Thank you."

He took in a deep breath. "I know you didn't want me to become an emissary—"

"It was your choice," she said, averting her gaze. *She seems more defeated than angry.* "You found your sister. That's what you wanted. I'm... happy for you."

"But about before," he said, "back in the Crossworld. I—"

"This isn't the time," Scarlet cut in.

"If not now, then when? Scarlet—"

"I don't know." Scarlet's fists were on the table, clenched tightly enough to make her knuckles white. "Later. After the battle."

"There might not be—" Dante had to pause to steady his words. "There might not be an after."

"You can't think like that."

"I do. Because I've seen the battle in my dreams a hundred times by now."

Scarlet's hands went limp, and her voice grew soft. "What did you see?"

How would things change if he told her the truth? He couldn't lie to her, but he also couldn't risk derailing them both from this path. "There are ways we can win... and more ways we can lose. Even if we do succeed, not everyone is going to get a happy ending."

"I know we're at a disadvantage, and not everyone's going to survive. But..."

"You don't want to face it." He knew the feeling well enough.

"How can I?" she whispered. "Everything's a mess, Dante. Including me. I just want... everything to be okay, somehow."

"I just want—" Dante stopped. What did he want? He was so far from what he wanted. Even though he had found Zandra and accepted his powers, he'd lost so much. His parents had died hating who he was. His first mentor, Ferrick, had nearly changed everything for him, but Dante's hopes of becoming an herbalist and living a simple life had gone out the window when Death had forced Ange to rat him out. His old master would shun him or worse if he knew what Dante really was. And then, Dante had become an emissary in hopes of saving Bronwen, and his new mentor's fate was... uncertain at best, now that Riordan had gotten to Death.

And then there was Scarlet, who he'd foolishly allowed himself to grow feelings for. It wasn't like she hadn't warned him away. Even though they'd had moments of closeness, she still held him at arm's length. Perhaps he had been unknowingly using the insight powers that Leandra told him about, and it'd built a false, one-sided sense of intimacy.

Maybe Scarlet had been right; he'd loved her because she was the only person around. He shouldn't be bringing all of this up again. Maybe he had nothing left other than the hope that he could make Saridian a better place for his sister.

No more could be said when Barek interrupted them. He came through the front door, crystalline sword in hand. Zandra was close behind.

"I'm coming with you," Zandra told Dante.

Barek eyed Dante apprehensively. "I can't convince her otherwise."

Dante nodded. "Come on, we'd better get out to the field."

Zandra gave him a tight hug before the four of them walked together out of Rosewood to the battlefront, an open field deemed appropriate for the confrontation. Most of the Vanguard was worried that Riordan wouldn't even show up. Dante knew for a fact that he would. Whatever Riordan wanted from Jarrett or the mage that had sealed his memories, it was enough of a draw that he arrived in every possible iteration that Dante had seen.

By the time they got there, most of the Vanguard and the Ravens had already assembled. *So many people, and yet... so few to fight a god.*

Since Barek had one of the magus swords, he and Zandra split off to take their place inside the circular formation. The magus sword wielders were spread out evenly throughout. Scarlet and Dante were on the outer edge of the circle where Dante would stay in case Scarlet faltered and needed to retreat to him.

It was nearly time, though Ange and Jarrett had yet to show up. Dante knew things would happen quickly once they did, though. Riordan would portal through the Crossworld to navigate over to them in nearly no time at all.

"Scarlet," he said. His nervousness made his voice shake. "You know what you have to do, right?"

Scarlet's forehead wrinkled. "What do you mean?"

"Take Riordan down with a magus weapon. You have to do it."

"I don't—Dante, I don't even *have* one of the swords."

"But you do," he said.

She furrowed her brow further. "Is this something you saw in your visions?"

"Yes," he said, but that was all he wanted to say. Too much more and it might change the careful balance of the path he was walking. He spotted two figures in the distance. "I think Jarrett's here. Ange, too."

Instantly, Scarlet glanced over to where Dante was looking. "That man—something about him."

"What?"

Scarlet shrugged. "I'm not sure. My mind is foggy. It's been getting this way for a while, but since I broke the Crossworld bond... it's so much worse."

"We'll get you back to normal soon."

Dante took Scarlet's arm so that he could transfer energy to her more easily, and make sure she was at full capacity for the battle. The tension in her body was easy to feel, she held herself stiff as they waited for Jarrett and Ange to take their places. He would give her everything he could.

Now that Leandra had pointed out his insight powers, they were becoming more obvious to him, especially with skin-to-skin contact. He wasn't sure it was a power he wanted. It seemed invasive and had led him astray with Scarlet. Yet, it was something he had apparently done his whole life without knowing. His magic subtly prodded at those around him, seeking out their innermost feelings.

Dante tried to restrain himself from reading Scarlet and to focus instead on channeling energy to her, but it was difficult while holding her arm. She flooded easily into him.

Scarlet was tense. Anxious, yet confident. She was a muscle coiled, ready to spring. A weapon honed for this very purpose. This was everything. It all came down to this moment. This intensity commanded her, even as her energy wavered. A chance to slay Riordan, rescue her mother, and keep Dante safe.

He managed to pull himself back from prying deeper. He needed to keep his distance. It tortured him, to be so close yet so far from her. He hadn't fully convinced his heart to accept the error of its ways. The tiniest things were sparks that reignited his hope—like how strongly she felt the need to protect him.

If only she could protect them all. But she couldn't. Truly, what either of them did or didn't feel for each other wouldn't matter soon.

Io was right. This requires a sacrifice.

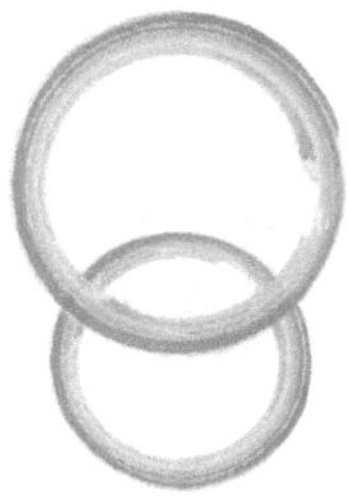

CHAPTER 39

Shortly after dawn, everything was nearly in place. Jarrett wiped his clammy hands on his trousers and resisted scratching his tattoo, which had been constantly itchy and worn raw by his fingernails. Today was the culmination of all his hard work, his efforts over the past years—both building up the Vanguard and searching for his memories.

Everyone was gathered out in the field just outside of Rosewood, ready for the battle—except for Jarrett and Ange, the last ones left at his house. She'd wanted one last briefing with him.

It was strange for his house to be quiet. For the past few weeks, it had been filled with the various newcomers. Zandra and Barek, then Ange and Dante, as well as the girl, Scarlet, whom Dante had brought last night. She'd barely been conscious.

"I still don't quite understand what's wrong with that girl." Jarrett had a hard time wrapping his head around everything that was happening so quickly now. It didn't help that he was anxious to have his memories unlocked. There was little room in his head for other concerns.

Ange sighed. "The short version goes like this: Death saved Scarlet's life, but not *really,* and she stopped being able to keep her stable, and now the bottom line is Scarlet is going to need substantial infusions of energy to keep going."

"Magical energy?"

"Magic *is* energy. How do you think healing works? It's one person giving their energy to another, allowing them to heal faster."

"I've never seen magic healing before."

"You *have.* You just don't remember."

Jarrett's frustration was beginning to boil over. If he could just get his memories back, he could understand what all of this meant. "Fine. But if she's in such bad shape, why is she fighting with us still?"

"Because I can't stop her, just like we can't stop Zandra."

Jarrett tensed. "I thought Zandra joined the civilians taking shelter in the town hall."

"That was the plan, but she's not following it. Same with Scarlet. And honestly, we could use them both, regardless of circumstances. We need every bit of help we can get."

Jarrett grimaced. They had so little control over anything that was about to happen. He tied his hair back into a warrior's tail and started buckling his leather armor on.

"I told you," Ange said, "You aren't going to need that."

Jarrett kept buckling. "We'll see."

"You aren't fighting today, Jarrett."

"We'll see," he repeated more forcefully. There wasn't any way he would let his returned memories stop him from the most important battle the Vanguard would ever face. Regardless of his past, the Vanguard was his present, this battle was the only chance they had for a half-decent future, and he was going to see it through. "Are you ready? Let's not keep everyone waiting."

"Keep some of those straps on the left unbuckled. I'll need access to your tattoo."

"Fine."

"Jarrett." Ange looked at him, deadly serious. "No matter how today goes, I hope we'll continue to work together."

"None of us are going to stop until Riordan is gone. And after that, there will be plenty of difficulties in moving Saridian past the era of his rule."

"I was thinking even bigger than that," Ange said.

Jarrett furrowed his brows, recalling Leandra's suspicion of Ange. "Is there something I should be worried about?"

Ange smiled. "We're about to fight a god. There's plenty to be worried about."

"Isn't that the truth," Jarrett grumbled.

"Are you ready?" Ange asked. "We shouldn't delay any longer."

Jarrett finished one last buckle. "I'm ready. I could have been ready sooner. You're the one who kept me back."

"Look, Jarrett, before we go, I just want you to know that returning your memories... it's going to be a painful process. In more ways than one."

"It doesn't matter." Jarrett hadn't forgotten Leandra's warning about continuing his chase. That woman was full of caution. "I have to know, no matter what."

"I just want you to be prepared, that's all. Breaking the seal might be painful in and of itself, and your memories—" Ange let out a long breath.

"You know more about my past than I do. Not that you've shared any of it in the meantime—"

"I only know pieces."

"Still. I know nothing. Is it that bad?"

"There are things that will be difficult for you, I'm sure. Exactly *how* difficult depends."

"On?"

"On why exactly Kiera did this to you."

Hearing that name made a pang run through Jarrett's chest. Ange had told him nothing more about the mage that had sealed his memories.

"You've been tied up in this struggle against Riordan for longer than you know," Ange continued. "If Riordan comes today, it's because he's going to sense Kiera's magic signature, and she is—or maybe was—his enemy."

"You mean she might be dead?" Jarrett's heart dropped. Would he never get the chance to confront the person who'd put him through years of this veiled agony? "Also—wait, you aren't implying that Kiera sealed me because I used to be on Riordan's side, are you?"

"What I want you to know, Jarrett, is that there are more sides to this conflict than you think. I'll put your fears to rest—you've always been plotting against Riordan. So have I. So has Kiera. Kiera and I used to be allies, but now we aren't. Not *all* of our goals align. I just have to wonder, whose side will you be on once the puzzle pieces lock into place?"

"Yours," Jarrett said immediately. "Why would I ever be on hers? She... she ruined my life."

"You might feel differently when you can see the whole picture. But I hope you're right. As I was saying, I'd like to keep working with you. So keep me in mind, that's all."

"Of course." Jarrett didn't know what else to say to that. He couldn't imagine a reason he'd forgive Kiera, let alone work alongside her, even if she was on their side. "Was that all? We really should go."

"That's it."

They left his house and joined the Vanguard and Ravens out in the field, where they waited armed and ready. They stood in a circular formation. Ange led him to the center to address his army. Micah, one of the Vanguard's strongest, joined them. Jarrett looked at Ange questioningly.

"If this process incapacitates you, Micah is to carry you home," Ange explained.

Jarrett grunted. He didn't care how much pain he was in, he was fighting today, but he was tired of arguing with her about it.

Mages and the magus weapon bearers were strategically placed throughout the formation. Hopefully, the rest of the soldiers could take the brunt of the god's attention and assault while the key players accomplished their part.

"Alright, Jarrett," Ange said. "Are you ready?"

For everything he had been waiting for? "Of course."

He could feel the eyes of every soldier and mage of the combined Vanguard and Raven forces boring into him. He wondered what they thought of all this, but it didn't matter. He was getting what he wanted, and if Riordan came, so was everyone else.

Ange reached her hand towards the raven emblazoned on his skin. "Deep breath."

As Jarrett inhaled, her cold fingertips touched his tattoo, the icy sensation digging its way through his body. Cold tendrils branched into his head before suddenly pulling away, ripping out blockages with their retreat.

Jarrett screamed as his mind split open. His head rushed with an intense thrum, a shockwave that emanated from his brain and wracked his entire being. He was barely conscious of Micah catching his weight as he toppled over.

Images began to flood his mind, playing at an incomprehensible speed. Overwhelmed, he lost himself in them. After a few breaths of being buffeted with the force of his visions, they slowed enough that Jarrett could pick something to focus on. What was the big picture here, what would give him the most information? He zeroed in on a woman who kept flashing by.

In some of the images, her dark hair was short. In others, it was long and wild. Her eyes were blue enough to drown in. Fierce, determined lines set around them, deepening as she aged. He must have known her for a long time.

A scene solidified. They were in the snow together, clumping together snowballs before throwing them at one another, laughing. When they were sufficiently cold, damp, and tired, she came and leaned against him. He wrapped his arms around her, trying to shield her from the wind.

Then, he kneeled before her, knees buried in the snow, and pulled a ring from his pocket. He had been carrying it around for some time now, waiting for the perfect moment. It was a simple silver band engraved with a garland of delicate flowers.

Her cheeks were red with cold and grew a deeper shade when she saw what he held. "Rings aren't the custom, where I'm from." Her wry smile told him she didn't really mind.

"Marry me anyway?" he asked, breathless.

She kissed him, and let him slip the ring onto the fourth finger of her left hand. He was glad he didn't have to see the tattoo on her right. Back in her homeland, Galapia, they would have gathered flowers to weave into crowns, a more temporary but no less meaningful symbol of their commitment. In Saridian, they might have been able to do such a thing in the spring, when flowers covered the countryside. But Jarrett couldn't wait that long. So instead he had carefully engraved flowers into the ring he had made for her; a blend of the two traditions.

She examined the ring on her finger, spinning it around. "It's beautiful," she said softly.

"Just like you."

She looked up at him, mouth set in a firm line. "You know I can't stay."

"I'll come with you."

"It's dangerous."

He put a hand on the back of her neck and gently pulled her in for a kiss. "I'd risk anything for you. What would my life be without you, Kiera?"

Kiera.

With the utterance of her name, Jarrett was yanked out of the vision, spiraling through the slideshow of images once more. His stomach churned. He couldn't comprehend how she could have done this to him. His wife erased his memories of her, and—

Oh, gods. His *daughters*. He had forgotten his own daughters. Viridian was *dead*. He wailed as the pain of the loss shook through him all over again.

He'd failed, she'd been killed, and it was all his fault. Why couldn't he have been stronger? If only he'd been born a mage.

And Scarlet. She was *here* and he hadn't even recognized her. The last time he had seen her, she would have been what, eleven, twelve? Unruly hair, eyes just like her mother's, an unbreakable spirit. A fierce little girl. Now she was here, struggling to survive something that he didn't quite understand, despite Ange's attempt to explain.

As their daughters grew up, they'd lived a life on the edge. Kiera was an emissary of Death and spent her time working on researching ways to kill a god. Riordan. They were always afraid that he would sniff them out and destroy them.

It became harder for Kiera to conceal them after Viridian, and later on, Scarlet, began to show signs of the gift—they would both become powerful mages, Kiera told him. Easy for Riordan to track by their magical signatures. Nevertheless, they settled down in Kindlespire for a while. Kiera, Ange, and a couple of other mages were working on a project. The magus swords, he realized now.

But then Viridian was killed when Kiera had been away. The next part was blurred by his grief. Did Kiera take his memories to spare him the pain of their lost daughter? How could she? Viridian was his daughter. He *should* have carried that sorrow.

Jarrett didn't know how to feel, so he felt everything. Angry, bewildered, filled to the brim with grief, completely lost, terrified for his daughter, ready to explode.

Five years without his remaining family. Was this Kiera's punishment for failing to protect Viridian? The abandonment, the excruciating pain of forgetting and then remembering all he had lost. How could his wife do this to him? He could feel his love for her now, twisted together with resentment for what she had done. And his living daughter—Scarlet.

Scarlet was here, and she was dying. Had Kiera sealed her memories as well? She'd barely been conscious when he saw her; would she recognize him now? He had to get to her, she couldn't be in this battle, his little girl. She was all he had left in this world.

He tried to slip back into his body, but everything running through him was an overwhelming jumble of emotion, pain, and confusion. He wanted to scream again, maybe he was still screaming, but he was lost, so very lost.

With great effort, he became aware of his body. He was in the fetal position on the ground. Words he couldn't quite comprehend barked an order, and someone hauled him over their shoulder. He blinked his eyes open. He was still surrounded by the Vanguard and Ravens. He looked around wildly for Scarlet but couldn't spot her. He tried to call out to her, but his tongue was lead; it couldn't form his daughter's name.

There was a presence. Foreboding, powerful, commanding. It loomed over Jarrett, a cold shadow examining him from afar. In the depths of his heart, he could feel it. Riordan had arrived.

CHAPTER 40

A thrum of power ran through Scarlet as Riordan ripped open a portal to the World. Battle cries rang out from the Vanguard and Ravens as the inner circle began to collapse in on the god.

"Hold!" someone cried out. Scarlet thought it sounded like Ange, but she couldn't see what was going on from the outer ranks.

"I need to get closer," she told Dante. "You're staying back, right?"

"Yes. I'll stay as safe as I can. Come back when you need a refill."

Scarlet nodded. "Give me all you can, for now."

Dante gave her a final burst of energy. Scarlet took his hand and squeezed it, her eyes meeting his for the briefest of moments before she pushed forward through the loosely packed formation.

Her mind and body still fought to stay connected to one another, but she felt more alive than she could ever remember, each nerve in her body ready to fire, her mind set on a singular focus: Riordan.

He was here. He had strangled the magic out of his own kingdom. His mage hunters killed her sister. He had tried to kill her, too. He had tormented Death, broken her down until he could capture her. He had taken her mother.

It's time. I'm going to end him.

She would do her job, her duty to Death, but it would never be for her patron god. It would be for herself.

Scarlet squeezed through the more tightly packed ranks toward the center of the formation and broke through to where she could see Ange, face to face with Riordan in the open middle of the circle. Ange stood in a wide, defensive stance, her magus sword drawn, her hand held out in a signal for the rebellion to hold their attack.

Scarlet hadn't seen Riordan properly before. He'd used magic to deflect her gaze back to the forest. His hair was brown, hanging down to his chin which was square and clean-shaven. She saw a flash of his eyes, light brown and as piercing as Death's, as he looked around to take in the combined Vanguard and Raven forces surrounding him.

Scarlet could feel his aura pressing in around her. *He's stronger now that he's drained all of Death's power.*

Though some feet away, Scarlet could also see the sweat dripping from Ange's forehead. She wished she had one of the magus weapons in her own hand. No matter how powerful her magic was, Ange told everyone that a magus weapon had to be the final blow against Riordan—it had to be a solid strike, too; the crystal needed a few moments of contact with his blood to entrap his soul.

She wondered what Dante had been talking about—something about her having a sword? As much as she wanted one, Ange wouldn't let her have one in her current state. She would have to settle for being the one who put Riordan in a position to be struck down instead of doing it herself. If she could create an opening for one of the magus wielders, that would be success enough.

Of course, that would also mean that I need the go-ahead to attack, which Ange isn't giving us. What is she waiting for?

The fighters around her were shifting around, muttering to one another. The tension was palpable. She circled closer to Ange and Riordan, trying to listen in.

"Let them go," Ange was saying. Scarlet realized as she approached that two men behind Ange were holding a third, unconscious man. Jarrett, who Ange had used as bait. He seemed so familiar to her, her clouded mind fighting to recognize him, but perhaps it was simply her exhaustion playing tricks on her. He hadn't appeared to know her at all. For now, all she knew was that Riordan wanted him. Tendrils of Riordan's magic tied the two men carrying Jarrett completely still, though they were trying to strain against the bonds.

"I have no reason to let them go, dear Angelise." The insidious smile plastered on Riordan's face made Scarlet's hate for him flare. Sparks escaped from her fingertips. "Jarrett is the key to the lock I've been trying to break. Really, I must thank you for bringing him to my attention. I thought he must have been long gone, but no, Kiera played one last trick on me, didn't she?"

Hearing her mother's name broke her last efforts at restraint. Fire rose within Scarlet, and she knew it was about to burst from her, whether she wanted it to or not. She hurled it at Riordan with all her might and rage. Without looking, Riordan raised a hand. The flames dissipated as he absorbed the energy into his palm, only adding to the reserve already contained within him.

The god turned to her, and Scarlet suddenly felt small. Diminutive. The immensity of his energy dwarfed her. "Ah. The daughter, too. How could I forget her?"

"Scarlet!" Ange yelled, a reprimand and an exclamation of concern rolled into one.

Riordan stepped toward Scarlet. Now that he was closer, she spotted a faint scar along the side of his neck. She wondered if that was the wound that Calder alluded to, the one that her mother had given to him. "The only thing better than one key," Riordan said, "is two."

Scarlet's blood boiled. "So, fight me."

Panic flashed across Ange's face as she signaled for the Vanguard to attack. This probably wasn't how Ange's plan was supposed to go, but Scarlet didn't care. All observations not directly related to Riordan dropped away. Flames blazed easily in her hands.

Riordan took another step closer. Scarlet could both see and sense the magic swirling in a vortex around him, growing stronger with each passing second. A god approached her; she should be afraid, but she wasn't. Ange might have forged the swords for this battle, but Death had forged Scarlet into a weapon for this very purpose.

If I'm going to die, I'm bringing Riordan with me.

The front-line of the Vanguard rushed at Riordan, but with a shockwave blast, he pushed them stumbling backward. Scarlet braced herself against the energy and kept her footing. She took a deep breath, then sent a series of fireballs careening toward her enemy.

Riordan quickened his tempo, dodging out of the way of most of the fire and absorbing the rest into his energy vortex as he dashed forward. Scarlet stood her ground. He was almost upon her now, twenty feet—Scarlet summoned a disk of fire, held high as a shield—fifteen feet, ten—

Before Riordan overran her, someone interceded. Scarlet saw the blue glint of a magus weapon as a young man leaped upon Riordan, bowling him over. Both god and man hit the ground hard. It seemed impossible that anyone had the strength to knock Riordan over like that through his aura of amassed power.

Riordan threw the man away from him with another shockwave. Scarlet realized as he skidded across the ground that it was Barek, his body shimmering with magic. Zandra was empowering him, so he wielded one of the magus swords and got close to the god without being thrown back by the energy vortex.

The other Vanguard fighters had no such luck. Riordan rose and was surrounded by troops once more, but as soon as they got near him, he easily flicked them away with no more effort than swatting flies.

He locked back onto Scarlet, raised his hand, and sent glimmering tendrils of his vortex at her. She failed to jump back in time and the tendrils latched onto her ankles. She gave them a zap of energy and shook them off. She and Riordan began to circle one another, each carefully watching for the next attack.

The mages from the Vanguard and the Ravens began shooting volleys of energy bolts, but Riordan's aura served as a barrier against these attacks; it was useless. Scarlet worried that each bit of magic that entered his vortex would only make him more powerful.

Still, attacking him with magic was all she could do to distract him, to create an opening for a strike from a magus sword. Her anger fed her power, and it would not be denied.

She hurled her fire disk, aiming for his neck. A sweep of his arm deflected it, sending it careening into the crowd instead. There was a yelp of distress, but Scarlet couldn't worry about it. She summoned another disk, hurled it, then another, each larger and hotter than the last. Sweat glided down her face.

Riordan began to boomerang her disks back at her, instead of into the other combatants. She danced through the returning barrage of fire, flames singeing her feet when she wasn't fast enough. It was worth it, though—Leon and Korene charged in together from the wings, each heaving their magus sword at Riordan.

They were surrounded by bubbles of energy. The Ravens must have a protection mage who had fortified them. They had a chance of getting close to Riordan, unlike the rest of the fighters who continued to be swatted backward.

Riordan's attention was on Scarlet, but he wasn't distracted enough to miss the approach. The next two flame disks Riordan deflected were sent hurtling at the two Vanguard fighters. Korene was struck across the shoulder and dropped to the ground. Leon ducked in time, but Riordan sent out an energy dart that struck him directly in the face. He collapsed just a few steps ahead of Korene.

Scarlet's breath caught. *Are they dead?* Her energy was flagging, she wouldn't last much longer at this rate, herself. She glanced behind her, hoping to spot Dante. Instead, Ange was right behind her.

Ange glared at Scarlet, shoving past her into the inner circle. "You're spent. Get out of my way."

Scarlet growled and slipped into the ranks of her allies—now only there to serve as a blockade to limit Riordan's mobility, as it was clear they could do no damage. Ange must have called off the mages, as they had stopped firing on Riordan. They were no threat to him, and only fed him more power.

Scarlet felt waves of heat rolling off of herself. Her energy was leaking, she couldn't control it. Everyone she passed jumped out of her way as she searched for Dante.

This is all Riordan's fault. The scar on her back ached like it knew she was near the one who had bestowed it upon her. Riordan had more or less killed her with that wound. He'd captured her mother, shortly after. Because of him, she was an emissary, that she was trapped, separated, stuck—he would pay. She would make him pay.

But first—"Dante." He was kneeling just outside of the circle of fighters, healing Barek. Zandra overlooked them, arms crossed.

Dante spotted Scarlet and rushed to her. "I'm here. Are you okay?"

Scarlet didn't know how to answer that, so she didn't. She was calmer now, less heat flowed off of her. Dante took her hand and poured more of his energy into her. She quickly felt more solid, more real again. "Dante," she said again. "You're using too much energy if you're healing people, and giving me—"

"I know my limits."

A twinge of worry streaked through her regardless. "It's dangerous to push them."

"Zandra and Barek might be able to do some damage. They're a good duo. I have to give them a fighting chance."

Scarlet glanced at Barek's magus weapon lying on the ground next to him. "Where's that Raven girl? The one they gave the sword to?"

"Fae? She's there." Dante nodded his head over to a girl standing near Zandra and Barek. "She's a protection mage. She's going to shield Barek before he goes back in."

Fae didn't look like much of a physical combatant. If the Ravens were going to give the sword to a mage, Scarlet wished she had it instead. Ange had originally planned for her to. She thought of Ange, fighting Riordan in the inner circle, trying to land a hit, just one, with the blade that would end this all.

A flash of power surged. It had Riordan's magical signature written all over it, and a few of the Vanguard cried out as they were knocked back. Riordan was getting more aggressive, and the circle containing him was coming apart. She let go of Dante's hand. "I need to get back in there."

His face was plastered with a pained look. "Good luck."

Scarlet glanced at Zandra, who was helping Barek up. "Send them in when they're ready." She turned to go and came face to face with Fae.

"Let me shield you," the Raven said.

Scarlet stood stiff as Fae weaved magic around her. "Why aren't you out there?" asked Scarlet.

"Patience."

Scarlet huffed, let the other girl finish the shield, and marched back through the quickly dispersing circle. Ange and Riordan were having at it. There was a flurry of magic and Ange's crystal blade was almost impossible to follow. Scarlet re-entered the battlefield, searching for an opening.

She circled to Riordan's backside and summoned a flame whip into her hand. She lashed it out and managed to wrap the flames around Riordan's ankle before he could sense the attack. He glanced back, sharply chopping his hand down as he broke the whip into pieces.

Ange took advantage of his brief distraction, charging at him at full speed. Scarlet's heart leaped to her throat as it looked like victory may be within reach—Ange's sword arched toward Riordan's neck. The moment before it made contact, Riordan summoned a tremor of magic that was more forceful than any of his previous onslaughts.

In an instant, the sword shattered. It was as if the rest of the world was silent as the crackle of fracturing crystal filled the air, followed by the slowing of time as thousands of glittering shards fell to the ground. A deadly weapon, now rendered useless. Ange stumbled when her weapon didn't make contact and collapsed on top of its remains.

"You're done," Riordan told her, his teeth glinting in the morning sun. "You have only two of your weapons left. Who's next?"

Scarlet looked to the spot where Korene and Leon had fallen. They were gone, hopefully carried away for aid, but sure enough, two piles of shards lay there. Her stomach turned over. Their chances were running thin.

She saw Barek approach from Riordan's back, shield in hand and closely followed by Zandra.

"Me." All she had to do was hold his attention for long enough. "I'm next."

Riordan turned to her. "Oh, yes. I suppose you must want to know how your mother is doing, after all."

Barek charged in faster than Scarlet could have imagined. Zandra's enhancements had given him speed and strength. Riordan could sense him, though, and threw out a hand, his bolt of energy shattering Barek's shield into metal scrap. He scowled, turned to face Barek, and with another precise movement sent a shot out that brought Barek to his knees. A third bolt knocked him prone.

Riordan huffed. "You're all getting rather annoying."

Scarlet circled back into Riordan's sightline, hoping to catch his gaze. If Barek wasn't dead already, he was at the god's mercy. Instead of finishing him off, Riordan's eyes locked onto Zandra. She was staring at Barek in shock.

"Stop!" Scarlet screamed and let the fire rise in her once more. She surrounded herself and Riordan with a wall of flames, separating them from Zandra and the rest of the Vanguard. She was sure to leave Barek's magus sword outside of the radius of flames. "You said you wanted me. So, come get me."

"It's difficult when your dear friends keep attacking me. But now, I suppose we have some privacy, don't we?"

Flames crackled, and the wall surrounding them was unbearably hot. Scarlet was flushed and slick with sweat.

"I won't let your mother live for much longer, you know. Not if she keeps refusing to give me what I seek."

"Guess I'll have to kill you first then," Scarlet said. She wanted it to sound intimidating, but the threat sounded flat even to her.

"Not likely, but I'll let you see her again if you'd like."

"Calder didn't make that offer sound too tempting. I won't let you use me against her."

"You're not going to have a choice. Either you, your father, or both of you are coming with me."

"My *father*?"

"Ha! Oh, my girl, you really are lost."

The truth knocked the wind from her lungs as she realized it. Jarrett was her father. The years apart and her drifting awareness had obscured her recognition.

She couldn't think of this now. With each passing moment, she grew weaker. The flames around them began to falter.

"Ah, perhaps only your father will be coming with me. I see now, Death was saving you, and now—well, now, she belongs to me, and you won't be around for too long. It's a shame, but I'm sure I'll be able to get the information I need out of Kiera with just one of you."

One final strike. That was all Scarlet had left. She channeled her rage, translating emotion into power. She funneled the wall of flames up and inward into a focused blast of energy coming at Riordan from directly above his head. At the last second, she felt her power slipping from her grasp.

Her mind flashed back to her backfire on the Dante's first day of training. She tried to refocus, but her anger had gotten the better of her, and her blast erupted too far above, and too wide. She was caught on the edge of the explosion.

The shield Fae had crafted around her shattered. Fire scorched over her skin. Her own energy zapped her, wracking her with pain. She cried out and dropped to her knees. She spotted Fae coming in from the side, sword leveled at Riordan, but he had only been caught in the periphery of Scarlet's attack, unharmed, and with a single blast, dispatched both Fae and the sword.

With the falling shards of the magus sword, Scarlet saw their chances of winning this battle fade.

CHAPTER 41

Dante's world froze as the flames and smoke cleared, and Scarlet crumpled to the ground in what seemed like slow motion.

He closed his eyes, only for a moment, but he needed that split second to steel himself. All of this would be worse than anything he had seen in his dreams; this time, it would be real. What he needed to do had felt impossible, but now, pushed by his desperation, it was time. It would take getting to the brink of utter disaster for things to go as planned.

He lunged forward, but Zandra caught his arm. He swung around to his sister. "Let go."

Zandra only tightened her hold on him. "Look. I have Barek's sword."

His eyes flickered to the crystalline weapon in her other hand. "There's no time for that now." No matter how much Io wanted him to do it, Dante knew he couldn't be the one to kill Riordan. Without the desperate rage that Scarlet's death would cause, he would falter, and everything would be ruined. Barek wouldn't be able to do it either. He would live, but he was too injured to continue fighting now.

"You have to heal Barek. I know we can do it, the two of us, we need one more shot—"

"I'm sorry. Barek is too hurt. I have to help Scarlet."

"It's too late for her! Help me. Help *us*. This is the last sword."

Dante glanced back to Scarlet. She was safe for now, but precious seconds were ticking by. Ange was nearly the last person standing between her and Riordan. All around them were dead Vanguard fighters and Ravens, the survivors desperately trying to escort the more severely injured away from the next clash between Ange and Riordan.

"Keep the sword and yourself safe, okay?" The hurt in his sister's eyes was immense as her hand went slack, releasing him. He wished he could help her. Turning her away felt like a betrayal of their bond. She was his little sister, the last of his family. But to protect her in the long run, he had to help Scarlet right now. "I'm so sorry, Zandra. For everything. But I have to go. I love you."

Dante fought back tears. *This is worse than leaving her in Briarglen. So much worse.* He pushed aside his rising emotions. He couldn't lose control now. He rushed toward Scarlet, dangerously close to where Ange was taking her last stand against Riordan.

Safely, he made it to her side and knelt down next to her. "Scarlet. Scarlet?"

She was just barely conscious. "Dante...?"

Dante tried to pour energy into her but it wouldn't stick, it ran right back out. He knew it wouldn't work, but he had to try. She was fading fast.

"I'm sorry," she said. "I couldn't do it. I don't have a sword. Even if I did—"

"You did everything you could."

Her eyes fluttered closed. He was losing her.

But he couldn't.

Dante took a breath, took Scarlet's hand, and began to press in with his newly discovered insight magic. On the surface, she was numb as her soul drifted away. Digging in deeper, he could feel her fear, her heart beating erratically. Slowly, she was surrendering to the void, to the stream of souls. He needed to dive even deeper now, straight into her consciousness, if he wanted to keep her alive.

He released his body, letting his mind flow freely into hers. No longer was he surrounded by the horrors of the battlefield, but instead he was in a dark, open space. It was like being in a vision, some sort of empty, similar to the white void of Io's realm. This dark void pressed in around him, heavy and stagnant, almost like he was underwater.

In his gut, he knew energy should be flowing here, moving, but instead, it was still. There was nothing but darkness in every direction. Dante was small, insignificant, and scared.

He took a moment to center himself. Where was Scarlet, in all this? He looked around, but couldn't see her. *Wait, there*—he spotted a thread, a thin string of energy. He latched onto it, closed his eyes within this vision, and traced it to its source, zooming through this strange space. When his eyes opened, Scarlet was in front of him.

She held her legs tight against her chest, curling into herself like a dead beetle. Her edges blurred, she wasn't solid.

"Scarlet?"

She didn't look up at him.

"Scarlet, let me help you."

Her response was muffled. "No."

He floated closer to her. "Please!"

She looked up and met his gaze. Her usually bright eyes were empty. "You always want to help. You want to *save* everyone—"

"You say that like it's a bad thing."

"—you don't even want to be here. You're afraid, you think you're weak. Just go home."

Those words cut him, but he didn't let himself waver. "Of course I'm scared. I wasn't made for this. You're right, I don't want to fight—but I have to."

Scarlet scoffed. "It was your choice to become an emissary."

"No. I don't have to do this because of Death. I can't go home, I'm fighting *for* my home. And I won't let Riordan keep Saridian in discord, killing mages, abusing other gods, everything, all of it! That's not the World I want to live in, and if that means I die and I go to the Nextworld, then so be it."

Scarlet said nothing for a while, staring at him dully. "Then go. Go fight, finish this. You aren't the one who's going to die. I am."

"You won't if you let me help you."

Her eyebrows drew in tight, her edges smudged a bit more as energy poured out of her at faster rate. "I don't need saving."

"You always want to do everything alone."

"I have to."

"Scarlet—"

"I have to, Dante! *I have to.*" Scarlet ran her hands through her tangled hair. "You don't get it. I can't rely on other people to stick around. I can't be the little girl, waiting to be rescued. If I'm going to do this, I need to do it *myself*."

Dante could feel her helplessness, her fear, swirling all around him. Her inner fire, her resolve, her stubbornness. "You're strong. Scarlet, you are the strongest person I know. That's why you're the one out there fighting Riordan—not me. It's not just because you're a better mage. You're braver, tougher, more determined. But that doesn't mean you can do it alone. No one can." He wrapped his arms around her, and she let him pull her close. "You don't have to do it alone."

Scarlet let her defenses crack. Her emotions poured out: her fear, her helplessness, and beneath all of it, her affection for him. He could sense now what was wrong: Scarlet was stretched thin, torn between two places. Part of her soul was trapped in the Crossworld, beginning to slip into the Nextworld, and trying to bring the rest along with it. Death was right, Scarlet was as good as dead—part of her had been gone. The rest only stayed attached to her body because of Death's tether.

Death couldn't figure out how to bring the rest of Scarlet back, but Dante had to. He had the advantage of being deep within Scarlet's psyche while her heart was held open. If only he could have done this before the battle. But he knew she never would have let him. It had to be now.

"I'll be back," he told her. Scarlet released him from the embrace and gave him a solemn nod.

He flew away deeper into her consciousness, following the trail of her torn soul. He arrived at a stream of energy that pulled him along swiftly. He was surrounded by souls, shimmering collections of energy and light that flowed along beside him. They were a part of the stream, but he was separate still, like oil in water.

Was this where Scarlet's soul met the stream of souls? He had to find her missing pieces. Dante tried to swim through the stream, but it was difficult to push through the rapid current. He reached out with his mind into the mass of souls, trying to pinpoint Scarlet, but everything rushed by too rapidly.

What had he done in his vision, the one where he succeeded? That too, had flown by so fast. In the dreams in which he failed, he spent too much time searching, trying to seek out the missing parts of Scarlet.

Then, it came to him. He didn't need to reach out and find her, he had to call her to him. He closed his eyes again.

Scarlet. The passionate one, the distant one. A fire that couldn't be quenched, for even her smoldering coals resisted—they would always sting with heat. She was strong, even in fear. Powerful, yet lacking control.

Come back home, he urged. *Rejoin yourself. I can take you there. I promise you can trust me. Scarlet—*

A half-solid hand met his. He opened his eyes to see a transparent Scarlet clutching onto him.

Bring me home, she said, not out loud, but he could feel the words resounding in his mind.

The stream of souls didn't want to let go of him now, and even more than that, of her. Death hadn't been able to pull Scarlet out of it, not all the way. But Dante had a connection to her, something that was beyond or at least different than the obligation of an emissary bond. He could do it.

He knew her enough that he could separate the parts of her from the nebulous stream trying to carry her away. He plucked all that was Scarlet out of the stream, then ripped himself out of its grasp too. With all his might, he stole them away from the stream of souls back to the shallower parts of Scarlet's inner self.

He landed back in the void, dizzy for a moment before he could sit up. When he did, Scarlet was sitting right in front of him in the dream space, her edges now solid.

"I feel... I feel like a person again. Like myself. I haven't felt this way since before I woke up in the Crossworld." Scarlet blinked, letting a tear run down her cheek. "Thank you."

He could see the inferno in her, blazing stronger than before. Life glinted in her eyes, along with her tears. She was more beautiful than ever.

"You're everything," he said. His heart burned as brightly as she did.

Scarlet leaned in toward him. Dante hadn't seen this part in his visions. One kiss was all he wanted before it was over. Their lips touched. Her fire poured into him, and this time, he didn't flinch from the flames. This was it. It was Scarlet. He knew, then, that he really did love her, every bit of who she was.

For a moment, he was at peace.

Then everything was pain.

He was thrown out of the dream space, screaming, thrust back into his body just in time for it to slump into the ground. Agony radiated from a point on his back, a vicious wound beyond anything he'd ever felt before. He managed to turn his head to see Riordan towering over him, grinning, power crackling in his raised fist.

And then the god brought his hand down.

CHAPTER 42

It should have been a moment of triumph.

Dante returned her soul to her body, and Scarlet could feel her heart beat again. She was whole. The snow in the quiet place in her mind was melting around them. And there, before her, was Dante. His green eyes were set on her, and he saw all of her. This time, she finally saw all of him.

His strengths were so different than hers. He lived with his heart open when she had shut her own, afraid of being alone and of being close. Dante thought things through, while Scarlet was impulsive. She was a fighter, while Dante was a healer. He would mend this entire broken World if he could. There was one thing they shared, though: they would both do anything to save the people they loved.

Her heart was finally open, too. They were still in the dream space, a moment suspended in time. She was whole again, and there was a feeling in her chest she had never felt before.

She kissed him. They were going to do this, together—

Then it was all swiped away as Dante's scream pierced through the vision they shared, thrusting her, disoriented, back into physical space, just in time to watch Riordan strike at Dante a second time with a fistful of pure magic. A wordless scream of her own left her throat as she lunged at Riordan.

Scarlet wasn't fast enough. The god's strike hit its mark. Life left Dante's eyes as Riordan's fatal blast of power ran through him.

Her rage rose out of her belly, flames poured out of her mouth as Scarlet rose to confront the god, the murderer, the man she would kill. In his victory over Dante, Riordan, in his conceit, was not expecting her. She slammed into him, knocking him onto his back and spreading flames over him as she did so.

His vortex neutralized most of the fire, but she saw that some broke through, scorching his skin. Perhaps he was weakening. It didn't matter. Scarlet would kill him all the same. Her fury would break through any barrier.

Riordan pushed her off. She regained her footing and gave him no time to recover his bearings. With a primal yell, she punched fireball after fireball at him, weaving complex flight patterns to keep him from predicting their path. With each dart of magic he threw at her, she sent out a return bolt to collide with it, neutralizing his offense, all the while continuing her relentless, fiery assault.

For all the pain she had gone through under Death's tutelage, she was going to use every trick the god had ever taught her. With her soul and body fully merged once more, she was more powerful than ever.

Changing tact, Riordan fed more energy into his vortex, then lashed out at Scarlet with it. He caught her wrist with a stealthy tendril of magic, limiting her movement, making it easier for him to latch onto her other hand, and then her feet.

Though she was bound, she didn't panic. She closed her eyes and fell easily into the place Ange had taught her to reach. There, she sought out Riordan's tendrils. She could have unbound herself from them. But, instead, she followed them to where they led and began to unravel the vortex itself. Riordan tried to shove her mental influence away, but she held on with all her might, using his grasp on her against him.

You killed Dante, she projected at him, as she dismantled his energy vortex. *And now, I'm going to kill you.*

She felt a sliver of fear underneath his arrogance. He was stripped of his defenses now. Scarlet opened her eyes and summoned more flame into her hands, ready to end this god. She poured her heart into a conflagration, a streaming wall of flames that would wipe him out.

Die, Riordan.

When she was ready to collapse from the effort, she stopped, breathing hard. Slowly, the smoke cleared, and Riordan was on the ground. He wasn't a pile of ash like she had hoped. Even without his vortex, he must have been able to absorb enough of her magic to survive. Yet, he did not rise.

"Scarlet."

Scarlet glanced at the source of the sound. Ange was stomach-down on the ground, blood pooled around her. While caught up in fighting Riordan, Scarlet hadn't taken an account of the battlefield. Dead and injured soldiers were scattered across the ground. The remaining rebel forces had retreated or were helping to pull away the injured. Ange pushed herself up enough for Scarlet to see that beneath her body she protected a magus sword—quite possibly the last one that remained intact.

"Take it," Ange gasped out. Blood dripped from a slash that ran diagonally across her chest.

Scarlet carefully pulled the sword out from under Ange. She had a sword now, just as Dante had said. With her heart hammering, she turned back to charge at Riordan, who was now pulling himself back up to his feet.

She swung at him, once, twice, but he dodged the blows. She cried out in frustration. If only she'd had more time to train. The crystalline sword still felt awkward in her grasp.

She heaved the sword at him again, but Riordan weaved around its arc, his unreadable eyes locked onto her. "You can't kill me, Scarlet."

But she could. Dante dreamed it.

She had Riordan on the defensive. It didn't stop him from throwing out energy bolts, but she was able to disrupt or dodge them. This couldn't last for long, though, she had to strike the winning blow soon before she was completely spent.

Then, she noticed what Riordan was focused on—he was keeping an eye on her sword more than anything else. She feigned a swing at him, and he moved out of the way—right into the fireball she shot with her offhand. The force of the blast knocked him off his feet.

She stepped forward and kicked his chest, pushing him down onto his back. She raised the sword with both hands, tip down, ready to drive it into his chest and claim what victory she could.

"Stop," Riordan choked out. "If I die, Calder will kill Kiera."

Scarlet's heart skipped a beat and she paused, sword held over the god.

Ange called out, "Don't let him get to you. *Kill him.*"

Ange was right, she had to do it and hope his threat was a bluff. But Scarlet's brief indecision was all Riordan needed. He reached up and the sword shattered at his touch, shimmering pieces that were once a blade clattering onto his chest. Scarlet was left holding nothing but the hilt.

With a blast of magic, Riordan forced her to stumble back, off his chest. As he heaved himself back up to his feet, he waved a hand and reality rippled at his fingertips as a portal formed. His other hand reached toward her and caught her wrist. The useless hilt tumbled from Scarlet's hand as he latched on tightly, and began to pull her toward the portal.

Her heart almost stopped. He would take her to the mage prison—

Riordan's grip broke. Scarlet hopped backward as soon as she was released. In her tunnel vision, she hadn't seen Ange draw a mundane sword and slash at Riordan with the ounce of strength she had reserved. She'd bloodied him, carving a deep gash in the god's side while he was distracted by Scarlet.

The god roared as blood poured from him. It was clear that he would need to staunch the flow swiftly or risk losing too much blood. But even if he died now, it would be a hollow victory. Calder would simply become the god's new incarnate.

Riordan leaped through the portal he'd already opened, stealing even this minor victory from them. The window to the Crossworld closed behind him.

It wasn't worth the risk to go after him. The magus weapons were destroyed.

Scarlet sank to her knees. Despair began to pour out of her, sobs of pure anguish born of misery so deep she feared it may be fatal. The World spun around her and the air was full of the scent of blood—but only of her allies, not of the god that had taken so much from her.

The moment had come, and it had passed. Scarlet had failed, and all was lost.

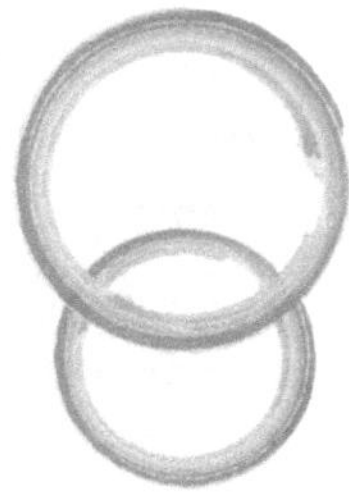

Chapter 43

Back in Deianira's library, there was a story Scarlet had read about the gods. The gods used to be a single entity who contained every aspect of existence. So powerful was this god, and yet, it was difficult to exist as a being with so many clashing facets. Every emotion that could ever exist was in constant conflict.

So this being decided to create vessels, smaller beings that could hold some of this weight. Thus, humans were created. The humans, indeed, took some of this burden. But these new mortals picked and chose their emotions, and ran rampant with them. Wars began between the humans. Pain and suffering took their toll. The powerful deity was left with love and empathy in their heart for these suffering mortals.

It saddened them to look upon their creations with love, only to see them ripping each other apart. Watching the humans endure such hardship while holding eternal compassion caused a crack to form in their heart, and eventually, it tore the god asunder.

It broke them.

Scarlet knew how they felt.

Her heart had been shattered so many times, into so many fragments.

A flood of ruthless memories returned to her as her soul did.

The first was Viridian. The scene played out so clearly in Scarlet's memory, forever branded, a scar placed on her soul. The mage hunter had been charging toward Scarlet and her father. Viridian swooped in from the side to intercept their enemy, clutching a fistful of concentrated magic. In another second, her sister would have blasted the magic at the hunter. Instead, the hunter angled her sword to pierce through Viridian's chest. Her arms fell slack. The magic she'd been ready to wield faded.

The last thing Viridian did was turn toward Scarlet and their father. Scarlet watched the life wane from her sister's eyes, their emerald glow dulling. She was gone.

Scarlet was frozen. Her father had to drag her away from the scene. They made it to safety, but she couldn't remember how. She was numb then, as she was now. Maybe numb was the wrong word. It wasn't that she felt nothing. Everything hurt so much that there was no room to feel anything else.

Shortly after, her father left. As if she and her mother needed anyone else to mourn.

That first crack, was it the beginning of the end, the catalyst to all the rest?

Scarlet and her mother survived well enough. For a while. But then Riordan had found them, hunted them through the forest, and struck Scarlet with that fatal blow.

That brought her to Death, to make a bargain: her life for her freedom. To Viridian, only to mourn her all over again. The loss of her mother, who doubtless was being tortured by Riordan to try to get whatever it was he wanted from her.

It had brought her to this moment. Dante. Just like Viridian, he died saving her, and then—

She could have defeated Riordan. But she hesitated, and now Dante's sacrifice had been for nothing.

Nothing, because that's what she was. Dante had helped her become whole, but now she was broken all over again.

How had she ever believed she could make a difference? She was mortal. Powerless. Useless. Pathetic. Death should have kept her in that dungeon. Maybe then Dante would have lived, at least.

The aftermath of the battle, her failure, was a blur. Someone took her to a house. Who took her, whose house it was, she didn't know. It didn't matter. There was a room. It had a lock. Scarlet made use of it. She shuttered the window. She collapsed into herself.

She wept.

CHAPTER 44

Scarlet didn't speak to anyone in the days following the battle. Forcing words out was more effort than she could afford. Force-feeding herself so she wouldn't perish was the most she could manage. She had to fight against herself to keep it down. A constant gnawing of inner pain made her lethargic and constantly nauseated.

She and Ange had been staying in a house together. They weren't told who it belonged to. The owner wasn't present. Scarlet had no doubt they were dead. She tried not to think about it. She spent most of her time locked away in a bedroom. *Her* bedroom?—at least for now. In the darkness, she tried her best not to let her reeling mind take over.

Since Dante had returned her soul to her, it seemed as if cobwebs had been dusted away from her mind, and everything around her was brighter than before. It was a vivid desolation, colors were too saturated for her weary eyes. So she stayed in the darkness. Anything else was unbearable.

Hopeless was an understatement. What else was left? They took their best shot at Riordan. It was the best advantage they would have on him. They lost.

She wanted to burn the whole World down, yet no flames came to her anymore. Her magic, her anger, was silent for once.

What was to happen next, Scarlet didn't know. Didn't care, either, though it was hard to avoid Ange's fervent planning whenever she ventured out of her bedroom to force some food down her throat. As soon as Ange was well enough to sit up, she demanded maps be brought to her. After they arrived, she poured over them constantly, muttering to herself and occasionally to Scarlet, when present, who ignored her to the best of her abilities. Eventually, she caught on to the fact that Ange was searching for magus crystal—a large amount of it.

The other person to avoid was Jarrett. He came calling daily, and each time he did, Scarlet locked herself in her room. He would knock, ask to speak to her, and Scarlet would hide under her covers and wish that she couldn't hear him.

Her *father*.

Her mind had been fogged by breaking her connection to the Crossworld. Too much of herself had flowed into the stream of souls. But now that she was put back together, she recognized him instantly.

She'd spent years furious at him for disappearing after Viridian was killed. The coward. Who abandons their family after a tragedy? But it wasn't like that. At least, not according to Ange, who claimed that her mother locked away Jarrett's memories, left him behind, then lied to Scarlet about it.

What in *any* of the gods' names was she supposed to think of that? Her mother had hidden so much from her, but this was confounding beyond all reason.

Kiera obfuscated, with magic and otherwise. But to *lie* about something so fundamental? It was beyond anything Scarlet could imagine. What was the purpose of it all? Did her mother blame Jarrett for Viridian's death? Was this her punishment for him?

She knew it was cruel to avoid Jarrett. Unless these were more lies, he had been the innocent one, in the end. But she wasn't ready to face him, to defuse the years of fury and anguish, and to come to terms with what her mother had done to him, to their family.

Whenever Jarrett came, Scarlet could hear Ange gently consoling him, and urging him to give her time.

Of course, Ange wouldn't let her avoid him forever. Scarlet woke one morning to a relentless knocking on her door.

"Scarlet, get out here. It's time."

Scarlet ignored her, wrapping herself tighter in the rough blankets. Unfortunately, doing so didn't make either Ange or herself disappear. Ange kept knocking.

"You know I can get into there if I want to, but I'm giving you a chance," Ange said. "Why don't you come out?"

If Ange wanted to break in, then so be it. Scarlet sensed the flash of energy and heard the crack of her shattered lock.

Scarlet looked up, squinting. Her eyes watered and stung with the effort of adjusting to the new light. A serious expression was plastered onto the woman's face. "Let's go."

Seeing Ange's expression, Scarlet finally spoke, barely croaking the word through her throat. "Where?"

"We're meeting with what's left of the Vanguard council and some of the remaining Ravens."

"Why?"

"To figure out a plan, of course. Our next step."

"No."

Ange seemed genuinely confused at Scarlet's lack of enthusiasm. "No?"

"No more plans. It's over."

"It's far from over." Ange's voice had an alarming hiss to it.

Scarlet rolled away so she wouldn't have to look at Ange anymore. "Maybe for you."

"You want Kiera back, don't you?"

Scarlet gritted her teeth together so hard her jaw ached. "There's nothing we can do. The swords are *gone*."

"*Think* for a second, would you?" Ange snapped. "Riordan has Death. That means she can't aid souls into the Nextworld."

Scarlet rolled back over. "So what?"

"It means that souls might not be crossing over. Which is bad, because they will be trapped in an eternal purgatory until she can return. But, there is an opportunity here. Anyone killed in the battle—well, they might not be gone yet. I took the bodies that I could and encased them in magus crystal down in the vault. They'll be preserved until it's time. We could bring some of them back."

A name sat unspoken between them.

Dante.

Scarlet remembered the last part of the story she'd read about the gods.

After the original god splintered, the new gods took on unique aspects and pieces of Quintras to oversee. The more of each gods' aspects existed in the World, the more power the gods gained in both the World and the Crossworld.

They started the Magus War. They fought for what they had and for what they wanted.

Even shattered, they formed new beings. It wasn't the end of their story.

Scarlet felt something. It was small. Not even a spark. But it was enough to get her on her feet.

CHAPTER 45

Scarlet and Ange were the last to arrive to the council room. A dozen or so people were gathered loosely around the council table, some seated, some standing. The Ravens in their dark garb stood out from the Vanguard. She recognized a couple of them from her visits to the Ravens with her mother, including the Ravens' leader, Leandra. Her mother had never let her speak with her, but she had caught enough glances of her over the years to remember her face.

Barek was there, standing next to Fae, the Raven woman she'd met during the battle. Ange introduced her to Hera and Leon, members of the Vanguard council. On their way to the meeting, Ange told her that the other members of the council, Korene and Rohan, had succumbed to the injuries Riordan gave them.

And then there was Jarrett, of course, at the head of the table. She avoided meeting his gaze and kept close to Ange.

Ange let the armful of maps she carried tumble onto the council table. "Any luck?" Jarrett asked.

Ange sighed. "None whatsoever. I can't think of anywhere that might have as much magus stone as we need. Saridian has so few deposits that are easily accessible, and I stripped most of them clean for the first batch of swords."

"And you're sure there's not enough left in the vault here?"

"Yes," snapped Ange. "The cavern looks impressive, but I covered it in only a thin layer of magus stone and artificed it so that the weapons wouldn't be easily detected by mage hunters. Even if I hadn't done my... interment project, it wouldn't be enough."

Scarlet cleared her throat. "What's going on?"

Ange leveled an annoyed look at her. "You would know if you had bothered to show up this past week. We need another magus weapon. But it takes magus stone, obviously—and a *lot* of it. More than you'd think. And there's nowhere nearby with enough of it."

"So we'll go farther," Hera said. Her hands were gripped into fists on top of the council table. "Outside of Saridian if we have to."

Ange shook her head. "Impossible. Celaigh's mountains are ripe with magus stone, but it's far too dangerous to risk extracting it. Riordan doesn't keep an eye on his magus stone. Trust me when I say that Meyrin does. Touching it breaks the Magus Treaty, and he'll have no mercy on us. Another god at our heels is the last thing we need right now."

Scarlet's memory stirred. "What about the missing sword?"

Ange barred her teeth. "Your mother was the only lead I had in locating it. We could keep searching, but we're running out of time. The flow of souls will become stuck without Death, not to mention that Riordan will come for us once he's recovered."

Scarlet caught Jarrett staring at her, and he quickly looked away. He cleared his throat. "Alright then. Any other alternatives?"

"The mage prison." Everyone turned to look at Barek. "Beneath Riordan's castle," he continued. "It's made entirely of magus stone. It has to be enough."

Ange bit her lip. Considered. "It might be our only option."

Leandra spoke up. "You want to crawl beneath Riordan's nose? That's a suicide mission." Scarlet had never been close enough to Leandra before to catch a glimpse of her hands, though she had always tried to. Leandra reached up to itch her face, and Scarlet finally got the confirmation of the suspicions she'd built up: Death's emissary mark was tattooed on her hand. She'd been right. It was the reason her mother had never let them meet.

A blanket of silence had fallen over the room.

"It's what we have to do," Ange said. She said it firmly like she had no doubt at all.

"Two emissaries, disconnected from their god's power," Leandra said. "A handful of Vanguard soldiers and mages. A few Ravens. You can't truly believe that we can break into Riordan's castle, succeed in forging a weapon, and kill him with it?"

Ange shrugged. "Riordan has been plotting my death for over a decade. He hasn't succeeded yet, as you may have noticed. The truth is as simple and as complicated as this: I refuse to fail."

After the meeting, Scarlet and Leandra both lingered in the council room while the others filtered out. Leandra remained seated at the council table, while Scarlet loomed by the door. For some reason, she felt better having an escape route. Maybe it was the way the woman's icy eyes seemed to bite into her.

"I was hoping you would stay and speak with me," Leandra said. "I was sorry I didn't get a chance to talk to you before the battle."

"I'm sorry I didn't get to speak to you years ago."

"Your mother had a certain way of shielding you, didn't she?"

Scarlet choked out a bitter laugh. "You could put it that way."

"While I haven't gotten a chance to get to know you, I have had the opportunity to enjoy your work. I must say, your flamescribing is quite masterfully done."

"Thank you." It had been so long since she'd hunched over her pages with letters endlessly flowing out of her. Though Death's concentration exercises had bored her, she'd always been enraptured with flamescribing. Would that still be the case now? The time when flamescribing had been her one connection to magic was far behind her.

Scarlet found herself missing the scent of charred paper.

Leandra gestured to the chair across from her own. "Why don't you have a seat with me?"

"No." Scarlet fidgeted. "I'm okay."

"Ah. I'm making you uneasy, aren't I?" A pressure Scarlet didn't realize she had felt faded away. "I must apologize. I use my insight magic somewhat unintentionally at times. I shouldn't pry without asking, so I won't. Will you sit with me, now?"

Scarlet cautiously took the seat opposite Leandra. "What exactly was that?"

"I'm attuned to Io. My gift is insight, specifically. I have a knack for being able to see things about people that they can't see themselves. Like Bronwen—he has a kind of insight as well, but most of what he sees are the powers of others."

"So you know Bronwen?"

"Of course." Leandra let out a long sigh. "We're the last three of Death's emissaries, you, me, and him. At least, I hope he still lives. Last four, if your mother still lives. Which I'd like to believe she does. She's a fighter."

"I hope you're right." Scarlet's words came out raspier than she expected. "How long have you been an emissary?"

"A long time. But we aren't here to talk about me."

"You'd rather talk about Death?"

"No. I'm interested in *you*. I'd like to do a reading if you'd give me your permission."

Scarlet's face scrunched. "And what exactly will that do?"

"As I said, I can see things that others can't see about themselves."

Scarlet shook her head. She was raw, empty. "There's nothing left to see."

Leandra raised her eyebrows slightly. "You think this is pointless? Dante saved you with the help of his insight powers. He didn't even know he had them until I told him."

"Dante has powers like yours?" *Has.* She couldn't bear the past tense. Not yet. Not unless she learned his soul crossed over.

"He could read the emotions and souls of others. Similar, yet different to my powers. But that's how he was able to find you in the stream of souls and pull you fully back into the World."

Desolation began to build up as a pressure in Scarlet's chest. "I can't—I don't... want to talk about this."

"That's fine. I just want you to know that this is something worthwhile." Leandra held out her hand. "If you're willing to be a little vulnerable with me, I might be able to help you."

Vulnerable was the last thing she wanted to be.

But where had that gotten her? She'd opened up to Dante too late, he'd been ripped away from her only a moment after she was able to let him in. If she couldn't bring Dante back, Scarlet knew she'd regret her denial of him and her own feelings for the rest of her life.

She placed her hand in Leandra's.

The uneasy feeling came back with the other emissary's touch. She felt like a book being rifled through for a particular passage. After a long minute, Leandra seemed to find what she was looking for and withdrew her hand.

"You're an interesting girl," Leandra said. "Or, young woman, I should say. How old are you now?"

"Seventeen." She'd almost forgotten that her birthday had passed in her months at Deianira.

"You're at least as tough as your mother. You're going to need all of that strength, every drop of it. And forgiveness."

"Forgiveness?"

"You'll drown in your pain, otherwise."

Scarlet swallowed. There was a lot of forgiveness she wasn't ready to give out yet.

"It doesn't have to be all at once," Leandra added softly.

A lump built in Scarlet's throat. Who exactly was she supposed to forgive?

Her mother for lying to her? Jarrett for being gone, even if it had been against his will? Dante for giving up his life to save her, when she'd rather he be alive instead of her? Viridian, for similar reasons? Death for deceiving her, controlling her, throwing her into a dungeon instead of explaining anything?

Herself, for hesitating when she could have killed Riordan and ended it all? For so many lost chances at connection.

"Is that all?" Scarlet asked. She barely waited for Leandra's nod before nearly knocking her chair over by standing abruptly.

This outing had been more than enough for the day.

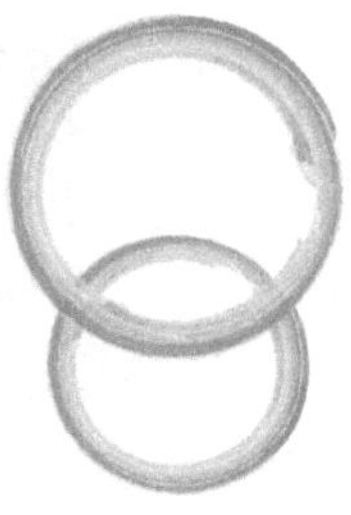

CHAPTER 46

J arrett waited outside the town hall to ambush his daughter.

She wouldn't speak to him by choice. He'd tried to be patient. *I have to talk to her. Even if just for a moment.*

They'd lost many in the battle. The deaths of Korene and Rohan weighed on him the most heavily. First Morgane, now them. At an increasing pace, he was losing the people closest to him.

He couldn't lose his daughter, too. Not again.

He watched everyone else leave the hall, but Scarlet didn't exit. Neither did Leandra, for that matter. They were both emissaries, he supposed, though that didn't put him at ease at the idea of them meeting alone. He couldn't force himself to trust Leandra fully.

Not that he would crash in on whatever conversation they were having—though he'd be lying if he didn't admit he'd considered that.

It wasn't too long before Scarlet came rushing out of the town hall, red-faced. He wondered if Leandra was responsible for his daughter's desolate look, or if it was simply the pressures and tragedies they were all suffering under.

"Scarlet!"

She stopped, turned to him, defeated. Her eyes were wary and struck him to his core. They were the same color as Kiera's.

"Can we talk? Please."

Scarlet looked away. "I don't know what to say."

"I didn't abandon you on purpose. I *swear* to you." What could he say? What could he do to make her stay, for even one more moment? "I don't want to lose any more time with you than I already have."

She looked like she was on the verge of tears. "I told you, I don't know what to do right now."

Jarrett's throat tightened. He knew he was upsetting her further, spiraling out of control, but he couldn't stop himself. "Neither do I, but we need to figure all of this out... don't we? I don't *understand*. After your sister... why would Kiera take my memories? She left and took you away. You won't even speak to me. What did I do to deserve any of this?"

Others in the street glanced over at the confrontation with curiosity.

"Let's... let's not do this here," Scarlet said.

"My house?"

Scarlet nodded almost imperceptibly and, by a minor miracle, followed Jarrett. He tried to compose himself, forcing air steadily into and out of his lungs. At his door, he fumbled with his keys before finally unlocking the door and shuffling inside.

He slumped into a chair, and Scarlet quietly took a seat across from him. For a moment, he worried that she wouldn't speak.

"I didn't recognize you when I first saw you, either," Scarlet started. She looked up at the ceiling, eyes searching. "I was nearly dead when I came here." She stopped, eyebrows furrowed, and she took a couple of long breaths with her eyes shut tight. "Dante was able to bring my soul back. He fixed me." She spoke each word with deliberate care. "But Riordan killed him while he was distracted saving me. And now, it's all so much, and I don't know what to do, what to say. I'm sorry."

Jarrett stared at her. His daughter. Her life had been in jeopardy only days ago. She just lost a friend. *She is in so much pain, how dare I make this all about myself?*

The past few days had been excruciating and that wasn't exclusive to him. The Vanguard and the Ravens were shadows of what they used to be. Riordan had done his damage, and they'd gained nothing to show for it.

Korene and Rohan, gone—and so many others. Ange had preserved some of their bodies down in the vault, with some plan to bring them back if their souls were delayed from crossing over. It was too faint of a hope to hold onto.

He had barely dealt with losing Morgane and everyone else who fell in the battle against Riordan's soldiers. It crushed him, as did the return of his memories. His own wife had betrayed him, locked away the memories of his family, and left him.

There were moments where he almost thought Leandra had been right about warning him away from seeking his past. The truth was a burden, but he never could have gone on without knowing what he was missing.

He had lost Viridian, and perhaps Kiera... but Scarlet was here. She was so familiar and yet so unknown to him. Jarrett wanted nothing more than to be in her life again—but he had to remember that being a parent meant he had to put her first.

"Scarlet, you have nothing to be sorry for," Jarrett said. "I'm the one who should be apologizing for pushing you to talk before you're ready. And I am so sorry about Dante."

Scarlet flinched when he said Dante's name. Jarrett wondered what the nature of their relationship had been—from his brief time with them both, things had seemed intense, but that may have been a product of the danger they were all in.

"Is there anything I can do?" he asked. "Do you want to talk about it, do you want to stay here instead of with Ange—"

"I don't think I'm ready for any of that," Scarlet said loudly. She cleared her throat and continued more softly. "But, thank you."

Jarrett couldn't help but feel hurt, though he knew he didn't have any right to be. He hadn't been in her life for years. Scarlet let her head drop into her hands. Her dark curls hid her face. She was shaking—crying?

"Scarlet—"

"Did Ange tell you?" Scarlet interrupted.

It only took him a moment to realize what she meant. "You aren't to blame. Riordan threatened Kiera—"

Scarlet's head snapped up. "It could have been *over*." Her eyes were dry but her pain was palpable, written in the strained lines on her face. "I—I had my chance. And I faltered. I failed." Scarlet's voice had an unnerving frankness to it.

"Scarlet." Jarrett's heart broke. What could he say to her? He had learned not to take the skills of the young for granted, but she was still just a girl. More grown-up than he remembered her, but certainly not experienced enough to hold the weight of this war against Riordan on her shoulders. She wouldn't want to hear that, though. This battle was deeply personal. The Tyrant had taken so much from them both. No platitudes could suffice. He needed a truth, but a different one.

"You were worried about your mother," Jarrett said. "You didn't want to lose any more than you already had. I, for one, could never blame you for that."

Scarlet's lips pressed together tight as she held back her tears.

"Riordan may not be dead, but neither are we. Or Kiera. We will fight to the very end."

Scarlet nodded firmly, then wiped the errant tears that had escaped from her eyes. It took a few moments for her to gather herself before steering the conversation to a new topic. "So. Mom was really the one who blocked your memories?" she asked.

"Yes. Ange could feel her energy signature on the seal."

"Is it still there? The energy?"

The image of the raven was still emblazoned on his chest, but Jarrett was no mage. "I'm not sure."

"Can I... can I see?"

Jarrett nodded and pulled down the neck of his shirt to reveal the tattoo. Scarlet came over and pressed her hand softly on the markings.

"Is it—"

"She's still there," Scarlet said as she stepped away. "Just a little."

Jarrett put a hand over the tattoo, trying to feel what Scarlet felt, a hint of his long-lost wife. He couldn't feel anything. "Do you know why she did it?"

He couldn't read anything on her face while she thought about how to answer. *I don't even know her anymore.*

"She lied to me. She said you left us. I don't understand it any more than you do."

That was like a knife in his back. Not only had Kiera stolen his memories, but she had convinced their daughter that he had *chosen* to leave? "You must have hated me. Or... still do hate me."

"I..." Scarlet brushed a lock of black hair behind her ear. "I'd like to be honest, which is more than what Mom did." She hesitated. "I did hate you. Viridian died and you *left.*" She took a shaky breath and composed herself. "But nothing is as it appeared. I'm trying to... unravel that. Put it back together in a way that makes sense. You remember now, though, right? Is there something that happened, an explanation of why she sent you away?"

Jarrett sighed. He remembered. But it was a deluge. "I have all my memories now, I think, but I'm still figuring out where they all go. How they're all connected. And I think, because of Viridian... some of it is hard to examine. I have years of grief to catch up on."

Silence lapsed between them. Scarlet was fidgeting. Was she nervous about something? He didn't want to push her, but his curiosity got the best of him. "I know you are about as lost as I am but... do *you* have any guesses about *why*?"

His daughter's eyes were stony. "It has to have something to with Viridian. Right?"

Viridian's death and Kiera subsequently sending him away soon after... he had figured the events must be related. "Was it my fault?" he asked, his voice so small he hardly recognized it as his own. He feared the answer to his very core.

He had been with Scarlet and Viridian while Kiera was away. It happened often that the three of them were left behind when Kiera was doing her most dangerous tasks. Death's missions weren't exactly family-friendly.

They were rarely in danger when Kiera was away. But... that time, mage hunters came. This was the main memory he couldn't bear to delve into. When he tried, all he could see was a mage hunter thrusting a sword into Viridian's chest. Her wide eyes. The blood, gushing—

He couldn't relive that horror. He was supposed to have protected her. Scarlet had been there, witness to this tragedy, as much as he hated that as well.

"No," Scarlet said, blunt. "It wasn't your fault."

Jarrett almost didn't register her words. "But... but I—"

"The mage hunters took us all by surprise. You and Viridian both fought your best." She was stoic. He didn't know what that meant. Was it the truth, or was she trying to absolve him, as he had tried to do for her? "It's true," she added, softer. She must have sensed his hesitancy.

Jarrett dropped his head into his hands. "Thank you. I just want to know, so badly, what happened. What it was that tore our family apart, when we all needed each other the most. I thought that when I got my memories back I would finally have all the answers. But now I just have more questions."

"We'll rescue Mom," Scarlet said. "And then we'll ask her to tell us the truth."

Her words lacked conviction. Jarrett couldn't blame her for that. Ange's insane plan... could it be anything other than a suicide mission?

But could he give up on his mission to free Saridian from Riordan? Could he give up on his wife? No. *I can't back down now.*

"I don't want you to get hurt, Scarlet." He shuddered at the thought of losing another daughter.

Determination flashed in her eyes. "I'm not staying behind."

"Please—"

"You have to understand."

She didn't explain further, but she didn't need to. She'd grown up in the intervening years since he'd seen her last. She was a fighter now, a mage. She'd lost Viridian, both her parents, Dante, and… who knew who or what else. Somehow, she became an emissary of Death, something Kiera would have done anything to prevent. She'd nearly died when Death was not able to save her completely.

Jarrett swallowed his pride, his fears. It was already too late to protect her.

CHAPTER 47

The chill air of dawn blew Scarlet's hair across her face. She brushed it out of the way and continued out into the open field that stood between Rosewood and the forest. The hooded cloak she had dug out of a musty chest wasn't thick enough to shield her from the brisk morning, but she found that she didn't mind. The cold air bit at her, made her feel raw, running in parallel to her emotions.

Tomorrow. They'd leave for Kingsmount tomorrow. It felt like an eternity. She wanted to go now, so she could stop glancing behind her, waiting for Riordan to appear and strike her down as he had back in the forest with her mother. But the waiting... it couldn't be helped. Even though the Vanguard and the Ravens had been preparing for the road as Ange schemed—they would have to go *somewhere* to find more magus crystal, though they hadn't known where. Finalizing everything still took time.

The bustle of loading food and weapons and organizing who would go in what wagon and what horses needed to be reshod and a thousand other details Scarlet didn't fully understand—it was all too much, overwhelming, and she didn't even know how to help without getting in the way. The Ravens, nomadic as they were, had their own packing down to an art. The Vanguard were a bit more scattered, but still, they had been working together for years. Scarlet was new. She wasn't a part of either group. She was underfoot, in the way, but she needed to do something, and so she'd ended up here. In a field. Alone.

At least, that had been the plan.

She didn't so much hear the approach from behind her as much as she sensed it. Her heart stopped for a moment as she assumed the worst—she had been a fool to wander off alone, and now she was being ambushed. As Scarlet spun around, she summoned flames into her clenched fingers, hot and bright embers at the ready.

It wasn't an enemy. It only took a split second to realize the woman who'd followed her was a Raven, dressed in black and overloaded with decorative jewelry and charms of both silver and bone. *How didn't I hear her, with all that metal on her?* Scarlet would have guessed she had muffled her approach with magic, except she recognized the Raven from the battle. It was Fae, the shield mage—attuned to Meyrin, not Cascara.

Fae quickly shifted into a fighting stance when she saw the flames but relaxed as Scarlet let the magic dissipate. "Sorry," Fae said. "Didn't mean to startle you."

"Then why'd you shadow me?"

"Fair point. I won't say I'm great at making friends." Fae flashed a smile. "I thought maybe if I followed you out here, you'd train with me."

Scarlet considered. She had come out to the field with the idea of training, something that could calm the restlessness she felt. The other reason, though, was to be alone. She hadn't quite emerged from her cocoon of solitude. It took so much to interact with others, to summon answers to their questions, to hide from their prying into her mourning and guilty conscience over the events of the battle.

Somehow, Fae seemed... familiar. Comfortable. It made no sense, she barely knew her. But it would be a good idea to sharpen her skills for the next battle. Having a partner to practice with would be helpful. Tentatively, Scarlet accepted.

To start, Fae practiced making barriers around Scarlet. "I'm not as good at doing them on other people as I am on myself," she explained.

Scarlet watched as the shimmering shields thickened around her. "It's that different?"

"It's harder to focus on when it's farther away from me. When I make barriers around myself, they're... they're like a part of me. A second skin. I can focus the energy where it is needed the most. Around other people, it's more complicated."

The effectiveness of Fae's shields became apparent when they moved to sparring. While Fae's offensive abilities weren't as good as Scarlet's, they often came to a draw when Scarlet couldn't break through the barrier and both of them eventually became too exhausted to continue. Scarlet grew frustrated at their draws. Maybe she was too used to winning against Dante. Her gut clenched madly at the thought of him.

They gave each other pointers—Fae gave Scarlet some insight into how to feel out weak points in barriers and Scarlet in return helped her increase her power output for her bolts. Though they worked together, there was an underlying tension—Scarlet could tell Fae was as driven as she was, and they both clearly wanted to win their spars. They fought until they collapsed.

"So how did you end up here?" Scarlet asked her when they were catching their breaths after another grueling tie. "Did you join the Ravens, or were you born into them?"

"I joined."

"Why?"

Fae shrugged. "Why did any of us join? Why are any of us here, embarking on a mission that is almost certainly doomed? Riordan is evil. Saridian and Death must be protected. There is no other option."

Scarlet saw the look in Fae's eyes—a hard determination, mirroring Scarlet's own. "But there's something more personal."

Fae didn't say anything back for a while. Scarlet's breathing finally returned to normal. She stretched out, enjoying the sun on her skin on this rare warm day.

"There might be more," Fae said finally.

Scarlet didn't press her on it, she just helped Fae back up to her feet. There were things she didn't want to talk about either, and Fae didn't pressure her, either. There was an easy kinship between them, though Scarlet couldn't pinpoint why. Regardless, it was a relief compared to how difficult it was to be with Ange or Jarrett or anyone else right now.

The other thing that caught Scarlet off-guard was the ease at which her magic ran through her. It made the whole time training with Death feel like she'd been moving through molasses in comparison. Now, everything came so smoothly, her energy no longer threatened to slip out of her control.

It was because of Dante. Her magic had new life, now that she did. Somehow, he had found the part of her that was lost to the stream of souls and made her whole again. She was stronger now, solid, even though she still felt like she was shattered into a million pieces.

He saved her, and now she needed to save him. Had to save him.

And when the time came, she wouldn't falter again.

The sun was high in the sky by the time Scarlet made her way back to her temporary home. Ange was outside, conferring with a small group outside of a large caravan. She looked up, caught Scarlet's eye, and beckoned her over.

"There you are. It's about time," Ange said. "Pack your things. We're leaving."

"Wait, we're leaving *now*?"

"Yes. Go, go." Ange waved her off and went back to speaking with the others. It was the rest of the mages, Scarlet realized, except for herself, Fae, and Dante's sister.

Scarlet went inside, to her bedroom, and then stopped. She didn't have anything to pack. Some extra clothes that'd been found for her, as well as her light leather armor, were already bundled. Old habit, from living her life on the run with her mother. Ready to go at any time. She slung her pack over her shoulder and grabbed the scabbard that held the sword Ange had given her. Her dagger was already strapped to her boot, as it always was, and... that was it. All her worldly possessions were carried easily in a single load.

When Scarlet emerged to the main area, Ange was there. The woman looked frazzled and ran a hand through her messy hair as Scarlet approached.

"Did something happen?" Scarlet asked. "I thought we were leaving tomorrow."

"We're ready now, so we're going. We've dithered too long already."

Admittedly, Scarlet hadn't kept track of the days since their confrontation with Riordan. Time had slipped by beyond her notice, distraught as she had been. It must have been... maybe a week?

"You're the one who cut Riordan—how deep did you get him? Could he have recovered by now?" asked Scarlet.

"If he was a mortal, I'd say no. Not enough to fight. But as an incarnate... there is so much energy running through him, doubly so now that he has control of Death as well—he would heal more quickly."

"So he... he could come for us at any time."

"But he hasn't. And honestly, that worries me more than anything."

"What do you mean?"

"If he's left us alone by choice, it's because he has something else more important to do. Something he considers more pressing than dealing with a force dedicated to his destruction." Ange grimaced. "He may not see us as much of a threat, as weak as our forces are. But, if his strength has returned, why take any chances when he could easily portal here and finish us off? He has the advantage now, he have no surprises left for him."

Ange was right, he could quash them like ants. Scarlet felt the pit in her belly deepen as she realized how much danger they had been in these last few days. She hadn't been thinking clearly enough to consider the implications of their precarious position.

Ange continued, "Perhaps he's sending soldiers if he is still too injured or is otherwise occupied."

"So... if Riordan is up to something, what is it?"

"Riordan needed at least one of two things in order to have enough power to advance his plans. The first is an artifact. The last known person to have possession of it is Kiera."

So that's what he wants from my mother. An artifact. "What does it do?"

Ange waved a hand. "Irrelevant." Scarlet bristled at the dismissal of something her mother was being tortured over. "He admitted he needed you or Jarrett as leverage over Kiera to get anything out of her. You two are still safe, and if he hasn't broken her in all this time, I doubt he has now."

"You're not going to try to keep us from fighting Riordan, are you?"

"No. We have limited resources, so we play all our cards. If you or Jarrett is captured, it is what it is. Plus, he already has the other thing that would advance his power."

"Oh. Of course. Death." Scarlet felt her gut churn with every awful realization. "And now... he's stronger than any of the other gods."

"Yes. And thus, the Magus War will begin anew if we don't stop him. The only thing the Magus Treaty meant to him was a respite—time to amass strength. He's been preparing for this moment, and I have no doubt his plans are in motion."

"But if he breaks the treaty, won't all four of the other gods rise against him? Even with Death, he can't possibly be powerful enough to take on all of them, together."

"The gods have never played nice with each other. This era, since the treaty, has been one borne of indifference to each other, more than one of active peace and cooperation.

"Meyrin will defend against Riordan, no doubt. He will have no tolerance for an uprising at or near Celaigh's borders. Kajiem... perhaps since the desert also shares a border with Saridian, she will rally a response. But she is fiercely independent and is... not always focused on mortals, let's say. It could take her some time to respond. Riordan has his army with him too, of course. The people of Suraskrit are not prepared to face such a thing, nor to work in tandem with Kajiem's forces.

"Who knows about Io. Always a mystery. They may not swoop in until they see a weakness to capitalize on. Then there's Galapia, so far away, and Cascara is the most committed to peace. Who can say if she will join the fight at all, unless she is sure it is necessary?"

"So you're saying that... that Riordan could take over all of Quintras?"

"It would be difficult, to be sure. The other gods will all rally eventually. But either way, mortals will die in the needless power struggle between the gods, and chaos will arise. Oh, and this is not including whatever haywire madness Death's absence will cause in the meantime."

Scarlet took a long breath. *Riordan is going to get everything he wants. People are going to die. All because I hesitated to kill him.*

"We need to make new swords. I'll have to do my best to train you and the rest of the mages in magus crystal manipulation on the way there. I took some from the vault to practice with." Ange patted a satchel on the table. "It's a slow process to learn. I should have started you sooner—too much time pouring over those maps..."

Ange started muttering to herself, then sighed and addressed Scarlet again. "You're a good mage. I'll need you. I mean, there's not many of us, I'll need all of you. Nine of us, in total."

"Whatever it takes," Scarlet said, resolute.

CHAPTER 48

Scarlet felt her muscles tighten as she saw her father approach. It had started to drizzle, and she'd thought perhaps he wouldn't spot her with her hood pulled up. But of course, she was standing right outside the house she'd been staying in, grouped with the remaining Vanguard and Raven mages. She'd be hard to miss if he was looking for her.

She broke off from the group to speak with him.

"Scarlet! I was hoping... uh, wondering... would you ride with me, on the way to Kingsmount?" He was even more frazzled than Ange. Scarlet supposed that made sense—he had to sort through his newly restored memories, in addition to preparing for their journey.

"I can't. I need to ride with Ange, she's teaching us about artificing so we can help her make the god-slaying weapon."

"Oh. Yes. Of course," Jarrett said. His tone was good-natured, but Scarlet caught a hint of hurt. "...Travel safe, alright?"

Scarlet wished him the same and he was off, retreating to whatever wagon he was riding with.

Guiltily, she was grateful to have a good excuse to decline his offer. Though the ice had broken between them, she still wasn't ready to jump into the father-daughter relationship. It was hard to wash away the years that she thought he'd abandoned them for, even if she now knew that it hadn't been his fault.

She'd missed her father when he'd first left. They had spent a lot of time together when she was young since her mother was often busy with her missions for Death. Over time, when it was clear he wasn't coming back, she'd sworn off hurting over his abandonment and looking back on her memories of him.

Every time she saw him, he was a splinter digging into her skin, a reminder. Her family had been broken for a long time, now. Some of that was Riordan's fault, and the rest was her mother's. Animosity toward her mother rose from the pit of her belly. She needed answers. She needed Riordan to be gone. Maybe then, it would be easier.

She rejoined the other mages. Fae had joined them now, and they nodded to one another. Leandra was next to her, along with the other remaining Raven mages. Two of them looked to be in their twenties or thirties, a man named Wilhelm and a woman named Ophelia. The last Raven mage, Elden, was closer to Scarlet's age. The Vanguard had only two mages left, Markus, who was present, and Zandra, who had yet to arrive. Ange had run off to do... something.

As they were preparing to leave, the mood was somber between the mages and the others nearby. Most of the people going on this mission were leaving with the assumption they wouldn't be returning. The folks remaining were tense, bidding farewell to their friends and family and wondering what would become of them all. Rosewood wasn't safe, not with the possibility of Riordan's soldiers cresting the horizon, ready to destroy the last of the rebellion. Scarlet had learned that of those who were not able to fight, many were evacuating. Others planned to stay, worried about the suspicions that might arise following a mass exodus from the town, or refused to leave their homes and resign themselves to live among those loyal to Riordan once more.

Ange emerged from the bustle of the street. She joined the group of mages, clasped her hands, and looked over the assembled crew. "Alright, we're about ready to set off." Scanning over them, she noticed their missing member. "Where's Zandra?"

Scarlet shrugged, as did most of the other mages. She hadn't seen Zandra since the battle. It wasn't surprising, considering Zandra was staying at Jarrett's house, which she had mostly been avoiding.

Leandra cleared her throat. "I insisted she stay behind."

Ange stiffened. "What?"

"I sensed something with my insight," Leandra explained. "It's difficult to explain in words but... there's a dark cloud. Something isn't right, and she's not ready, Ange. Coming too close to Riordan again, I fear it will destroy her."

Scarlet could feel Ange seething, even from feet away.

"We *need* her," Ange insisted. "Call me cold-hearted, but I don't care whether this is good or bad for her. If Riordan wins, it'll be a moot point. She's a mage. That means we require her to succeed, and if we fail, she'll be destroyed anyway."

"You'd have to convince her, and you can't." Everyone turned to look at Barek, who had appeared behind them. "I came to stop you from trying. I wasn't able to stop her from joining our previous bout with Riordan. But now... she agreed to stay behind. Easily."

"Why the change?" Ange asked.

"They *tortured* her in that prison," Barek snapped. "They were draining her very life out of her. She explained to me what it felt like. It's... it's horrible." His face wrinkled into a disgusted sneer, then it settled into a somber grimace. "And now, her brother was killed. She's not in any shape to join us."

"Let me talk to her." Scarlet wasn't entirely sure why those words came from her mouth, but they did.

There was ice and doubt in Barek's voice. "I don't think that's a good idea."

"Why?"

"She blames you for Dante's death."

A wave of anguish ran through her because it was true. Dante had been a sitting target for Riordan while he fished her soul out of the stream. He was dead because of her. Every time she thought about it, she felt as if her entire being was being crushed and ground into oblivion. Tears sprung into her eyes, she couldn't stop them.

Crying felt like weakness. But trying to hide it, trying to wipe her tears away, felt even weaker. Concealing her vulnerability and denying her feelings had gotten her nowhere. So she let them fall down her face as she continued. "She's right. It's my fault. But Riordan struck the killing blow, and he won't stop there. I can convince her to come, and she might make the difference between our victory or the death of many, many more."

"But she *shouldn't* come," Barek bit back. "I *promised* her she'd never have to go back there. She's one person, she's nearly just a child. Leave her out of this."

"I understand your instinct to protect her," Ange said, "and if she wasn't a mage, I'd agree with you. But Barek... you're looking at the remaining mages in this battle. This is it. Without us, there are no more magus weapons. Without a magus weapon, it's over. You know what Riordan is capable of. This is our final chance. If we fail, there will be war. There will be needless death. There will be utter chaos. We need every tool we have."

"She's a person, not a *tool*," Barek nearly spit the last word.

"If we lose, she'll regret not coming," Scarlet said. "She will hate herself for not trying to avenge her brother or make it safe to be a mage. And Ange is right. She'll still be killed anyway."

Barek shook his head. "I can't... I can't ask her to come. Leandra and I are right, she needs to stay here." He was softer now, they were breaking through his armor.

"Let me talk to her," Scarlet repeated. "You think I'm not likely to change her mind, right?"

Barek shrugged. "I... I doubt it."

"You and I will speak to her, and then she can make her decision. Whatever she chooses, we won't push her any more than that. Right?" She pointedly at Ange and Leandra in turn.

Ange scowled, "Are you sure you're the right person to—"

"Yes," Scarlet said.

Ange and Leandra both scowled but nodded their assent.

Barek sighed. "I'll take you to her," he said, "but I can't promise she'll speak with you."

Scarlet accepted that, and Barek led her to Jarrett's house. Once inside, Barek knocked on one of the bedroom doors. "Hey, Zandra. We need to talk." He put a finger to his mouth, indicating that Scarlet should stay silent. *Probably smart, if she hates me she probably won't be willing to come out and chat.*

A wavering voice came from the other side. "I thought you'd left."

"Not yet. I wanted to say one more thing."

Zandra opened the door and tried to slam it back shut when she saw Scarlet. Scarlet flung an energy bolt at the door hard enough to jerk the doorknob out of Zandra's hand as it flew wide open.

Zandra stared at her with wild eyes and clenched fists. "Just leave, with the rest of them." Her voice was venom.

Scarlet stood fast. "Do you want to save your brother, or not?"

"My brother is *dead*." Zandra punched a dart of energy at Scarlet's face. Scarlet, not realizing the situation would escalate as quickly as it did, didn't flinch fast enough to completely avoid the blow. The bolt scraped along her cheek, slicing her skin open.

"We're going to bring him back," Scarlet said, unflinching. The warmth of blood trickled down her face and dripped down onto her clothes. "Ange saved his body, did you know that? Once Riordan is dead, Death will be free, and she can help us bring Dante's soul back to his body."

"I don't know a lot about being a mage, but I do know that magic can't just... *bring someone back*. I saw him *die*."

Scarlet held up her hand, her emissary marks facing toward Zandra. "This symbol... you've seen it on your brother's hand too, right?"

"Yeah. So?"

"It means we're Death's emissaries. We're connected to the god of death. Riordan tried to kill me. I should have died... in a way, I think I did. But Death and Dante saved me. So I know Death and I can save him in return. But we need every single mage to take down Riordan and make that happen. You coming, it could make the difference."

"Even if that's true..." Zandra shook her head. "I can't go back there."

Barek spoke up. "I don't want to make you face that place again. I know how afraid of Riordan you are—"

"No." Zandra's bloodshot eyes hardened. "I'm not afraid of *him*. I'm afraid... of how much I *want* to go. I want to tear every last one of the Tyrant's soldiers to shreds and break the mages free. I want the mage hunters to pay in blood for what they've done. I want to watch Riordan die as I curdle the blood in his veins. Is this what I am now? *Bloodthirsty*? I don't know what I'm becoming." Her voice was barely a whisper now.

Scarlet and Barek shared a look. *This girl is tougher than any of us gave her credit for.*

"Zandra, you aren't a monster for wanting revenge on an evil man... an evil god," Barek said. "He's destroyed our lives."

"You still have friends there," Zandra said. "And your brother. What about them? If we run into them, will we kill them, too?"

Barek turned pale. "I hope it won't come to that. But it... it might. When we fled, I accepted that doing the right thing meant that I may have to hurt people I care about. Trying to save Saridian and the rest of the World from Riordan... it's bigger than me and what I want for myself."

Zandra took a long moment to think. Her gaze flickered from Scarlet to Barek as she considered. Then, she closed her eyes and took a slow breath. "I know what I want for myself. And I'm not ready to give that up."

Barek furrowed his brow. "And what do you want?"

"Revenge," Zandra's eyes opened suddenly. "On everyone who has caused harm to me and my family." Her voice grew louder, firmer with each word. She turned to Scarlet. "If we win, you're sure you can bring back Dante?"

Scarlet couldn't know for sure if Dante's soul remained within the Crossworld where it could be recovered the same way he had returned Scarlet's soul to her body. And yet... perhaps she was only imagining it, desperate to grasp onto hope, but she thought she could feel a connection still—a bond between their souls. He was still there, her heart told her. "Yes," she told Zandra.

"Would you bet your life on it?"

"Yes. I'll save him or die trying."

"I'll come," Zandra said, "but if you can't save Dante, I'll kill you for being the reason he's dead." The cold certainty with which she said this chilled Scarlet's blood; she didn't doubt for a second that she meant every word.

Zandra scooped up a knapsack and a crystal orb that was sitting on top of the bed, then pushed past Scarlet and Barek. The front door slammed shut on her way out of the house.

Scarlet swallowed hard. She had hoped to attain Zandra's trust, not nurse her vitriol.

"Well," Barek said sheepishly. "...I guess you got her to come."

CHAPTER 49

As they entered Kingsmount, Jarrett hoped that he was ready to lay down his life. Despite their plotting back at Rosewood, and throughout their journey to the capital, their mission was still a death wish. At least he had been reunited with his daughter once more, though their relationship was lukewarm at best. As for his long-lost wife, well—if he perished now, Kiera would have to explain herself to him in the Nextworld.

Morgane had died for the Vanguard, for the cause. Jarrett could at least follow in her footsteps. If the Tyrant finally fell, the sacrifices his friend and many more of the Vanguard had made would be worth it.

This plan had two prongs, both dangerous. Jarrett was on the distraction crew, along with a troop of about forty Vanguard fighters. Their job was to let the infiltration crew get the best possible chance to sneak into the mage's prison and form the weapon. If all went well, they'd join them for the final battle against Riordan.

Scarlet was in the infiltration crew. She had to be—she was a mage. Jarrett wished he could watch over her, but Ange needed as many mages as possible. They needed at least one mage in his crew, and unfortunately, the only one who could be spared was Leandra. He wished it could be anyone else, except perhaps Fae, but Leandra wasn't as spry as the younger mages and didn't have the dexterity to aid the other team.

They had left their wagons and horses at different inns near the outer gates of the city, hoping that they had spread themselves out enough to avoid suspicions that would arise from such a large group arriving all at once.

The infiltration crew would have gathered, and by now they should be waiting near the castle for an opening. Barek would take them around the back to one of the service entrances. Jarrett and his squad would be making a bold entrance. They were disguised as Saridi soldiers, repurposing what tabards they could salvage from the initial onslaught at Rosewood. That battle seemed so long ago to Jarrett's weary mind. Morgane's death. Discovering the vault, the weapons. Time had so quickly catapulted forward to this moment. Their last stand.

Riordan's resplendent castle sat in the center of the city. Even in this darkness, its grand and macabre structures promised the dominance and repression of an egomaniac god's empire. Jarrett had seen it in the daylight once before when he was a child. His father brought him to Kingsmount, though Jarrett couldn't remember what errand they had been on that day. His father had been a blacksmith, perhaps he'd needed new equipment that he couldn't source in one of the closer, smaller towns.

A pang hit him now. His father had died from an illness when Jarrett was young. Was he about to leave Scarlet to the same fate, missing her parents before she was even properly an adult?

The castle made an impression on him back then, as it did now. In the sun, the spires glittered, a spectacle that didn't reflect the oppression that the god sowed throughout his country. In the darkness, they loomed forebodingly over the Vanguard, spikes to impale them all.

The group approached the extensive gardens that surrounded the castle. They were groomed meticulously, not a branch nor vine out of place, everything neatly ordered. It was utterly unnatural and completely reflected Riordan's will to control all of life in his image. Plants as well as people could not be trusted on their own.

Leandra's voice broke him from his brooding. "You doing alright?"

Jarrett stifled a sardonic laugh. "You know I'm not." He wished it was Hera at his side, not the Raven mage, but she was placed at the back of their formation.

Leandra shook her head. "It takes energy to pry with my insight if that's what you're accusing me of. I'm not always spying on your feelings, you know. Though sometimes I don't even have to use my insight when your mood is written all over your body."

Not *always*. What a relief that was. But it didn't matter. He was tired. "Do you think we'll make it out of this?"

"To be honest, it seems unlikely. But then again, I did not think you would be reunited with your family. You've already found your daughter. Maybe, with luck, you'll rescue your wife today."

Jarrett's stomach churned. What would it feel like to be victorious? He hadn't let himself so much as imagine it in all his years with the Vanguard. The impossibility of it all had never stopped him, but he had held himself back from really, truly, believing it could happen. He'd always thought he would die in pursuit of this goal, and he'd been at peace with that. When he'd had no past, what was there to lose? At least he could do something honorable with his life.

Then suddenly, meaning returned to his life. His memories. His wife, his remaining daughter, his chance to confront Riordan and save Saridian from the tyrant god, and all that he held dear. It happened so fast, all at once, after years of biding his time.

Jarrett had rediscovered what he had to lose, just in time to lose it.

They were approaching the castle now, and they were a conspicuous lot. Even disguised as soldiers, their large group would stand out from the guards who were patrolling the grounds. They split into a few groups in an attempt to minimize any attraction.

Jarrett had Leandra and a handful of soldiers with him as they weaved through the gardens. It wasn't long until a pair of guards moved to intercept Jarrett's group, but Leandra didn't give them a chance. Her blast of magic made the approaching soldiers stumble back, and the two Vanguard archers finished them off with well-aimed arrows. Somewhere else in the garden, a guard yelled out a warning. More shouts rang out in the distance, as well as the telltale clang of colliding metal.

Jarrett cursed. Were they going to get slaughtered before even entering the castle? He couldn't get an overall grasp of the situation; there were too many hedges and meticulously trimmed shrubs blocking his line of sight.

His group appeared to be making some progress toward the castle. The garden path they followed became watered with blood as the Vanguard fighters crushed Riordan's guards who came to confront them. These guards were disorganized, just mooks unprepared for a brazen frontal assault such as this. Jarrett was relieved, but he knew things would only get more difficult the further they got.

Before long, they were at the castle doors. *We're really here, at Riordan's doorstep.* Another group of their fighters had already dispatched the guards and were beginning to hack away at the thick wooden door. Jarrett and his crew joined their effort, but then Leandra waved them back a safe distance. With some blasts of magic, she splintered the reinforced wood into pieces. By the time Leandra had broken through enough for them to squeeze through, more of the Vanguard had arrived. Some groups had lost members, but most seemed intact. Not all of them had made their way through the garden, at least not yet, but they couldn't wait for everyone. Either their whole groups had been killed or greatly injured, or they'd have to catch up.

The goal was to push as deep into the castle as they could and for Leandra to use as much magic as possible. They had lured Riordan to them in Rosewood, and now they had to lure him to to fight them here, in his castle. This time, their bait wasn't quite as tempting. It would be easier for Riordan to realize it was a trap, or for him to simply leave his soldiers to handle them. Despite all odds, they needed to convince the god that they were a threat that he had to deal with personally. Drawing Riordan to them was vital to buy the infiltration group more time.

"More magic, Leandra," Jarrett called to her as they entered the castle. They needed Riordan to sense energy, enough to alarm him.

Leandra obliged by summoning a swarm of light orbs, illuminating the hall as they charged in. Her lights were a ghostly blue, adding color to Riordan's bleak abode. Everything was gray and sharp, the marble floors shined to perfection. *Soon, we'll soak it in blood.*

They rushed into the grand hall. A massive chandelier hung in the center of the room, composed of wrought iron. Its decorative metal tendrils were barbed. Smaller versions of the brutal fixture were placed around the hall, above long tables and lavish space for dancing and frolicking—as if such a thing were ever to happen in the Tyrant's castle. A different type of dance would take place here tonight.

Saridi soldiers rushed in from various entrances to surround the smaller Vanguard crew. There were too many of them. They were armed and armored, more soldiers than expected for an average day in the castle.

They had been prepared for an attack. It was all going downhill.

If the whole castle was on guard, the infiltration team would come across trouble, too. *Scarlet.* How could he live with himself if this insane plan got his daughter killed? *But if I want to live to see her another day, I need to focus.*

The forces clashed, Riordan's soldiers funneling the Vanguard in between two of the long tables, trapping them. Jarrett hacked away at each soldier who confronted him. The confined space was both a blessing and a curse. The soldiers couldn't easily come at them from every direction, but they were also being crushed into close quarters, constraining their movements and trapping them.

Leandra took notice of this and directed a blast of energy at one of the tables. It flew several yards, taking some of the surrounding soldiers with it. She climbed onto the remaining flanking table and began to level wide blasts of energy at the soldiers to keep them at bay as the Vanguard fighters dealt with as many as they could.

Jarrett lost himself in adrenaline and anger. His sense of time melted away, replaced by sweat and blood and the exchange of blows. He fought with a vigor he hadn't felt since he was a younger man. Each strike he landed was for his family, for the pain of years lost, for the hope of a future with them. Each soldier he struck down bore Riordan's face, the source of all this hurt.

He didn't see the sword coming down at him until it was too late. A soldier had rushed at him from the side, and Jarrett was caught flat-footed against the deadly blow.

Suddenly, Leandra was in front of him, and the soldier's weapon plunged into her chest instead of Jarrett's.

"Leandra!" he cried.

The Raven woman collapsed, Jarrett stepped over her and took swift revenge on the man that had struck her down. The immediate danger dispatched, he kneeled to assess Leandra's injury. Too much blood was gushing from her chest. They couldn't save her.

Leandra raised her hand to touch Jarrett's face. "Don't you worry... about me. This is my time. If I must die, then I die for you, Jarrett. A man who has already lost so much."

"Leandra," he choked out. Why would she sacrifice herself for him? "No, no—"

"Go." She patted his cheek, a gesture that held finality. "Fight for us all."

He rose, and flowed back into battle seamlessly, battling alongside his comrades to protect everything and everyone that Riordan endangered. Without a mage at their side, the battle was more difficult. Thankfully, Leandra had leveled the numbers enough that they had a chance.

Jarrett had held so much animosity for her. But she had died for him, for them, in a desperate attempt to salvage their mission. His anger for her melted away.

More of his compatriots were lost before it was over. Jarrett shouted with rage each time one of his own fell. He wouldn't stop, not until every last one of the Tyrant's soldiers had joined them on the blood-soaked floor.

Eventually, there were no more enemies to fight. He and eight of his soldiers had survived. Leandra and the other half of the Vanguard fighters lay lifeless, either here or out in the gardens. They had won the battle—at a steep price—but even so, they had failed in their task.

Riordan hadn't come to fight them. Perhaps they had protected the infiltration crew from the wrath of many soldiers, but that would mean nothing if Riordan sniffed them out instead.

Now they could only pray that the mages were safe from the god until they had forged the weapon and were ready to face him.

CHAPTER 50

In the darkness, Riordan's castle looked much like Deianira. It loomed over Scarlet with a portentous presence.

It wasn't until she placed her fingertips on the cold, dark stone of the castle that she actually felt like she was *here*, that this was real. Throughout their covert journey through the gardens, she'd felt dissociative, separate from her body. But now they were here, literally at Riordan's doorstep, and reality was sharp again. There was a layer beneath the subtle floral scents of the garden, something acrid, something... rotten. The clangor of metal rang in the distance. Jarrett and the others were successfully diverting the guards.

Lit only by the starlight overhead, Scarlet and the other mages had followed Zandra and Barek to a service entrance at the back of the castle. Barek slipped inside, gesturing for the rest of them to follow.

It suddenly struck Scarlet that Barek and Zandra had had the bravery to do this alone. It would have made them harder to spot, but still, if anyone had seen them in the halls of the castle or out in the garden… they had no backup. They didn't have the benefit of a distraction.

How had they managed to scuttle so neatly out of Riordan's grasp? And beyond that, how was it that no mage hunters had tracked them down after the fact? They'd made it all the way to Rosewood, and no one had caught up to them.

Maybe Riordan didn't care. The god hadn't come back to wipe out the Vanguard, either. He underestimated them… hopefully.

Zandra, Barek, and Ange took the helm as they navigated the halls of Riordan's castle. Ange summoned a single orb that brightened a small radius around them. Scarlet and Fae were close behind, followed up by Ophelia, Wilhelm, Markus, and Elden. Quietly as they could, they skulked through the castle.

Inside, it was an austere palace, its starkness a different flavor than Deianira's. Death's castle was undecorated and empty. Riordan's home was decorated, but with such strict precision that it gave no real sense of warmth. Nondescript landscape paintings and carefully clipped floral arrangements lined the halls, somehow void of any personality.

Ange glanced back at Scarlet. "Pay attention," she hissed, obviously noting Scarlet's distraction.

Scarlet growled, but Ange was right. She needed to focus, completely.

Zandra stopped and turned to face a wall. She pointed to it. "Here. This is where the entrance is hidden."

Ange put her hand to the stone, and it started to melt away beneath her fingers.

"An illusion?" Scarlet asked.

Ange gave her a sly grin as she finished dispelling the magic. "Just like when we first met."

Scarlet grimaced. "Wait," Scarlet said, "who cast it?"

Ange's brow furrowed.

Ophelia spoke up, "Maybe Riordan forced a Cascara-attuned prisoner to do it?"

"No," Barek said. "The mages in there are in no shape to use magic."

Ange shrugged. A mystery, but not one they could solve in this moment. The barrier was removed and a passageway was now open. A dark tunnel yawned before them, the illumination of the light mote barely penetrating a few feet into it. They descended slowly, staying in a tight group. Thin veins of magus crystal ran along the tunnel's walls, thickening as they went deeper. The tunnel allowed only two of them to walk side by side. Scarlet found herself next to Zandra, who set her on edge. The younger girl's threat lingered heavily between them. Scarlet was sure she could take her on, but she didn't want to fight Dante's sister. And if it came to that, it also meant she failed at reviving Dante.

I can't fail. I have to be strong enough.

The darkness and the earth around them pressed in on Scarlet. She found herself lightheaded. *It's worse than Death's dungeon. Who knows how long the mages have been down here, and what Riordan has been doing to them. Solitary confinement is bad enough, but who knows what they've been through?*

Suddenly, she found herself acutely missing Viridian's presence. Though she had pushed her sister away when she was in Death's prison, there was still a small amount of comfort in knowing that she wasn't truly and absolutely alone. She wasn't alone now, in theory, but... no one here knew her. At all. Viridian had missed out on a lot, but she was still Scarlet's sister. And Viridian deserved to know the fate of their mother. Scarlet hoped she could at least give her that.

Ange's light suddenly snuffed out. Fae stiffened and made a small noise of surprise. Scarlet reflexively summoned another light orb. It only lasted a moment before the energy was consumed and they were left in darkness again.

"He's here," Scarlet blurted.

Ange swore. A cold blue light appeared behind them. The mages all turned to see Riordan. He grinned, the light glinting off his teeth. The strength of his presence pressed in on Scarlet, the aura of his power overwhelming. "You've all saved me some trouble, taking yourselves most of the way into my prison."

Scarlet's heart stopped.

Suddenly, a domed barrier formed over Riordan. Fae made a sharp movement and the barrier shrunk, hitting him in the head and taking him to his knees. With a punch, Riordan shattered the barrier, but Fae quickly formed a new one, and then another, collapsing them together to create a thick layer.

Riordan banged on the barrier and it cracked, hit it a second time and it shattered. "What do you think you're doing?" He began to call his energy forth, his vortex coming alive around him. The god smirked. "You think you can fight me?"

Fae flashed an angry look at the rest of the mages. "Go! I'll hold him off."

Wilhelm's eyes were wide. "You can't possibly—"

"Just"—another barrier formed around Riordan, then another—"go!"—and another. Riordan was encased in a thick shell of magic. Scarlet knew how much energy this was taking Fae. Riordan would keep breaking out, or absorb her power. Fae couldn't last long. She was sacrificing herself so they could continue.

They couldn't leave more than one mage behind, not when they had to make the new magus weapon. Barek stepped forward, drawing his sword, but Fae shot him a death glare in between her outburst of barriers. He couldn't stay either, he was the best swordsman and meant to wield the magus sword, once forged.

"I said, *go.*"

Scarlet and Ange were the first to obey Fae, the others close behind. Barek had looked so determined that she was almost surprised when he followed the mages as they barrelled into the tunnel, a swarm of newly summoned orbs lighting their path.

The twists and steep decline of the tunnel were perilous with such haste. Each heavy beat of Scarlet's heart counted down another second until Riordan caught up with them. She had to concentrate hard on every step.

The magus crystal veins in the tunnel walls grew thicker with their descent, then abruptly the entire tunnel was formed of crystal instead of the rough earth. As Scarlet's boot hit the crystal and slid, she almost lost her balance. They were in an unnatural, rectangular tunnel, and the ground had been formed into a perfectly smooth, glasslike surface.

Ange signaled for them to stop. "There's so much magus crystal here," Ange said, smiling to herself as she patted the walls. "Good. Good. We can start."

"No," Zandra said. "We have to go farther. Let some of the mages free."

"That's not the plan," Ange said.

Zandra was visibly shaking. Barek took her arm. "Are you alright?" he asked.

Zandra's face was pulled tight. "We have to get some of them out of their cells. They can help us fight Riordan!"

"No, they *can't*," Ange's voice was slowly rising. "Their magic is being drained into the crystal, just as yours was. They'll be useless, and Riordan is going to be here any second. We have to begin." Her tone was firm, unquestionable.

The other mages formed a circle, preparing to work the crystal as Ange had been teaching them to do. Condensing the crystal was a difficult process, and their lessons had not been entirely successful.

Sweat dripped down Scarlet's neck. They hadn't even come across a cell yet. She too felt the pull to run further into the tunnel, to try to find her mother, but she knew it had to wait. Every aspect of this plan was so fragile, so delicate that any deviance from it, no matter how small, could bring it all crashing down.

Zandra stayed a couple of steps back from the circle, shifting her weight from foot to foot as if she would bolt away if not for Barek's presence holding steady behind her. "No. I have to go."

"Zandra!" Ange was clearly out of patience. "*Stay*. Make the weapon. Mages later."

"I promise you," Barek told her, "we will free the mages as soon as we can. Okay?"

Zandra, silent, stepped into her place in the circle between Scarlet and Ophelia.

"Pull crystal from the ceiling," Ange instructed.

Scarlet drew a deep breath in unison with the other mages. She reached out with her magic, trying to dig into the crystal above them. It was difficult to penetrate the surface, she could feel the other mages trying to pry at the crystal alongside her, though Ange was the only one doing so with any success as a small amount of the ceiling began to liquefy.

"Don't try to break it," Ange said, a phrase often uttered during their practices. "You're all still trying to chip away at the crystal. Instead, mold it. Guide it, melt it."

Melt it. Scarlet knew how to melt things. Suddenly, it clicked. Instead of prying uselessly at the crystal, Scarlet wrapped her energy around it, focusing tightly on it, imagining it boiling and melting into a pliable form.

Nothing happened.

Frustration smoldered in her chest. She clenched her fists, fingernails bit into her palms, and with another breath, she redoubled her efforts. *Melt.* She could feel the fire, it lived in her blood. *Melt. Transfer into this crystal so you can do my bidding.* She spent so long under the control of Death, now it was her time to make something else obey her. *Melt.*

Liquid magus crystal pooled above. Ange and Scarlet controlled it as it gathered into a giant teardrop, dripping down into the center of their circle. Connected to the magus crystal now, Scarlet could feel the magic coursing through it, connecting... connecting to pain. She could feel multiple sources of agony through it.

The mages. Her mother, maybe. Perhaps Bronwen, too, if he had stayed at Deianira with Death only to be brought here.

She wanted so badly to delve into the streams of magic to search, but that would spell disaster for them now. Scarlet recentered herself on the current task and helped Ange draw more of the crystal down from the ceiling.

Ange nodded to Scarlet with approval. "Good. Hold that in place. I need to gather more."

More? By volume, the large drop of liquified crystal looked like enough to forge dozens of swords. Even if they condensed it significantly, it seemed like a lot, more than enough. Then again, Scarlet supposed there was a very good reason they needed to come here, of all places, to have enough crystal to create the weapon.

Scarlet used her energy to hold the crystal drop in balance, with the small amount of help the other mages could provide, as Ange brought down more crystal. And more, and more. By the end, Scarlet strained to keep the crystal in place and was grateful for the weight her compatriots were able to hold. Her whole body was slick with sweat now.

"Okay," Ange said, finally. "It's enough."

The blob of crystal no longer dripped down from the ceiling of the tunnel, it was now held independently by the mages. There was now a cavity where they had pulled the magus crystal down from. Luminescent energy flowed in circles inside, trapped but beautiful.

Their next step would be to pull the energy out so the crystal would have room to absorb a soul instead. Then, Ange would do the delicate part of artificing, calibrating their soon-to-be artifact to serve the purpose she meant it to. After that, they would condense the crystal and shape it into a sword.

"What's wrong?" Deep in concentration as she reached into the crystal to draw out its energy, it took Scarlet a moment to register the voice as Barek's. "Zandra, what's wrong?"

Scarlet glanced at the girl beside her, just as Zandra withdrew her magic. Scarlet clenched her teeth as the extra weight of the crystal transferred to her.

From next to Scarlet, Ange glared at Zandra. "What are you doing?" Ange asked.

"I can't do this," Zandra said, so quiet Scarlet barely heard, though she was a couple of feet away.

Scarlet felt like she was being crushed by the crystal; it drained her energy so quickly. After her and Ange, Zandra had been holding most of the weight. Elden's grip on the crystal slipped, and he sank to his knees, drained. The burden on Scarlet and the remaining mages increased.

"You can do this," Scarlet said, as she strained. "You have to help us."

"*No*," Zandra said, louder this time, her sharp word echoing through the cave. Barek tried to put a hand on her shoulder but she swatted him away. "I'm not—I can't—I'm not helping *you*."

With a precise motion, Zandra infused her leg with magic, and then kicked Scarlet in the shin, hard. Scarlet's eyes widened in surprise as the enhanced blow threw her off-balance, and she landed on her back as air forced its way out of her lungs. She lost her grip on the crystal, and without her, it crashed onto the floor of the tunnel, solidifying mid-splash.

Barek snatched Zandra into a restraint. "Zandra, what the—" She bit him through a weak point in his leather armor, making him flinch away and release his grip.

Zandra's voice was raised and raw. "My brother is *dead*. And it's because of you." Her angry green eyes bore into Scarlet from above. With a punch, she launched a bolt of magic at Scarlet's face. Scarlet rolled over and up onto her knees in time to avoid it.

"Riordan killed him!" Scarlet yelled, standing back up. "You just destroyed our chance at taking vengeance!"

"It's too late," Zandra said. "He's coming, and he's going to kill all of you." She laughed a little. "He might not kill me, not if I help him." Everyone stared at her in horror, but Barek most of all. "And if someone is going to kill you today, *I'm* going to be the one to do it."

Before Zandra could make another move, Barek lunged at her again. He tackled her to the floor, pinning her effectively. Zandra infused her arms with magic and threw him off of her, despite him being twice her size. She giggled again, verging on maniacally. "Join me, Barek. He'll spare you too. It was his plan for us all along."

"Riordan's controlling her," Ange said. "He has too much power, especially here with all of his captured mages to draw energy from." She muttered a string of swears under her breath. "He *let* Zandra and Barek escape, so they would tell us about the mage prison. So we would come here. There's a seed of manipulation magic in both of them."

"I'll never join Riordan," Barek said, but Scarlet could see a glazed look in his eyes. He was fighting something, and that something was a power-hungry god, whose magic was thick in the air.

"Join me, the prisoners, or the dead," Riordan said, pacing toward them, his vortex of energy picking up more force with each step. "It matters little. One way or another: you are mine."

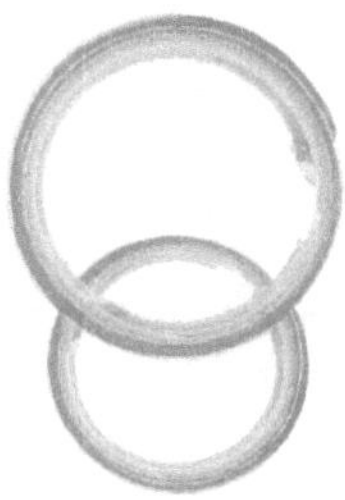

CHAPTER 51

"We aren't going to surrender," Scarlet said. She tried to swallow, but her mouth was too dry. She and Ange were the only ones left standing. The rest of the mages were slumped on the ground or trying to hold steady on their knees, exhausted from their attempt to work the magus crystal. Barek was also on the ground, his eyes glazed over. He'd lost his struggle against Riordan's magic. Zandra had snapped completely. She sat on the ground, rocking back and forth, mumbling something incomprehensible to herself.

"Most of your friends have already given up," Riordan said. The vortex of magic surrounding him grew and Scarlet could feel it swiping at her, draining her energy. "Fighting me will only cause you both more pain."

Ange gritted her teeth. "If I die, I'll die on my feet."

Riordan chuckled. "Years ago, I would have been happy to kill you." He leaned casually against one of the crystal walls. "But now, that would just be a waste. You mages are all worth keeping, you'll join my grid and feed me your power."

The last thing I need is another god trying to use me. Scarlet reached into the core of herself, summoning every last scrap of power she had left. *I'm strong enough now, I have to be.* With all her might, she thrust a concentrated ball of flame at Riordan.

He held up a hand to meet the fireball. It exploded into harmless sparks at his fingertips. The remaining embers were sucked into his maelstrom of power, quickly fading into wisps of smoke.

Scarlet felt Ange drawing power to make an attack when Riordan struck each of them with a swift blast of energy. The one aimed at Scarlet struck her directly in the gut. She was thrown back and tumbled onto the floor as her remaining breath was forced out of her lungs. She didn't get the chance to even sit up before Riordan landed a follow-up blow, a blast of magic that pushed her against the tunnel wall, smashing her head against the magus crystal.

Reality faded. She came in and out of consciousness as soldiers dragged them the rest of the way to the prison. When she managed to pry her eyes open, her vision was doubled. *Do I have a concussion?* For a split second, she thought of how Dante could heal her if he were here—

But he wasn't.

She had finally accepted that she couldn't do this alone, but now she *was* alone. Ange and the rest had been dragged away, she was the last one left to be taken to the prison.

A soldier came for Scarlet and hoisted her over his shoulder. Desolation washed over her as he carried her limp form roughly down the tunnel. She wanted to see if they had gotten to the cells, but her head spun in dizzy circles every time she tried to open her eyes.

After a couple of minutes, her captor tossed her back onto the ground. She bit her tongue as she landed, and the metallic taste of blood flooded her mouth. Her head hurt so badly from the whiplash of being thrown that she couldn't even hear properly, ears ringing sharply.

How many times could she dance this close to death and avoid that fate? She spat out a glob of blood. Not many more, it seemed.

"Sit up."

Before Scarlet could even process the words, a sharp kick to her stomach disabled her further. Pain flashed through her body, she coughed and hacked trying to get air back into her lungs.

"I said, sit up."

Breathing ragged, she managed to pull herself up. Riordan himself looked down on her. She spat a mouthful of blood at him.

"You little—" He grabbed a fistful of her hair, and Scarlet screeched as he pulled her up to her feet. Face to face, he snarled at her. "I'd kill you right now if I didn't need you."

He dragged her by her hair and arm to the back of the cell, where spikes of magus crystal protruded from the wall. He spun her so her back faced the spikes.

"If Kiera hears you scream, maybe she'll finally stop holding out on me." He shoved Scarlet to the ground, then with a foot pressed against her chest pushed her backward into the spikes. The pointed crystals pierced into her skin across her ribs and shoulder blades. The jolt of pain caused her vision to tunnel, and she fought against her body's urge to wipe out her consciousness.

Then, it got worse. Her magic rushed out of her, drawn out by the crystal as it met with her blood. She was left with nothing, a dry husk. Sick to her stomach and utterly void, she couldn't move a muscle, not even to vomit. Riordan might want her to scream, but she couldn't bring herself to summon the breath to do so.

"Welcome to my power grid of mages." Through her off-kilter vision, she could see Riordan's grin, his wolfish canines bared at her. Suddenly, flames began to outline his body and their immense heat bit at Scarlet's skin. "How do you like having your power turned against you?"

Scarlet had caught a glimpse of the god's bare feet. She now understood why. He was pulling her magic into his feet. The energy of each mage was drained into the crystal, then he could use it to supercharge himself with all their powers.

He didn't need a mage attuned to Cascara to cast the illusion. He could just drain their magic and do it himself.

"Once your mother gives up the amulet, I'll be able to channel all of the energy stored in the crystal down here into myself from anywhere. Between the power I drain from you *mages*," he spat the word, "and from Death... the other gods, they'll have no chance against me, not this time. All of Quintras will be under my control."

It was going to happen. The Magus Wars, all over again. Mortals were doomed. The other *gods* were doomed. Scarlet prayed her mother would be able to keep whatever amulet Riordan needed safe from his grasp... but now Scarlet was captured, and maybe her father, too. If Riordan used them as leverage...

Scarlet strained to move, to get up, to do anything—the best she could manage was to wiggle a toe.

"You're just a little, foolish girl. Did you think you stood a chance?"

Riordan was right. She was alone, and she couldn't stop him. Not before, not now. Her magic was drained, her body lethargic. Blood trickled down her back. She could feel one of the spikes driving into her scar, the wound Riordan nearly killed her with. All that healing only to have it ripped open again. With each shallow breath she took, the agony pulsated from that point was nearly unbearable.

You aren't alone.

Riordan flinched at the voice, evidently hearing it as clearly as Scarlet did.

I'm here.

The words weren't coming into her ears, but rushing into her from the crystal piercing her skin. For a moment, she thought it was Viridian. The voice was warm and familiar, but it wasn't her sister.

"Mom?" she whispered, the word her mouth had endured so much to even get the chance to say again.

Scarlet. I'm here.

"Quiet!" Riordan clenched his fists. "You'll have some *time* with your daughter soon, I promise you that."

Kiera's voice remained steady. *You have everything you need to defeat Riordan.*

"I don't have anything," Scarlet said. Her words were quiet, but she felt them pulse out through the crystal. "There's nothing."

Trust me. I've given you everything you need.

What had her mother given her? She hadn't taught her magic, and even if she had, her powers were drained.

It's time.

It was a different voice. *Dante?* It couldn't be. He was dead... but that hadn't stopped Viridian. Or maybe she was just imagining it as she faded away. Everything hurt, but sensations were becoming dull, detached.

Scarlet, it's time.

What had he told her, the day they'd lured Riordan to Rosewood? That she had to take down Riordan with a magus weapon. That she had one.

And suddenly, she understood.

Riordan snorted. "What cruel hope your mother gives you." He couldn't hear Dante, then. His voice was just for her.

Riordan leaned down and grabbed Scarlet by the chin, forcing her slack head to look up at him. A tear was running down her face. "I don't need you to cry. I told you, I need you to *scream.*"

His power flowed into her. Scarlet felt her muscles reactivate and tense. It began to feel similar to Death's compulsions—he was trying to control her body, to force her to scream. She fought it, trying to retreat from his internal grasp. Then, the tendrils of energy within her became barbed. She yelped as a thousand thorns of pain ran through her.

No, don't let him win. Scarlet wasn't sure if the voice was her mother's, Dante's, or her own—or perhaps all three of them.

She had to get free of the magus crystal spikes in her back. She took a slow breath, acclimating to the pain Riordan was inflicting. *Focus. You can do this.* She looked down again at Riordan's bare feet. How was it that he could draw energy out of the crystal, while it stole her energy? There must be some way she could reverse the flow.

"That's not enough for you?" Riordan barked. His hand balled into a fist, and the internal thorns of pain doubled in their agony. They began to rotate and twist, and Scarlet felt as if her insides were being shredded to pieces. This time, she couldn't help it; she screamed like she never had before, her spittle spraying her chin.

Is the pain only a feeling, or is he killing me? It would be so easy to let unconsciousness take her, however long it would remove her from this torment. But if she let go now, she might not get another chance. She would be dead, or Riordan could get the amulet. *I have to end this, and I have to do it now.*

She was too weak to manipulate the magus crystal. But maybe she didn't have to do it by herself. Closing her eyes, she reached for her mindscape, her quiet place, the place where Dante had drawn her back from the stream of souls.

She fell into the snowy dreamscape. In the distance, she could sense her body and the torrent of agony Riordan was putting it through. Perhaps she was even still screaming. But this place was separate from her physical form, it was a place of refuge. Her breath was visible in front of her, the chill from the air biting into her skin. She looked around. No longer was the snow around her pristine and untouched. There were tracks—exactly what she'd been hoping for.

She could hear Riordan's words echoing faintly in the distance. "Passed out, have we?" Her body was slumped and still. He slapped her across the face, almost jolting her back to physical reality. She held on tight, locked onto the tracks, and regained her focus.

The footprints in the snow were easy to follow, but she had to move quickly. She couldn't keep her attention from Riordan's assault forever.

The landscape rushed by her as she pursued the tracks, wet clumps of snow kissing her face. Scarlet braced her physical body against Riordan's blows as he tried to wake her, the immense pain threatening to pull her away from her mind.

And then she was there, at the banks of the stream of souls. Here, it was warm, the air electric. Trepidation rushed through her as she approached and waded in, spirits of the dead rushing around her feet. "Dante?" she called.

"I'm here," he said, echoing the words of her mother. She couldn't see him, but she could feel his presence.

"I want to save you, bring you back, I promise I will, but—" She took a ragged breath. "Before I can, I need your help again."

"I'm with you."

I'm with you, too, Viridian's voice echoed, fainter, but there.

With an electric jolt, Scarlet was thrust back into her body. She cried out as Riordan kicked her in the gut once more. She spat out the blood that had filled her mouth and looked up at the god, the man who had caused so much death and pain.

She was strong again. The crystals that dug into her flesh grew warm, and then searingly hot as energy rushed out of them and into her body. Her mother, sister, and Dante were helping her reverse the power grid Riordan had built. She heard her skin sizzle and smelled burning flesh.

Fire was alive and well in her blood. She opened her mouth, and this time instead of blood, she exuded a jet of flames. Riordan yelped and stepped back, away from the inferno. Scarlet pulled herself away from the wall of spikes, her scar pulsating with magic that had been injected into her body through it. As she stood, she drew the knife from her boot sheath.

She leaped at Riordan, her full weight catching him off-guard and throwing him to the floor. She landed on top of him, just in time to force the air out of his lungs.

"This is for all the pain you've wrought!" Scarlet plunged the dagger into his throat, panting heavily, her eyes blazing.

He gurgled, blood pooling from his mouth, then went limp. The energy from his body rushed into the dagger, its hilt growing searing hot. His body became dull and gray, and almost looked smaller, no longer having the presence of a god within its confines.

When the transfer was complete, Scarlet withdrew the dagger from Riordan's throat. It burned her fingers, but she held it tight regardless.

The obfuscation was broken—even coated in blood, it was clear the dagger was made from magus crystal, not the metal that her mother had disguised it to be.

The missing sixth weapon. Her mother had secretly entrusted it to her. Now, filled with Riordan's soul, the dagger gleamed with a bright blue light.

Scarlet. You did it.

Her mother's voice brought tears to her eyes once more.

"I'm coming to set you free," Scarlet promised. "Tell me where to find you."

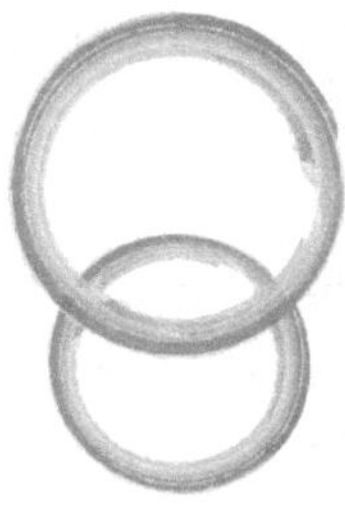

CHAPTER 52

With the bloody battle in the great hall concluded, Jarrett and the other surviving Vanguard fighters patched themselves up as best as they could. Not one of them had escaped injury. Jarrett had suffered a cut to his side that throbbed with each breath.

A dozen of his friends lay dead, including those who had fallen in the gardens. They had to leave their fallen comrades behind and hope that they could come back to retrieve them. For now, they had to see what had become of his daughter and the rest of the mages.

The smaller, culled group followed Jarrett as he charged through the halls, searching for any sign of the infiltration crew. The halls had been cleared of guards and any other activity. It seemed they had drawn all of them to the great hall. But then, where was Riordan? Why hadn't he come for them?

Perhaps he had come for his daughter instead. Jarrett gulped as the worst-case scenarios took hold of his imagination.

Eventually, their investigation revealed the entrance to a tunnel. They lit their lanterns. As they descended the tunnel, the stone walls turned to crystal, confirming it as the right direction.

Not far into the crystal portion of the tunnel, there was a spot where a conflict had taken place. Blood streaked the glimmering floor in several places. A large dome had been carved out of the ceiling, and below it, crystal had been frozen mid-splash, as if it had dripped down from above and then solidified partway through its landing.

"They tried to make the weapon here."

Jarrett's ears were still ringing too loudly for him to tell who made this observation. His grip on consciousness was precarious. The outcome of this battle didn't appear to be in favor of the mages who attempted to morph the crystal.

No, it was too early to make that assumption. He had to have hope. There were no bodies, either way. If they had succeeded, perhaps they had gone further in, to find the prisoners and free them.

Jarrett beckoned the others to follow him farther in. As he suspected, they began to come across prison cells carved into the crystal walls. Even the vertical bars jailing each prisoner were hewn from crystal. Vicious spikes lined the back wall of each cell. In every occupied cell—which was most of them—the prisoners were slumped back against the spikes, most of them unconscious. Dozens of mages, incapacitated and in constant torment.

The Vanguard fighters started the process of breaking prisoners free. If mining into the crystal vault back at Rosewood was any indication, it would take them a while to chip away at the bars with their weapons.

Jarrett didn't stop to help them. He needed to continue his frantic search. Where was Scarlet, and the other mages? And... Kiera. He wanted to cry out for her, but his throat was tight. What would he say to her, if she were here? In equal parts, he wanted to hold her close and yell at her for everything she'd done.

He peered into each cell long enough to confirm that none of them held anyone he recognized. His obtrusive light made a couple of the conscious mages glance up at him, lethargic and curious.

"We're getting you out," he reassured them quietly before moving on.

Jarrett was far into the prison complex now, probably farther than he should be from the others. He could faintly hear the chinking of axes and swords against the crystal bars. He should turn back and rejoin them, or bring them forward with him. He glanced into one more cell, reflexively turning away with disappointment when he saw blonde hair and not the black of Scarlet's or Kiera's, before spinning back to face the prisoner.

"Ange!"

She looked up at him, slowly. Jarrett couldn't imagine the pain of the spikes embedded in her back, sucking the life out of her. She smiled. Blood dribbled out of her mouth and down her chin. "So, you made it," she groaned.

"What happened? Where are the others? Riordan?"

Ange shook her head. "Dead."

Jarrett's heart stopped and his eyes stung.

"*Riordan's* dead." The clarification came from a faint yet angry voice. Jarrett spun to see Scarlet a few feet down the tunnel, hollow-eyed, a light orb and the glowing dagger she held illuminating the space around her.

His heart started again, and he felt himself breathe. "He's really...?"

Scarlet nodded. His daughter was streaked with blood. *What has she just been through?*

"But we weren't able to make a new weapon," Ange said. "We have a reprieve, but he'll bond with Calder."

"No." Scarlet came closer, and showed Jarrett and Ange her crystal dagger, glowing luminously.

"Impossible." Ange's eyes locked onto the weapon. "Where did you get that?"

"My mom gave it to me. She had put an illusion on it. I didn't know it was a magus weapon until the moment I needed it."

Ange let out a sharp laugh. "So, you brought me the last weapon after all. Kiera transmuted it into a dagger."

"Where *is* Kiera?" Jarrett asked. "Did you find her?"

"She found me," Scarlet said. "She spoke to me through the crystal. She's farther down in the prison. Much farther."

Jarrett's heart pounded hard, his ribs feeling like cell bars mirroring the prison's entrapments. "Then let's go."

Ange cleared her throat. "Want to break me loose before going to rescue your traitor of a mother?"

Scarlet swung around and gave Ange an icy glare. "*Excuse me*? You're going to accuse my mother of being a traitor, at a time like this?"

"I've made it clear to both of you that I've had disagreements with Kiera," Ange said. "There are things you need to hear before you speak with her, especially now that you have Riordan's soul—"

"No. This isn't—it's not the time for any of that. I haven't seen her in months, and my—Jarrett hasn't seen her in years."

Scarlet's dodge of the word "dad" strained Jarrett's heart.

"Scarlet, this is *important,*" Ange said. "You have to listen to me—"

Scarlet shook her head sternly. "We'll come back for you."

Ange looked to Jarrett pleadingly. He shrugged at her as he followed Scarlet away. He didn't have to decide right now how much he trusted Ange. Scarlet was the one who could use her magic to break Ange free. His manual hacking would take too long, and he wasn't about to leave his daughter to wander this place alone, especially when they were so close to freeing his long-lost wife.

For now, the tension of the search for Kiera was held taut between him and Scarlet. They were silent as they paced down the seemingly endless tunnel. They passed the cells holding the other mages that had gone with Scarlet and Ange. The bars had been melted away. Jarrett assumed that Scarlet had set them free on her way out to him. The mages were slumped on the ground, free of the spikes but still lacking either energy or consciousness. It was particularly difficult to see Zandra crumpled on the floor, as well as Fae in the cell next to her, who looked in worse shape than the rest of them.

Jarrett gestured to the fallen Raven. "Is she... alright?"

"Maybe. Barely. I bandaged her wounds the best I could for now, the bleeding isn't too bad, but there might be internal damage... Riordan seems to have kept her alive so that he could drain her power, but he may have gone too far."

"And what about you?"

Scarlet's nose had been bleeding, dried flakes of blood she hadn't fully wiped away remained. Her face was bruised and her lip was split open. As he had been following her down further into the prison, he had noticed the blood staining her dark clothing from the puncture marks he could only imagine were from spikes of magic crystal.

"I'm... pretty banged up. But I think I'm okay."

"Leland, our medic, will make his way down soon. He'll do whatever he can for Fae and everyone else."

"I found another friend of mine, too. Bronwen. He's a healer. I'm sure he will need some time to recover as well, but hopefully, he can aid those who need it most with his magic."

Leaving Fae and Zandra behind felt wrong, but with Fae already bandaged and Zandra freed of the spikes, there was nothing more they could do for them right now. The strained look on Scarlet's face made him wonder if she was thinking of Dante. If Jarrett remembered correctly, he had been a healer too.

As they continued, Jarrett wondered how Scarlet had gotten free, and how she had recovered so quickly compared to the other mages. Recovered enough to kill a god.

It was strange to feel pride in his daughter for killing someone. But he was immensely proud of her strength, courage, and wits. He felt his chest fill up with the feeling.

The crystal tunnel led them deep within the earth. The cells lining either side of them were empty after they passed the Raven mages, and then there were no cells at all, just bare crystal. Scarlet seemed distracted as if honed in on something that only she could hear.

"Can you tell how much farther?" he asked.

"We're close."

After a couple more minutes, they turned a corner and abruptly came to an end. The crystal tunnel terminated into a lone cell. It was identical to each of the previous ones, except it held the woman he didn't know if he loved or hated. The mother of his children. The stealer of memories. *My wife, if I can still call her that.*

Kiera was pressed against the crystal spikes. Her head hung limply, but as he and Scarlet approached she raised it sharply. Her eyes, mesmerizingly blue, bit into his soul.

She and Scarlet looked so much alike. The relentless force behind their gaze, their dark curly hair. She had new scars—most prominently, the vertical burn marks down her cheeks. A flare of anger rose. *Of course they magebranded her.* He wasn't sure why it surprised him.

Maybe it was just the shock of seeing her so changed. Other scars marred her face too, silver lines denoting where a blade had cut. She wore tattered clothes and Jarrett could see that her forearms were similarly scarred.

Riordan has been torturing her.

His heart burned with a flurry of feelings he could barely comprehend. It was too many things, all at once. Anger and pain, of what his wife had gone through... but also what he had been through. The fleeting joy of his family being together, finally. Except Viridian. A pang of loss rang through him. *My family will never be complete again.*

It was the most bittersweet moment imaginable.

Once Kiera was in sight, Scarlet ran to the cell and liquefied the bars. With nothing between them, Scarlet ran to her mother, pulled her from the spikes, and then into an embrace. In Kiera's arms, Scarlet began to sob.

"It's alright," Kiera said. Her voice was scratchy and soft. "Everything's okay."

Jarrett stood at the mouth of the cell, watching them. He didn't know what to do, what his place was in this. He was only an onlooker to their reunion. He was irrelevant, an intruder in this intimate moment.

He could name the core of what he was feeling now: loss.

Nothing would ever be the same. Viridian's death, Kiera's betrayal, his estrangement from Scarlet—there was no going back to how it was before. His heart ripped as he stood on the edge of his own family.

He had waited so long for this. All three of them had been through so much, and they were finally together, and... there was no relief. Not for him.

Kiera stroked Scarlet's head, tenderly squeezing their sobbing daughter close, despite her obvious weakness. She met Jarrett's gaze with her unreadable eyes. "Jarrett... I can't believe you're here. Do you...?"

"Remember? Yes."

Her voice broke as she told him, "I'm sorry."

For the briefest of moments, his love for her swelled. Then, the anger overtook him. "You have no idea what you put me through."

"No," Kiera whispered hoarsely. "I don't. But I did what I could to protect you. To keep you away from all this. I... I thought it was for the best."

"You were wrong." His voice rang hollow on the cell walls. He felt cruel, he didn't want to inflict any more pain than any of them had already had to endure. He wanted the perfect reunion. But this wasn't it. It couldn't be, not after all that had happened. Tears stung his eyes.

Kiera's eyes closed, sparing him from the intensity of her gaze. "We did this wrong. I realized, eventually. I never should have agreed—"

"What are you talking about?" Jarrett's voice shook. His hands were trembling uncontrollably.

Kiera's eyes fluttered open. "You're still piecing it together, aren't you? You don't remember—"

"I remember *everything*!" His control was slipping. "This was your fault, you sent me away—"

"If you remembered everything, you would know." Kiera paused. He didn't want to hear it. She didn't want to say it. But she did. "Me hiding your memories... it was your idea."

"No." Jarrett took a step back. The world around him spun. "That can't be right. I wouldn't have done this to myself. You're... wrong, you're lying."

"I'm not lying. But I am sorry. I never should have done it. Please, let's make things right, together. We'll get to safety, and we'll talk. All of us."

He couldn't help his voice from rising. "I lost years. Years of time, of life, of connection with our daughter, *my* daughter. I spent them *suffering,* so lost that I threw myself into harm's way just so that I could feel *something.*" Scarlet sniffled, her tears on hold, and unburrowed from Kiera's shoulder to look at him. "My family was ripped away from me, something so essential to myself was gone and I didn't even know what it was." He gestured to Scarlet. "She won't even call me 'Dad'."

"I'm so sorry, Jarrett." Kiera's earnest words fell flat.

"I don't know exactly what you did to make Ange consider you a traitor. All I know is that you betrayed *me.*"

With that, Jarrett turned his back, walking away from the family he had found only to lose all over again.

CHAPTER 53

In her mother's arms, Scarlet finally felt the tension leave her body. She had been hanging onto it for so long, ever since they had been separated. Tears ran freely down her cheeks.

She had spent a long time being mad at her mother. For holding her back, trying to keep her from the fray when all it did was make her more vulnerable. The secrets, the lying.

But none of that mattered right now. She loved her mother fiercely, despite it all, and finally they were together. Safe. As they held each other close, Scarlet let her anger go. At least for now. For this moment, all she needed was this. The complicated parts could come later.

This was it: victory. Riordan was dead. Her mother was saved. She had heard Dante's voice, and soon she could bring him back, too. Even Viridian had managed to reach her. Everything was going to be okay. It was too much to process, too perfect to be true.

But then, there was also Jarrett.

She won't call me "Dad."

Those were the words that echoed in Scarlet's head as Jarrett stormed off. Guilt washed over her.

"Mom. I don't understand. Did he leave us, or did you send him away?"

Kiera sighed and loosened her embrace on Scarlet so they could look at each other face to face. "It's... complicated. A bit of both? I think it's best if he has some time to sort out his memories—I had to block so many years from him, I'm sure it's a lot to process—and then... the three of us should all talk. Together. We'll sort it out. Okay?"

Scarlet paused. "Okay." She burrowed her head back into her mother's neck again.

I should be angry, but I can't be right now. She was too tired. There had been too much. Her mother was safe, and she wanted this moment of happiness to be unspoiled, no matter how complicated their situation was.

Her mother squeezed Scarlet tight. Her voice was layered, pain and happiness both shining through. "I'm so grateful you're safe."

"We're both safe," Scarlet said.

"You're... you're in the World. Death said that... you wouldn't be able to survive leaving the Crossworld."

"That was true. But I don't need to be tethered to the Crossworld anymore. I have my soul back, all of it."

"I still feel your tether. Just a thread."

Scarlet shrugged. "In any case, it's alright. I'm alright, as far as I know."

She hadn't been able to sense any connection to the Crossworld, other than her emissary bond, since she had broken the tether. It made sense that there would still be a faint connection, otherwise she probably would have died instantly, unable to hang on until Dante saved her. How subtle it must be though, for her to not notice it. And how strong a mage her mother was, to be able to sense it.

"Why did you give me the dagger?" Scarlet asked. "It would have made more sense for you to have it."

"I had it when Riordan attacked us. It was my chance to kill him. I did manage to cut him, but not deep enough. I'm sure he felt something though, because he ran. It gave me a chance to escape. But, ultimately, I failed that night. You almost died and I gave Riordan a reason to keep after me. I knew I didn't have a chance anymore, he was going to hunt me to the ends of the World.

"When I left you in the Crossworld, I switched the magus dagger with your own, in case you ever had to face him again. I would have retrieved the other weapons for myself... but Riordan ambushed me before I could get them."

Scarlet considered all this for a moment. "You trusted me to fight."

Kiera let out a short chuckle. "I suppose I finally gave in, in a way. I should have always known you were going to fight, whether you were trained to or not. I'm sorry. I should have taught you how to use your magic. I just didn't want... didn't want you to fight, to lose you like we lost—"

"I know. I guess in the end... it worked out. It's over." Scarlet laughed shakily and drew the dagger from her boot sheath. The light it emanated was a reminder of the power of the soul it held.

As if on cue, footsteps tapped on the crystal floor, and Ange rounded the corner. Evidently, she'd found a way to escape her cell.

"I would beg to differ." Ange was disheveled and her face was blood-streaked. "It's just begun."

"I'm afraid she's right," Kiera said.

Scarlet said, flatly, "Riordan's dead. How is it *not* over?"

Ange held out a hand. "Give me the dagger."

Scarlet loosened herself from her mother's embrace and stood up. She didn't like Ange looking down at her like that. "You need to explain yourself before you can ask anything of me."

"We made a *deal*. You owe me that dagger."

"I told you I'd find the weapon, not that I'd give it to you."

Ange's face darkened. "Don't try to twist my words."

"You weren't straight with me, so why should I be with you? You knew Jarrett was my father and you didn't tell me. And I need to understand why you think my mother is a traitor."

Ange waved a hand as if she could brush away Scarlet's worries. "That's all inconsequential, in the grand scheme of things."

"What is this 'grand scheme'? Why do you want the dagger—Riordan's soul? Why isn't this *over*? Tell me!"

Kiera broke in, "She wants power. To take the strength of the gods for herself."

Ange raised her nose, unabashed. "I want to make the world *better*. Can you deny that it's a mess, the way things are now? The gods rampage through the World as they see fit. The Magus War is over, but still, they linger, manipulating us to their will. No. It's *our* time. It's time for mortals to reign supreme."

"Perhaps," Kiera said, "but not with you at the helm."

"Who else has the guts to do it—or the power?" Ange asked. She turned to address Scarlet. "I'm the only mage who is attuned to *all* the gods. I was born for this, whether Kiera wants to acknowledge it or not. You want to know my plan? I want to capture each one of the gods, and then reunite them within myself. No more division, but instead a single god, as they started out. Incarnate of all, but *I* will stay in control, not give myself up as a simple physical vessel. To have but one ruler of Quintras—it's the path to peace."

"You'll become another dictator, just like Riordan. No one should have that much power," Kiera said. "Scarlet, you can't give her the dagger. We must destroy Riordan's soul, so he cannot return, and no one else"—she looked pointedly to Ange—"can wield his power, or give him form as an incarnate again."

Before Scarlet could respond, Ange flew into a rage. "*Destroy him*? Everything will be thrown out of equilibrium! Everything. The gods *balance* the World. That's why they must be one being, again. Separated, there is conflict. Reunited, we have a chance to end the constant power struggle. Destroying any one of them would bring destruction and chaos."

Kiera's voice got low and soft, though her words carried a heavy weight. "We need to destroy all of them. *That* will bring balance. Then, truly, our World can be free from the shadows of divinity."

"All of them, except Death," Ange said. "Isn't that right? You could never bring yourself to kill *her*."

"The flow of souls would cease without her. Unlike the other gods, she serves a function, and she doesn't interfere with mortals."

Ange looked at Scarlet, once again eyeing the dagger she clutched to her chest. "We seem to forget the decision isn't currently ours."

Kiera held out a hand. "Give me the dagger. I know what I'm doing. Ange wants power for herself, she doesn't care about the cost."

"Kiera will tear the World apart if she has her way."

"*Stop!*" Scarlet paused, swallowed, and steadied herself. "I... I'm keeping the dagger." She didn't know what she would do with it, but both her mother's and Ange's plans seemed dangerous. Neither felt right or like it would fix things. There had to be another way. But for now, she had to keep Riordan's soul safe. *Now* that's *a new sentiment.*

Power crackled from Ange's hand. "You think I can't take it from you?"

A moment of tension stretched across the cell. Scarlet wasn't worried about the dagger being taken by force—at least, not immediately. She was the least drained of the three of them, considering the burst of energy she had received when the magic flow of the spikes had been reversed.

Then, a bolt of energy came from behind Scarlet, crashing into Ange with such force that it blew her backward. Scarlet spun to look back at the source, her mother, who was barely holding herself up. *She's been imprisoned for so long, how does she have any energy left?* Scarlet rushed to her side and steadied her.

"If you *ever* harm my daughter," Kiera choked out, "I will hunt you to the ends of any World you run to."

Ange, ever resilient, picked herself up off the ground, panting. "I don't need to harm her. Nor do I want to. She'll be helpful to my cause when she comes around."

With that, Ange left, and Scarlet was left with her soiled reunion. She wanted so badly for everything to be alright, but it wasn't. Riordan had been taken out of the equation, but Ange was right: it wasn't over, as much as Scarlet yearned for it to be.

Chapter 54

Scarlet helped her mother out of the depths of the mage prison to where the Vanguard had gathered to recuperate, closer to the surface. Those who could were moving the remaining mages out of their prison cells to a makeshift triage area, where a medic was hectically tending to all the injured.

The couple dozen mages who had been freed from the prison were all in rough shape. She was glad to see that Fae and Zandra had been retrieved and were being cared for. Scarlet had done her best with Fae, but she knew little about treating injuries.

Thinking about how useful Dante's healing abilities would be sent a flash of pain through her chest. *I can still save him. It will be okay.* She drew in a deep breath as she tried to reassure herself. *And, thinking of healers, where did Bronwen end up?* She didn't see him as they rose through the tunnels and he wasn't in the triage area either.

Scarlet examined the faces of the Vanguard and Ravens resting and milling about. She faltered when she realized how many people were missing. Both the distraction and infiltration crews had lost much of their numbers. *More blood spilled because of Riordan. This victory cost so much.*

Her mother put a hand on her shoulder. "Are you okay?"

Scarlet nodded. Her throat was tight and she didn't trust her voice.

She couldn't see Leandra anywhere. Another emissary had fallen. Now it was only her, her mother, and—

"Bronwen!" Scarlet cried out, spotting him off to the side of the tunnel, gaunt and pale.

He smiled weakly and held a hand out to her. She took it, and he squeezed her hand harder than she expected him to be able to. "You came for us. I... I don't know how you accomplished all this, but...thank you." He noticed Kiera beside her. "I'm glad to see you are alright, as well."

"It's good to see you, Bronwen," Kiera said.

"Where's Death?" Scarlet asked, wary. "Is she locked away here?"

Bronwen dragged his weary gaze back to Scarlet. "No. Riordan imprisoned her in his realm. We'll have to jump to the Crossworld to free her." Bronwen glanced around. "And where's Dante? Is he with you, too?"

He didn't know. Of course he didn't.

Scarlet couldn't quite choke out an explanation, but her pained silence and a shake of her head spoke for her. Bronwen squeezed her hand a bit tighter, his face crumpling as he understood.

"Scarlet. I'm so sorry."

"Who's Dante?" Kiera asked.

Agony burned in Scarlet, sharp and impossible to ignore. Suddenly, she couldn't face Bronwen. She couldn't answer her mother. She released Bronwen's hand, and continued onward, her mother following behind with an air of concern, but didn't push Scarlet on the matter. She had always known when to leave Scarlet alone and let her come to her when she was ready.

She spotted Barek, sitting against the crystal wall, Zandra slumped unconscious in his arms now that the medic was done tending to her. *Are they free of Riordan's influence, now that his soul is sequestered?* She hoped that she didn't have to find out the answer the hard way. Zandra's inexorable betrayal had almost ruined everything.

Ange was out of sight. Scarlet wasn't sure whether to be relieved or concerned about that. Probably concerned. But there was no time for that.

"We have to get everyone out of here," Kiera said from behind Scarlet. "Riordan may be defeated, but he has an army, and supporters across the kingdom. Calder may not be able to become Riordan's next incarnate, but he will still lead in his absence. We aren't safe."

Scarlet nodded. She never thought she'd be looking forward to returning to the Crossworld, but she was absolutely done with being in Saridian. "Do you think the injured will be able to make it back to Deianira?"

"We may have to spend some time in Riordan's realm before they can travel that far," Kiera said. "And we have to free Death from the prison there, of course."

"Of course," Scarlet said, neutral.

"I don't think I can muster a portal right now," Kiera said. "Can you, while I gather everyone?"

Jarrett emerged from the crowd. "Wait, don't do that yet."

Kiera stared at him, an eyebrow raised. "Why not?"

"Because I think we should stay," he said. "This may be the only chance we have to take the capital from Riordan's supporters. We hold the castle, we can't let go of this opportunity."

"I wish this could be more of a victory than it already is," Kiera said. "But you'll never hold the castle with less than a couple dozen troops and a handful of mages. You have to know that. The only reason you were successful today is because Riordan sent Calder and his army to the border. With Death captured, he hoped to have enough strength to take over the other regions. They underestimated you, and you won, but Calder will bring the army back and crush you."

"Don't *lecture* me," Jarrett snapped. "I know staying is probably a death sentence." He looked up to the Vanguard and Raven fighters and mages around them who had stopped what they were doing to listen to their argument. "Our friends gave their lives for this victory! Leaving now would dishonor their memories. I won't tell you it's safe, but I will tell you that it's the right thing to do. The city will be in chaos when they hear of Riordan's downfall. We must hope that those who are tired of Riordan's rule will join us, and help us overcome the misguided."

Silence reigned over the tunnel.

"I think he's right," announced Barek. Zandra was alert now, sitting up next to him. She nodded her approval.

"I stand with you, Jarrett," Hera added.

One by one, the Vanguard members voiced their agreement. Some of the newly freed mages seemed eager as well, though many stood back, barely conscious enough to comment or fearful of the consequences of staying.

"You're a valiant group, I will say that," said Kiera. She seemed hesitant, but Scarlet could hear the admiration in her voice as well. Scarlet wondered if she was proud of Jarrett's leadership, or the bravery of those who were willing to stay. *Perhaps both?*

"The injured should come with us," Kiera continued. "They can recuperate in the Crossworld, and rejoin you later if they'd like."

"Thank you," Jarrett said curtly.

Scarlet squirmed as both her parents turned to her, wondering who she would join. She was the only mage in decent condition, she would be valuable in the stand to hold the castle, but... she couldn't stay. Her mother and Bronwen would need help transporting the injured, and she had to save Dante before his soul was swept to the Nextworld.

"I have to go," she told Jarrett. "I'm sorry."

He stared back at her blank-faced like he hadn't expected anything different. Scarlet's chest ached.

Two groups began to form, one around Jarrett, and another around Kiera, gathering to travel through the portal Scarlet would make.

"I wish we had more healers," Kiera muttered to Bronwen as he rejoined them. "Not that I doubt your abilities, but... there's just so many who need help."

The comment was jarringly insensitive before Scarlet remembered her mother barely knew Dante's name and had no idea he had been a healer. Regardless, her heart twisted. She would give anything to have Dante here with them. He had made this victory possible.

"Don't worry, Kiera," Bronwen said. "Once Death recovers, I'll be able to pull power from her again. We'll get them all through this."

Those who decided to stay with Jarrett didn't look much better than the injured who would be fleeing. All but two of the Vanguard fighters stood with him, regardless of their wounds. There were about five newly freed mages who had the grit to join him as well.

All of the mages from the infiltration crew made their way to Kiera with help from Vanguard members. Fae had to be carried very gently, the worst off of them all.

The exception was Zandra, who was with Barek still, near Jarrett.

"You should come with us," Scarlet told her.

Zandra's sidelong glare bit into Scarlet. "Barek's staying, and so am I."

"What if Riordan's manipulations remain active?"

Barek stepped in. "Riordan's gone now. I don't feel anything left of his magic," he said. "She should stay. We need all the mages we can if we hope to hold the castle."

Scarlet didn't have the energy to argue. Plus, they were right—Riordan's soul was captured, so hopefully he couldn't continue to cloud their minds with manipulative magic.

"But... Dante," Zandra added. "You'll get him to come here after you bring him back, right?"

What will Dante want to do once he's back? What... what will I do? Scarlet hadn't pondered much past her goal of reviving him. "I'm sure he'll want to see you."

Zandra nodded. "I want to come with you, to know he's okay, but... if this is our chance to help Saridian, I have to be here. Tell him I'm alright."

"I will," Scarlet said. "You two haven't seen Ange, have you?"

Both shook their heads.

"I think she's gone, for now," Kiera said, resigned. "But, Jarrett, if she comes back—you can't trust her. She wants to rule the World, as Riordan did. It would be trading one tyrant for another."

"And why should I trust your word?" Jarrett asked stiffly.

"Because she's right," Scarlet said. "Ange admitted she wanted power for herself. She thinks it's the only way to stop the gods from ruling over us."

"And if that's not enough for you, she threatened our daughter," Kiera added.

Jarrett's gaze flickered over to Scarlet. "Is that true?"

"She... she said she wouldn't hurt me but she wants Riordan's soul. I don't know what she'll do when she realizes I won't change my mind about keeping it."

Jarrett gave her a nod. "Then I'll be wary if she returns."

It was time for Scarlet to create a portal. She closed her eyes and sought the thread that still connected her to the Crossworld. Scarlet sank deep into herself and found it: the thinnest of threads, tying her to the realm of the gods. It gave her the feeling of the Crossworld, the flavor of it that she needed for this task. She dredged up the last of her power and cut a hole between the Worlds.

"Jarrett." Scarlet overheard her mother as the last injured mages were being helped to the portal. She had never heard her voice so filled with regret and longing. "Please, let's speak when I return. We need to talk about what happened. It's complicated, all of it, but I want us to get through it. As a family."

"I'll wait for you," Jarrett said. Hesitation lingered in his voice.

The mages were through the portal, then her mother, and then Scarlet was the last left of the retreating party.

"Are you coming back, too?" Jarrett asked. "Whatever happened, I'd like... to get to know you again."

Scarlet didn't know what she wanted. Her mother was right, that this was complicated. It seemed that Jarrett did have some part in leaving, after all, reopening the wound of abandonment that she had carried for so long. But her mother did play a part in his disappearance as well, though Scarlet didn't yet understand the details.

One way or another, after losing Viridian and nearly losing her mother, could she really turn any of her family away?

"I'll return when I can," she answered. "Hopefully with reinforcements."

Jarrett nodded. Scarlet couldn't hold the portal open any longer, her strength was fading. She gave Jarrett a wave as she stepped through to the Crossworld.

One day, maybe it would be easier to think of him as her father again.

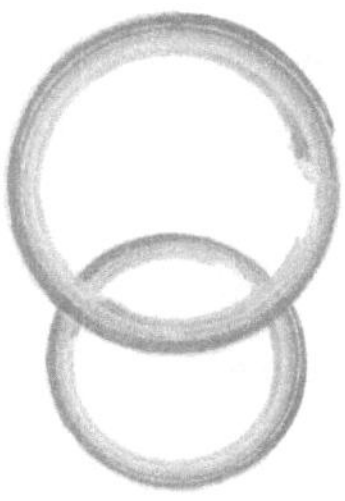

CHAPTER 55

Scarlet stepped through her portal into another tunnel. Her mother had already surrounded them with orbs of green light. Their luminosity was dull because unlike in the World, the walls here were natural rock and dirt instead of reflective magus crystal. The ground was rough beneath her feet, so much different than the smooth crystal floor.

There were no cells here in the Crossworld. And, if Ange had portaled through, she was long gone—no signs of her remained.

The incline was slight, but enough for Scarlet to orient herself with which way was up and out and which led further in. Something was tugging her towards the depths of the tunnel. Her emissary bond pulled taut, guiding her.

"I have to go down," Scarlet told her mother. She paused for a moment. "You said Calder is away with Riordan's army, right? He won't be here?"

"Riordan could have misled me, but I do believe that Calder is away. Now that Riordan's soul is captured... I don't think Calder would have

access to manipulation magic anymore, which also makes him less dangerous."

"So what you're saying is, even if he is here, I can take him," Scarlet
flashed a smile at her mother.

Kiera remained stone-faced. "I... suppose so, but, be careful. The lesson
of today has been to not underestimate your enemies."

Scarlet summoned a ball of flame into her hand to light her way. It was
more comforting to have fire ready on hand than a harmless orb of light.

"I'm going to have to get used to that, aren't I?" Kiera commented. "You
fighting, using magic..."

A lot was going to be different, now. *Jarrett isn't the only parent I've lost
touch with.*

"I'll keep an eye on everyone while you go," Kiera said. "Then we'll
sweep the castle and... if it's safe, we'll stay here, as strange as that might
sound. Just until there are enough of us recovered to transport the most
injured back to Deianira."

Scarlet shivered. The last thing she wanted to do was stay in Riordan's
realm, in his *castle,* even with him... subdued. Plus, regardless of the safety,
she needed to search out Dante's soul as quickly as she could. But one way
or another, the first step in their journey was to free Death.

Scarlet followed her emissary bond like a rope as it led her deeper into
the underground. Her sense of foreboding increased as she continued. Just
like the World, there was a cell at the end, but this time it held a different
woman.

Death stood behind a barrier of magic, awaiting Scarlet. Her red hair
frizzled out wildly. Scarlet had never seen her hair out of her signature braid
before. While her appearance was frazzled, Death herself seemed calm.

They stared at each other through the barrier, only a couple of feet away
from each other. Scarlet didn't know how to feel, standing in front of her
god. Death had saved her, tormented her, trained her, controlled her. Much
like her mother, Death had held her back for the sake of trying to protect
her. But the god had also given her power, so much power, the strength

that Scarlet had always wanted—both by teaching her how to use magic and by lending Scarlet the true power of gods.

A long moment passed.

Death spoke first. "I felt it. Riordan. He's... *gone*?"

Scarlet reached down and drew her dagger. She held the glowing blade up for Death to see.

The god bowed her head. "I owe you my life, and much more," her rich voice intoned.

Scarlet resheathed her weapon. "I didn't do it for you."

"Regardless, thank you," Death said. "I don't have enough power back to break free."

"Together, then."

Scarlet had to dig deep to access enough power at this point, and together she and her god blasted the barrier with a barrage of flame and pure energy. It broke like an exhalation long-awaited, a deep gust of power dissipating as it shattered.

Scarlet wiped the sweat from her brow. "Riordan made that energy barrier?"

"Yes. He took complete control of my powers."

Scarlet didn't like the thought of Riordan having his own skills, forget having Death's ability to shape pure energy, and of course all the powers of every mage he had captured. The god's soul, even trapped in her dagger, still felt too precarious to be safe.

Death stepped free of her confinement. Her face seemed different—softer, maybe, if that was possible. "I want to say I'm sorry—for everything I put you through."

"It's a bit late for apologies." Scarlet couldn't help but let the bitter words out. Maybe she got that from her father. She didn't want to cry again. Enough tears had been shed for today.

Instead, she began the journey back out of the tunnel. She could hear Death pacing behind her, but the god said no more.

Scarlet tried to work up the courage to ask about Dante—if he could be saved, pulled from the stream of souls, or if it was too late: if he had crossed, gone from this World. *I heard him. He has to be there still. And Viridian, too.* But she was afraid of the answer, of closing the final chapter of hope.

Other questions lingered on her tongue, not ready to be formed either. The dagger strapped to her ankle was light, but the decision of what to do with it was a weight difficult to ignore.

When they reached the mages, Death and Kiera took a long look at each other. The emotion behind their eyes was difficult to judge. Scarlet thought back to Ange telling her that her mother and Death had been romantically involved. It was a strange thing to believe.

Perhaps Death had been less cruel, back then. Scarlet hadn't expected Death's apology—maybe that was a glimpse of who she used to be. A person with compassion instead of a relentless god.

"Death," Bronwen said, looking up from where he was tending to Fae. He gave her a small smile. "It's over."

"Thank you, my friend," Death said. They clasped hands. It was the first time she'd seen Death show any kind of physical affection, even one so small.

Death and Kiera said nothing to one another. Death paced around the fallen mages, taking account of their conditions.

"Much of their energy will return soon, now that they are free." She lingered at Fae as she passed her by. "With Bronwen's help, even she should be able to travel soon."

"And then we'll get you back to Deianira," Kiera said. A long pause, and then she added, "And my debt to you is forgiven." Scarlet sensed that it was verging on being a question.

"Yes," Death said. "You're free, Kiera. I'll remove the emissary marks from you and Scarlet when we get to Deianira."

Riordan's castle in the Crossworld was similar to its counterpart in the capital, but boasted many more floors, towering up into the dark ether. With some searching, they discovered an infirmary and took over the beds and supplies there for the night.

Scarlet patrolled the halls, paranoid that danger could still be lurking around every corner. *I'm almost free,* Scarlet thought as she wandered. *It doesn't feel real.*

She'd gotten many of the things she wanted already. Her mother was safe. Riordan wasn't a threat to her anymore. She knew magic, and how to fight with it. Soon, Death would have no control over her.

And what would she do with her freedom? It could still mean nothing. She was starting to understand what her mother meant when she said that power doesn't make you safe. Scarlet was stronger than she'd ever been, but now she held a god's soul in her hands. It was already a target on her back if her conversation with Ange was any indication. Unless she surrendered control of the dagger, the circumstances would still limit her.

And then there was the hole Riordan had ripped into her heart when he had struck down Dante. If he couldn't be saved, if he was truly gone... What use was freedom, if she couldn't be with the best friend she had ever known?

She should have told him that she loved him.

Why did he have to put her on the spot like that? *We were out of time,* she admonished herself, but it didn't make her any less frustrated. It'd been too soon for her to be sure. She hadn't been whole then, her soul scattered between Worlds. But then he put her back together. He'd reached into her soul, and she knew it then: his love was real, and so was hers.

Dante knew her, he saw her even through her defenses, and he still wanted to be with her. He'd sacrificed himself for her. And then it was too late to say everything she wished she would have said.

She adored his tenderness, the quiet passion with which he cared for things, from the plants he tended to the people in his life. He had the patience to take things slowly—most of the time—to tackle problems with purpose and care.

And Zandra was right—he'd died because of her. She couldn't let that be the end.

After her feet were sore and her body too heavy with exhaustion, Scarlet finally chose a room across from the infirmary to stay in for the night. She lay in bed for less than a minute before she realized she wouldn't sleep until she got an answer. She got back up and searched out Death. She wasn't hard to find, she was exactly where Scarlet had last seen her, on a balcony at the end of the hall.

The door to the balcony was open, so Scarlet crept up behind her. Even though her footsteps were silent, she knew Death could sense her presence. Yet, the god didn't turn to face her. Scarlet joined her against the railing, looking out toward the twin moons of the Crossworld. She hadn't missed them.

"Death," she started.

"Don't," the god said, though not sharply. She shifted and looked at Scarlet. "Please, would you call me Eva? I want to... feel that part of myself a bit more, right now."

Death—or, Eva, she supposed—seemed so different now. More gentle. Scarlet was taken aback. "O-okay. Eva."

"You had a question for me?"

"Ange thought that, maybe..." Scarlet paused. Somehow, saying his name aloud was too hard right now. "The souls that needed to cross over while you were gone—"

"You're wondering about Dante."

Scarlet's chest thumped. "There are a few others whose bodies Ange preserved too—but—yes."

"The others, I won't know until we return to the stream. My powers are still recovering."

"And Dante?"

"He's an emissary. So, of course, I have a connection to him."

Every decision Dante had made, even those that went against everything Scarlet had wanted for him, was right. If he hadn't become an emissary, there would be no chance for him. Each moment Eva put off giving her a straight answer, Scarlet's heartbeat quickened. "Just tell me. Please."

"I don't know."

Scarlet narrowed her eyes. Was Death trying to dodge her questions once again?

"I sense his soul in the Crossworld. But I don't think that he's in the stream of souls."

"Where else would he be?"

"I'm not sure. I might have a better idea once I recover further."

So he hadn't crossed to the Nextworld—that should have been a relief. But what could it mean if his soul was missing from the stream? Even Eva didn't seem to know the possibilities.

"When you figure out—"

"I'll tell you as soon as I do," Eva said. "I promise."

CHAPTER 56

The next morning, they set off toward Deianira. There were ten of them in all: the Raven mages, Fae, Ophelia, Elden, and Wilhelm; the two most injured Vanguard, Dalton and Garth; and then of course there were Bronwen, Kiera, Scarlet, and the god that she had slowly started thinking of as Eva.

None of them were in the best shape, but Bronwen had managed to stabilize all of them enough to handle a slow trek through the Crossworld. Though it would be a painful journey, no one wanted to linger in Riordan's realm, especially not in his castle.

The first night, they huddled around a small fire to keep warm. The weather was turning cooler, day by day. Tinges of yellow had been appearing on the edges of the leaves in Riordan's realm as well as in Saridian proper.

Scarlet's mother pulled her from the fire, taking her far enough away that the others couldn't hear them speak.

"I know that things have been... intense." Kiera hesitated. "But now, you do need to give me that dagger."

Scarlet stared cooly at her mother. "I don't *have* to do anything." She wasn't ready for this fight yet. She'd hoped her mother would leave things be at least until they were back at Deianira.

Kiera seemed taken aback. "This isn't a *discussion*. We can't risk letting Ange get her hands on it."

"I don't intend to let *anyone* get their hands on it." After hearing that her mother wanted to destroy Riordan's soul, Scarlet realized that she couldn't let the dagger go. As much as she wanted to keep Riordan from mortal interference, destroying his soul seemed like a dangerous solution—and Ange's plan to take his place wasn't much better. But if stripping Death of her power threw the souls' crossing into chaos, who knew what outright destroying a god might do?

"*Scarlet*," her mother said in a voice that meant she was serious. She held out a hand expectantly.

Scarlet crossed her arms. "A lot has changed. You can't just... tell me what to do anymore."

Kiera slowly lowered her hand. "Everything I've done," she hissed, "I've done to *protect* you."

"How?" The word came out louder than Scarlet expected. In the periphery of her vision, she saw the heads of some of their allies by the fire turn to look at them. "All you did was *hide* things. You kept me from learning how to defend myself. You never told me anything about being an emissary, barely anything about what you were up to. And you took away Dad's memories. Where did that get any of us?"

"Here! It got us *here*. I won't deny that I've made mistakes. But Riordan's gone, and we're *alive*."

Scarlet let out a bitter laugh. "Barely."

"But you are. And now I want to make sure you stay that way. So hand over the dagger. Please."

For a moment, the pleading look in her mother's eyes almost convinced her. But then Scarlet shook her head. "I can't."

"You can be angry with me if you want. I know I've done some questionable things. Part of it is just... I didn't want you to have to live the same life I did. Full of loss. Bound to a god. But I failed, in the end. You lost your sister, your father, you became an emissary. I wanted to protect you from so much and I couldn't. I succeeded in keeping you alive, and you defeated Riordan—which is incredible. And now... this can be over for you. If you give me the dagger, you don't have to be involved anymore. You can be safe, and free."

Scarlet shivered as the wind buffeted her. They were too far from the welcome warmth of the fire. The flame in her heart felt distant, too, like it was hibernating. She felt more calculating than passionate, for once. "Is that really why you want me to give up the dagger?" she asked. "Or are you just afraid of what I'll do with it?"

Her mother's face was stone, unreadable. "It's both. I want you to be safe, and even with all you've managed to accomplish, this is a responsibility that is beyond you."

The heat flowed back into Scarlet's body. "I'm keeping the dagger. I think that Ange is right about one thing: destroying the souls of gods can only cause more chaos. So if that's your goal... I can't let you do that."

"So what's your plan, then? You think you can defend that dagger from Ange and whoever else wants it?"

"I don't know yet. But it's too late to keep me from being involved." Scarlet accepted her own words as she said them. So much of her wanted this struggle to be over with Riordan's death. She had witnessed the horrors that came from Riordan's reign and the death of two of the most important people in her life because of the struggle against the tyrannical god. Riordan had almost killed her, too, and had tortured her mother. He may be gone, but if his soul fell into the wrong hands...

She was caught up in this, she was the one with Riordan's soul, and she wasn't ready to cede control over the fate of the god to someone whose plans she didn't agree with. *I have to accept that I am a part of this, still, whether I want to be or not... and I think... I want to be. The World needs to be a better place than it is. I can't allow for things to go back to the way they were—or worse.*

"So then, let's figure this out together," her mother offered. "But let me hold onto Riordan's soul."

"No. I'm sorry, Mom. But after everything... I don't know that I can trust you."

Kiera bit her lip. "You *can*. I promise."

"You always do what *you* think is right. No matter the cost to anyone else." Scarlet had to look away from the hurt look in her mother's eyes.

"You have to understand that I was only trying to protect you—"

"But you couldn't! And I don't know if you've changed. And I *have* changed." Scarlet could tell her words were cutting into her mother, but still, she couldn't stop. "I should be dead right now."

Scarlet looked back to her mother to see silent tears streaming down her face. "I tried to keep Riordan from getting to you—"

"I'm not sure that's even the worst part."

"Was she that bad to you?" Kiera whispered. "Please, don't tell me I made the wrong decision. I never wanted this life for you, but I wanted you to live."

"I don't know."

Scarlet found that her face was wet with tears as well. She barely knew what she was saying anymore. Death—Eva—had been awful, yet had also brought her some of the best things in her life. Magic, a way to be in control for once. Knowledge of the world in the books, in what Eva and Bronwen taught her. And, companionship—Dante, though each thought of him dug a knife deeper into her chest. If she had just died when she was supposed to, he would probably be alive right now.

Then again, so would Riordan.

"No, that's not true, actually," Scarlet said. She sighed. "It was my decision to become an emissary, wasn't it? You got me to the place where I had the choice, but I chose it. In the end, it wasn't up to you."

The memory of it was vague, but snippets of it had returned over time. Death had fished her soul out of the river and given her the choice: let her soul flow to the Nextworld, or stay and become an emissary.

If she could go back in time, and hear Death's deal again, knowing everything it would bring, would she still take it?

It was a difficult question to grapple with. The past months had been intense, full of pain and anger, but also connection and love. She'd been at both her weakest and most powerful. So much gained, and yet much lost, too. All of these opposites were intertwined. Had it been worth it?

Her mother took her gently by the shoulders. "You're going to have to accept that I've had to make sacrifices. Not all of them have been my own. But I did the best that I could with what I had."

"You're going to have to accept that I'm a different person than that girl you left at Deianira. I've been through a lot, but I'm stronger for it. And I'd do it all again if I had the choice. So you made the right decision, and so did I." Scarlet took a shaking breath and looked up at her mother. "But who I am now... I can't give you the dagger."

It took four days for them to reach the center of the Crossworld. The journey was much slower than Scarlet's first jaunt through Riordan's realm since many of their group were still injured. It felt even slower, still, with the tension running between her and her mother and her anxious impatience to learn the fate of Dante's soul. She'd been gone for long enough that she worried that Viridian would be gone, too. She desperately wanted her sister to know that their mother was finally safe.

The sun was high in the ethereal purple sky as they approached the stream of souls. A boat sat waiting for them—it was painted blue and gold, Riordan's colors, from when he had stolen Eva away. Eva insisted on being the one to ferry them across in groups.

Eva, Kiera, and Scarlet were the last group to cross the river. Scarlet peered down into the stream of souls as Eva paddled them closer to Deianira. Part of Scarlet had been floating along in the stream until recently. No wonder it had pulled at her energy like it did when she was swimming across it to get to Cascara's realm to meet Ange.

She longed to let her fingertips brush the water. *But what if I don't feel either of them?* If Dante and Viridian were both gone, she would be shattered all over again. She didn't want to be stuck in a boat with her mother and Eva if that happened.

As they neared the shore, she watched her mother stare up at Deianira. *What's it like for her, to return here? Are her feelings as complicated as mine?*

They disembarked, and Scarlet immediately reached for Viridian. There were wisps of her energy, but nothing solid to latch onto. *No. She can't be gone. Not now, when Mom is finally back… Maybe she's just harder to reach now that I'm not tied to the Crossworld as I once was.* Scarlet grasped tightly to this hope as they trudged through the swamp to Deianira.

"Eva," Scarlet said, her voice unsteady.

The god didn't make her ask the question. "I don't know yet," she said softly. "Give me some time."

More time until she knew whether he was gone. The waiting threatened to break her. Kiera glanced back and forth between them, but she didn't inquire. *I wonder how long things will be strained for,* Scarlet wondered. She and her mother had kept some distance since their argument over Riordan's soul.

They made it to the castle. Scarlet helped her mother get the injured settled in various rooms near Bronwen's quarters—conveniently located for him to heal and keep an eye on them—while Bronwen went to the pantry to prepare them a proper meal from whatever was available there.

"Where's your room?" Kiera asked her afterward. Scarlet led her there and swung the door open to the closest thing she'd had to a home for the past months.

"This was my room too, back when I lived here. I wasn't much older than you, then." Kiera wandered in and brushed the curtains back to take in the view.

Scarlet tried to imagine her mother as younger, living in the same room she had. It was a strange thought. This place was filled to the ceiling with her loneliness, her depression, her anger; it drowned everything else out. Scarlet knew suddenly that she couldn't be in this room, not for another night, not another second.

"You can stay here," Scarlet said. "I'll take the room across the hall."

Her mother stared at her, appraisingly. "Dante's room?"

Scarlet flinched, just a little. She hadn't spoken of Dante to anyone since her conversation with Death. "How do you know that?"

"I spoke with Bronwen. Scarlet, I'm so sorry—"

"I don't want to talk about it." Scarlet left her mother and went to Dante's room, slamming the door behind her.

She sat on the edge of Dante's bed, the place where she had sat to comfort him through his visions. How could she think this room would make her feel *better*? It was so empty without his presence, yet its walls pressed at her. Most of the plants he had carefully tended to had long since wilted from neglect. Only a couple remained, succulents that had thrived even without care.

Scarlet felt more like one of the withered plants than the hardy cacti. She was worn down, sucked dry, and still, she had to keep going.

Would he ever come back to these rooms? Or was she cursed to haunt these halls, alone, all the while making decisions on the fate of the World that she didn't feel the least bit qualified to make? A World she didn't even know her place in. She'd been thrust into all of this, never having the privilege of getting to decide what she wanted for herself.

She kicked off her boots, unstrapped the dagger from her ankle, and tossed it to the other side of the bed. She pulled her feet up and nestled into the bed. Wallowing in Deianira. In Dante's room. Familiar, but new. She had squandered the time she could have had with Dante.

She shut him out for so long. Why had she been that way? Her anger was acid, always eating away at her, leaving her worn thin, too translucent to let anyone else see her presence. Could she have done it another way? Accepted friendship, love, truly, before it was too late?

Her mother was back and now Scarlet was wasting that time away too, letting her bitterness overtake much else. She thought back to her conversation with Leandra, back in Rosewood, when the other emissary had told her to forgive.

How do I forgive when I'm still so angry? How does any of this get better?

Leandra's words rang in her mind: *It doesn't have to be all at once.*

There was a knock at the door. For a moment, Scarlet thought about yelling, sending her mother away. Instead, she pulled herself up.

She didn't want to wallow in loneliness anymore. The battle was over, but a war had begun. There would be no peace as long as Scarlet had the soul of a god confined in her dagger. Even in her rage, and all of the complications, she couldn't waste the time she had with her mother. They could lose it again at any moment. Scarlet opened the door.

"Scarlet—" her mother started.

Scarlet embraced her. Her mother, surprised, was stiff for a moment, then pulled her in tight. "I'm sorry," Kiera said. "I'm sorry." Her voice broke on the last word and she began to shake.

When they released each other, both of their faces were wet with tears.

"I spoke to Viridian," Scarlet blurted. She suddenly felt guilty for keeping it from her mother for so long. A kind of emotional retaliation, in a way.

"W-what? How? When?" Her mother's eyes were wide.

"Ever since I came to the Crossworld, I've been able to hear her voice. Only in Death's realm... and... I can't reach her now."

Kiera's face turned white. "I've read about this before. Sometimes, if someone dies with unfinished business, part of their soul remains in the World or in the Crossworld. A... ghost, they call it." She began to pace around Dante's room.

"Her unfinished business was... us I think. Our family." Scarlet paused. "Maybe that's why she's gone now? We... we were all back together."

"It could be." Kiera ran her hand through her hair, a mannerism that Scarlet abruptly realized she had picked up from her. "I miss her. I'll miss her every single day until I join her in the Nextworld."

"I'm going down to the stream," Scarlet said. "I want to see if I can still reach her, maybe from there."

"Can I come with you?"

Scarlet hesitated for a moment, then nodded. The part of the tension between them that still lingered tempted her to decline. But she pushed away that feeling. She needed her family to be as complete as possible, for just a moment. She regretted that Jarrett couldn't be with them, too.

Scarlet fetched her boots and made sure her dagger was strapped in tight, unwilling to leave the weapon unattended for any amount of time. As they made their way out of the castle and to the stream of souls, Scarlet focused on her breathing, willing herself to be calm, to be connected to the energy around her. On the muddy embankment, close enough to touch the water, she dropped to her knees. Her mother stood steady next to her.

"If you speak to her, I don't know if I'll be able to talk with her too so... tell her... I don't know." Kiera laughed a little. "Everything. Tell her everything. Tell her I love her."

Scarlet grabbed her mother's hand and squeezed it. "I will."

Her fingers shook as she held her other hand out, but she stopped before they reached the stream.

Scarlet closed her eyes. She laid down, pulling her mother to the ground next to her, heedless of the dirt that would cake her clothes and hair. She felt the energy in the air, in the earth beneath her, in the water rushing next to her through her mother beside her. She had never felt so connected to all the magic that ran through everything. She took one more breath and plunged her hand into the stream.

The stream didn't call to her like it did before. It was sharply cold and buzzed with energy, but it didn't threaten to pull her soul into it anymore. She reached out, first trying to call out to Dante, but there was no trace of his energy. Death was right; he wasn't here. Thorns pressed into her heart.

Now, she searched for Viridian. There were echoes, traces of her sister—her strength, the comfort in her voice, the way she smelled. A bittersweet melody of their sisterhood, fading more by the second.

Viridian. I hope you're at peace. Me, Mom, Dad… we're okay now. As okay as you can be in this World, anyway. We love you. You deserve to rest, now.

For a moment, the water burned hot as it rushed by Scarlet's hand. A wave of Viridian, burning bright as she exited this World. Their mother gasped, and squeezed Scarlet's hand tighter—she felt it, too. Scarlet laughed, cried, let her tears run down her face and fall into the stream of souls, and gasped as her grief overtook her body.

Goodbye.

CHAPTER 57

“**S**carlet.”

The voice broke Scarlet's trance. How long had she been lying at the stream's edge? She opened her eyes, but the world was too bright. “Mom?”

Scarlet blinked a few times and refocused. It wasn't only her mother standing over her, but Death as well. Eva. A smile pulled at the god's lip, amused at her confusion. She had braided her hair again, her lips were painted bright red like they used to be. After a moment, the smile was replaced by a more serious expression. “I have to say goodbye.”

“Goodbye? Where are you going?”

“To the Nextworld.”

Scarlet scrambled up from the muddy ground with her mother's help. Eva had already started toward the castle by the time she was back on her feet. “So, wait—”

“Crossing was always her plan, once she was free,” Kiera told her as they followed the god.

Finally regaining her bearings, Scarlet let it sink in. "She's going to find Deia."

"Yes."

"But—can gods go to the Nextworld?"

"No," Eva broke in. "The gods are the fabric of this World. The divine part of me will stay in this existence. But... my mortal half. Eva. Eva will go."

When they got back to the castle, the obsidian doors already stood open for them.

"I want to give my farewell to Kiera first," Eva said. "Scarlet, I will fetch you from your room after we're done."

"O-okay." Scarlet met her mother's gaze, wondering how she felt about Eva's departure. She knew that the history between the two of them had to be more complicated than she could imagine. Kiera grabbed Scarlet's hand and squeezed it before disappearing into the castle with Eva.

Scarlet made her way to her old room. She changed out of her muddy clothes, her mind in a daze. Her insides all felt raw. Viridian was gone now, truly gone. She was infinitely grateful that she and her mother had been able to say goodbye to her, to share that moment of closure. But now, that chapter closed, she felt an emptiness.

Now, they each had a turn to say goodbye to Eva. Scarlet wasn't sure how to feel about that. Her relationship with Death had been so adversarial for so long, but all of that tension had melted away when the god was freed. There was nothing left to fight about. But there was still history, imprinted in Scarlet's memories. The training injuries, the dungeon, the compulsions controlling her. Recounting her time in this castle made the feeling of dread rest in her bones.

Soon, Eva would be gone, and Death would no longer have an incarnate. Scarlet would be free from her influence. It was exactly what she had longed for. And yet, the thought of Eva departing left streaks of grief, too.

For all of the pain the god had made her endure, she'd also given Scarlet a gift. Magic. Power. After years of helplessness, Scarlet finally felt confident in herself. Strong. And it was because of Eva.

A knock came at the door. Scarlet answered it, finding Eva in the hall, but not her mother. Wordlessly, Eva led Scarlet through the halls and up to the top of the castle. They reached a door that Scarlet knew was locked from her previous explorations. Eva pulled a delicate silver key from her pocket and unlocked it.

Through the door was a circular room, in the center of which there was a wrought iron staircase, spiraling high. Blue light orbs were inset in regular intervals on the banister and were the only source of illumination in the room. Eva began to lead them up the steps gracefully.

"What is this place?" Scarlet asked, looking around in wonder.

"You'll see."

Scarlet shivered as they became surrounded by darkness and blue like the staircase was suspended in a void. With each step higher she felt the weight of the dagger strapped to her boot. "Will Riordan's mortal half be able to find you in the Nextworld? Or is his soul trapped in my dagger, too?"

"When an artificer creates something from magus crystal, they calibrate it to their specific purposes," Eva said as they spiraled higher and higher yet. They must be going to the very apex of the castle. Scarlet had always been curious about what was up there. "Ange seems to hold a special talent for this. Only Riordan's soul is caught in your dagger. His mortal incarnate was named Regan. He has passed into the Nextworld. I... hope not to find him there, though Riordan was the dominant personality of that pairing."

It was strange to think of two souls joining together as an incarnate. Scarlet was suffocated enough as an emissary, she couldn't imagine wanting to *join* with a god, to share a body with them.

"Who is the dominant one for you?" Scarlet asked.

Eva didn't hesitate to answer. "Neither. I'm equally both. We joined so the immortal could experience the mortal, and vice versa. As a god, I wanted to know what it was like. To be human, to fall in love, to feel pain. I got all of that when I chose Eva. Many times over, in fact." Her voice was wistful.

Finally, they reached the top of the staircase. It was a small platform, and a door, hewn from obsidian just as the front and throne room doors were. It was inscribed with profoundly intricate runes. Scarlet wondered what they meant as Eva touched the door and the designs lit up with a soft silver glow.

They went through and came out into another circular room, this one large and bright. Instead of the stone that formed the walls of every other room in Deianira, there was only glass, tall windows stretching high, at least twice the height of Scarlet until they converged, forming a domed ceiling above them.

Through the windows, the Crossworld was laid out before them in every direction. The swamp trees below were miniaturized. The sun would set soon, but for now, Scarlet could see across the river of souls to the gods' realms. She paced around, staring out at each of them.

Cascara's scattered islands, groves of trees abound.

Io's sprawling grasslands that would eventually lead into a jungle.

Kajiem's desert of red sand—perhaps there was an oasis, so tiny and far she almost couldn't spot it.

Meyrin's mountains towering around inside passages through the realm—whether to shelter or terrify those below, Scarlet didn't know.

Riordan's evergreen copses, the plains full of flowers beginning to wilt from the cold. Thankfully, she couldn't see the towering monstrosity that was Riordan's castle from here.

Then, she found herself drawn back toward the inner part of the room. In the center, a circle was carved into the otherwise smooth stone floor. Scarlet realized that it matched the flat, circular panel at the top of the glass dome above them.

The air here felt sacred. Quiet, barren, important. Familiar. Scarlet couldn't place why. She didn't dare step too close to the circle.

"This is the observatory," Eva said. "The other realms, they all are connected to the World. My slice of the Crossworld, here in the center, is not, as you well know. You can't open a portal from here to the World."

Eva wandered over to a window and pressed a palm to the glass as she stared out toward Kajiem's realm. "This place is different," she said, quieter. "You must have wondered about the differences between the realms here and the World. The gods can have some play in that. But many of these things—the odd coloring of the flora, the second moon—come from the Nextworld. Things from there, leaking into here.

"This place is connected to the Nextworld, as am I. I can make a portal here, where the connection is the strongest."

Was that why this place felt so strange, so familiar? The Nextworld had called to her soul for so long. Suddenly, she wanted to leave, to get as far as possible from that circle.

"Why did you bring me here?" Scarlet asked, unsettled.

Eva shrugged, still looking out at the desert realm in the beyond. "I wanted to show you this before I left. I think it's quite beautiful. The atmosphere here holds a lot of weight, I know. But it can be a good place to gain perspective."

It was a stunning view of the realms below. But Scarlet couldn't enjoy it with her stomach so knotted. "I don't know what to do with Riordan's soul."

Eva turned back to her, fidgeting with the loose hair at the tip of her braid. "You want my advice?"

"Maybe. Yes."

"Don't throw it away."

Scarlet snorted. "Really?" she said dryly. "That's all you have to say?"

"Riordan is no longer trapping me here, keeping me bound to the Crossworld. Soon, both parts of me will be somewhere that he won't be able to reach even if he does return. I doubt I will choose another incarnate. So, I have nothing to lose or gain, whatever you do."

"You can't tell me you don't have an opinion, after everything he's done. Or that you think it's a good idea for Ange to try to rule the World, or for his soul to be destroyed—"

"Alright, you got me," Eva said, a sly grin on her face. It was the closest thing to playful that she'd seen from the god. "I'm not above having feelings about it. Opinions, even."

She paused. "For what it's worth, I think you'll make the right decision. You've done well enough already, keeping the dagger from Ange and Kiera. You're right in thinking both of their ideas are dangerous and ill-founded. Ange isn't fit to rule the World. And, while the gods are disruptive to mortals, eliminating them isn't likely to fix anything, only throw the World into a new kind of chaos. Balance is kept by their powers flowing through the Worlds. Destroying, or even keeping them contained for too long will have chaotic effects. It might tear the World apart."

Scarlet huffed out a breath of frustration. "But what are the alternatives? Let everything go back to the way it was?"

"I can't answer that for you."

"There's no good answer, is there?"

"I didn't say that. Just, that I don't know it. I'm a god, Scarlet, but I'm not infallible, nor omniscient. You know that well enough already."

While true, it wasn't helpful. "I read a tale about how all the gods were once one. Ange mentioned it too. Is that true?"

"It is, though it's lost knowledge to most these days. The other gods don't like to think about it much. So much strife between them, now."

"Do you think you all could ever reunite?"

"To be one again..." Eva took a long moment to consider. "It would be hard. We may only tear apart again. The dualities we hold, as one being, it is difficult to reconcile, even for a god."

"But not impossible."

"There's something you would need to reunite us... an artifact, of sorts," Eva said. She bit her lip. "Something we all made, together, very long ago. Your mother had it. An amulet."

"Where is it now?"

"Oh. Long gone. You'll have to ask Kiera."

"Wait," Scarlet said. "An amulet. The same one that Riordan wanted?"

"I didn't know he was after it, but that does make sense. It's very powerful. And a good reason to keep Kiera alive, if he wanted to find out where it was."

"I'll find it with or without her."

"You'll never find it without her. Maybe not even *with* her."

"I'll find a way," Scarlet said, mustering more confidence than she felt. How had it fallen to her, to fix a broken World? She wasn't even sure if reuniting the gods was the right way to fix it. But there didn't seem to be a reasonable alternative.

"I don't know how much it means, coming from me, but I do believe in you, Scarlet," Eva said, her gaze piercing into Scarlet. "You have a resilient spirit. And I do realize that I have firsthand knowledge, having put it to the test. I have to say that I'm sorry, I really am.

"I know you probably see me as no better than Riordan, and maybe that's true. I feel like I lost myself, trapped here for so long. I've been here for decades. Incarnates do not age while in the Crossworld. There was no end date to this imprisonment, not until Riordan was taken care of.

"I did what I thought best—I was trying to save what I had left. With Deia gone... I feel like I've done everything the wrong way. I didn't want to save you, at first, to get back at Kiera—then, I became desperate to keep you safe, because I realized Kiera would never forgive me if I let something happen to you. And then Riordan, I wanted, *needed,* to defeat him so badly, I pushed you so hard..." Eva sighed, an exhalation that lasted a few heartbeats. "I was in pain. It's not an excuse for my actions, but, there it is."

Scarlet thought of Dante and the agony she felt in his loss. The crushing feeling of being trapped in the Crossworld when there was so much she wanted to do. Unable to fight back, to free herself, to rescue her mother. The added fear of falling prey to Riordan. Then she imagined that pain multiplied over decades.

It came back to the question of forgiveness, once more. Was under-standing Eva enough?

Some of what the god had done *was* to protect her, though Scarlet hadn't known it at the time. She couldn't have left the Crossworld without dying.

But even so, Eva could have told her *why*.

There was a level of cruelty that was pointless. The dungeon. Every brutal injury Scarlet sustained in training. The use of compulsions. Con-cealing things, just like her mother had. There were wounds, physical and emotional, that still ran deep.

"I can't forgive you," Scarlet said. "Not... not yet. But I understand you better now."

Scarlet wondered what was happening behind the god's emerald eyes. Eva blinked and nodded. "That's the most I could hope for. Thank you."

Silence lapsed between them.

It couldn't be avoided anymore. Whether the finality of knowing would crush her or not, she needed to know the answer to the question that constantly buzzed at the back of her mind. Scarlet hesitated, she almost avoided his name again, as she had done frequently since his death. But it was time for her to face it—the hope, the pain, anything and everything that followed. Scarlet could already feel her world crumbling away. "Dante," she exhaled. "Eva, I have to know. Did you find him?"

"Yes... and no."

Eva clearly saw Scarlet tense. The god held up her hands. "I'm not being avoidant. I promise. It's just... more complicated than I expected."

"Is he like I was? Caught between the Worlds?"

"No." Eva placed a hand on one of the expansive windows and looked down at the steam of souls. "The others that Ange hoped to save... their souls have all crossed, so her efforts were in vain." Her voice was heavy with grief. "Dante's soul would have too, but... someone else got to him first."

"What?" Scarlet did her best to hold steady, but her whole body shook. "*Who?*"

"Io."

What did another god have to do with any of this? "Why would they want Dante's soul?"

"Your guess is as good as mine. They do not have an incarnate at this time. You could travel to their realm and seek an audience with them in their divine form."

Scarlet had expected that she would find out Dante's fate, one way or another. In a way she had, but her head spun with new questions. She hadn't even known that it was possible to communicate with the gods if they didn't have an incarnate. The last thing she wanted to do was get tangled up with more gods, but avoiding them seemed more impossible with each new piece of information.

Her emotions started pouring out. "I feel like it's the end. If he's gone, if I can't get him back then... then I don't know. It's *over*. How am I supposed to do this? I feel so alone, all over again."

"Loneliness doesn't have to be permanent." Eva reached behind her neck, and she unhooked the clasp to the necklace she always wore—the piece of crystal Scarlet now unmistakably recognized as the magus variety. "A parting gift, for you." She held the pendant out to Scarlet.

Scarlet accepted it and turned the crystal over in her hands. It was empty, no magic flowed through it.

"It's like the swords. Designed to hold a soul. I thought to use it to trap Riordan, but it isn't large enough. A failed project, but I believe it sparked the idea that Ange used to eventually forge the magus weapons." Eva put her fingers to the indent between her collarbones, where the pendant used to sit. "It wasn't always calibrated to be a soul-stone. It used to just be an ornament, a pretty thing. Deia made it for me. It's always held hope for me, and perhaps it will for you, also. It will fit a mortal soul. Go to Io. Bring Dante back."

Scarlet put the necklace on, feeling the crystal cold against her chest. Empty now, but not forever. "Thank you."

Eva held out her hand. "One last thing, before I go."

Scarlet placed her left hand into Eva's outstretched one, emissary mark facing up. Eva held it tight while she traced the tattoo with her other hand's pointer finger. It burned as the magic that bonded them was ripped out, but it was a satisfying pain, one that let Scarlet know that something was being fixed. When Eva was done, only a faded mark was left behind, almost unnoticeable. A faint scar of the past.

They both looked back up at each other, and Eva released Scarlet's hand. "You're free. And it's time for me to go. Deia has been waiting long enough."

"Wait. So I'm your final goodbye?"

Eva nodded.

"Why me?"

"Ah." Eva closed her eyes and took a long breath. "It felt right, somehow. There's... another reason I became passionate about trying to keep you safe. You remind me of myself. The passion that drives you, the intensity of the love you feel, the lengths you'll go to to save those you hold dear... it's the reason I chose Eva to be my incarnate. As a god so far removed from mortals, I didn't understand these things—but I wanted to. And you, like me, feel these things deeply."

Eva took Scarlets' hands. A ripple of power passed between them, though Scarlet couldn't tell which of them had been the source. *Are we truly so similar?*

"I hope you find her," Scarlet whispered.

Eva smiled. "Thank you. I hope you find him."

Scarlet felt the god gather her power, so she stepped back from Eva and the room's center. Eva began to sweep her arms in large, circular gestures. The circle carved into the floor began to wake, shimmering and swirling with the growing flow of magic. Scarlet watched with rapt attention until finally, a radiant blue light burst from the circle, momentarily blinding her. When she had blinked away the overwhelming brightness, a slightly duller light emanated from the circle, a column of blue that stretched up to the matching circle on the ceiling, and beyond.

A portal to the Nextworld.

"Will you remember each other in the Nextworld?" Scarlet asked.

"Not even I know what lies beyond," Eva said, the blue light illuminating the determined lines drawn across her face. "I'll find her," she said with a renewed confidence that contrasted her last statement. "I know in my heart, my soul. I'll never forgive Riordan for taking away what Deia and I had in this World, because in the Next... things could be entirely different. But it doesn't matter. I'd recognize her in any World. It won't be the same, and I'm prepared for that. But, I *will* find her."

Eva stepped toward the light and held her hand out, her palm lingering against the edge—just barely outside of its radius. She looked longingly into it, the precipice, a whole new World. "Deia's death was an end. So was Dante's. Mine is another, though for me, it is truly time. But, Scarlet, remember this: *an* end is not *the* end.

"I am Death, but what people do not see is that I am also Life. I'm not a line, something with a termination point—I am a circle. Souls leave this World, but they also enter it. So, do not be afraid. An end leads to a beginning leads to an end. It is the way of things. It is the cycle."

With that, Eva entered the pillar of light. With another brilliant, blinding flash, she was gone from this World, leaving behind her divinity and a girl who stood on the brink between an end and a new beginning.

Bonus Scenes and More

For new release alerts and exclusive content, including bonus chapters, deleted scenes, and more, sign up for my newsletter at:
www.signup.emilydevereuxbooks.com/VIP

Thank you so much for reading Death's Emissary!

Acknowledgements

Thank you to my early readers, who gave excellent feedback and were the first to share in this journey with me: Samantha Allan, David Driessen, Katie Cunningham, and Frances White. Thank you to my friend and editor, Hannah Brown, who was invaluable in polishing my words and helping me get to the finish line. And lastly, thank you to my family, who have always encouraged my creative endeavors—in particular, my mom, who fostered my love of books by reading to me every night when I was young and transcribing my stories before I could write them down myself.

About the Author

Born with a passion for storytelling, Alberta-based author Emily Devereux has been reading and writing fantasy from a young age. Her first published story was featured in the Isabel Miller Young Writers Award Anthology. As a queer woman, she champions diverse representation and strives to challenge stereotypes in her work. Her life is full of nerdery, from her hobbies playing D&D and video games to her day job as a chemical technologist working in environmental research.